Despite the Buzz captures the contemporary essence of our ever-evolving technology ensconced classrooms. Ms. Davis captivates a broad audience with her witty and succinct observations of daily events reflected through universal themes. A quick read and terrific resource with intelligent perspectives for parents, students, and educators to communicate with compassion and savvy. Everyone will be richer with this bright and diverse spectrum of humanity!

— Deby L. Tygell, Educator, Sign Language Interpreter, Environmental and Social-Justice Activist, Artists in the Classroom Coordinator

Like it or not, technology in our daily lives is here to stay. It has evolved from something of a frivolous pastime into a constant presence that has the power to influence daily decisions, for better or worse. This book examines the consequences this power can have, and it encourages a sense of personal responsibility over our online behavior. A great dive into the murky waters of social (media) ethics.

— Alisha Gonzalez, BA in Philosophy, citizen of the planet

Tamara Davis has taken on a monumental issue of our time ~ she deftly uses the characters and this story to highlight some of the biggest challenges facing youth and our culture today. She creates a compelling story in which she weaves believable characters as they navigate cyber issues using information, modeling, direction, and compassion in their lively dialog. She invites us to start reflecting and begin to have real and important conversations about the interweaving realities of the impact of internet usage on young peoples' (and our) lives. Tamara's persistent and diligent commitment to bring this conversation forward for our children and their mental health is truly heartfelt and inspiring.

— Katherine McClelland, author of *Power Coupling: Coming Together*, co-host of *Two Gals Soul School*, creator of The Love Intelligence System, co-founder of the Interfaith Alliance, Spiritual Psychologist and Ordained Minister, Certified Relationship and Mind/Body Coach

Interesting and relevant! A thought-provoking read examining the impact of prominent issues in today's society, on our lives, and within our families and communities. This story explores the ongoing, internal struggle for morality that we each face.

— Briana McCarthy Skei, lawyer, activist, spouse, mother

Tamara Miller Davis' *Despite the Buzz* is a timely and well-crafted novel for educators, parents and teenagers alike. We all need to examine and re-examine our relationship to technology, weighing the costs and benefits of the choices we make daily for ourselves and our children. A diverse gathering of characters in this story prove to be excellent mirrors for our process of reflection.

— Aurelia Ureño, Educational Research and Evaluation Consultant, mother of two, degrees in Anthropology (Social Sciences) and Holistic Healing Studies

Despite the Buzz gives the reader a glimpse into some of the biggest challenges for teachers in today's world. Like many educators who are still trying to fully understand the effects of technologies, the main character, Ms. Gabby Oliver, encourages her students to spend more time socializing in person, creating connections, and respecting privacy. It touches on the topics many find taboo but are actually in greatest need of our attention. Students have so much access to information because of tech advances; we need to teach them how to sort through it, process it and know what is factual, educational, and worthy of our time. Ms. Oliver does a great job reminding us of this, while also encouraging her students to show vulnerability in the classroom, create a sense of community, and recognize the need for digital citizenship. This book is an entertaining quick read that is both educational and thought provoking!

— Tara Hengesbach MEd, LLPC, Wife, Mother of Four, School Counselor, Professional Counselor

Despite the Buzz is the book that we all needed and didn't even know it. Tamara Miller Davis, aka "Tami" to me, creates a unique perspective of varying cultures, personal expectations, and the blend of the inner workings of teens and adults. Tami thoughtfully invites the reader to be more mindful of their own process and relationship with social media use and the ever present presence of our "smart" devices (phones, watches, TVs, thermostats, etc.). Tami's debut novel is a true work of love, devotion, growth, and opening. As someone who uses social media on the regular, maintains long distance relationships with people through the internet, and works with teens, this book provided the nudge I needed to evaluate my own life and look at how I might bring back "old school" ways to communicate, a.k.a. "snail mail." I thoughtfully invite you to dive into this book, "despite the buzz" in your pocket.

— Jennifer "Liz" Butler, Certified Youth Life Coach

I'm speechless, shocked, humbled and enlightened. Such an educationally fictional story. Intellectually fun and fierce. Never did I see the twist coming! Completely surprised!! And I love the lyrics. Awesome!

— Jessica Corner, fan, friend, mom, daughter, progressive thinker, antiracism activist

As adults, we struggle with the tough issues of screens, social media, gun violence, and other matters affecting our world. Rarely are we given a realistic day-to-day glimpse of how these topics affect our youth. *Despite the Buzz* is an intimate view of how these issues influence our children through the lens of a new high school teacher. Educators today have an enormous load on their shoulders. And this book gives a name, Gabby Oliver, to the face of thousands of teachers struggling with educating our children in today's world. If you stay up on current events, this book is for you. If you have children, this book is for you. If you enjoy the representation of modern women in a modern world, well…you get the idea. Happy reading!

— Randi Harvey, BA in Media Studies, Author of *The Core Series &* *The Bone Gatherers*, TV Personality on HSN

Tamara Davis' new novel *Despite the Buzz* takes us inside a modern high school English class to reveal a range of developing personalities dealing with examining their true feelings via reflective writing in the digital age. We get to know our protagonist - new teacher Gabby Oliver - as she attempts to reconcile the reality of today's social media with the richness of classic literature. Meanwhile, she learns a great deal about herself.

Davis does a nice job of demonstrating the immense impact of social media's lure on impressionable young people who have grown up knowing technology as the new reality and driving force in the formation of their personalities, values and interactions with their peers.

The contrast between deep reflective reading and writing and the artificial world of social media is explored with interesting and stunning results. Parents and teachers are well aware of the total absorption today's teens (and younger children) have with their smart phones, and this book explores not only the worst examples of technology's influence on those generations but also the surprising positives as well.

This is a cautionary tale of the extremes of social media's impact on young minds and personalities and the need for normal life, actual social interaction and the ability to appreciate a lot more than the second-by-second developments on a tiny hand-held screen.

— David Wilk, author of two novels and fifteen biographical books specializing in the rich lives and extraordinary adventures of people who are not necessarily famous but have impacted the world profoundly

Tamara Davis captures all the turmoil of a teacher's first year—and then some. The personal idealism of a beginning teacher and the harsh reality of teaching a diverse class of students collide to create ripples of conflict that extend far beyond the walls of Miss Oliver's classroom.

Davis presents a protagonist with a simple plan and a clear goal: to show her students the power of writing. However, the classroom is not a vacuum, and the outside world suddenly exerts its influence on Miss Oliver's plans. The students of Miss Oliver's class come from a variety of backgrounds with many different lived experiences along with their own personal plans and goals, all of which test Miss Oliver's resolve.

Davis' writing is compact and nimble, encapsulating what is needed while teaching. She manages to capture the wide array of voices and struggles that exist within a classroom, while never forgetting the much larger social and cultural context which education is a part of. Additionally, the mix of narrative elements makes this an engaging read, giving the lay-reader a taste of the dramatic highs and lows that come with standing in front of a classroom full of students.

Despite the Buzz is much more than a narrative about a teacher's first year teaching. It is also a well-researched and thoughtful conversation about important issues that affect us all in one way or another. It raises critical questions about our relationships with technology and each other through a lens that any current or former high school student can relate to. Readers are invited into a conversation with these students and their teacher about these topics that have become unavoidable for us all.

— Greg Raney, High School English Teacher

It's clear that the author loves teaching and that Gabby has thrown herself into her work with both feet. Gabby really strives to contribute to a better community, a stronger and more vibrant society of thinkers and doers.

— Dr. Mary Adler, author of *Building Literacy Through Classroom Discussion* (Scholastic)

With *Despite the Buzz*, Tamara Miller Davis brings us into a world that anyone who has spent time in front of a classroom can recognize. Through the eyes of her passionate protagonist, Gabby Oliver, we lose ourselves in a school where pain collides with privilege, where disabilities bring new possibilities, and where everyone has to adapt to the onslaught of technology. Though she's new at this game, Gabby has enough confidence in herself, dedication for her students, and love for the world to take it all on.

— Sean Carswell, CSUCI professor, author of *Madhouse Fog*

Current. Creative. Poignant, especially as the world was forced to turn to social media & IM to connect to others. This book should be on every teacher's bookshelf and required reading for parents with teens or tweens. Ms. Davis gets the reader into the hearts and minds of each character as they explore the dynamic high school years. The educator and protagonist in this tale, Ms. Oliver, will inspire readers to relate to this next generation of writers as they expand their genre from texting to typing and from 280 keystrokes to the whole story.

— John Rowan, parent, middle school teacher, academic advisor

Well prepared and well-intentioned, Gabby Oliver designs her Reflective Writing class in *Despite the Buzz* to free her students from the narcissistic mayhem of their social-media driven worlds. Sure of herself and brazenly naïve, the diversity of her students' experiences and voices, as well as a potent reckoning with contemporary challenges, soon impel her to realize that "teaching" is as much what we learn from our students as what we impart to them. Gabby's structured lessons about media awareness and reflective living are an explicit counterpoint to the unarticulated, implicit education she and her students stumble through in the unpredictable classroom of life. *Despite the Buzz* is a thoughtful exploration of an educational landscape few of us could have imagined 20 years ago, but a perilous one which we must help our youth navigate in this moment. Tamara Davis has created a fictional classroom that is useful, elevating, and entertaining.

— Crystal E. Davis, Educator, Administrator, Poet, Author of *Hazard Reduction* and *One Owl*

I had the privilege of reading an excerpt of *Despite the Buzz* by author Tamara Davis. I found what I read to be intriguing and can't wait to read the rest of this novel. The story is realistic and likewise in the characters portrayed. The dynamics of real-life situations regarding youth, emotions, peer pressure, interactions, intentions, life-changing decisions, and the notion of "popular and unpopular" students meshes the story together well in what could be a current news story of the times. The author was careful to depict the scenes accurately, and she brought the perspective of each character forward clearly. I am eager to read the novel in its entirety, and I'm certain this will be well received by all who read it!

— Mary J. Kelley, poet, mother, grandmother, Legal Affairs Administrator for the Tribal Government of the Grand Traverse Band of Ottawa and Chippewa Indians (GTB), Chairperson of the GTB Green Committee, Council Member, Supporter of the Great Lakes Water Walkers

A good storyteller plays an important role in the transmission of information from one generation to the next. Under the supervision of a well-trained classroom teacher, sharing becomes possible. Miss Oliver represents the legions of educators who introduce students to critical thinking. Through the creation of a cooperative and collaborative learning environment that makes connections beyond the classroom, students learn to stand in another person's shoes. Miss Oliver adapts her interactions depending on what she learns about students. They want her approval and are willing to work for it.

— Michael High, retired high school English teacher

DESPITE
THE
BUZZ

A Novel By
TAMARA MILLER DAVIS

BLUE JAY INK

Book Design: Ojai Digital | Cover Art: Julia Weissman

Published by:

Blue Jay Ink, 451 A East Ojai Ave., Ojai, California 93023

bluejayink.com

This is a work of fiction. Creative characters, pretend places, and make-believe incidents are either the product of the author's imagination or used within the fictitious setting. Aside from the honorees mentioned in the epilogue, any resemblance to locales or between characters and actual people is either incidental or coincidental.

This book is rated for readers ages fourteen and older.

Library of Congress Cataloging-In-Publication-Data

Names: Tamara Miller Davis, Author

Identifiers: Library of Congress Control Number: 2021908151

ISBN 978-1-7363722-0-3 (paperback)

Subjects: | BASIC:FICTION / Literary. | FICTION / Contemporary Women. | FICTION / Coming of Age. | FICTION / Mothers and Daughters | FICTION / Technology | FICTION / Language. | FICTION / Academic. | FICTION / Teaching. | FICTION / High Schools. | FICTION / Emotions.

Printed in the USA

Dedication

This book is dedicated to my kids. They are Zs of Generation Z. May they peacefully navigate these modern times. I can only hope to serve as somewhat of a compass for them. Their father has always been better behind the helm. And as all parents (and educators) must accept, a child's future is uncharted water.

The novel is also dedicated to my resilient mom as well as thoughtful teachers, motherless children (of all ages), families impacted by cancer, and brain injury survivors.

Acknowledgments

Thank you to everyone who encouraged me as an aspiring author, including my Artful Editor Ashley Henshaw (and her editorial director Naomi Kim Eagleson), book designer David Reeser, local Writers and Publishers Network (WPN), consultants, contributors, beta readers, husband, mom, mother-in-law, stepmother, dear friends and family members, uplifting dance group, inspiring instructors, and, although we don't know each other personally, Elizabeth Gilbert via her podcast "Magic Lessons."

Thanks to those who have supported me as a credentialed, substitute, and summer-camp teacher: college professors, empowering bosses, kind coworkers, mentors, and students. Without that work experience, I couldn't have filled these pages.

Gratitude also goes to loved ones who believe in my capability: my dad, brother, grandparents, godparents, stepfather, in-laws, and extended family.

Dear Readers,

Thank you for your time and interest. I think you'll find these characters and pages compelling. I sure did when creating the content! And I sincerely tried to include something special for every aged reader: gifts of relatability. Enjoy!

I incorporate a variety of viewpoints in order to diversify storytelling and the characters therein. But a book can't tell the whole story behind a person's wider existence. Only so much can be revealed—on stage, on the page, through dialogue, and via social media. Please forgive any perceived stereotypes or misrepresentations within this novel. I cannot speak for anyone else, really. I can only try to imagine the hardships someone might face based on my limited exposure to the big world.

Furthermore, I wrote this over the span of four years. Seasons changed in our country. As did the national landscape. Throughout this experience, I strived to stay current, considerate, mindful, and attentive. Of inclusion, inequities, and injustices. As I received feedback from thoughtful beta readers and carefully edited the final draft, I realized there were sensitivities I previously couldn't see within the parameters of my perspective. The process of writing and revising helped broaden my outlook.

Since the tale is set in recent times, characters allude to actual happenings, and some public figures are mentioned or implied. If leaders should read my researched interpretation and abstract application, I hope the fictional context causes them to think more about their conceivable influence.

With humility and respect,
The Author

P.S. To round out the novel after reading its fiction, kindly consider the Epilogue for Commentary, Citations, Resources, Honors, the Coda, and follow-up Discussion Questions. Please note, this story is loosely set in the fall of 2019.

"Anyone who is even slightly familiar with the history of communications knows that every new technology for thinking involves a trade-off. It giveth and taketh away, although not quite in equal measure. Media change does not necessarily result in equilibrium. It sometimes creates more than it destroys. Sometimes, it is the other way around. We must be careful in praising or condemning because the future may hold surprises for us."

- Neil Postman, *Amusing Ourselves to Death, Public Discourse in the Age of Show Business*, Page 29, Published 1985

Looking Back

"I WON'T LEARN TO TYPE!" I resolved and declared in my brattiest teenage voice. With hands on hips, I went on strike in a ninth grade typing class. The year was 1996. My parents didn't use computers or typewriters in the home, and email was a rather new phenomenon—for me, anyway. Granted, we lived in the woods. My school was appropriately named Forest Area.

I put my head down on the keyboard and resisted. I thought about all the diaries I'd handwritten inside, all the printed photographs I'd scrapbooked with cursive captions, all the folded letters I'd given to friends. And, deep down, I worried that learning to type, using a computer, and accessing the formidable World Wide Web would diminish my attachment to a handwritten culture. It threatened my homeostasis. My hormones were erupting, I'd just moved up the hallway from middle to high school, I'd changed lockers, and now this. Teachers couldn't make me adapt again!

I'd survived the upheaval of moving four hours north three years prior. I'd weathered my parents' divorce. This was all written down— by hand. All the emotion, every word. Entering the electronic realm somehow compromised that; it invalidated the time I'd spent recording life by cursive. Typing was too modern for my rural upbringing; it felt foreign. And, I was not going to do it! Not that day, anyway.

Eventually, the computer teacher won. I acquiesced. ASDFGHJKL. Home keys. "Home" got bigger. I acquired an email address. And another mailbox. Friends sent jokes electronically. I went to class early in order to read the funnies online. That semester, my classmates and I threw a surprise birthday party for Mr. Rawlings. After all, he was our gatekeeper. As was Mr. High, the journalism and college-composition teacher there. His classroom also offered internet access.

Six years later, I won an award for being an "advanced typist" in Yeoman "A" School as I took up an administrative position for the U.S. Coast Guard. Payroll and per diem were all figured electronically. By then, I owned a laptop and relied on email to communicate with family and friends 2,500 miles away. Snail mail took second. Digital scrapbooking, text messaging, smartphones, evites, and social-media posts soon became the norm. But, I still journal—by hand—almost every day.

TABLE OF CONTENTS

"The networked culture is very young. Attendants at its birth, we threw ourselves into its adventure. This is human. But these days, our problems with the Net are becoming too distracting to ignore. At the extreme, we are so enmeshed in our connections that we neglect each other. We don't need to reject or disparage technology. We need to put it in its place."

- Sherry Turkle, *Alone Together*, Pages 294–295, Published 2011

DESPITE
THE
BUZZ

Week One

Back to School

Teacher's Desk

Seating Chart

Subject: 11th grade Reflective Writing   **Teacher:** Miss Oliver   **School:** Heart High

★ ★

Kenn	Adam			Leeland
				Ember
Rhonda		Binah	Nadia	
Lillian	Lucy	Stephanie	Matt	
				Robert

— Window —

Doorway)

Week One, Monday

"Who in here enjoys writing?" Miss Gabriella Oliver asks her new class. Some students sleepily raise their hands. "Only ten of you?" she questions in response to the poll. "Who in here has a cell phone?" All but two hands go up. "Am I right to assume everyone who uses one also texts? Is messaging not a form of composition? Is it not a compulsion that incites us to read and reply, urging communication in a written form?"

"True, true," Kenn, an attractive athlete, chimes in from the rear. "I do like to text the ladies," he says with a smirk, his flashy jersey as showy as his smile. A boy sitting next to Kenn laughs. The teacher notices a young woman named Stephanie rolling her blue eyes from the second row.

"Why do you like writing?" Miss Oliver approaches Rhonda, a seemingly studious girl playing with a purple ballpoint pen.

"I do it to clarify the—um—frustrations in my life, I guess. It helps me see them more clearly, so I can try to improve things."

Miss Oliver writes "clarify" on the board. She thanks Rhonda for contributing, nods toward the back of the room, and adds "text the ladies" to the list. Students laugh.

The teacher is building a rapport with her class. She is also highlighting the importance and abundance of writing within their lives, which is the purpose of the day's lesson plan. This informal survey serves as the engagement or "hook" piece of a larger unit.

A directive is on the board: Write your name on your new notepad. Red, green, yellow, and blue spiral-bound books decorate the desks. A plastic box of colorful markers sits atop a table near the front, the range of colors reflecting the spectrum of teenage emotions.

"Writing can take several forms, especially these days," the bespectacled instructor says in response to the laughter. "I suppose texting can also provide some clarity at times, Kenn." She cocks her head and forces a smile.

"Yeah, especially when it's sent with a sexy picture!" he jokes.

"Ah, shit," Kenn's buddy Adam happily remarks in support.

Miss Oliver reprimands the seventeen-year-olds: "Let's keep the language appropriate to an English class." She walks around the room, arms folded behind her back, high heels tapping the floor as she traverses the aisles among an array of eleventh-graders. A hint of rose-scented perfume follows her. "But why else do we write? For which purposes?"

Rhonda speaks up again from her seat by the window. "I blog in order to get my thoughts out. About politics and whatnot. I used to be religious. I find writing helps me explain why I—um—left the church."

"Explain to others? Or to yourself?" Stephanie asks sincerely.

Rhonda clears her throat and squints while debating how to answer. "Well, both, I guess."

Miss Oliver adds "blog" to the list. In parentheses beside it, she puts "politics and religion."

A lanky boy at the front of the class catches her eye and then looks down. Miss Oliver glances at the name tag he has artfully designed on his notebook's cover. "Robert, why do you write?" As the words leave her lips, she realizes she's made an assumption about him based on his looks. Wistful eyes and long hair don't always suggest a poet. But, this time, she's right.

"I, um," he fidgets in his seat, "write songs."

"Really?" The teacher joyfully inquires.

"He's in a band," Matt tells her as he taps the back of Robert's chair with his foot.

"Cool," Miss Oliver comments as she jots "poetry and lyrics" on the whiteboard.

"A laptop keyboard is the only instrument I've ever played," Rhonda weighs in again. The communicative teen is heavyset and confident; a thick, amber-colored braid drapes over her shoulder.

"I like commenting on people's pictures," Lucy, a stylish student sitting next to Stephanie, says as she shrugs. Her thick black eyeliner makes its own statement.

"Okay," the teacher responds neutrally.

"Like, on Insta-Face, a.k.a. IF," Lucy spells out.

"Right," Miss Oliver replies, dodging the implication that she doesn't understand social-media functions. "Commenting on pictures" is added to the inventory.

More hands go up. Students go on to say they take notes for school, others email, Ember turns in essays, Lillian has written letters to the editor of a local paper, Nadia sends postcards to family in Mexico, Binah edits scripts for plays she performs in, and Leeland addresses letters to his dad who is deployed overseas.

A minute before the bell, Miss Oliver stands up front and gestures to the long list of examples. "See," she summarizes, "you do like writing!"

Week One, Tuesday

A quote on the board reads:

> "Opening up a conversation about technology, privacy, and civil society is not romantically nostalgic, not Luddite in the least. It seems like a part of democracy defining its sacred spaces."[1]
>
> -Sherry Turkle, *Alone Together*, P. 264

Students meander into class after break. Some are finishing snacks and drinks as they sit down and pull out their notebooks. The last bell rings, and the chatter quiets. Miss Oliver is nowhere to be seen. Announcements start, and in walks the teacher carrying an oversized bin. She muscles it onto a vacant desk up front and opens the lid. As the school secretary talks over the loud speaker about the upcoming football game and dance, Miss Oliver begins to unpack journals. Four, eight, twelve high. Students watch curiously. Eventually, three stacks teeter on the tan tabletop. Announcements finish; she wipes sweat from her forehead and twists her tresses into a clip. A small gray streak contrasts with her otherwise copper-colored hair. The updo gives her a sophisticated look. With an audible sigh, the teacher stands tall and greets her class.

"Who in here journals? Writes in a diary of sorts?"

Four hands go up. "Nice," she nods, engaging the students who admit their hobby. "These were my mom's. They were given to me by my father. My mother died when I was five. This is how I've come to know her." The room falls completely silent. Up front, Robert, the contemplative band member, locks eyes with Miss Oliver. He gives her a warm smile.

---

1   Sherry Turkle is a clinical psychologist, author, and professor at MIT: https://sherryturkle. mit.edu/. Excerpts are reprinted by permission of Basic Books, an imprint of Hachette Book Group, Inc.

Composing herself in front of thirty teenage onlookers, the woman of medium stature takes a deep breath and places her palm on the middle stack. "In these journals, Rose Oliver recorded her observations and insights about life. She reflected on her weaknesses; she celebrated her achievements—big and small, public and personal. She wrote to me. Letters to friends and family. Correspondence that never got sent. Undelivered mail that needed to be written, regardless. She wrote poetry. Quotes—from songs, books, conversations. She documented memories and expressed heartfelt words. Here in these archives. She wrote about cancer. And impending death. She wrote about motherhood and marriage." A tear runs down the teacher's cheek. "Through these efforts, she lives on." Gabriella gestures toward the treasured artifacts. "Class, meet my mom."

Several students sniff, but no one speaks. Not at first. An orange-haired girl in the fourth row shuffles uncomfortably. The instructor glances at the seating chart to recall her name: *Ember*. Finally, Stephanie, who is sitting closer, raises her hand. "Doesn't it feel awkward to read those, though? I mean, aren't they private, personal? I know I wouldn't want my secrets shared."

Miss Oliver presses an inhaler to her mouth before answering. "Yes, sometimes it does, depending on the content. But, before she died, my mom wrote a letter and trusted my dad to keep these for me." The sentimental teacher pulls a yellowed business envelope from the bottom on the empty bin. On the front, it says **Give to Gabby when she is in high school.**

"Wow, that must be nice," Ember evaluates while readjusting her seated position.

"This letter gives me permission. To learn about my mom—her flaws, vices, anxieties, and beauty. Her humanness. Sure, it took courage for her to share these with me, albeit posthumously. But doesn't all communication between sender and recipient, giver and receiver, writer and reader, require an act of courage?"

WEEK ONE, WEDNESDAY

The new hire spiffs up her desk as adolescents enter. This being her first real teaching job, she's eager to do it right, to stay organized, to keep on track. She tidies piles into right angles, arranges clips and pens into drawer compartments, and quickly looks over the day's lesson plan: The Students Will Be Able To (TSWBAT)… Stephanie sits down in the back corner nearest the teacher's workspace.

"Have you read them all?"

"What?" Miss Oliver asks in response, turning toward the inquisitive girl.

"Your mom's journals. Have you read them all?"

"No," she replies. "I have not."

Miss Oliver smooths her skirt and moves to the front where she takes attendance via a laptop. As she marks absences, a counselor escorts a tall bearded boy into the room.

"Miss, this is Scott. Did you get my email about him, ma'am?"

"Yes, I did, Mrs. Bach. Nice to meet you, Scott. Welcome."

The teacher had indeed received notification that this new student would be joining her Reflective Writing group on a provisional basis. The counselor explained that a brain injury, resulting from a bicycle accident, had left Scott somewhat "eccentric," yet "witty and charming," and though he'd attended special needs classes before, he is mainstreaming into regular courses this semester. Supposedly, Scott demonstrates enough proficiency for inclusion within the Junior Class, though he'll get assistance in the learning center and will be granted alternative test-taking allowances through his Individualized Education Plan (IEP).

Walking with a limp, Scott ambles to an available desk and collapses into the chair. The teacher notices his unzipped backpack with papers spilling from it. She also sees that his collared shirt is buttoned askew, and his trousers are too short for a teen of tremendous height. Scott fishes through his bag and piles books upon the desk. Miss Oliver approaches, crouching down beside him. "You don't need anything at the moment. You can relax," she assures him quietly, gently patting his shoulder.

With a friendly smile, Scott begins to sing. **"Suddenly I turned around, and she was standin' there…Come in, she said: 'I'll give ya shelter from the storm.'"**

Miss Oliver then remembers another tidbit from Mrs. Bach's description of Scott. *He mostly speaks in musical lyrics.* These, she knows, are Bob Dylan's.

The educator thinks about her introduction to the class so far. She'd been personable, nice, firm but not overbearing. *Is this the way I want to be perceived? Should I wear a different hat, project a sterner voice?* Within the induction program Miss Oliver would be completing this first year, instructors were encouraged to try a variety of pedagogical approaches. *Will this introductory unit be effective and engaging?* Time would tell. Conscientiously, she begins the lesson.

"Stephanie asked me if it feels intrusive to read my mom's personal diary entries. And my answer was 'Yes, sometimes it does.' I want to explore that idea further. When should something be kept private and intact versus made public and distributed? These days, people tend to share their inner thoughts online. What used to be written in journals, kept secret between friends, or never uttered at all now makes its way onto the Internet and becomes open to interpretation.

"What if the school secretary voiced frivolous thoughts over the intercom? What are some positives and negatives of oversharing? Please pause to consider both sides and then discuss your thoughts with a classmate sitting near you."

Without hesitation, students begin chatting. Matt uses his phone to record his partner's commentary as if he were conducting an interview: "So, Stephanie, what are your thoughts?" he asks the blonde belle beside him.

"Alright," Miss Oliver calls the class to order after a few minutes. "What did you discover in your—ahem—interview, Matt?"

"Stephanie said one pro is reaching people quickly, like in the case of an emergency or something. She said she saw a shady guy on campus and texted her friends to stay away from the quad."

"Yeah, that shady guy was Adam!" Kenn points and laughs at the muscular light-skinned boy sitting next to him.

The teacher acknowledges the potential good of sending alert-type messages and ignores the silly accusation.

"Stephanie also said sometimes you send a message to the wrong person, though, so hopefully it's not too delicate. One time her friend wrote, 'Are you wearing a dress to the dance?' and accidentally texted Mr. Nelson, the soccer coach."

The class roars. Miss Oliver can't help but laugh, too. Scott sings, **"Girls will be boys, and boys will be girls. It's a mixed up, muddled up, shook up world. L-O-L-A, Lola."**

"You're on key with The Kinks," Rob recognizes.

"Ha! Okay," the teacher settles them, "so texting can be a source of confusion, depending on whether it reaches the intended recipient or how it's written."

"In the case of my blog," Rhonda adds, "sometimes I get readers I didn't expect. They may not like what I've written; they might disagree, and it creates some—um—anxiety. Not much, but still. Keeps me awake at night. I think about what to say in return."

Scott sings a familiar Beatles' tune, **"You say, 'yes.' I say, 'no.' You say, 'stop.' I say, 'go, go, go.'"**

"You bring up some good points, Rhonda, and well, Scott. Responding versus reacting to online posts. And the consideration of purpose and audience. I'm sorry you lose sleep over your blog, but I'm glad you take time to develop a thoughtful reply. When you address an individual, there's a clear sense of audience; when you write publicly, there isn't.

"Without looking into a person's face to see how something you've said affects them, without an immediate exchange, apprehension can build. Who in here has sent a text, commented on a post, or written something online and then sweat the reaction or waited impatiently for an answer?"

Almost every person raises a hand, except for Kenn and Ember. Kenn rolls his eyes and remarks, "Shit, if they don't like me—screw 'em!"

The teacher glares at Kenn and admonishes him with a single word: "Language."

"A non-like is a dislike, in my opinion," Lucy suggests. "It means you saw it and scrolled by, didn't deem it worthy of reaction."

"Not everyone sees everything!" Ember exclaims.

"Yeah, and if there's an apostrophe or comma out of place, I'm not liking it. Not showing my support of bad writing, sorry," Rhonda righteously rebels.

Stephanie adds, "It's like ignoring someone's smile or wave. Performing and not getting applause. Cheering…and no one showing interest in the chant."

Miss Oliver clears her throat. She wonders if these girls crave attention, recognition, or reciprocity. *Maybe all of the above.* "Interesting takes on the subject, girls. By the way, I think you can actually turn off likes and comments in your social-media settings."

Lucy scoffs, "Who would want to do that?"

"Well, I believe it's an option, a design intervention, and a way to opt out of feedback—positive, negative, or neither." The lecturer lets listeners think on that while she considers something herself: *The intention behind likes might've been to acknowledge and appreciate one another—to spread love, but it seems like an absence of hearts has led to disappointment and perceived disapproval.* "Speaking of," she resumes, "the title of this first unit is Technology's Toll." She writes it on the board. "There are definitely positives of electronic communication and easy access to the World Wide Web, but it's also impacting your age group in new—and sometimes negative—ways.

"I'm not that much older than you, but I did not use a cell phone in high school. I did not 'check in' to places, electronically share my location, or publicize my whereabouts. There was an element of mystery back then. It wasn't so evident who liked whom or who would be where when. I treasured that. I miss that. It is a nostalgia you'll never know. It's a generational thing, and that's okay. Times change.

"Technology is definitely changing the way we think and interact. Even so, I want you to go more consciously into the world of writing and sharing. I want you to consider purpose and audience in your own lives as well as within school essays. We will eventually use a website on occasion, but we'll do most of our journaling by hand.

"Please take out the two-part notebooks I provided and asked you to bring back to class. For those who don't have them today, here's lined paper. There is a pocket you can insert loose pages into later. The first section is for submission to me; I will read those entries. The second section is private. I will not read those. *Promise.* I invite you to write for different reasons: one has an audience; the other does not.

"Here is a prompt to get you started," the teacher continues. She projects a prepared quote onto the board. "You don't have to respond to this specifically," she says. "But sit with this passage for a moment before you begin writing."

"Today's adolescents have no less need than those of previous generations to learn empathic skills, to think about their values and identity, and to manage and express feelings. They need time to discover themselves, time to think."

- Sherry Turkle, Alone Together, P. 172

Miss Oliver ponders past and present teenage tendencies. During her school years, before the distractions of handheld devices, students seemed to have longer attention spans. Teachers didn't compete with cell phones. *Our reputations weren't subject to social-media likeability, either; we were less emotionally vulnerable before Insta-Face weighed our actions and appeal.* She wonders how generational differences would affect her as an educator.

On the drive home, Gabby spots a school bus next to her on the highway. She contemplates: *What do children do on bus rides these days? Do they still stare out the window and process the school day—their lessons and interactions mulled over as sunny sights pass by? Do they giggle with friends and share snacks? Read books and start homework? Or...do kids go on devices and perhaps look at things they shouldn't see behind those tall seatbacks?* Gabby knows the answer to this rhetorical question: It is a probable modern-day reality. As she exits onto an offramp, the yellow bus whooshes past.

Week One, Thursday

Miss Oliver sets down her book bag and coffee in order to open the classroom door. She feels a sense of gratitude as she unlocks it. *Her door.* The school key now hangs on a ring, among her apartment key, car key, and other shapely silver dangles. She notices an old dorm key and decides, *I guess I don't need that anymore!* She reflects on how far she's come since starting college back East: a bachelor's in English, a master's degree in education, applications, letters of recommendation, interviews, a long-term part-time job at the local bookstore's coffee shop in Aurora, Illinois, and *now this.*

She thinks back to her high school days in the Midwest near Chicago. Gabby remembers the enclosed hallways with one or two entrances to a building where freezing kids bustled inside. *Californian classrooms are different: open-air passages, skateboarders maneuvering between them, and kids hanging around outside.* A rose-colored sunrise greeted her on the drive along the beach this morning.

"Starbucks, ay? I thought English teachers were supposed to avoid clichés?" Miss Oliver turns to see Mr. Ritter opening the door next to hers. She hadn't officially met him before. He wasn't part of her department, and she didn't see him at the schoolwide meetings in August.

The newbie knows her neighbor is a math instructor, but the only mention she'd heard of him was when a female colleague winked and said, "Ooh, you're assigned a room next to Mr. Ritter!" For all Oliver knew, the woman was being sarcastic, and Ritter was a curmudgeon buried in a world of algorithms. Instead, the man standing nearby takes her breath away.

"Yeah," Gabby shrugs sheepishly. "Guilty." She notices he brought a mug from home.

"Have a good day," the male teacher bids as he enters his room.

Miss Oliver catches her breath, picks up her belongings, and walks inside.

First and second periods give Gabriella the push she needs to prep for her third-period class—the one after break, the group she is focusing on as part of her orientation. She doesn't want to say it's her favorite class, but it's her favorite. The students seem interestingly varied when compared to other periods. The dynamic offers opportunities for unexpected teachable moments and growth on her part as well. It wasn't the safest section to report on, considering their distinctive differences, but she'd already designated them. And she felt grateful for their span of apparent Multiple Intelligences.[2]

"Well, I look forward to reading your journal entries this weekend. I will not be grading for grammar and punctuation so much as for content, but please proofread and fix glaring errors before you turn them in tomorrow. Also, I want you to title and date your pages. The caption may not come at the outset, but usually when you finish, you'll get the gist of it.

"We *will* have grammar and punctuation lessons in here, and I hope you can improve upon those aspects in time. We will also play with sentence structure, tense, perspective, and genre as well as build our vocabularies. You can look forward to vocab tests on Fridays and workshops on Wednesdays." The eager teacher beams.

"I'll be absent those days, then!" Kenn snarks from the rear.

"Then, your grade will reflect it," Miss Oliver responds seriously. "And you and I both know if you want to remain on the football team, you have to earn good grades."

Stephanie laughs, tips her head back, and utters, "Earn, ha!"

---

2   American developmental psychologist Howard Gardner proposed the idea of Multiple Intelligences in his 1983 book *Frames of Mind*. He divides human intelligence into types, instead of thinking of it as one ability. The types are meant to be empowering and inclusive: musical-rhythmic, visual-spatial, verbal-linguistic, logical-mathematical, bodily-kinesthetic, interpersonal, intrapersonal, naturalistic, existential, and moral.

"Maybe if Stephanie tutors me," Kenn teases flirtatiously. Stephanie blushes, her blonde locks framing pink cheeks. She is sporting a red cheerleader uniform atop a white turtleneck shirt. She wears thick black tights beneath her pleated skirt, a conservative approach to the "wear uniforms on game day" mandate.

Scott sings, **"Roxxxxanne, you don't have to put on the red light!"**

"Way to call The Police," Rob gives a thumb up to the bearded soloist.

"Okay," the teacher redirects her students. "Let's talk about your homework. Did you notice any differences between writing for me versus writing for yourselves? The public versus the private realm?"

From the middle of the classroom, Binah raises her hand. "When I write for myself, I just sorta ramble. But when I was writin' in the other section—the one you read—I felt like it should make sense, be 'bout somethin' specific."

"Can I ask what you wrote about?" Miss Oliver queries.

"For you or for myself?" Binah clarifies.

"If you're comfortable sharing, then both topics, please."

Binah opens her two-subject notebook. "In the part you read, I wrote about tryin' out for a play. In the other," she smirks, "I wrote about a guy."

"Ooh, let me see, Bee!" Lucy nudges her, peeking over Binah's shoulder.

Matt raises his hand.

"Yes, Matt. Go ahead." The teacher invites his input.

"I was confused. I mean, are we supposed to write poetry or personal stuff or a description or…?"

"Yep," Miss Oliver answers informally. "All of the above, if you want to. We will write and revise within those genres. But that'll be more academic. You have freedom within your journals. The personal section should read like a conversation between you and yourself. The tricky part is," she points to framed artwork on the classroom wall and reads the caption aloud, "I think my life would be easier…if I could just get my *selves* to agree on something."

"That's funny," Matt smiles.

"Yes and so true," the teacher agrees. "At least for me. That's why I bought the piece by Brian Andreas."[3]

"Well, I'm just not used to printing," Matt confesses.

A girl with freckled cheeks and tangled hair raises her hand.

"Yes, let's see…" Miss Oliver studies the seating chart. She traces her finger along the second row. "Lillian!"

"Do you mean instead of cursive?" she wonders.

"No, I mean instead of typing or texting," Matt clarifies. "I haven't written much by hand since I was little. Even school essays are typed. We have laptops in almost every classroom. Teachers usually use a smartboard, unlike you, Miss Oliver. No offense."

"Hey," she responds playfully, "I prefer the dry-erase board. Call me old-fashioned, I guess. But at least it's not a chalkboard! And I get what you're saying, Matt. So much of our writing—and even communication as a whole—is done electronically nowadays."

Matt had stumbled onto the point of the class: to give adolescents an alternative to instant communication within an otherwise digital world. Most teachers were utilizing online forums for students to correspond, email and interactive websites as a way to submit paperless assignments; messages were becoming the norm instead of face-to-face interaction. One instructor even projected himself into parent-teacher conferences! Students were using smartphones to conduct research or listen to music, and they routinely read from screens instead of books. There was a general emphasis on technology in school, but Miss Oliver

---

3   American author of poetic short stories and sentiments which are complemented by inventive colorful drawings called Story People

was encouraging the opposite. The elective course was a response to the detriments of social media, texting, and other forms of modern exchanges.

A group of counselors and fellow staff thought up the novel class, which would fulfill three units of College Prep English. A task force was formed when two students committed suicide after an unfortunate social-media exchange last year. *Teachers had to do something.* They wanted to help kids express themselves another way, despite the buzz in their pockets. The school hired a second social worker, and she taught monthly "life-skills" lessons on campus. Considering Miss Oliver was the English department's newest educator, seemingly hip enough to understand the electronic compulsion of current times, she'd been assigned the Reflective Writing course. And so, she aims to encourage old-fashioned cursive penmanship in the process. Owning her passé preferences, Gabby thinks the assignment fitting.

The teacher feels the effects of her espresso and suddenly has to go to the bathroom—*pronto!* This has never happened during a class before. She wonders if it's okay to leave them unattended by an adult. She decides she has no choice and announces an assignment.

"Students, tonight's writing will be more focused. You can start on it now. Please write a description *for me*: A place where you enjoy going and why—maybe it's an area inside your home, within the community, or outside in nature. Write it in first-person perspective, how you see it. The more adjectives, the better! And please write about your first week at school so far—in the other section. That's *for yourself.* On your mark, get set, go!"

The instructor impatiently waits until students busy themselves writing, and then she sneaks out. As she heads toward the restroom, she passes Mr. Ritter's class. His door is ajar, and she can see the seats are empty. He sits at his desk, looking at his phone. It must be his prep period. She asks if he'll chaperone.

"Hi, um, can you…?"

"…Watch your class?" Mr. Ritter finishes her sentence. "Coffee catch up to you?"

"Yes, please," she bobs anxiously.

"Of course." He removes his feet from the desk and sets his phone down. She briefly takes in his messy, darkish-brown hair, small goatee, sparkly eyes, and sparse mustache. He is almost the same age as her, maybe a couple years younger, she guesses, but he seems comfortable with his position at school. When he stands, Gabby estimates his height to be about six feet. He reminds her of someone, *an actor, maybe.* She doesn't mean to check him out, but….

Oh yeah, the teacher remembers, *the bathroom.*

Week One, Friday

"Well, students, we've made it through the first week," Miss Oliver begins. "I hope your other classes are going well. We've discussed writing and its different types. I'd like to tell you about my own experience as a writer."

"Do you blog?" Rhonda asks.

"You a playwright?" Binah wonders.

"Can we be friends on Insta-Face?" Matt picks up his phone and pretends to take a picture of the teacher. She poses with a cheesy grin.

"No, I will not accept any 'friend' requests from my students; sorry, Matt. I may be friendly, but I am not your buddy. No, I do not keep a blog, Rhonda. And I'm not sure why you'd peg me for a playwright, but I could only aspire to it, Binah. I consider myself a good correspondent, for one. I still send handwritten cards and letters. I was in the journalism club in high school, and I contributed articles to a college newsletter. I've also attempted to write two books."

"What sort of books?" Lillian asks.

"One fiction and one biographical account. The biography includes a collection of my mom's precious poetry."

"Why did you stop writing or—um—compiling?" she pries.

"I didn't. I just put those projects on hold for now because I'm busy teaching. But I learned a lot about writing in the process of those beginnings."

"Like you can't get a date if you're stuck behind a computer screen?" Kenn jeers.

"That's the only way *you* can get a date, Kenn!" Matt insults. "How many friends do you have on social media, pal? How many do you actually know? Your relationships are purely fiction, brotha."

Miss Oliver is surprised by the poignant comeback. Instead

of explaining what she learned about the writing process in both the fiction and memoir realms, she decides to make the most of the teachable moment and address Kenn's rude remarks.

"You're right, Kenn." He looks up at her. Instead of calling attention to himself, someone else is shining the spotlight upon him. "Writing a story involves dedication and loyalty to a project instead of people, which can sometimes mean that real human interaction diminishes. Thoreau asked, 'How vain is it to sit down and write when you have not stood up to live?'[4] Authors have to maintain a balance of living and reporting on their experiences. And though social networking doesn't require the same amount of sacrifice, being a good correspondent is also time consuming. By that, I mean keeping in touch with folks you know, despite distance. I'm not talking about random followers. Furthermore, you're also right, Matt." He returns a smile toward the teacher, his gelled black hair framing his attentive face. "Storybook characters are idealized, similar to love interests on social media."

Ember laughs out loud. The braces on her teeth catch the electric light shining down from overhead fixtures. Drawing her attention, the teacher notices the girl's overgrown orange highlights look wild but becoming.

A boy in the back with a crew cut volunteers, "Standing up to live could mean joining the police force or military."

"I suppose it could, Leeland." Miss Oliver honors the alternative viewpoint.

Rhonda raises her hand. "What you said about Thoreau reminds me of a poem I recently read."

"How so?"

The astute student opens a slim book and relays a title from inside. "It's called 'The Paradox' by Sarah Kay." Rhonda looks it over.

---

4   Henry David Thoreau, American author, 1817-1862

"It begins with, 'When I am inside writing, all I can think about is how I should be outside living. When I am outside living, all I can do is notice all there is to write about.'⁵ It speaks to the demands and sacrifices of authorship."

"Plus gathering material, finding a balance between living life and writing about it, right?" Lillian voices her interpretation from the left.

"True," the teacher agrees. "Nice, girls. This conversation brings us to an important topic: the reason for this class. Who knows why the school instituted Reflective Writing?"

Lucy raises her hand eagerly: "It's an option for English 11. It gives us college-prep credits."

Ember elaborates: "Yeah, but I heard it's partly because of what happened last year with those senior girls who committed suicide."

"You're both right," Miss Oliver clarifies. "This class is meant to give you an outlet for expressing yourself. Unlike other writing courses, some of the assignments will be less academic in nature; instead of writing formal and analytical essays, you'll be more introspective of your own lives. We'll explore a variety of writing practices. But not everything will be shared like it is online."

"Gee, I thought this would be easy," Kenn reacts.

The instructor ignores the negativity and continues talking as she walks around the room. "Today, we're going to discuss some disadvantages of overusing social media." She passes out an article from NPR entitled, "Uptick in Teen Depression Might be Linked to More Hours Online."⁶

"Please get out your highlighters. You can follow along while I play the podcast." Miss Oliver feels good about employing multiple modalities in order to accommodate different learning styles: audio,

---

5   Sarah Kay, American poet known for her spoken-word delivery
6   By Patti Neighmond on November 14, 2017

visual, and kinesthetic. She waltzes over to the computer and cues the four-minute episode from *All Things Considered*.

When the audio file finishes playing, the teacher asks for input. "Okay, what did you highlight and why does it matter?"

Ember quickly comments. "Toward the end, it says, 'When people spend less time on electronic devices, they tend to be happier and less lonely.' I would mostly agree with the happy part, depending on life stuff. You all know I don't use a cell phone. So, I don't suffer from the OMG look what he said, she said bullshit. But here's the problem: *Everyone else* has a mobile phone! So, when I want to talk—say at lunch or whatever—they're busy texting, taking selfies, or posting online. It's as if they can't just hang out or stay focused on one conversation. Probably too awkward for them."

Lucy raises her hand. "I think cells connect us. I mean, at the beginning, this says people experience 'symptoms of alienation' after spending long hours online, but I can talk to a lot of friends and family about a bunch of things. It's…what's the word? Efficient! I don't feel alienated. I feel like I'm right in the mix of what's happening. And I've had a phone for a long time. For safety. And well, entertainment? Since both of my parents work. That's your choice for not having one, Ember. Your choice for disconnecting."

Lillian interjects: "Whether you believe phones are connecting us or not, Lucy, the study shows increased time spent with devices might be contributing to depression and even suicide, especially for girls. It says here, teen suicide went up between 2010 and 2015."

"True," the teacher confirms Lillian's evidence. "And adults use social media differently—for networking, business, events, inspiration, recipes, politics, displays of gratitude, and…picture sharing with distant relatives. Whereas, teens seem overly concerned with appearance."

Rhonda critically comments: "Politics, ha! Now that's something to talk about. You mean propaganda? People re-sharing memes without thinking? And then getting all negative by defending a so-called stance or sense of truth. It's not just adults who do that."

"Okay, some of those habits apply to all ages, Rhonda; you're right. Actually, malicious content can be an irksome issue online. Before social media, it was impolite to talk about politics in certain company. Because values vary. Personal opinions were ordinarily kept private. That has certainly changed!"

"Yeah, really," Rhonda maturely agrees.

"Even good intentions can get misrepresented and misconstrued. Message boards are a decent way to see and share interesting info, and there's value in independent thought, but not everyone can easily discern fact from fiction. Hence the need for media literacy. Many get taken at times."

"By BS, you mean?" Rhonda qualifies.

Miss Oliver continues the conversation: "Sometimes. Simple scrolling can require research to be sure. Because when people post inflammatory memes or rancorous rants, they're generally looking for an argument and/or support, right? I've seen this happen among midwestern friends, and it can get ugly. Especially when commentators spit harsh generalizations, talk in absolutes, make simple-minded statements without context, distort reports, get fired up about issues, or attack an individual's character. So, my advice is that you try to avoid 'BS' traps, including outrageous headlines and logical fallacies, a.k.a. argumentative missteps, such as extreme attitudes, errors in reasoning, and irrelevant estimates lacking evidence." She mentally tabs the loaded lingo for later.

"Wait, but what about jokes between friends, sent by direct message?" Kenn surprisingly differentiates.

His teacher thinks before speaking: "I suppose that's fine, in good company, but some social-media users could behave better online."

"I hear you," Lucy voices. "I hate negatrons!"

"What's a 'negatron'?"

"It's someone who's always stirring stuff up," Lucy defines.

"Oh, you mean an agitator, an antagonist, an adversary, maybe even an anarchist?" Miss Oliver specifies, "a contrarian."

"Yes, like an electron with a negative charge. I dunno. I think my friend made it up."

"I like the play on words, Lucy, and you bring us to another worthy point. Pessimism on public forums. If you're going to speak up on behalf of a common concern, please do your best to present the matter without getting vile. In other words, don't get sidetracked by spitballs."

"Ha!" Stephanie shrieks.

"When people engage in faceless arguments, they tend to write insensitive things they probably wouldn't say in person. That can affect someone's day and interactions offline too, their energy. Sometimes it's just not worth the fight. Not without shared understanding. Consider the suicide stat Lillian spoke about."

"Better to be kind than to be right," Lillian theorizes.

"Yes, I love that famous quote! It's been said by many. Something to live up to. Let us be neutrons, or better yet, protons! Since we're talking subatomic particles." Lucy laughs. "Personally, I'd prefer to see positive—rather than political—posts. Thanks for your contributions, girls. And Kenn. Do others have anything to add?" Miss Oliver gestures toward the co-ed class at large.

Robert speaks up. "This article claims the 'screen experience' is different for boys. It says boys play games while girls worry about popularity. But I believe both do both. From what I've, um, seen."

The teacher concurs: "Good point; boys care about image, too. And girls like games. That's fair," she says to the kid with long hair.

Kenn adds, "Yeah, Stephanie's always trying to get me to play Candy Cram." He tosses a Jolly Rancher wrapper toward Stephanie and smiles. She looks back at him bashfully.

"Don't get a big head, Kenn. You're probably not the only boy she plays with," Lucy jeers.

"Oooh," Adam accentuates the rumor. "Hashtag hustler!"

"Just joking," Lucy retracts, dismissing the insinuation. "But what are we supposed to do? Not go on our phones?"

The students look to her for wisdom. "I understand that you feel a tug from tech, as if you're leashed to your phone, but don't let it pull you down. I recommend you use restraint, limit yourself. Practice time management. Prioritize. Stay positive. As the study shows, more time online increases the risk of depression. There is a price for so-called progress. Plus, the fact is, your brains are still developing, and information overload can cause fatigue. In other words, constant connection can wear you out. So, give your brain a break!"

"But I have to maintain my Snappy-stream," Matt lightheartedly rebuts.

"Do you?" the teacher challenges. "Why not invest time in something else you're proud of? I just watched a documentary about surfing that features a man who surfed every day for twenty-five years. Now that's dedication!"

"True that, Miss O. I've seen that flick, *Step into Liquid.*[7] Good point." Matt gives her props.

"What about taking pictures?" Lucy raises her shapely eyebrows inquiringly. "I mean on family trips and such; I like to use my phone for that. It's convenient."

"You can set the cell to airplane mode in order to carry it like a camera without being distracted by other things," Matt differentiates.

"Look, a squirrel!" Ember mocks.

Lucy argues: "Yeah, but what's the point of taking pictures, if I'm not going to text or post them?"

"For memory's sake, duh!" Ember answers with annoyance. She drops her forehead into an upturned palm and looks downward in disbelief. Her right elbow supports the cynicism.

---

7   2003 movie, directed by Dana Brown, produced by John-Paul Beeghly

"You don't have to share them that instant," Matt elucidates. "You can upload and catalog them later."

"Great ideas," the teacher applauds. "Lucy, you could also put your phone on 'do not disturb' or better yet, turn off notifications in general, so they're not tugging at your attention when you're on vacation.

"Actually, this mindful practice goes beyond pictures, students." Miss Oliver looks around. "If you want to read articles or look at updates within an app, you can deliberately do so on your own time. And send social-media emails to spam! You don't need to be bothered from multiple angles. I'm not saying don't use your cell; I'm saying don't let it use you!"

The room quiets as teenagers appear to process forthcoming suggestions. "Yeah, it's like tech companies are trying to program people, to manipulate us into thinking we *need* mobile phones," Ember critically observes.

"I believe that's called conditioning?" Rhonda advances. "We learned about it in a psychology class I took last year. Everyone accepts device dependency as normal. Yet some apps are *designed* to be addictive."

"Exactly," Miss Oliver responds. "Be sure to check settings in your frequently used apps." She hopes her students try to make healthier choices instead of simply surrendering to unconscious habits. "Hey, who in here sleeps with a smartphone nearby?" Half of the hands go up. "Well, I think that's unnecessary, sorry. Most news can wait until morning—social, national, and otherwise."

Matt raises his hand. "I get what you mean, but what about our alarm clocks?" A choral "ye-ah" rises in response to Matt's question.

The educator shakes her head in exasperation. "I'm pretty certain you can still buy one that plugs into the wall."

Stephanie asks, "But what if the power goes out?"

"That hardly happens," Miss Oliver defends. "Besides, your bio rhythm should wake you."

Adam argues, "How 'bout when the time changes, yo? Wall clocks don't know."

"That's only twice a year, Adam." She curtails the stocky student's confutation.

"Well, what about emergency alerts, like we got during the fire," Matt rebuts. "People had to evacuate. Their phones were their lifelines."

"He's right," Binah affirms. "I can't take chances on electricity with my dad's health. He's gotta get his pills on time, every time." Binah says her dad relies on reminders for his medication.

"My dad wears one of those new smart watches for work. He's always on call, within an arm's reach, as a first responder. Forget about spending uninterrupted time with *him*," Ember irritably includes.

"During the last big fire, I used my phone a lot," Lucy adds. "Like for information, but also to check on people."

The teacher is stumped. Being from the Midwest, she'd never experienced such an emergency. She couldn't quite relate. Snow days and tornado drills were the only worries from Mother Nature during her school days. Unlike massive wild fires. "Okay, there are exceptions, I suppose. But research shows sleeping with your phone can lead to insomnia, irritability, and anxiety." Miss Oliver hadn't even considered electronic watches! She can't imagine being that constantly connected.

"Well students, I hope you at least have the courtesy not to text at night. Please don't let your sleeplessness disturb someone else's slumber. For those of you who snooze near your cells, tell me, is it the first thing you look at in the morning?"

Her pointed question is met with shrugs. Adam nods his head and says, "hashtag duh." Miss Oliver is speechless. That is not her routine, never has been, and she can't relate to engaging with tech that early. She chooses to wake up gently. *Without immediate calls for attention.*

"I'm not so hip on hashtags, Adam. But I suggest you use discretion: think about where you want your pictures to post and with whom you prefer to associate. Okay, moving on," she continues.

"Who in here subscribes to more than one social networking site?" Three quarters of the students indicate they do. "Wow, well, I personally think people could try to engage in more face-to-face activities and verbal dialogue instead. It's becoming a forgotten pastime. Talk with Ember, for starters!" The teacher makes eye contact with Ember. "I challenge you all to resist your devices while waiting in lines this weekend: at the grocery store, at the movies, in the lunch line today, inside the office, at the library checkout after school, wherever. See what conversations naturally arise when you're not preoccupied with your phones."

"Is that a dare?" Matt jokes.

"Yes, it is. A double-dog dare, in fact!" She smiles. "And then you can tell us the *truth* about what happens next week."

"Deal, Miss O." Matt happily accepts the challenge, despite his techy tendencies.

"Truth or Dare? Gee, can we play Spin the Bottle next?" Kenn kids.

"No, Kenn. But I like that you're thinking about old-fashioned adolescent games in contrast to modern-day screen interaction, which can be isolating." Several students snicker.

"You want us to talk with strangers?" Stephanie clarifies.

"Sure. Within reason," the teacher qualifies.

"Well, I guess I do talk with randoms online, so what's the diff?" the girl aptly analogizes.

"Whoa, what?" Kenn stares at Stephanie.

"Students, my point is when you need to gather your thoughts and express yourself, consider talking out loud with a friend or writing in your journal before posting online."

Scott looks at Ember and sings a familiar tune by Bob Dylan: **"When the rain is blowing in your face, and the whole world is on your case, I could offer you a warm embrace."**

"On that note," Miss Oliver resumes, "please respond to the prompt on the board. You can use the rest of the period to finish writing. Don't forget to turn in your composition books. I'll be waiting by the door for them. This weekend's reading homework is noted on the class website. It's titled: 'Correspondence between Frederick Douglass[8] and President Abraham Lincoln.'[9] There is a stack of printed copies here. Please pick up a packet on your way out, after we journal."

As the students unpack their notebooks and writing utensils, the teacher picks up a dry-erase marker from the shelf and then sets it aside. Instead, she begins typing the prompts to be projected via her laptop. *Sometimes it's just more efficient to type*, she decides. *After all, these are modern times.*

For yourself: Who is more of a fictional character than a real one in your life and why? Do you want to get to know this person better, or would you prefer to keep his or her character a mystery? What are the pros/cons of both?

For me: Who are you on social media? How does your profile compare to the "real" you? Give three examples of how you think you're portrayed accurately through pictures. Give three examples that may extend or confuse the notion of who your friends and family believe you are.

A couple of minutes before the bell, Binah raises her hand. "Miss O, can I eh, make an announcement?"

"Sure, go ahead."

"Hey, y'all, I'm in this play on Sunday. It's not at school, but there are some homies you might know in the show. It's at the theater

---

8   Frederick Douglass (1818-1895) escaped slavery to help lead the abolitionist movement. He was a human rights activist and author.
9   Abraham Lincoln (1809-1865) was the 16th president of the United States (from 1861-1865).

on Seventeenth, downtown Palm Oak. Show your student I.D. card, so it only cost you three bucks. Two o'clock matinee."

"What's the show about?" Stephanie asks.

"It's called *The Tomorrow People*. 'Episode Two, Season Two: A Changing Picture.' But it's a radio drama. That means we don't really act; we just read our parts. We get in character, though. It's cool. Based on a TV show back in the '70s. British. Sci-fi. About people teleporting, and I play a chick named Elizabeth M'Bondo. Actually, she's a teacher like you, Miss O."

"That's great, Binah!" Miss Oliver commends. "Congrats on the part. I'll try to make it. Seventeenth Street, you said?"

"Yeah, that's right."

The caffeine fades. Periods four and five tire the ambitious instructor who struggles with meeting her daily objectives when unique occasions arise. The last group turns in assignments, and she bids them farewell. Wearing a velvety green v-neck shirt atop a long khaki skirt, Miss Oliver slouches under a weighty stack of notebooks. The fresh dose of lip gloss she smeared on before last period didn't revive her. Nor did the Altoids or the spritz of rose water. Her feet ache from a week in heels. She is 5'6" naturally, so the teacher resolves to forgo the wardrobe detail next week. Now that a heightened professional tone has been set, flats would do fine.

Miss Oliver reaches for the door handle. Shut herself in, that would be the way she'd work. She'd stay until one set of journals was graded. *Two tomorrow. And two more Sunday. Then, I'll be done.* That was her plan, the only way she could foresee reading all 140 over the weekend. As she grabs the round brass handle, the spiral stack begins to slide. She shifts her weight, but it's too late. The notebooks topple onto the ground outside her doorway.

Just then, as luck would have it, Mr. Ritter exits his class. Closing the door behind him, he notices the scattered stationery. Miss Oliver is picking it up, piling one pad of paper onto another in the outdoor passageway. Wisps of wavy hair fall from the clip holding her bangs back. A teardrop shaped amulet dangles from her neck. She looks up at him with green eyes, peering through bronze wire frames.

"Hi," Miss Oliver greets her colleague. It is the only syllable she can manage at the moment.

"For an English teacher, you're a woman of few words," Ritter teases as he bends over to help. She notices the contour of his tan arms.

They both stand and carry the journals inside, setting them on top of a desk near the table up front. Mr. Ritter looks around, apparently taking in the décor. Gabby follows his gaze, feeling proud of her tissue-paper tree and its literary leaves. A student project, each quote is written in different handwriting.

"Well done," Mr. Ritter compliments. "The room looks nice, tidy. It being your first year—pre-clutter—of course."

"Thank you."

"I value the charm a female adds," he smiles. Indeed, Miss Oliver has worked hard on color coordination and decorative framing around bulletin boards.

There is a sign with purple calligraphy lettering by her desk that asks: "Is it true, is it necessary, is it kind?" Next to it hangs her "I Pledge Allegiance to the Earth" poster with its blue and white world. It's a bit wrinkled from bygone days in Gabby's dorm.

The visitor extends his hand. "We haven't been formally introduced," he says. "I'm Brandon Ritter, math teacher extraordinaire."

"Well," she titters with a casual curtsy, "nice to make your acquaintance. I'm Gabriella Oliver. Gabby for short."

"I know," he winks and turns, leaving her blushing. "My door is always open," he calls from the hallway.

"Well, well, well, if you're not already making a friend out of Mr. Ritter!" Mrs. Marie Burrows confidently saunters in, her long red hair swaying behind her fearless figure. Her black boots tap quickly against the tile.

"How'd it go?" Marie asks as she sits down and pulls an e-cigarette from her purse. She takes a long drag and rises to exhale out the open window. "Shit, this has been a long first week back," the weary woman continues. "I had a punk kid tell me to 'shove it,' a pregnant girl puke on my boots, and a physical fight between transgender teenagers! What the hell? You'd think that after sixteen years of teaching, it would get easier!" She shakes her head. "Ugh, kids these days."

Dr. Burrows is the director of the English department. She was assigned mentorship of Miss Oliver. The women met several times over the summer, and the newcomer cherishes the veteran teacher's realistic recommendations. Marie has a reputation for being cutthroat. Gabby considers her captivating.

"Give me half," Marie gestures toward the notebooks. "Come on, hand them over," she urges, revealing a pen from inside her sock. "Always," she instructs with a wink, "have a red pen handy!" Marie opens the first journal and guffaws. "Ooh, this is going to be good!" she exclaims, showing her coworker a sketch inside the front cover.

A promiscuous-looking teenage girl is depicted there. She is wearing a very short ruffled skirt and a low-cut midriff shirt with Heart High's emblem on it. However, this version has cupid's arrow going through it. The cartoon attire only slightly resembles the school's more modest cheerleading uniform which shows less skin. The girl's thick hair and big eyes look familiar. Gabby peeks at the cover. It's Kenn's from third period. Gabby guesses the drawing represents Kenn's fantasy adaption of Stephanie's game-day appearance.

"I appreciate your help, but since it's my first time reading student work, I really should be the one to comment on it."

"Okay, fine. How very conscientious of you. But I already texted my husband that I was staying late to help. So..." the tall woman picks up her purse. "I think I'll use the time to shop. I need some new boots. Ones that haven't been puked on." She places a hand on her hip. Gabby notices Marie's dark red hair is the exact match of her lip color.

"I applaud your motivation and integrity, Miss Oliver. Words of wisdom: Be watchful of cocky boys who are distracted by sensitive girls. Both are vulnerable due to social-media culture and limited life experience. Are you ready for the highly charged emotions you'll be privy to in these journals? Wait, don't answer that! Just show us you can handle it. Stay alert: Some kids will surprise you."

The young professional feels nervous and excited by her supervisor's implications and expectations. "Thanks, I'll try." Marie turns to go.

"Oh hey," Gabby calls. "One of my students—Binah—is in a play, or radio drama rather, this Sunday: *The Tomorrow People* at two o'clock. Do you want to go with me? It's at some theater downtown."

"Ha! Sure, my oldest son is in the show. I'll be there."

"Perfect, see you then."

Gabby reads Kenn's entry:

Who am I on social media? I'm an f'ing God. Girls love me. I show them my bulging biceps, and they can't resist. This is the real me. I'm the star of the football team. My physique proves it. Pictures show me running fast and catching the ball. Touchdown, mofos! My mom tries to confuse my manly image by posting "Throwback Thursday" pics of me as a silly kid. 1) me with my arm around my sister 2) me at the fair 3) me playing ball with my dad before he left. Whatev. Biatches know, I ain't that kid no more.

Geez, Kenn seems narcissistic, chauvinistic, conceited and…wait a minute, his dad left. Hmm. This is the area he may need to explore. Should I prompt him? In red, she writes:

Nice use of punctuation, Kenn. I'm glad you have a positive self-image, but "f'ing God" is a stretch, and it's inappropriate. What do the "silly kid" pictures convey about you? Are you close with your sister? How do you feel about your dad leaving? Is he still a part of your life?

Eventually, Miss Oliver cuts herself off from grading and packs the rest of the notebooks into two grocery sacks. She hauls them out to her purple Pathfinder and drives a quick ten minutes home. On the drive, she debates calling Marie to see if she wants to meet for a drink, but Gabby predicts her colleague is probably home now, making dinner for her family. In a way, Gabby longs for a family to greet her after the workweek, but then again, she has Eddie. And he's easier to feed.

Inside the apartment, a dog paces at the door. He suspects his owner as she unlocks it. The cocker spaniel jumps up and invites her inside. Gabby unloads the bags from her shoulder and sets her purse down as she opens the sliding glass door to let fresh air inside. Eddie has used the doggy door and puppy pads on the porch. "Just a second," she reassures her furry friend, "we'll go on a walk soon." She gets the pup a treat, fills up a water bottle, and grabs her cell. On the face of her phone, there's a message from an unknown number.

Have a nice weekend, the text reads. *Hmm*, she wonders who it is. *Maybe a wrong number.*

Oh well, she thinks and responds, **You too.**

Gabby leashes Eddie, and they head toward the beach. It is a bit of a walk from the residential part of town she lives in, but the teacher wants to clear her mind and exercise Ed. In contrast to the current of teenage drama at school, walking her dog is a calming retreat. Together, they stroll peacefully through the apartment complex. Gabby notices the leaves of a maple tree, not ready to turn color even though autumn has begun to set on September. It is still dry and hot outside, unlike the brisk air during fall in windy Chicago. She loved walking beside the waterway there, too. Thankfully, the weather wouldn't get nearly as frigid along the Pacific as it did on Lake Michigan. Without an ice barricade, Eddie could enjoy the shoreline all year.

On the way back, Gabby and Eddie stop for a bite to eat at a burrito shop. The weather warm, they sit at an outdoor table where Gabby munches on chips while browsing the laminated menu. Eddie patiently awaits scraps of pollo y guacamole. Meanwhile, a man talks loudly on his cell phone. He discusses Thanksgiving dinner and who would be bringing which items to his family's holiday meal, even though it is months away. *How rude*, she contends. *I don't want to listen to all those details! This is a public place. What makes him think he can dominate the din? Why is his future meal more important than my current one? Does he not see me sitting here?*

Across from the talkative man sits a woman—presumably his wife—and their baby. The lady is texting, and the baby is playing games on a tablet. It lights up, and colors flash across the screen. The little boy is less than two years old. He follows a figure with his finger, laughing. The child's entertainment rests atop a paper menu and unboxed crayons. Next to him sits an uneaten cheese quesadilla and untouched carrot sticks. Gabby stares at the family. *Three devices. One for every family member. The baby is pacified because his parents are preoccupied.*

After the long walk and somewhat unpleasant experience at the restaurant, Gabby collapses on the couch back home. She decides against grading, pours a glass of red wine, and begins to read instead. She only has eight "great books" left on her to-read list. A professor once joked that if she did not tackle these twenty classics, she could not possibly become a worthy English teacher. And so, she'd been chipping away at the list, hoping to develop a sense of greatness within a few years.

Gabby recalls she was supposed to call her dad and tell him about her first week at work. She picks up the phone but realizes it's probably too late to call him: Chicago time is nine, ten o'clock—two hours later there. She sees more messages from the unknown number. First, a smiley face, probably in response to her "you too" reply. And more recently, **Did you get my friend request?**

What? Gabby thinks. *Who is this? Friend request…am I back in elementary school?!* She reminiscences about a note a kid once gave her in sixth grade. It read, "Do you like me? Circle yes or no." Rolling her eyes, Gabby opens up Insta-Face, undoubtedly the social-media site the anonymous texter is referring to and the only one she subscribes to for time's sake. Since she checks it so infrequently, there are several pleas for her attention: appeals to join groups, including Book Readers USA and Sunset Apartment Community Forum; invites to events, such as an art show and a local poetry reading; a notification alerting her to a political post her friend "liked," and so on. There are also three friend requests awaiting her acknowledgment.

Gabby imagines people putting friend requests in each other's purses or lockers. "Circle yes or no," she says aloud and laughs while shaking her head. The three suitors include a barista from the local coffee shop, Kenn from third period, and Mr. Brandon Ritter. *Well,* she wonders, *which of these people is especially eager to become "friends?"*

Gabby denies Kenn's request. *What audacity that kid has!* Ultimately, she doesn't want him privy to her personal life. And she need not meddle in his. But first, she clicks on his account, out of curiosity. Scrolling down his page, she sees crude jokes, selfies from all angles, and pictures of Kenn posing with various scantily clad girls, everything set to public viewing. Surprisingly, his profile picture is not a selfie. It's older—grainy from a time before high-resolution digital photography. Kenn looks to be about four years old—freckled and scrawny, hair spiked in "I just woke up" kid fashion. His arm is around a handsome man, presumably his father. They are standing in front of a Christmas tree.

Before moving onto the next request, Gabby pauses to contemplate the array of images on Kenn's unprotected page. Unlike with intended email or private message recipients, he attempts to appeal to an ambiguous audience, possibly everyone he's ever known or wanted to know.

Gabby bookishly ponders, *Is social media a utopia or dystopia? Is it a pretend playground where friends can connect or a place of criticism and hence suffering?* She decides it is probably both comic and tragic for certain characters at times.

She navigates to the barista's page. There are advertisements for events happening around the community, pictures of costumed women dancing, inspirational quotes, and links to feminist-type sites, such as Choosers R Us, Bold Blondes, and Daring Divas. Gabby also notices a haiku the woman posted earlier that day: Drink coffee today/One dollar off for a poem/Share yours with me, please. "Cool," Gabby tells her dog and approves the request. The teacher feels a little less alone now that she has a local friend outside of work. Technology confirms their online friendship, but she wonders if they'll become closer in person as a result.

Gabby clicks on her own page, anticipating how it might be perceived by the barista, assuming she even takes the time to look. Her neutral timeline is not too telling. She realizes it's actually pretty dull by contrast. Considering her Christian relatives, teaching mentors, college associates, and midwestern friends from yesteryear, she deems the spread of viewers too vast for pointed posts. So she sticks to common ground.

Well, I hope the upbeat artist likes what I've simply conveyed here. Gabby muses: *What else, besides social-media profiles, could be compared to such disparate reception? What else is subject to disjointed judgment?* "Oh hey, art is!" she exclaims to Eddie. "Especially when it's graphic or wordy. Like a movie or book!" *Because creatives certainly can't please everyone.*

Lastly, Gabby hovers over the confirm/deny options for Mr. Ritter. *Would it be unprofessional to befriend a workfellow online?* Though she easily accepted a near stranger's request, she strangely feels ambivalent about "friending" the man who teaches right beside her. She decides to evaluate Brandon's profile first: the storybook of a person's character these days. And what she finds there is seemingly predictable—for a Californian male about her age.

Brandon has posted pictures of surfing competitions, impressive waves, beachside seascapes with "far-out" captions, and beer drinking with friends. No sign of a girlfriend. *At least not within the last week.* And he doesn't seem overly egotistical. *What the hell*, she concludes, swallowing a mouthful of wine. *This is how people get to know their neighbors.*

Weekend One, Saturday

Gabby lounges in bed, avoiding the stack of journals. Eventually, she wills herself to make coffee and begin reading. There are only a few remaining from third period. She starts with Ember's:

#1   *Technology is not taking much "toll." On me anyway. I don't have a "smart" phone. I don't waste my time on social sites. I don't care.*

Coming into school this morning, the guy friend I walk with asked me if I was going to the funeral. I said what funeral? He said "Lucy's grandma. Duh. Isn't she your neighbor?" I had no clue. I felt like an idiot. I should've checked Insta-Face.

But you know what, screw Insta-Face! It's like everybody is expected to know about their friends' news feeds, the school dance, football games, who got elected to city council and how that will affect my dad's job, the damn drought and the fires and who's running for office and what's happening in the world, and it's too much. It's just too much! I can't keep up. My dad sometimes puts the news on the TV but it's mostly about which celeb dyed her hair or broke up with whoever.

#2   *Who are you on social media? How does your profile compare to the "real" you? Well, I don't know because I don't regularly use it. I mean I have an Insta-Face account on the home computer but whatever. It's not in my pocket.*

#3   *I went to Baja José's restaurant last night, and I didn't "check in." The sophomore I sometimes walk to school with comes up to me and says, "what's with you livin under the radar, girl?" Donny wasn't here in middle school. He doesn't know what happened to my family. He is a nice guy. But I didn't feel like telling him why I hate phones. So I ate my taco.*

#4   *Well, if you want my perspective or whatnot to make sense, I might as well tell you. My mom got into a car accident. While texting my dad. About the groceries. She was t-boned at an intersection while driving home from college. She was finally going to finish her degree in Biology. And then she died. Because she wasn't sure which kinda milk we needed. I was thirteen. And out of soy milk.*

Gulp. Gabby can't help but feel depressed. *Ember's mom is gone. Lucy's grandma passed away, and apparently, it's news on the net. But unknown to her classmate neighbor.* Teens feel more pressure than she'd realized. Stress from a virtual world she never knew in high school. And yet, she can relate to the sense of overwhelming accountability Ember describes.

Gabriella considers her life's timing unique—on the cusp of technology's cutting edge while reminiscent of a time before electronics dominated. *Both in-person and online friendships offer opportunities at connection,* she thinks. *Both have exchange currency. But do we really know our virtual selves, our virtual friends? Are connections made over brief texts and across social media as meaningful?* English teacher that she is, Gabby deliberates on the definition of the word virtual: *almost, nearly, apparent but not actually. Simulated.*

With that in mind, she looks up Ember on Insta-Face. Layered behind a pretty orange-haired profile picture, the banner image spanning across Ember's page is a colorful quote: "Be kind, for everyone you meet is fighting a battle you know nothing about." *The source is missing, but the sentiment is clear.* Gabby responds accordingly by pen.

"BE KIND, FOR EVERYONE YOU MEET IS FIGHTING A BATTLE YOU KNOW NOTHING ABOUT."

Dear Ember,

I'm so sorry to read about your mom's death. I can relate to losing a parent at a young age. I respect your choices to not have a smartphone and to rarely use social media. I hope you are still able to console Lucy about her grandma. I agree there's a lot to keep up on within various forms of news these days. If you want some reputable sites, I could recommend a few. I also like the independent publications (the free ones you can sometimes find outside coffee shops). Thanks for your willingness to impart personal matters. Balancing the use of electronics with written and in-person communication is the focus of this course.

Sincerely,
Miss Oliver

Gabby continues commenting on notebooks into the late afternoon. Being that this is the first time she's read student work, she merely responds to content and doesn't measure the writing against much criteria, per se. Her overall goal is to stimulate artistic and introspective expression. This first round only requires informal feedback. She handed out a syllabus on Friday, and formal evaluations would soon follow.

Reflective Writing

In this class, we will compose within several genres that lend themselves to thoughtful reflection, including:

- Autobiographical - via daily prompts and in consideration of multiple audiences (self, teacher, peers, and/or beyond)
- Personal narrative - polishing and furthering selected autobiographical pieces
- Poetry - using a variety of devices, rhythms/patterns, and styles
- Imitation - learning from model authors/poets/musicians
- Biographical - third-person, about someone else's life
- Process writing - chronological and sequential
- Monologue - oral performances
- Exposition - explaining matters
- Persuasive - recognizing and utilizing elements of persuasion (ethos, pathos, logos)
- Letter writing - formal and informal
- Multi-media collections - using artifacts to convey meaning aesthetically

* Most projects will go through sharing, editing, and revision phases.
* Students will identify and strive to include standard components of a solid paragraph and larger piece of writing: introduction, thesis, supporting details, and conclusion.

Vocabulary - Students will highlight words they don't recognize within reading assignments, list and define them in a log, and audition at least three per week; every **Friday**, we will write a paragraph for the purpose of trying out new vocab.

Grammar, spelling, and punctuation - Formal writing will be graded along a spectrum (unclear references to minimal errors); bonus points for neat cursive writing. Content will be graded separately.

Wednesday grammar/spelling/punctuation lessons will include:
A. Using apostrophes (plural doesn't always mean possessive)
B. Utilizing commas properly and for readability
C. Quoting correctly
D. Homophones/homographs (homonyms)
E. Dashes, semicolons, and colons
F. Sentence structure variation
G. Shifting tenses
H. Mastering modals
I. Revisiting spelling rules (since auto-correct is disabling our memories)

In general, you will be graded on the following:
- Two-part notebooks (private and shared)
- Formal writing
- Multi-media piece
- Grammar/spelling/punctuation worksheets
- Reading responses
- Vocabulary usage
- Participation in discussions

Entries start to run together. Teenage drama leaves Gabby feeling dizzy. She makes notes on seating charts to remind herself who sits where. As the ambitious teacher packs up three class sets of journals, she notices one remaining at the bottom of the sack that held writing from third period. It is Stephanie's:

Technology is taking a toll on me for sure. I get "friend requests" from guys I don't know all the time. It's weird. I'm like dude, I don't know you. But sometimes, I'm like dude, you're hot—let's be friends. It's not as if I put out, though. I mean some girls show cleavage in their profile pics. I could never do that. Ms. Queenie (our coach) reminds us how we have to be respectable and "wear the uniform with dignity" and all. I mean, she's right, but can't I have a little fun?

On social media, I'm portrayed as a cheerleader—which is accurate. There are pics of us at games and at camp, one of me at the top of a pyramid—shit, that was scary. Many of the photos just show me and the girls. We're together a lot for varsity practice. Ms. Queenie is a big health nut, so we have to strength train in addition to practicing cheers, dance routines and stunts. There's a lot to cheerleading, actually. I'm not sure if people realize it. They tend to think it's just a bunch of airheads following boys around, but that's bull. I don't really care about the boys on the football team! I'm dating an older guy online. And I've told him I prefer cheering because it's not competitive. I'm just a person who wants to promote her school team! Plus I like the musical beat of cheers and chants.

The other day Kenn said, "cheerleading isn't a sport." Then, I out-planked him in the gym—in front of everyone. Ha! He thinks he's so strong! Cheerleaders have to be mentally strong to put up with players.

Oh yeah, back to the prompt...so that's the "real" me, I guess, but I'm more than "just" a cheerleader. Duh. I'm also pictured at the beach with my little sis. I like boogie boarding, parties, and acting onstage. Btw, I'm in the drama club.

A cheerleader in the drama club? Haha! That's funny. Gabby guesses Stephanie must mean school theater. *This is the last journal I'm commenting on today*, she decides. *I'm getting giddy.*

> *Hey Stephanie,*
> *I'm sorry you feel judged. Keep trying to dismantle the stereotype of cheerleaders as wimpy airheads. I get what you mean about cheering on the school team and participating in a non-competitive sport. I'm glad your coach encourages respectable behavior and strength training. Way to out-plank one of the football players! Relish the girl time, and good luck with stunts. Oh, and be careful of guys you meet online. People can be different in person.*

Based on her life before and after smartphones, Miss Oliver knows a sense of wellbeing now includes digital wellness. Maybe through raised awareness and reflection, her students could avoid some plugged-in pitfalls. *But would it be enough to keep them on higher ground?*

"Come on, Eddie!" Gabby motions toward the front door. The black cocker spaniel prances anxiously around their small leather couch. "Thanks for waiting," she says, patting the pup. He gazes up at her expectantly.

Gabriella likes living in the midtown apartment. The construction is newer, and since she'd only resided in college dorms and shared apartments after adolescence, she has enjoyed decorating her own spacious living room and full kitchen. Looking beyond her small deck space out back, Gabby can see a glimpse of the ocean from her raised hillside vantage point.

When Gabby moved into the one-bedroom last June, she opted for a "rose bloom" theme, reminiscent of her mom. She picked up new and used items to suit her fancy: flowery hand-towels hang in her kitchen opposite the front door; rose magnets affix school schedules to her fridge; a matching fruit bowl sits atop the counter that separates the kitchen and passageway; floral-inspired knickknacks adorn the fireplace she's never used.

Gabby's favorite decoration hangs above the mantel. It is a symbolic painting gifted by a family friend back East.[10] Two variegated roses extend from one transparent vase. An older flower droops slightly, spreads widely, and has begun to drop its petals; the younger blossom is upright in budding bloom. Baby's Breath filler whispers, "Your mom will be with you wherever you go," which is what the artist had assured before Gabby left home. She said, "You two grow from the same root, you know."

10 https://paintingandvine.com/page/11/about-us

Gabriella calls her dad on the walk and tells him about her week. Boat captain that he is, Mr. Oliver isn't surprised by the cocky boy or other student personality types she describes. He's seen it all onboard. "Good luck with your crew," Mr. Oliver says encouragingly. "And remember what Socrates said, you 'cannot teach anybody anything.' You 'can only make them think.'"

"I'll try," she tells her father. She admires the longtime fisherman for taking time to soak up great philosophy. He's been quoting it her whole life. His love for books inspired her to read and later teach. Or ask Socratic questions, anyway.[11]

When they arrive, Gabby pauses for a puff from her inhaler and then snaps a shot of Eddie on the beach at sunset. She sends it to her dad. He would appreciate the familiar—yet different—beach scene when compared to his commercial fishing ventures near Chicago. Lake Michigan is also vast and beautiful, but palm trees aren't present on Navy Pier.

And maybe because she'd spent the day grading papers about teenage addiction to social media, Gabby decides to post the picture of Eddie online. "That way my midwestern friends can see our local hangout," she tells her canine companion—his black curly hair now tangled in a wet sandy mess.

When Gabby opens the social-networking app, she notices an invitation to a function that very evening. "Brandon Ritter invited you to Beer and Bands at the Beach," the notification reads. In addition to the sound of small waves greeting the shore and rippling against rocks, she hears music playing in the distance. "Arrr," she says in a feigned pirate's accent, "there is life down yonder, matey." Eddie pants in response.

---

11 Named after the ancient Greek philosopher Socrates, the method involves asking, rather than telling, when teaching. Students can thoughtfully discover answers through dialogue and idea exploration.

Emboldened by the salty night air and yearning for adult inter-action, Gabby leads Eddie to the sound of music.

It's dusk as Gabby and her dog make their way through the crowd. The main event is apparently taking place on a grassy area along the bike path. People stand in line at beer booths and mingle with each other. Two women hula-hoop near the stage. A circle of drummers sounds off from the coastline. Gabby thinks, *How delightful. A true California experience.*

"Hey, rad, you came," a voice calls. Gabby turns to see Brandon walking toward her on the path. He is dripping wet and carrying a surfboard under his left arm. A black wetsuit clings to him. "I didn't really expect you to," he says smiling. "Let me change, and then we'll grab some beers. This next band is going to be great!" Brandon pushes stray hairs back and shakes his head of excess water. "I had to catch that last set."

"Were they good?" Gabby asks, signaling at the stage.

"I dunno; I was in the water," Brandon winks. "Here, follow me. Where are you from again—Minnesota?"

Gabby then realizes Brandon meant set of waves, not songs, and she feels embarrassed as she trails behind him toward the nearby parking lot.

"No, Illinois, but it's funny, most people equate the Midwest with Minnesota. Our accents are different, though."

"Oh yeah, tell me a-bowt it!" he taunts as he lifts the surfboard into the back of a vintage orange Volkswagen Thing. Brandon secures the board and grabs a towel from the backseat. "Here, can you hold this?" he asks her, demonstrating she drape the towel while he changes between it and the car.

Gulp. Gabby doesn't move.

"What, you Minnesotans don't know how to change in a park-ing lot?" Brandon kids. "Fine. I can manage without your help. Watch."

He reaches behind his neck and unzips the suit down to his waist. The surfer stares at her as he quickly removes his arms one at a time, eventually revealing his bare chest. "See, I don't always wear a collared shirt." With a smirk, he grabs a gallon jug of water from the front seat and douses himself from overhead. Instinctively intrigued but also uncomfortable, Gabby turns toward the sea.

Dressed in board shorts and a faded Rip Curl T-shirt, Brandon tosses his towel into the Thing. "Wait," he remarks, "let's give this guy some water." He motions for Eddie to drink from his cupped hand as he pours fresh water into it. "Now that he's had a drink, let's get one ourselves."

Gabby hesitates. "I didn't bring my wallet. I didn't intend to come, actually. We were just out for a walk..." Suddenly feeling insecure, Gabby remembers she's wearing lousy yoga pants and an old T-shirt from college. She reaches up to smooth her bangs back into a headband.

"You look great," Brandon reassures. "And don't be silly, my treat. After all, I invited you."

The teachers sit atop a green hill, slightly removed from the rest of the crowd. They face the stage where a new band is setting up. Dusk has turned to night now; the recent colorful sky is beginning to speckle with stars. *How quickly a scene can change*, Gabby observes. She pats Eddie who nuzzles next to her in the cool air. Brandon looks up from his phone. "Sorry, I just had to respond to that."

"It's okay." Gabby dismisses. She's used to people dividing their time between the life in front of them and the temptation at their fingertips. When she worked in the coffee shop at a bookstore, people would pass time in line by busying themselves on their phones. As a result, they often missed out on the special of the day, even though it was cheerfully advertised in chalk calligraphy.

"What kinda beer do you like?"

"Oh, I don't know," Gabby waivers. "Whatever."

"Whatever?" Brandon responds with raised eyebrows. "Well, which brewery?" He gestures toward the vendors. Each booth offers selections from someplace local. Being new to California's craft brew infatuation and not really caring for beer besides, Gabby is stumped.

"You pick."

Gabby enjoys the music with Eddie while Brandon fetches drinks. The band plays bluegrass beautifully. Reaching inside of a small pouch, she finds a few forgotten items beside her phone and inhaler—Kleenex, keys, etc. She freshens herself with sheer lip-gloss and rose-scented lotion. *Is this a date*, Gabby ponders? *I mean, I was invited. But we just happened to walk here.* She smiles at Eddie as if he can read her mind. "Destiny," she whispers to the dog.

Brandon cheerfully returns with two brown beer bottles. He plops down beside Gabby and kicks his feet out, careful not to spill the drinks. "Here," he says, handing her a beverage. "Oh wait," Brandon pulls the bottle from her hands and sets it beside his own on the grass. He positions himself belly down and pulls out his phone. Brandon turns the labels toward himself and alters the angle of his camera. "There," he says with a flash. "Check it out," showing Gabby the picture as if she can't see what's in front of her. Admittedly, it is a nice shot of the beer, beach, and band in the background.

"Sweet," she comments with mild enthusiasm.

"Yeah, I got you this dark one from Stone. I hope you like it. Wait, let me share this with the beer club." Brandon fiddles with his phone.

Gabby shakes her head and sips the beer. "Beer club?"

"Yeah, they'll be stoked. Me and some guys started an online group. People who like hops. We can see what each other has tried that way."

Gabby raises her eyebrows and tries to focus on the music. *Did he just say, "me and some guys?" Did he really insert 'me' into the nominative position?* She swallows the stout.

"What, not a big beer fan?" Brandon sets down his cell and nudges Gabby flirtatiously. He sits right next to her, perhaps closer than he needs to, considering they're not infringed upon by other concertgoers.

"Beer is okay sometimes," Gabby replies while remembering her dad's drunken crewman Bob—the one who fell overboard in a stupor. "Thank you for treating us. This is fun."

The folk music invigorates Gabby, despite the sedative effect of the alcohol. A harmonica and mandolin mingle sounds on stage.

"What brought you here—I mean, besides me?" Brandon winks in Gabby's direction. "What took you to California?"

"A job interview."

"That's it? No family? No...boyfriend?"

"Nope. Just a longing to leave the Midwest and stretch out toward the sea." Gabby's dream had come true.

"Far out. So, you're here alone? That's brave."

"Maybe." Gabby reflects on the attribute. *It was brave of her father to navigate his fishing boat in rough waters, courageous of her mom to agree to chemo when she knew another round would wreck her, daring of little Eddie to tempt the tide as he runs along the shore. But brave of her to start a career in a distant coastal state? Maybe.*

"How about you?" Gabby deflects.

"I grew up here."

Of course, he did, she thinks, *with his surfer's confidence and beach-swept appearance.* "You seem comfortable at work. How long have you been teaching?"

"Um...four years full time. This is my fifth. I took a long-term sub job and stayed."

"Did you know you wanted to teach math then—while you were subbing?"

"Well, it was either math or English. But literature bores me, dude. I find equations more exciting," Brandon teases.

"Whatever," Gabby spars. "Math is fixed. The answer is either right or wrong. Literature is open to interpretation. It varies by a reader's experience and exposure. I find that very enthralling."

"Hey, math has variables!"

"Touché!" Gabby exclaims. She enjoys her colleague's quick wit.

"Do you want to dance?" Brandon extends one hand toward her and another toward the makeshift floor in front of the stage.

"Me?" Gabby questions coyly. "I'm not really a dancer."

"Oh, come on," Brandon insists.

Gabby is turned on by the man's desire to dance, to interact intimately. "Okay," she reluctantly agrees, taking a deep breath and finishing her chocolatey beer.

"Wow," Brandon laughs. "Bottoms up! Way to hang loose! You know dark beer is stronger, right?"

"Mm-hmm," the tipsy teacher responds, hoping it gives her strength.

Close by, on a small starlit surface, the two teachers mingle. An older man is swaying comfortably. His silver shaggy beard shimmers in the moonlight. Middle-aged Hispanic women mirror each other with call-and-response sass. They laugh and pose. Brandon pulls Gabby's hand and coaxes her into him. He slides a hand behind her slight back and presses his hips toward hers. The messy-haired man leads them in step. Gabby nearly melts as he impressively moves them back and forth, easily, gracefully, impulsively.

Gabby sweeps her bangs back when the song ends. She looks relaxed and naturally pretty. Her green eyes glimmer. They ascend the slope toward the beach towel where they were sitting. "That was fun, and you're a great dancer!"

"Well, I had a good partner," Brandon smiles brilliantly in response. He grabs her hand and squeezes it. "I have to use the bathroom. I'll be right back." Gabby sits down next to Eddie and sighs happily. Both the beer and boogie have intoxicated her. She leans back on her arms and peers out toward the ocean. A sudden vibration interrupts her thoughts.

Gabby glances down to see Brandon's phone abuzz beside her leg. It must've fallen from his pocket. The screen is lit up, and a new message reads, **"Suzan Zimmer: Who's your date???"** There is an emoji beside it with two beers.

She sighs again, this time irritably. What felt like their private experience had apparently been shared or seen and now questioned, judged, intruded upon. "Can't anything be lived firsthand anymore? Kept sacred?" Gabby asks Eddie quietly. The pooch pants indifferently.

"Hey," Brandon returns, straightening his shirt and patting his pockets. "Did I leave my phone here?"

"Yes," Gabby says sullenly, handing him the device. He looks at it, the bright screen illuminating his anxious face.

"Ohh," he groans. "Sue Z."

"Who's Suzy? Is she here?" Gabby boldly inquires.

"No, she's not here." Brandon sits down beside Eddie who lays between them. He pats the dog and looks outward. "She must've seen my post with the two beers."

"Okay, well um, I think I'll head home soon."

"Wait, Gabby. Let me drive you. It's too late to walk alone—I mean with Eddie; he doesn't look like much of a guard dog," Brandon jokes, trying to lighten the mood.

"Alright, that's fine, thanks. I'm tired anyway," she accepts the offer. They stand and gather their belongings. The band has begun playing a new song, and silently, they walk to the beat.

"Here's the Thing," Brandon motions toward his vehicle. Gabby carefully steps down off the cement curb and lifts Eddie into her arms. Brandon opens the passenger side door for them. "Where do you live?"

"Down off of State. In those newer apartments. Thanks for giving me a ride."

"Sure, thanks for the dance." Brandon shuts the door.

As they drive along the coast, Gabby recollects a question she had wanted to ask her coworker. "So, why weren't you at school meetings this summer? I don't recall seeing you."

"Ha! That seems so long ago now," Brandon taps the steering wheel to the tune of a Ben Harper song playing on the local radio station. "They gave me a permission slip, an out. I mean, I didn't have to go. I read all the updates via email."

"That's nice," she curiously concludes as they pull into her apartment complex. "Lucky for you, especially being a newer employee and all."

"Yeah," Brandon exhales. "I suppose. I was in Hawaii; I was, um, supposed to get married."

"What?" Gabby faces him in the dark. "That was just a few weeks ago! What happened? I mean, if you want to tell me. Why didn't you get married?"

"Oh…variables." Brandon turns and parks the Thing near her entrance.

"I see. What's with math teachers? So many unknowns," Gabby jokes. *And an unsolved x,* she thinks to herself, exiting the orange car. "See you Monday."

Gabby brushes her teeth and undresses. She pulls back the soft bedcover and realizes she forgot a cup of water. As Gabby fills her glass, she hears her cell ding. *Who is bothering me this late?* she wonders and untucks the phone from her pouch. There is a message from an anonymous person: **Goodnight Gabriella.**

When she opens the text, she sees it was sent from the same nameless number that wished her well and pestered her about a friend request the previous day. Gabby calls upon a skill she learned in college when she had to determine which Shakespearian character was talking within a play: *When I only have the lines, I have to ask myself, "Who could it be?*" Like on that British Lit test, Gabby guesses: **Goodnight Brandon(?).**

A smiley face greets her in response.

How did you get my number?

She waits impatiently.

The employee directory.

WEEKEND ONE, SUNDAY

Dear Mom,

It's been a while since I've written. I know you've been there with me (in spirit) at my new job, and thank you for saving me from that accident on the highway last week. Everyone needs an angel like you! Like Dad used to say, I'm lucky to have my own guardian angel.

So, my teaching job is exciting. There are so many students, though! I can hardly keep up with grading. And as you might expect, there are some bratty teenagers who keep me on my toes. Probably payback for the way I ran Dad ragged. Ha! I feel old drinking coffee to keep going. But I suppose that's typical for a person in her early thirties. Still, school is so different from when I was growing up, Mom.

You've been gone awhile…Everyone uses cell (handheld, cordless) phones—for everything. These things can take pictures, do research, play music, videos, and instantly share it all with everyone a person knows. They're called "smartphones," actually. They're great but also annoying at times. Greatly annoying. Admittedly, they're often necessary to thrive in today's world. Anyway, it's interesting to think that photography used to be a profession! Now everybody believes they have a knack for it—since we conveniently carry cameras.

Oh and…I met a guy. Well, I didn't meet him out of the blue. I work with him. Next to him. At school. He teaches math. He's a few years younger than me. And he asked me out. Eh, kinda. Maybe he was just promoting a local event? But I ended up meeting him there. It was fun! Outside, near the beach, so CA! Although, he was distracted by his device at times, which, well, sort

of hurt. I mean, wasn't I enough? He was apparently talking to
another girl while out with me. Modern times are tricky, Momma.

Love,
Gabbers

P.S. The guy's name is Brandon Ritter. He's a handsome surfer. And
a great dancer. Plus, he has a convertible.

XOXO

Gabby tears the sheet of lined paper out and slips the notebook
and pen back under her bed. She carefully folds the letter, kisses it,
and gets out of bed. Reaching into her bedroom closet, Gabby lifts a
pile of jeans from the top of a wooden trunk. The crate barely fits into
the closet as it takes up most of the carpeted floor space. The tawny
colored wood is framed with wrought iron, and a three-by-six-inch
slot is carved out of the flat-top cover. A gold plate is affixed above the
opening with the inscription, "Letters to Heaven."

When Gabby was little, her dad told her he emptied the trunk
every week and mailed the letters each Friday. She was never supposed
to open it. When she was about twelve, Gabby willed herself to peek.
She borrowed a screwdriver from the garage and looked inside. All of
her letters were still there. Every. Single. One. Seven years' worth. She
marched into the den that day and called her father's bluff. "You said
you'd mail them, Dad! You promised."

Gabby can still hear the response her dad tearfully gave. The
one that would have to do. The only answer her dad could muster.
"Gabriella, I'm sorry. They wouldn't take them at the post office. The
postman told me, 'Heaven has no address.' I tried." So, Mr. Oliver
reassured his deflated daughter the best he could by saying he'd prayed

to God, asking Him to relay the messages to her mother.

Eventually, young Gabby shrugged off the delivery debacle; she preferred the heavenly fantasy to her motherless reality. She wrote another letter. It was a way to reach out to her mom, and she'd written dozens of letters since.

Gabby feels a contrast between their longhand relationship and today's typical speedy connectivity. Despite the buzz of current alerts, their kinship endures. With an ongoing faith in magical delivery, she drops the folded note into the trunk.

Later, Gabby does a little research before heading to Binah's performance. She learns that the character Binah will play is also of African descent. And it was a big deal for the original actress to star as a female lead back in the 1970s. Moreover, she reads that the supernatural television show was set in London.[12]

Gabby finds a parking spot near the old-fashioned brick playhouse and pays her admission at the door. She walks into the auditorium from the top and looks down toward the stage. The venue is beautiful: a dark cranberry-colored curtain cloaks the stage, and the carpet is of the same hue. Plush black seats fill the room.

She scans the area for Dr. Burrows and finds her in the second row. "Hi," Gabby greets. Her supervisor doesn't immediately look up. Hunched over, she finishes sending a text message first.

"Hey, sorry, it's my husband, Todd. Stan—our middle child—is sick, so they're not coming."

"That's too bad."

"Yeah, back-to-school germs. Happens every year in our household."

The lights dim, suggesting audience members take their seats. "So what role is your oldest son playing?"

---

12 *The Tomorrow People* by Roger Price, 1973, starring Elizabeth Adare and Philip Gilbert

"He's a biological computer named Tim."

"Oh wow."

"You actually won't see him because his voice will be projected."

The curtains split, revealing a panel of actors sitting in mahogany chairs. Futuristic music plays in the background. Binah screams! Gabby gasps! The student actress cries dramatically as the show begins.

Binah has straightened and divided her shiny black hair into two low pony tails. She wears a simple dress, but others sport space suits. The story is about people evolving to have paranormal capabilities. Gabby listens in awe. *By God, Binah has perfected a British accent! What verisimilitude!* The girl is transformed by the role. Her typical vernacular is completely undetectable.

Binah, as Elizabeth, reads effortlessly from her script: "It's the same in every classroom. Wild. I want to be a teacher because I believe in the young, but that belief took some pounding today, I can tell you." At that, Gabby taps Marie's leg.

"So good," she whispers in response.

An amplified voice asks, "May I ask you a question, Elizabeth?"

Marie elbows Gabby. "That's my son, Steven, as Tim," she mouths excitedly.

"Are you going to keep your job? Qualify to be a teacher, I mean?" He continues.

Elizabeth answers, "Yes, and then carry on teaching, I hope. If we're going to discover more tomorrow people, what better place to look than a school, and what better way to look than being a teacher?"

"I am glad you are not choosing the easy option, Elizabeth."

"Thank you, Tim. But I wouldn't mind it being a bit easier."

Week Two

Causes for Concern

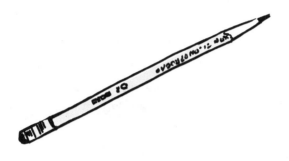

Week Two, Monday

"Good morning. I got to see Binah's radio show! Anyone else go?" Nobody replies. "She was amazing as Elizabeth M'Bondo. What a linguistic range you have with the believable British accent, Binah! Just wonderful, transporting," the teacher applauds. Binah takes a quick bow.

"I enjoyed reading your journal entries, too, everyone. Thanks for sharing. Please take a moment to look at my feedback before we get started. And here's today's prompt. Respond with your interpretation."

"In the next decade, we may see more adults who know just the right emoji for a situation, but not the right facial expression."
From "Have Smartphones Destroyed a Generation?"
Published in *The Atlantic* (2017) by Dr. Jean M. Twenge[13]

A few students trickle in late. One boy walks by the podium wearing a shirt with a grocery store logo. His name tag is pinned on it: Nico Hernandez. "Sorry I am tardy," he politely says as he finds his seat.

"Just get off work?" Miss Oliver asks quietly as she approaches his desk.

"Sí, profesora."

"No problem. Your peers are just reading my feedback in their journals." The teacher crouches down beside Nico and lays her hand on the notebook she placed there before class. Passing out materials during break has helped Miss Oliver learn the seating chart. The girl sitting beside Nico blows a kiss at him.

"Alright, last week's assignments should've gotten you into the mode of reflection. And I hope you're able to notice a difference be-

---

13 American psychologist, author of *iGen,* and professor of psychology at San Diego State University: http://www.jeantwenge.com

tween writing for yourself versus an audience, which has only been me so far. Any thoughts on that?"

"Well," Lillian begins, "when I write in the 'for myself' section, I have more, um, what do you call it…liberty. I can write freely. There are plenty of things I don't want people to know about me. I never considered writing them down before. Like the things I care about. But, I dunno…it feels good, I guess."

Rhonda raises her hand. "I get what you mean; trust me, I'm a writer. I keep a blog. But, I mean, if no one is going to read it, what's the point?"

The young woman sitting next to Nico looks as if she's going to say something. She tentatively opens her hand and then sets it back down on the desk. Miss Oliver takes note of her interest and scans the seating chart.

"Nadia, did you want to say something?" she prompts.

"I write descriptions of our daughter in a baby book." She looks at Nico. "Most of you know I had mi niña last verano. Anyway, mi tía got me el libro. In it, escribo what Cielo looks like, how she is, and how much we love her. I picture her reading it someday. It's bueno."

Miss Oliver smiles. She understands that code-switching across languages, or even dialects, is normal, depending on different speaking situations. Although she felt nervous before the academic year began, she appreciates the challenge of teaching English Language Learners, or ELLs, in her classroom. She aims to provide scaffolding and specially designed instruction for English Language Development (ELD). Presently, she's touched by Nadia's imagined future with her daughter, the act of documenting baby's growth now, so it can be enjoyed later. "So, the *point* is documentation, Rhonda. Remembrance. Curiosity. And imagination."

"Hey, my mom had me young, too," Stephanie relates. "I love looking back at my baby book. I'm glad she took the time to make it."

The boy with a high-and-tight hairstyle raises his hand. Miss

Oliver welcomes the male contribution, hoping it won't be a chauvinistic comment like some of the outbursts last week. Leeland hasn't spoken up much before. From the fifth row, he stands. "I write letters to my dad in Afghanistan. They take a while to get there. By the time he reads them, the things I told him about school or whatever are old news. But he's not allowed to use electronic communication this time, I mean on this deployment. It could compromise him, pinpoint his whereabouts."

Kenn turns his way. "Whoa, top secret, bro," he mocks.

"Yeah…bro." Leeland raises his eyebrows and replies, "It actually is."

"Thanks for sharing that, Leeland. I'm sorry you can't communicate with your father as instantly as we're so used to through text messaging these days. Speaking of old-fashioned letter writing, let's take out last weekend's homework." The students pull a blue packet of papers from their belongings. At the top of the first page, the heading reads:

Correspondence between Frederick Douglass and President Abraham Lincoln

"Hopefully you read and annotated like we talked about. You should've looked up and noted vocab as well. I would like you to highlight the respectful words Douglass uses to address President Lincoln. Notice his etiquette. For example, his letter begins:

"Your Excellency was pleased to honor me a few days ago, I have freely conversed with several trustworthy and Patriotic Colored men concerning your suggestion that something should be speedily done to inform the slaves…

"Granted, some expressions were regional and particular to that period in history. We will be analyzing this letter[14] and interpreting his narrative.[15] Eventually, you will be asked to mimic similar styles—meaning, formal letters and expository writing. Regarding a reflective aspect, you'll see how Douglass details an interview with the president and explains what his own life was like as a slave."

"Hey, Teach." Marie walks into the room after school lets out. Gabby is busy on the computer, detailing lesson plans for the next two days. She wanted to write them a week in advance, but then she realized that too many teachable moments arose and delayed or changed plans, thus making the process tediously recursive.

"Hi," Gabby looks up from her work. "Do you think I'm planning far enough out if I only have detailed plans for two days at a time? I mean, I have the unit and the pieces already laid out. It's the day-to-day I'm asking about."

"Umm, that's a day more than I plan out. Of course, I've been doing this longer and could wing it on a whim." Marie pats Gabby on the shoulder as she squints at the lesson plan on her computer screen. "You're doing a good job, even though school is subject to change.

"I think we're off to a nice start this year. Well, with the standards being broader and with your new class. I expect it's encouraging writers? Beyond texting, the lil' shits...." Marie sits down at the desk nearest Gabby's. "I tell you what, I took a girl's phone today. I warned her twice. She was being so disrespectful, not only to me but to the students in her small group. They were supposed to be discussing the book!"

"Which book?"

"Gatsby.[16] I thought we'd start out with something dramatic in

---

14 The American History Project of the Lehrman Institute: Online Library archive by Richard J. Behn and Kathleen Packard.
15 *Narrative of the Life of Frederick Douglass*, Chapter Two. Page by Page Books (public domain), Copyright 2004.
16 *The Great Gatsby*, a novel by F. Scott Fitzgerald (husband to Zelda), published in 1925.

American Lit. And we're going to have a dress-up day!" Marie beams. "Should I go as Daisy or Myrtle?" She playfully sticks out her tongue and raises her eyebrows.

"Go as Zelda." Gabby grins.

"Yesss! You're brilliant." Marie stands and poses, hand on hip, chin over shoulder, long red hair framing her face. "I'll wear something jazzy. Speaking of fearless women, wanna smoke?" Marie untucks an e-cigarette from her bag, takes a hit, and blows it out the window.

"No thanks," Gabby declines. With a few keyboard strokes, she saves the lesson plan and closes her laptop.

"Say, how was the rest of your weekend? We didn't really get to catch up at the theater. Sorry I had to run afterward. Motherhood called. Were you buried in schoolwork on Saturday?" They casually chat as friends.

"Yes, somewhat. But I went out and did something fun Saturday, too…believe it or not."

"Oh yeah, where'd you go?"

"To that surf-and-brew thing on the beach."

"Fun! But you don't seem like a surfer. Or a beer drinker, for that matter. How was it?"

"Spontaneous." Gabby leans back in her upholstered chair. She feels grateful to have someone to confide in.

"Christ, I'm jealous!" Marie retorts. "I almost never do anything impromptu anymore. It takes foresight and childcare arrangements in order to go out. And then, after it's all planned, I'm almost too tired to go. I tell you, every day, I wake up and wonder how the hell I'm going to accomplish it all—work, groceries, meals, sports and clubs with the kids, laundry, phone calls, appointments. But it all gets done. Well, mostly. Last week, I told Steven to pull his damn jersey out of the dirty clothes and spray it with Febreze before the soccer game. Ha!" Marie laughs. "Wouldn't you know it, on Friday, I wore a skirt inside out! All day! Parenting, I tell you; when it comes to multitasking, it's even more demanding than teaching. When my kids were younger, I preferred a class of thirty high schoolers to my three toddlers at home. Nowadays, though, with ubiquitous cell phones, teenagers have shorter attention spans than children! But anyway, I'm glad you got out. Did you go alone?"

Gabby can't help but smile. She tries to act cool, though. "Kinda."

"That face is *kinda* telling me you did not go alone. You think after sixteen years of teaching, I can't tell when a girl is blushing? What's the story?"

"I ran into someone there. That's all. That's the story."

"Oh okay, well, you can keep your secrets then. But you haven't lived here long. You can't know that many people. It wasn't a student, was it? You look young, but be careful, Gabby."

"No, not a student! Geez." Gabby is appalled at the insinuation. She considers her gray highlight: *I don't look that young!* "A teacher. It was a teacher I ran into." She signals to the side, toward Brandon's room.

Marie's brown eyes bulge. "Are you kidding me?" she whispers and points in their colleague's direction as if he can hear them through the wall. "Mr. Ritter?"

Gabby nods her head.

Marie leans in close. "Girl, if I was younger and single and didn't have three children following me around, and if I was cute like you, well, hell, I'd be after Mr. Ritter, too. Mr. Ri-diculously hot!"

"Wait a minute," Gabby purses her lips. "I am not *after* him. I'm here to work. To teach. To experience California. I just went on a walk and happened to run into him at an event."

"Oh yeah, right. You're probably besties on Insta-Face by now," Marie teases.

Gabby giggles. "Whatever." She cradles her head, leans on the desk, and looks whimsically outward through wire-framed glasses. Tiny rose decals decorate the sides of her spectacles. "Besides, aren't you supposed to be my mentor? Shouldn't you discourage this, um, behavior—dating coworkers. Isn't that against the rules or something?"

"You're an adult. He's an adult. What rules? Unless he's violated some sexual harassment code—which for your benefit," she winks, "I hope he does—you're free to date." Marie gets up and straightens the desk. She positions a purse strap over her shoulder and turns to go. On her way across the classroom, she adds, "Don't forget to send me your lesson plans this week; after all, I am your mentor!"

Gabby prints out her agenda, tucks it into a binder, and prepares it for projection come morning. She picks up trash, shuts off the lights, closes windows, and wipes the board clean. As she collects her belongings—purse, water bottle, shawl, lunch bag—Gabby hears her phone ding. She had almost forgotten it inside the top drawer. There's a message from Marie.

Wasn't Ritter supposed to get married this summer??

Week Two, Tuesday

"What up, Miss O?" Matt greets the teacher casually as he sits down. He is a few minutes early. Gabby is shuffling papers at the podium.

"Just another great day in paradise, Matt," she cheerfully replies.

Overhearing them, Robert comes in and sets his books down with a thump. "Jimmy Buffet's cheeseburger version or Phil Collins' realistic one?"

Matt high-fives Robert, and they sit down near each other.

"Good point, nice distinction," Miss Oliver acknowledges thoughtfully.

Scott seizes the opportunity, "**It's just another day for you and me in paradise. Paradise. Just think about it.**" He happily makes a production of Collins' lyrics.

Matt humors his classmate: "Hey buddy, you should be in Rob's band!" Looking toward Robert, Matt smiles and shrugs.

Nadia and Nico enter, hand in hand, as the bell rings. As students settle in, Miss Oliver notices that Stephanie is sitting in Adam's spot next to Kenn. They are chatting amorously. "Assigned seats, please," she reminds them. Stephanie rises and sits down in the second row, her bright blonde ponytail bobbing.

"I can check you out better up there anyway," Kenn flirts loudly for everyone to hear.

Lillian walks in late. She is carrying a green smoothie and wearing a blue shirt that says "Earth's Temp Matters."

"Sorry, sorry," she apologizes, as she sits down next to Lucy and slurps. Lucy fixes her dark hair into a symmetrical bun and looks curiously upon her peer's loose dreadlocks.

"Welcome back, class. Day two of week two. How is everyone?" Miss Oliver compares the seating chart with the roster, noting absences along the way. "So, it looks like Binah and Adam are absent."

"I think Binah's setting up for the art exhibit," Rhonda gestures toward the empty chair next to her. "They should be done soon."

"Yeah, and Adam's probably watching porn," someone comments as Miss Oliver notes Binah's apparent whereabouts on the roster. She ignores the audacious assertion about Adam.

"Shut up, dude," Kenn retorts from the back. "Adam's home pumping iron."

"Ahem, let's get started. Please note that I'll be collecting notebooks midweek—tomorrow after our grammar lesson. And the vocab review is coming up again on Friday. With any luck, you're keeping up with the reading assignments, responses, and journal entries. So, how about the letter Frederick Douglass sent to President Lincoln? What did you notice?"

Stephanie raises her hand. "I noticed it was very formal. The language, I mean."

"Of course it's formal," Ember insists. "He's writing to the president."

"I just mean we're so used to snippets of information, quick and casual-like, sent over text messages and social media," Stephanie defends.

Ember looks annoyed. "Maybe you are. I don't text. And if I were writing a letter to the frickin' president in hopes of bettering the lives of slaves, you better believe I'd treat him respectfully and try to make my case intelligently."

Stephanie looks as if she's about to cry, her big blue eyes blearing with moisture.

"Alright girls, good points," Miss Oliver mediates. She writes "language, purpose, and audience" on the board. "I know we've discussed these concepts before, but I'll come back to them time and again."

"Oh, goodie," Kenn says rudely.

"I'm glad you're looking forward to it," she returns the sarcasm.

"Now, Ember, you're right. The audience, or recipient of the letter, was obviously Mr. Lincoln, the president of the United States, Commander in Chief of the Union Army. So, yes, the language was formal, well-mannered, appropriate." Miss Oliver glares at Kenn and then records information on the board. "What was the purpose of their interview and Douglass' follow-up letter?"

Leeland stands, instead of raising his hand.

"Yes," the teacher politely acknowledges him.

"As I understand it, Mr. Douglass was encouraging Black soldiers to enlist, but he wanted confirmation that they'd be protected, paid fairly, and recognized for their work."

"Precisely, that's how I interpret it, too. Thank you. I can tell you read carefully."

"Douglass laid it out sequentially. He was like a military man. A strategic thinker."

The group listens to his refined input. "Good observation." The instructor is impressed by the boy's attention to detail and admiration for the late freedom fighter.

Leeland sits down in the back corner. Binah walks in, handing Miss Oliver a signed pass slip.

"Hi Binah. We are discussing Douglass' letter to Lincoln which was in reference to their interview. Now, class, let's think about how this might compare to correspondence with our current president." Several students laugh.

Lucy clears her throat. "I thought we weren't supposed to debate politics in English. This isn't Political Science or Government."

Miss Oliver slowly inhales and collects her thoughts. They all wait for her response. "Of course not, Lucy. We're looking at language. And reflecting on the past. Deferring to our elders. Let's stay on task."

Rhonda raises her hand. "Do you mean our president's misspelled Chirps? His insults and unprofessional reactions blurted out to the masses? His angry attempts at announcing a partisan position in defense of his ego? I've written plenty about it in my blog, actually."

"No, I mean appreciating the words of our celebrated forefathers, Rhonda, with regard to the present."

"Well, it's socially relevant, regardless," she deduces.

Scott sings, "**Come senators, congressmen: Please heed the call…It'll soon shake your windows and rattle your walls. For the times they are a-changin'.**"

The teacher quietly thanks Scott for the Bob Dylan song.

She reminisces about middle school field trips to President Lincoln's historic home, tomb, library, and museum in Springfield. She remembers how revered he is in her home state, where he worked as a lawyer and served on the House of Representatives. Every seventh grade class visited these important sites while studying American History, and every student played a part in the school's Civil War reenactment. Gabby got the lead role, complete with top hat and fake beard. *Honest Abe*. She easily recalls the memory from "four score and seven years ago."

The notion of equality and social justice were novel ideas to her then, something from history books and slavery days of old. Now bound to this diverse group of learners, some Californian kids more privileged than others, Miss Oliver knows that, as their teacher, she is "dedicated to the proposition that all men are created equal." And over 150 years after Lincoln's address at Gettysburg, she's still "dedicated to the great task remaining" because she recognizes the deep-rooted impacts of ongoing racism. While his record isn't perfect, Gabby admires the 16th president for being a thoughtful and ambitious leader who helped advance human rights, a symbol of equity.

"We've been focusing on Frederick Douglass' powerful rhetoric; I want to give you a taste of President Lincoln's. You may have heard or read this speech in history class. It was presented in dedication of fallen soldiers in 1863, about four months after the Union Army won the Civil War at Gettysburg, Pennsylvania." She recites a paragraph from memory,

"The world will little note, nor long remember what we say here, but it can never forget what they did here. It is for us the living, rather, to be dedicated here to the unfinished work which they who fought here have thus far so nobly advanced..."

"Wow," Rhonda comments. "President Lincoln apparently thought through his talking points."

"Yeah," Lucy chimes in. "His speech is all about others, not so concentrated on himself like we're used to with our president."

The teacher takes the mic, so to speak. She doesn't mean to berate the current commander, per se. But in light of Rhonda and Lucy's input, she hopes politicians do more to create a future that further heals the nation's past. *With compassion, concern, and kindness.* Miss Oliver intends to focus on language, but she also wonders if the significance of Lincoln's life, cause, and death resonate with Californian students as much as it did her back East.

"Abraham Lincoln was a celebrated orator. His anti-slavery views were highly contested through warfare, and his promotion of freedom resulted in his assassination. And you're right, Lucy: He's honoring the dead and encouraging equal treatment of the living. He's focusing on what was accomplished through a tragic but heroic three-day battle. And it's true, Rhonda, his ideas were carefully outlined and delivered."

With that, the bell rings, dismissing the class.

Week Two, Wednesday

"Good morning. Yesterday, we talked about modern-day communication with regard to history, and hopefully, you all took the time to annotate and reflect on Douglass' writing style. I'll be collecting your journals today after our grammar lesson. Let's take a few minutes to write right now."

Scott adds cinematic song lyrics to the prompt: **"Tell me somethin', girl. Are you happy in this modern world? Or do you need more? Is there somethin' else you're searching for?"**[17]

Miss Oliver projects questions from her laptop onto the whiteboard.

Let's think about purpose, audience, and language in contemporary communication. How does it compare to the correspondence between Frederick Douglass and President Lincoln?

Leeland's Journal

I think actions speak louder than words. Look at Douglass' actions. He encouraged his sons to enlist. He escaped slavery. He was big into politics and spoke publicly. He was proud. Upright. Not only did he stand for blacks, but he stood for women's rights as well. He was a self-made man. Mostly taught himself—and then other slaves—to read. He had/has an audience, despite the risks back then. And, his purposes were clear because of his actions. I'd salute him.

---

17 "Shallow" by Lady Gaga and Bradley Cooper, from the musical movie *A Star is Born,* 2018

Binah's Journal

Upon close reading of the letter, I notice the tone. Frederick is tryin to make a point, but he's framin it with respect for the pres. He refers to him with such titles like "your Excellency" sir and so on. And Fred is optimistic that his plan will work so the tone is positive. I also see that he capitalizes random words, including Colored. I like that. He's drawin attention to the adjective as if it's a title worthy of respect. Mad props to Fred. I'm a fan of his style. Also, I like his striped fro.

Rhonda's Journal

Purpose, audience, language. Modern day comm.

People used to write long thoughtful letters. You wouldn't just pen a line or two because you wouldn't waste the paper. Or stamp. You can't send someone a nice letter with only 140 Chirped characters! Although one time I sent an old friend a note that just said "hi." But, my <u>purpose</u> *was to reopen communication with her, since we hadn't spoken in a while. Anyway, salutations alone take up space. They're sincere. "With sympathy." "Yours truly."*

Letters are personal and singular. Even a prayer meets this criteria: Dear God, please protect/forgive me, Amen. But Chirps don't have addressees. They are a cry out to social media masses! And a wide mix of subscribers at that.

In a way, old fashioned letter writing was like essay writing. Paragraphs. Points of intention. A conclusion. "See you this summer." "Best wishes on the new job."

Even letters to an editor take time. But the local editor must be bored these days. It seems like people would rather post their concerns in brief. At large. And in hope that some random follower will find them entertaining.

Dear Frederick Douglass,
Thanks for your contributions. And your formality. You set a precedence. Too bad it's gone by the wayside.
Sincerely,
The future
P.S. That last bit is about 140 characters counting spaces and punctuation.

Hey, check out my blog! It's called Opal Mood.

Miss Oliver then realizes that Rhonda invalidates herself a bit when she condemns others for using the net as an easy mode of expression, and yet she does so herself. *Granted, Rhonda might tailor her blog toward a specific set of subscribers? And,* the teacher wagers, *I'll bet she uses more than 140 characters to make her proofread points.*

Ember's Journal

Purpose, audience, and language in modern day communication... As you can tell from my journal entries, I don't do much high-tech communicating. The <u>purpose</u> *of social media seems like a big f.u. to so called friends. It's kinda like saying, you're stuck in the snow, f.u. I'm at the beach. Or, you didn't think I was athletic, f.u. I just ran a marathon! Or, you don't think I'm pretty, look at me now with my 10,000 selfies and 86 likes. Ha!* <u>Audience</u>*...It's all about audience. These dweebs believe they're on stage with their followers. Maybe they are. In a sense, I guess. But Insta-Face ain't Broadway.*

Sorry if my <u>language</u> *is offensive. I grew up with a fireman father. He tells it like it is. He says if a fireman beats around the bush, he lets the house burn down.*

Hmm, comparisons do come up when scrolling, Miss Oliver concurs. *Ember's right: Contrasting oneself to others can heighten a person's insecurities and sense of inadequacy or exclusion. A "must be nice" feeling may arise from the depressive effect. And some individuals surely like to show off! But by talking themselves up, they might inadvertently—or purposefully— make friends feel down?* She sympathetically questions: *Do social-media sharers send gifts by letting viewers live vicariously through their vacation pictures, or do they rub exotic getaways in their followers' Insta-Face?*

Miss Oliver extends her thoughts on the matter: *The world needs entertainment, and particular people are natural performers, some more tal-*

ented than others. Social media gives them an opportunity to develop their "on-stage" presence. Ambivalently, she decides: *there are certainly pros and cons to life online! Timely trade-offs. In theory, individual strengths and accomplishments would be measured independently, though. Not against others. And without inflation.*

Nadia's Journal

It said Lincoln respected Douglass back by not treating him like a black person back then. The president seemed to really like him. Douglass said that when he was around Lincoln, he wasnt reminded of his "unpopuler color."

I liked the romantic part about Frederick and his first free wife. To bad she couldnt read or right well though. Its surprising they could be a thing when he was such a good righter. My Tía says you cant help who you fall in love with.

True, the teacher agrees. *And come to think of it, his second wife was white! That was sure surprising at the time.* She looks up from reading third period's responses, stands and stretches at her desk, and then grabs an iced tea from her mini-fridge. She has to keep close tabs on this class and certain "at-risk" learners because they are the focus group of her preliminary-teacher program. *But the selection of students is so varied in personality, upbringing, and aptitude.* How could she paint the proctor a picture of diversity with a single stroke of description? She goes outside for some fresh air.

Gabby admires the calla lilies, poppies, and birds of paradise along the landscaped property. *What a neat learning space,* she thinks. *There's so much in bloom.* She walks down the sidewalk to smell a rosemary bush. Its aroma lingers on her fingertips. *Schools back East were often snow-covered, cold, and icy outside. But inside, the warm rooms offered an inviting refuge.* Gabby ponders the positives of both educational environments. With that, the teacher remembers to turn off the air conditioning before she leaves for the day. She walks back to class.

At the end of the passageway, a giant red heart is painted onto the white brick wall. Inside, it reads "HHS," an abbreviation of the institution's name: Heart High School. She recalls seeing a cartoonish version of the sign hanging up on a poster in the main office.

To Gabby's surprise, Mr. Ritter is waiting inside her door. He leans against the frame, watching her as she nears him. His hazel eyes penetrate her, intimidate her, excite her.

"Well, hi," Gabby greets her coworker with an inquisitive look. "What brings you all the way over here to Room 18?"

"Room 17 bores me at times. I came to see you. To see how your week is going. It being 'hump day' and all."

Gabby guffaws at the insinuation. "That's right," she affirms. "It's Wednesday; we are technically over the hump. And it's going pretty well, thanks. I was just reading a set of notebooks."

Blocking the doorway a bit, Brandon peeks inside at her desk in the back. "I can tell."

Gabby smiles at his interest in her work. "It's nice to see you. How are things?"

"Oh, fine. Math test today, so I stayed late to grade, too."

She nods in acknowledgment of their common pastime. "Well, good luck with it. Thanks for stopping by." She takes a step toward him, intimating she'd like to get back to work. Eddie-dog is waiting at home, and Gabby wants to call her artist friend before it gets too late back East.

Brandon is still imposing on her doorway. She senses him look her over: from heels to hair, he seems to notice her bare legs, black skirt, belted waist, tight top, pearls, glasses, bangs. She watches his eyes move up her body. "I'm done evaluating today," he says as he turns to leave. "But I realize it takes more time in the English department."

Lucy's Journal

Modern Day communication is tricky. If I post a selfie, girls think I'm "vain." But they're all posting pix too. So whatev. My dad tells me to get off my phone, but there's so much to do. I try to hit people back with texts, just to be nice. I'm in contact with a lot of kids—from my old school and such. And homework is often assigned online. Sometimes there's an email to check from student council or the organization I volunteer for…and I've gotta keep up with my biz (I sell clothes online). Snap-Speak filters are funny. I got my first phone when I was ten. To stay in touch with my parents and all. But I've had to block some numbers and some people. Guys can be weird. Just because I'm fashionable doesn't mean I'm horny. They write all kinds of sick things. Even back when I was like 13. It can be uncomfortable.

The teacher adds a quote in response: *"We are consumed with that which we are nourished by."* - *Shakespeare (Sonnet 73, slightly reworded)*

P.S. If you put too much of yourself out there for others, there's little left in reserve. Consider time, energy, priorities, and privacy, Lucy. Remember, posts and photos could be re-shared with unintended recipients. Please protect yourself.

Lillian's Journal

People don't wanna communicate. They just pass judgement. They look at me and think my dreadlocks are a fashion statement. And, I'd like to think they are. :) But, I started growing them out when we were homeless. I guess my "troll hair, don't care" is in fashion now. Trollish because I lived beneath a bridge? Before, I could only shower in the locker room at school. But, my mom and I have a place now. Still, some high schoolers see me as a hippie because I care about the environment. I wish they saw me as a friend. But, I don't have a cell right now. And, I definitely don't have a computer. So, I'm not sure who my friends are. I feel more comfortable among characters in books. When I walk the hallway, people are on their phones. And if they bother to look up, some teens can be mean. "Eww, gross," I heard a girl say in the hallway last week. And then, she took a picture of me..

That's a lot to process. She closes her eyes in contemplation. *Although we enjoy different levels of access, we all live within this newfound digital experiment,* Miss Oliver muses. Routinely surrounded by students who grew up on screens, she would try to help them navigate life on and offline. *Just because people can take photos doesn't always mean they should. Especially not if the images are exploitative or malicious!*

The last journal doesn't have a name on the cover. Gabby flips it open irritably. *Why can't kids just follow directions? Teachers have so much to read. We don't have time to play detective when it comes to figuring out who wrote what.* On the first page, there is beautiful cursive writing. A short letter is addressed to her.

> *Dear Miss Oliver,*
> *I like you. Will you go out with me? Circle yes or no.*
>
> *Yes   No*
>
> *Hopeful,*
> *Mr. Ritter*
>
> *P.S. Since you don't regularly respond to my Insta-Face or text messages, I thought I'd try this old-school approach.*

Gabby leans back in her chair and considers the sweet proposal. She picks up a red pen and writes "maybe" between the options. On her way out, she slips the notebook beneath Room 17's door.

Week Two, Thursday

"Hello, class. Thank you for your journal entries. I appreciate your input, bearing in mind that I'm, ahem, a bit older and maybe not so hip to the selfie culture. But I will say that my high school friends—way back when—were just as concerned with image and identity. We captured life by 35 mm film and only as often as our budgets could spare the cost of development. It was fun waiting for those pictures, especially because you never knew how they'd turn out or if you'd even get them back."

Stephanie asks, "What do you mean, 'if'?"

"Well," the teacher clarifies, "there was a time when pictures were censored in a dark room. A film processing center had the right to dispose of prints if they were obscene."

"Like nude photos?" Stephanie questions.

"Yep," she responds. "I can remember a friend not getting all of her beach pictures back from our senior trip to Florida. Because girls were wearing bikinis."

"What?!" Kenn tunes in. "The dude developing those shots probably just kept them. I would. Or maybe pass them out to my friends."

"Possibly developers did," the teacher mulls over. "I'm not sure, but there was a standard, and photo stores could choose not to print certain images."

"Wow." Matt tilts his head in contemplation. "But no one ever saw your printed photographs. I mean, besides the pervert processer guy. You couldn't upload and share them."

"True, Matt, less people saw them. Average strangers definitely didn't. But we'd scrapbook and show the pictures to close friends. And we always ordered doubles. So, there were two copies: one to keep and one to give away." Gabby feels happily nostalgic.

Scott sings, "Every memory of looking out the back door. I had the photo album spread out on my bedroom floor."

"Nickelback, nice," Robert applauds Scott's lyrics.

"Alright," Miss Oliver interrupts the repartee, "as you can see on today's agenda, we're going to practice old-fashioned letter writing."

Stephanie looks perplexed. "Like cursive?"

"Sure, you can use cursive. Or print lettering. But no abbreviations. You can choose to type or handwrite the final draft. And I want it formatted appropriately. I've projected examples of salutations."

Binah raises her hand. "What's a salutation?"

Nico momentarily lifts his head from the desk. "Hola, hasta luego."

"Sí, Nico, gracias," the instructor responds in Spanish. She has been reviewing a manual from college called *Spanish for Teachers: A Quick Reference Guide for Today's Multicultural Classroom*. By bridging language barriers and encouraging engagement, she hopes to build ESL comprehension within the otherwise fully immersive environment.

Leeland stands in the back. "A salutation identifies who's being acknowledged, and the gesture usually pays respect. Like a salute." He raises his right hand and bends his elbow at a 45-degree angle to create a sharp example.

"Good point, Lee," Miss Oliver commends.

Ember raises her hand. "So, who are we, um, addressing?"

Stephanie asks, "Are we just writing to you?"

The teacher composes herself and considers the potential reception of what she's about to say. *This could go badly,* she worries. *Or well. We'll see.* "Like Frederick Douglass, we will be writing to the president of the United States. His letter is our model."

Rhonda rolls her eyes. "You think it'll make a difference?" She is wearing a black ballcap with the letters ACLU spanning across it. At first, Miss Oliver wonders which college that is. And then, she realizes it stands for the American Civil Liberties Union.[18]

"I don't know if it'll make a national difference, but it's worthwhile for other reasons. Since this is a reflective writing class," the teacher continues, "I want you to reflect on something that's happening in the world. Something you'd like to see changed. Just like Douglass did."

Kenn complains: "So, we can't just write "Whaz up? How's it hanging?"

Miss Oliver shakes her head. "No. Here are the details of the assignment. There are essentially three pieces: the worksheet, a short essay, and the letter. You'll have this period, tonight's homework, and tomorrow to work on it. Remember to do your best when speaking up about your concerns." She passes out a graphic organizer. "You can type up the prewriting and research, if you want, since it might contain links." She points toward a class set of available laptops. "This assignment is partly persuasive and somewhat expository; you will take a stand on an issue and possibly propose a solution."

"Can we just write it on our phones?" Lucy asks. "I can text type a lot faster than I can computer type." Miss Oliver deliberates on the proposition. *Both methods could accomplish the research and documentation necessary to write official letters. But the craft of writing is better done on a large screen or blank page where details can be manipulated and moved around. Plus, phones are so distracting. While using them for research, students might be tempted to text.*

"No," the teacher responds definitively. She doesn't want teens to feel like texting is the only form of communication or composition. Miss Oliver knows there's value in the long-winded writing process: brainstorming, drafting, rethinking, revising, proofreading, and polishing.

---

18 Founded in 1920, the ACLU is a non-profit organization dedicated to defending constitutional rights and individual liberties.

What are you concerned about in the world, particularly in the United States? This could be related to the environment, the economy, education, homeland security, foreign matters, trade, terrorism, the military, healthcare, energy, immigration, etc.

A) List three details as to why this upsets or excites you.
1)
2)
3)

B) Record your research about the topic. Document sources. Explain the subject.

C) What would you like to happen or to change, if you could help the cause?

D) How would you respectfully advise the president on the matter? List three main points.
1)
2)
3)

E) Write your letter. Incorporate the prewriting.

F) Bibliography: Note sources you look at for information (links are okay) on a separate sheet of paper. If they are pertinent to your point, mention them in the body of the letter itself.

Ember raises her hand. "Are we actually sending these?"

The teacher passes out the last of the papers and returns to the podium. "Maybe."

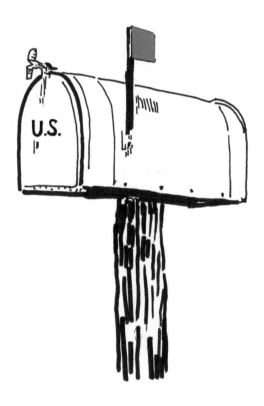

Week Two, Friday

When Miss Oliver walks into class after the short break, several students are already in attendance. They're looking at laptop screens or writing quietly by hand. Pleased by the early birds, she happily hands out gummy worms before the bell.

The whiteboard reads: Research complete? Prewriting done? Letters due at the end of the period!

"Hi, all. Happy Friday. I hope everyone made a dent in the work yesterday and homework last night. Today, you're finishing your letter-writing assignment. If you have extra time, share it with a friend before committing to the final draft. Please include your prewriting worksheet when you turn in your letter at the end of class."

Stephanie raises her hand.

"Yes?"

"What if we don't want you to send it. Like, to the *actual* president of the United States?"

"That's completely fine. I often write letters I don't—or can't—send. It helps to clarify what I'd like to say if given the chance. Maybe you'll eventually take action through that intention. In fact, I have something to give you in exchange for your letters as you finish. Think of it in terms of Civics, a resource to use if you so choose." Miss Oliver holds up a half-sheet of paper.

Got something to say? Start with your **Senators!**

Senators can be emailed via a form on the website at:
https://www.senate.gov/general/contact_information/senators_cfm.cfm?State=CA

You can also look up **Representatives** by address online. California has 53 representatives, based on 435 congressional districts.

You can contact the **Governor** at:
https://govapps.gov.ca.gov/gov40mail/

1303 10th Street, Suite 1173
Sacramento, CA 95814
Phone: (916) 445-2841
Fax: (916) 558-3160

"And if you don't want me to send your letter," she instructs, "simply write, 'don't send' at the top of it. What's the expression, 'NBD'?" Matt laughs. "You'll still get credit for writing it," Miss Oliver ensures. "Oh, and vocab paragraphs are due today, as well."

Kenn grumbles, "What? There's a test?"

"No, Kenn," the teacher corrects. "You should have a log of new words for the week. Choose three and try them out. Write a simple paragraph with them."

"About what?" he asks.

Matt turns around. "About anything, dude. NBD."

As the students busy themselves writing, Gabby preps a lesson on modals for the following Wednesday. *Should I cover modals?* she wonders. *Maybe so. A good teacher would. Indeed, I will!* She silently smirks at the English-y humor of this thought process.

She then circulates the room, initialing and recording completed vocab work—both the log of new words and the sentence extension assignment. Bloom's Taxonomy[19] meets public-school-teacher efficiency. Students consult Miss Oliver about their writing and exchange work for exit slips.

---

19 Named after educational psychologist Benjamin Bloom, specified learning objectives are classified into a hierarchical system of description, action, and assessment. Levels includes knowledge, comprehension, application, analysis, synthesis, and evaluation (also known as re-member, understand, apply, analyze, evaluate, and create). Activities ranging in complexity correspond with each level.

Thinking back to her Gateway to Education classes, Miss Oliver remembers that professors stressed keeping up with the latest tech trends in order to engage learners "on their level." They touted that teaching meant competing with handheld entertainment and breaking news. With so much drama happening online, advisors said lessons would require extra energy to gain and hold attention. *But does everything have to be dramatically performed? Is that the only way to interact? Just how it is these days?* Gabby questioned the supposition— then as a student and now as a teacher two weeks in.

I can't be the only one who feels this way. While she plans to utilize tech when necessary, Miss Oliver doesn't believe it should be a main method. She isn't adopting a digital approach. Not yet. Not unless she has to. And in fact, this class lends her the liberty of choice. *I can convey meaning and assess learning in different ways*, she reminds herself while recalling other college courses. *There is value in slower-paced instruction without soundbites and video input.*

Weekend Two, Saturday

Groceries purchased and apartment cleaned Friday night enable Saturday's workday. Gabby sits down to an uneven stack of letters coupled with prewriting pages. She takes a sip of fresh coffee, crossing her legs and fingers in hopes of reading thoughtful insights from students. On a large, lined sticky note, she creates a rubric. She assigns value to the criteria, and with cinnamon toast in one hand, Gabby reaches for the first pair of papers with the other.

<u>Letter Assignment:</u> 1 to 5 points possible for each aspect

Awareness of Audience	
Clarity of Claim	
Development of Ideas	
Mechanics	
Appearance	
Research	
Total (out of 30 points possible)	

Dear Mr. President,

Hey, how's it goin in the White house? I'm a Black teenager with a sick dad. Stop reading now if you want. But if not, I'll tell you that my dad is better now. Somewhat. Thanks to insurance, social security and financial assistance. The story is he worked hard all his life. He worked in the oil industry down south. At a refinery. He never smoked… that I know of. He's older. But he got lung cancer. Probably from work. Bronchioalveolar carcinoma. BAC. The White coats said it's just in his lung. And, it might come back. They did a transplant on the lung with the tumor, thanks to the Affordable Care Act. So, my dad couldn't work. He had to collect. And he gets Meals on Wheels now. He and my mama split a long time ago. So, my dad's income is very limited.

He's got medical bills with deductibles, copayments, prescriptions, home nurse checkups, physical therapy, blood draws and now dialysis. I know this is just a story about one Black man, but he's my dad. Thanks for reading.

Don't cut money from social security, Sir. Especially not for the Disabled. Keep medi-Care insurance and medic-Aid assistance programs goin. Pay subsidies that provide low-income people with insurance. Cost sharing helps pay premiums. Please keep life affordable so my dad don't die.

"This is but an imperfect outline of the plan — but I think it enough to give your Excellency an Idea of how the desirable work shall be executed" (Frederick Douglass).

Peace out,
Binah

P.S. I dig your hair style. It flows.

Wow, Gabby reckons. *Thoughtful? Yes. Paragraphing? Yep. Research? Seemingly extensive, though some of her knowledge was learned through life. Polished language? Not terribly bad.* With some allowance for lingo and individuality. Gabby fumbles for her red pen. She rolls it around on the table. *Do I make her rewrite it? According to my sense of style? My meticulous notion of mechanics? Nah,* she decides. *Let it be.* Gabby calculates the percentage and, with black ink, writes a B+ at the top of the prewriting page. She also wishes Binah's dad well. Next...

Dear Commander and Chief,

With all due respect, sir, I think there is a need for gun reform in our country. Recent attacks demonstrate this. Especially in schools. Because it's not safe enough. Students should feel guarded from harm and free to relax at school. I'm writing you because I'm not sure what else I can do.

I'm concerned about gun violence domestically. Based on my research, I believe the federal government, particularly the Department of Homeland Security, could do this. The Feds. It goes beyond people on watch lists not being allowed to purchase guns. It is about widespread safety and the protection of our people…here on American soil.

One of the missions of the Department of Homeland Security is to prevent terrorist attacks. But as we know, not all aggressors are foreign, and though we have gun laws, they vary from state to state. Based on my reading, it seems there are several gaps and "loopholes" in the current system. I will address three: assault weapons, background checks, and gun sales.

Improvements have been made over time and especially since recent incidents, but it's not enough. "When access to assault weapons is restricted, deaths due to mass shootings decrease" (smartgunlaws.org). Most agree that weapons with high-capacity magazines should only be used in military operations. Maybe it's time to require national compliance with semi-automatics and regulate modifications to existing weapons while upholding a federal ban on fully-automatic guns from civilians.

Secondly, statistics show states that require background checks on every sale—licensed and private—have less gun deaths, mass shootings, gun trafficking, and firearm suicides. Gun shows could be better organized in order to follow the rules of proper sale. Disclosing mental health records (including incompetency to stand trial) and criminal activity to the FBI's National Instant Criminal Background Check System (NICS) could be required of each state, not just encouraged. Reporting limited information apparently isn't enough. Background checks would be more thorough if federal law required them from all states and for all sales.

Thirdly, gun and ammo sales should be from a licensed seller and to a permitted recipient who has undergone firearm safety. That way, buyers are screened. Firearms ought to be registered, and transfers documented. It would improve accountability. These actions won't solve everything, but they would do something to save <u>innocent</u> lives.

I appreciate LE efforts within the DHS. They help to keep our country secure. However, the federal government could do more to prevent gun violence by collaborating with the Department of Health and Human Services, the FBI, ATF, state officials, and other agencies. I think we need nationwide standards.

My dad is serving in Afghanistan. Throughout his military career, he has witnessed lawlessness overseas. We have the power, infrastructure, and law enforcement to block bad guys from buying and rapid-firing guns. Here in the US. Are you brave enough to stop them? For the sake of schoolkids?

Respectfully,
Leeland Farbinski

Did this kid just call the president to action? Perhaps. Is the letter respectful? Of course. It is also researched-based, polished, passionate, and personal. Accurate? It seems so. Gabby reviews the rubric. Accuracy isn't part of the criteria. She skims Leeland's list of sources. *Hmm, looks thorough. But is gun control under the purview of the DHS? If not, could it become so?* She wasn't sure. *And what degree of mental-health issues are concerning?* She doesn't think maintaining mental wellness—such as getting treated for depression, anxiety, or PTSD—should qualify as grounds for report. *But severe disorders, sure.*

Gabby's device dings in the distance. *A-ha, an opening! Shall I let myself deviate from homework?* She fishes for her phone inside a canvas work bag across the room.

How about tonight? Pick you up at 7:00...MAYBE?

She smiles at Brandon's text. *Possibly,* Gabby prospects. *If I finish grading these papers.* Next...

Dear Mr. Prez,

I'm writing about trade, energy, the economy, and well, the environment. You know money talks. Resources talk. A graph on U.S. Energy Information (eia.gov) reports that we import around 10 MILLION barrels of petroleum a day. A flipping day! Wowsers. And we consume about twice as much. If I could help the cause, I would consider how we could rely less on other countries, how this might improve worldwide relations, and how Americans can be leaders in innovation and renewable energy.

Crude oil is messy and our need for it complicates foreign matters, including war, intervention, and all that grown-up political stuff. So, how can we be independent without drilling through protected lands and pissing people off? Natural and renewable resources, bro. Promotion of renewable energy—in the home, in the automotive industry, and in our daily lives.

We've got to 1) use less plastic 2) have widespread recycling programs 3) be able to drive affordable cars that don't take as much gas 4) build smarter roads 5) construct, heat, and power our homes more efficiently. This helps our economy and the environment.

I don't have all the answers. I'm just a teen with ideas. Please turn to the experts, meaning civil engineers, environmentalists, car manufacturers, energy enthusiasts, and chemists.

Thanks,
Matt

"Wowsers!" Gabby says aloud and laughs. *Does he realize that's from the 1980s cartoon detective show "Inspector Gadget?" Do kids still watch that? But wait, what about "flipping," "pissing," "bro?" What about Frederick Douglass? What about respect? What about…Chirps in contemporary times?* She twirls her red pen. A baton between her fingers. A majorette in the English marching band. Poised to circle the inappropriate language, Gabby's phone dings again.

She looks down to see a picture of Brandon at the beach. He's holding a single daisy against his bare chest, his wetsuit unzipped and pulled down to the waist. The Pacific Ocean glimmers in the background. Rays of sunshine illuminate his sandy face, sparkly eyes, long eyelashes, and wet hair. *OMG*, Gabby reacts. *Flipping A. Wowsers.*

Refocusing on the task at hand, the distracted teacher writes "conference!" at the top of Matt's prewriting page, followed by "language!" And lastly, she adds "organized and passionate!" Thus, giving it a mixed review.

See you at 7:00. I hope to be done grading by then. Nice picture. Enjoy the sunshine. She snaps a shot of her work, sends it in response, and continues on.

Gabby is intrigued by the next paper's introductory paragraph.
She sits back in her kitchen chair and reads Lucy's letter with curiosity.

Dear Mr. President,

My name is Lucy and I am a Latina. My mom was
born here, but her parents came from Puerto Rico.
My mom teaches Spanish—at a charter school. I've
been on the waiting list to go there. When I was
little, I went to a private school. It was nice.
They even had horseback riding! Plus outdoor ed.
Tech-free camps. And academic advisory groups. My
grandpa paid for it. But, he passed away. So, I
attend public school now. The teachers are great.
The lessons are good. But, it's not so easy to ask
questions or get help with homework. Luckily, some
stuff is posted online.

My parents said classes were smaller when
they were kids. Class averages were established
in 1964. According to the California Department
of Education, the average size in Kindergarten
is apx 31 students. That's a lot of littles!
For first through eighth grade, it's about 30. I
realize that our growing population is a factor.
That's one reason why I volunteer for PP, Planned
Parenthood.

At the charter where my mom works, she really
gets to know the kids. She comes home with funny
stories about them. I wish I felt more connected to
instructors and classmates. That's partly why I'm
on SC, Student Council. But public-school teachers
are tired, so they sometimes get frustrated
easily. Especially when we're on our phones. Or
they are. Anyway, if public education had funds to
hire additional staff, classes could be smaller.
Plus, teachers wouldn't feel so stretched. I have
no idea how they read and grade so much.

If there was more money available, maybe
people wouldn't feel like charter schools are
"stealing" from the public budget. Charters are

cool because they can frame things how they want, and my mom has always told me that people learn differently. So what if a school has an alternative approach, as long as it works? And sure, I think there should be general standards, but not all schools have to run the same way. For example, my mom's elementary does "little buddy" leadership (where older students help younger ones read and craft) and "magic circle" (a routine where kids share their likes and concerns respectfully).

I like that charters are an option for some, but I'm concerned that public class sizes are getting too big for the rest of us. As students, we are future college applicants, future workers, future leaders. If there's anything to invest in, it's us. Right?

Sincerely,
Lucy

Teary eyed and proud, Gabby circles the "A" at the top of Lucy's assignment. Next…she picks up Nadia's notes.

Dear President,

I am not an immigrant. My boyfriend is. He is a teenager. We have a baby now. You have money, resources, everything. Not everyone is born that way. Mi novio Nico got to stay here because of Deferred Action for Childhood Arrivals (DACA). The program allows Mexican kids to live in the United states with there parents. Last year he got a work permitt. Im trying to help him with English. His dad picks fruit. His mom cleans houses. They are nice people. Nico works at a store. There jobs matter to the comunity. They matter to there jobs. We try to better our lives. We are thankfull for DACA. We want a good life for the baby.

Let Nico stay. Por favor. He will become
a citisen wone day. Our baby needs her daddy, a
sitter, and money. Mi tía helps us, pero necesito
Nico también.

Gracias,

Nadia

Gabby takes a long inhalation. She stares off into the distance, out the window, toward the horizon. Late morning sun filters through the wooden lattice and trailing vine framed by a sliding glass door. The teacher studies Nadia's minor mechanical mistakes. *Was her paper less effective because of spelling errors and such? Or was it more?*

The educator knows Nadia wants to improve her English abilities. But she doesn't want to shame the struggling student and henceforth hinder her vocab acquisition. Coming from the less linguistically diverse Midwest, Gabby thinks learning a second language is an awesome feat, an impressive skill to be admired. Reluctantly, she circles the misspelled words and kindly directs her to "please rewrite" it. On the top of Nadia's paper, she inscribes "best wishes," then adds a star for heart. And hope.

Dear President,

Gender prescription, identity, sexual attraction…
chromosomes, genes, hormones, sex organs and
social conditioning. It's not simple or assumed.
There's a lot of research and opinions on the
subject. I read "Beyond XX and XY" in *Scientific
American* (September 2017).

I'm concerned about LGBTQ rights.

Some politicians want to move backward when things
just started to go forward, especially in the

military (Don't Ask Don't Tell Repeal Act of 2010 vs the Transgender Ban announcement in 2017). Un- informed people can make mean generalizations about uniformed people. Life is not binary. Male and female. People vary for multiple reasons. And they/we should be allowed to stray from simple categories. It shouldn't limit us in work choices.

So, think before you Chirp. Read before you need. To vote. Watch, listen, and ask before you cast. Judge-ment. Consider consult. Before you insult. Again.

1) Stand up against discrimination of LGBTQ and non-binary people
2) Expand rights instead of denying them (make the Equality Act of 2019 a national standard)
3) Read, watch, listen to alternatives

Please,

Robert/Rob/Robbie/Bert/Berta/Roberta

Whoa. Gabby gasps. *I had no idea he was…Wait, what should I call him? Her? They? Ahh! Well, the letter is short…but poetic in part? A re- search article is mentioned. As is policy. The grammar, spelling, and punctua- tion are fine. The content is authentic. The demeanor may be a tad accusatory, though.* She gives Robbie a "B" plus.

As she grades, Gabby vacillates between assigning more worth to content, mechanics, or character. *This is difficult, hard to judge such variety against one set scale.*

Mr. President,

Those in power have sometimes sought more. For centuries, The Church fought to establish its power over the people, either with the help of

kings or regardless of them. Supposedly, knowledge
was controlled. Many people were illiterate, so
whatever information was available to read wasn't
usually wide spread. It's been said that writing
was discouraged back then because it usually led
to independent thought. It's no coincidence that
this part of history is known as the Dark Ages
(or at least that's one general take on the time
period of apx 500-1000 AD/CE).

In more recent records, slave owners feared that
literacy might prompt slaves toward wanting
freedom. Indeed, it did. For good reason. Knowledge
was part of a path forward for African Americans
like Frederick Douglass. After escaping slavery,
he published an abolitionist newspaper in 1847,
and he and his black wife helped slaves traveling
north through the Underground Railroad.

Now we live in the Information Age, yet some of
those in charge are still trying to limit people's
access. Humans are more connected than ever, and
this could potentially pose a threat. I'm asking
you to restrain from passing policy which aims to
censor online content and to take a stand against
foreign rulers who keep their citizens in the
dark.

Censorship is not simply a matter of passing harsh
legislation. It works in sneaky and harmful ways.
Clouding the truth is also a type of control.
Labeling news as false or fake simply because it
goes against one's beliefs or agenda discourages
some from interacting with certain valuable
sources. The late author Ray Bradbury once
wrote, "You don't have to burn books to destroy
a culture. Just get people to stop reading them"
(*Fahrenheit 451*, published 1953).

I think 1) Everyone deserves the right to express
themselves and communicate. 2) This is especially

true and even more important for minority groups. 3) We could have a more united, equal, and productive world if we were able to share, accept, and understand different stories and experiences.

Please protect the press and media outlets to allow free flow of information for the world's citizens. I want the 1st amendment, or something similar, to be applied widely. Perhaps the UN can get involved and create an Internet Bill of Rights (like in Brazil and Italy).

Regards,
Rhonda

Miss Oliver is impressed by Rhonda's research application and eloquence in addressing timely issues. She is aware that Rhonda is articulate; she knows the girl enjoys writing and actually publishes some of it online, but she didn't expect this level of concern from a teenager. Rhonda is paying attention to the world, to history, and to the politics of the World Wide Web. *But she also demands a lot.* The teacher envisions the determined student with fists on her hips.

Curiously, Miss Oliver wonders: *Could there ever be a global internet agreement? Aren't rights relative to region? Is complete free flow a stretch, even in our own country?* She acknowledges that the pros come with the cost of cons. *Some things online push the limits of acceptable.*

Dear Mr. President,

I am concerned about device dependency. Statistics show that increased time online can lead to depression, anxiety, and even suicide! Especially for teens. Social networking is encouraging addictive behavior partly because opinions are shared, argued against, and misinterpreted. Personally, I barely use it. I don't even carry a frickin phone. Social media tends to piss me off.

I read "Me, myself, and iPhone" from the Mental Health section of *The Economist* (November 25th-December 1st, 2017). It is reported that 3/4's of teens use smartphones. During the last decade, the amount of teens and kids admitted to hospitals for suicidal thoughts doubled. This could be related to social networking, seeing as how a recent study found that people who gave it up for a week felt less depressed when compared to a control group who did not give up the habit.

We also read "Uptick in Teen Depression" and listened to the NPR podcast in class (11/14/17, *All Things Considered*). In it, a study from the journal *Clinical Psychological Science* showed that extra time online was connected to signs of depression, but face-to-face activities decreased this. The researcher said that the finding should come as a warning to parents. Duh.

I read a *New York Times* article entitled "How Evil is Tech?" by David Brooks (November, 2017). Here are some quotes that I agree with: A). "Social media promises an end to loneliness but actually produces an increase in solitude and an intense awareness of social exclusion." B). "Since the spread of the smartphone, teens are much less likely to hang out with friends, they are less likely to date, they are less likely to work."

San Diego State University psychologist Ms. Jean Twenge is the researcher cited in all three of these articles. In "Have Smartphones Destroyed a Generation?" published in *The Atlantic* in 2017 (and it's also in the NYT article noted above), she says teens who spend three or more hours online a day are thirty-five percent more likely to be at risk of suicide.

Please address these issues 1) by reaching out to today's kids and encouraging limits regarding time spent online/texting and 2) by example. Leading by example might mean depending less on social networks, not hiding behind a screen, dealing with tough issues in person, resisting the urge to defend yourself online, talking with people directly, accepting other viewpoints, agreeing to disagree, and focusing on what matters. Maybe you'll get real smiles instead of electronic likes or angry emojis.

Personally, I hope that in time there are less car accidents as a result of decreased dependence upon devices. BTW, my mom died while texting. Unfortunately, when people compulsively check the news—including their personal messages and social sites—anxiety, depression, and sometimes even death follow.

Concerned,
Ember

Another stirring letter with real concerns facing today's teenagers. *Ember is on fire here!* Gabby pictures the girl with her fiery orange hair telling it like it is. The teacher agrees a president should model communication techniques that unify and stabilize instead of divide and dismantle. Such strategies could improve habits from the top down.

She stands and stretches. Gabby thinks about how she can better address these issues in her classroom. How can she convince students to disengage from habits that both inform and depress us? *A simple Venn-diagram-driven discussion wouldn't be enough to account for the spectrum of issues.*

At least Ember is able to channel her grief, Gabby realizes. *As a result of her mom's death, she's choosing to abstain from phone usage. And she's trying to raise awareness about the harmful effects of overuse. She even does it rather politely here, considering her normal angry stance.* In this case, the teacher lets the swear words slide.

Dear Mr. President,

I'm over global warming. Climate change and all. I'm sick of hearing about it, sick of people trying to shame miners and refinery workers, sick of other countries trying to call the shots for the U.S. It's about money, either way—money for renewables or money for fossil fuels. But we all depend on fossil fuels. And workers depend on jobs within that business. It's just the way it is.

Keep standing up to new age environmentalists who are trying to overthrow the old system. The Paris Climate Deal might cost our country. Let's focus on us instead of the world for once! Like EPA admin dude once said, "Our EPA puts America first." Extreme pollution laws would harm businesses like coal, natural gas, and oil. My uncle Ralph owns oil rigs, and he's always complaining about regs.

Of course we can keep trying for energy independence. If we don't agree with the Paris group, why should we uphold standards they set? To lower the earth's temp by a couple measly degrees? We already have the Clean Air Act and the United States Climate Alliance to keep pollution in check, right? Why let other countries bully us into doing more? I'm glad The Clean Power Plan is under review.

Life is pretty good here with burning coal, using oil and natural gas, driving big cars, carrying plastic bags, and sipping sodas from straws. People are wasting their time trying to save the earth. I think you agree.

You've got this,
Adam

The teacher is appalled. *Doesn't Adam recognize the benefits of the Clean Power Plan?*[20] *Doesn't he know that the U.S. is a major player in the Paris Agreement?*[21] *What we do—or do not do—environmentally may influence other countries. How could someone prioritize outdated norms over world preservation? Renewable energy will eventually save Americans money in bills. It will create jobs! As will renewable agriculture.*

Adam's concerns are only the tip of the environmental iceberg regarding global warming, climate change, population growth, different types of pollution, and diminishing resources. Being from a Great Lake state, water cleanliness is important to her. *His straw comment is the last straw!* She would like to assign Adam a research report on the 5 Gyres![22] Gabby pulls out her inhaler. Her asthma is worse when she's agitated. And the worst when she's near smoggy cities.

But Gabby can't grade Adam according to her beliefs. She knows she can't dock points for disagreement. But she wishes he wasn't so resistant to change at such a young age. *Sure, she reasons, oil has its place in our society, and hardworking people rely on jobs in that industry, but cleaner fuels and innovative alternatives should also be valued. And encouraged.* Gabby consults the rubric and notes his paper is well researched. Although, through her own cursory investigation, she realizes Adam must've overlooked aspects of the articles cited in his bibliography. For instance, the Clean Air Act had undergone recent rollbacks.[23] *I guess sometimes people only see what they already believe to be true.*

---

20 The Clean Power Plan is designed to address climate change and intended to lower carbon emissions, proposed and reviewed by the Environmental Protection Agency (EPA) in 2014 and 2017, respectively.
21 Under the Paris Agreement, one requirement is for each country to report emissions to the United Nations. The goal is to curb climate change.
22 The 5 Gyres Institute is an organization dedicated to reducing plastic pollution, namely garbage patches, floating at sea, moving with ocean currents and wind patterns.
23 The Clean Air Act is supposed to help reduce greenhouse gasses, toxins from automobiles, power plant smoke, and drilling site pollution.

Gabby uses the restroom. She broods over the naivety of certain students, their immature rationale about complex matters. *I can't expect these kids to think like adults. They haven't had the experiences yet. Some of them may be parroting their parents or things they've heard on the news.*

She continues to read papers into the afternoon. Some pleas she agrees with; others she does not. The teacher marks students down for undocumented research, incomplete work, thoughtlessness, overly sloppy writing, incoherency, and disregard for audience. One boy wrote a letter to his mom, which was funny, but it wasn't the purpose of the assignment. She tries not to judge them on their concerns, although some have political leanings, some letters are rhetorically charged, and some writing is shallow. Alas, she picks up the last paper...Lillian's.

```
Dear President,


    "The number of climate related disasters has
more than tripled since 1980" (Nat Geo). This is
affecting other animals and plants, too.
    I'm concerned about climate change and global
warming. The world is getting warmer, scientifically
and statistically. Weather is getting worse. More
humans could assist with efforts to slow this down.
2016 was hotter than 2015. And 2015 beat 2014.
We are heating up the earth with Carbon Dioxide
(CO2). Because of melting ice, sea levels rose 8-9
inches since 1900 (NOAA).
    Through research, I learned that Carbon
dioxide is created because of fossil fuels (coal,
oil, gas). Methane comes from agriculture and
landfills. Nitrous Oxide comes from agriculture
and industry. Fluorinated gasses also come from
industrial processes. These create the "greenhouse
effect" (concentrations of trapped gasses in the
atmosphere). Cutting down trees doesn't help
because trees filter air.
    The National Park Service says we can reduce
greenhouse gasses by: getting dual paned windows
```

in homes, insulating doors, using renewable energy (solar, wind, and water), using less heat and a/c, buying energy efficient lightbulbs, turning off electronics when not using them, hanging clothes out to dry, and planting native plants.

I can do some of these things, although my mom doesn't have money to change much in our HUD house.

Please don't hurt the Earth. Help it. Limit greenhouse gasses and global warming. Set the example by trusting scientists and upholding policies like the Clean Power Plan. Allow the EPA to set and enforce limits. Spread the word to businesses. Even informed kids could make changes in their homes! You are a world leader who can help reduce carbon emissions at a presidential level.

Hurricanes, flooding, drought, fires, and weather extremes cost money, end lives, and devastate regions. Coastlines are threatened by rising seas. This is a real problem, as much of a threat to our health and safety as any other.

I will try to do my part as a Californian teenager and global citizen. Will you do yours?

Peace,
Lillian

A. Well done.

The teacher thinks about the letters overall. *Students seem to crave both decisiveness and thoughtfulness from the president and his administration. Are the two notions mutually exclusive?* Gabby's momentary musing leads her to a memory of a clever toy she spotted in a gift shop recently: a collection of plastic green army men practicing yoga. Strong and calm, each soldier posed in a mindful position.

Miss Oliver recognizes that research findings may create internal conflict for some. She relates it to a story her dad recently told about her own learning process. A parable of sorts. He reminded her of it after she earned her teaching credential and accepted this job out West.

"The notion of the sun was a foreign concept to you," she remembers her father's voice saying. "First, you learned about the moon. You'd point to the moon in books and in the night sky. Then, I read to you about the sun, and you'd shake your head. You'd argue with me in your tiny-but-mighty voice. 'No, daddy, moon.' It was all you knew about celestial bodies then."

Life certainly gets more complex with age, Gabby determines. *It's hard to assimilate the known with the new.* She pictures the twinkle in students' eyes at times when they're unsure but speak up anyway.

Gabby jumps in the shower. While shaving her legs, she deliberates on how to dress for the evening. *Should I ask him where we're going? No, I'd rather be surprised. But what to wear? Will we be inside or out? Does he even have a plan? I could text him a few pictures of outfits? No, that's silly. I want him to be surprised.* She realizes devices with easy access have the potential to diminish a date's anticipatory set.

Before walking Eddie, Gabby lays out a few options on the bed: short flowy dress with brown belt and heels, long sleeveless gown with chiffon scarf, or fitted blue jeans with lacy top and big earrings…she throws on an old Chicago Bears T-shirt and cutoff shorts.

Despite her asthma, the active woman has always enjoyed walking. It works out nervous energy, and it burns off calories. Walking tends to mentally straighten Gabby's thoughts whether or not she strides in a straight path. She misses the lush windy trails of the midwestern woods, but she also appreciates the succulent-lined cement sidewalks of her current surroundings. *Beauty takes many forms*, Gabby thinks as she recalls Chicago's architecture and the unique exhibits inside Millennium Park. She and little Eddie pass an overweight man led by a giant groomed poodle, its calico curls bouncing on top the dog's pitched forehead. *And preference for companionship varies as well.*

The doorbell rings just as Gabriella finishes polishing her nails, so she turns the knob carefully. Brandon greets her with flowers. Gabby beams from inside the doorway.

"Hi. Thank you. These are beautiful." She accepts the bouquet and welcomes her colleague inside. Relating romance to academics, the English teacher analogizes: *First impression jitters lure lovers like engaging lessons lead students.* Brandon is wearing a red collared shirt, stylish blue jeans, and cowboy boots. *Wait, cowboy boots.* Gabby pauses to take in his western footwear. *I guess we do live "out West,"* she concludes vis-à-vis her suburban setting.

"Here, sit down," Gabby gestures toward a stool under the entryway's granite island. "Let me put these in a vase." She sets the carnations on the counter and walks around to the other side. Brandon watches speechlessly as her straightened hair falls over the wide neckline of an off-white dress, her long bangs framing pinkish cheeks. The colorful petals complement the hue in Gabby's girlish face. "How was your day?"

"Pretty rad, thanks," Brandon replies. "Got up early, went for a run, caught some waves, met a friend for a beer."

"Oh, that's nice." Gabby wonders about the friend: *male or female?*

"Yours?"

Gabby points to the stack of graded papers teetering on the small dining room table.

"I'm sorry," Brandon sympathizes.

"It's okay," she assures him. "That's the nature of my job, and these papers were actually pretty interesting to read."

"Oh, really?" Brandon humors her.

"Yeah, students wrote letters to the president." Gabby freshens the flowers, arranging them neatly into a fanned array.

Brandon shakes his head as if to clear water from his ears. "What? Do you mean the president of the United States?"

"Yep," Gabby answers curtly.

"About what?"

"Things they're concerned about: the environment, economy, education, homeland security, foreign relations, trade, guns, healthcare, renewable energy, immigration…typical teenage worries."

"Wow, way to drop in! Ride the wave, so to speak. That's impressive," Brandon applauds. "To get them to think beyond parties, football, and social media."

"Yeah, well, some of these kids have big ideas. Sure, they're idealistic, but their pleas to the president were research based, albeit limited and somewhat biased. Anyway, I still figure it was a good assignment. It was supposed to be about language—getting away from abbreviations and slang, a.k.a. text talk. But in the end, I decided to let some of that slide."

"Did they write the letters in 140 characters or less?" She knows he's referring to social-media parameters because on some forums, you can only say so much.

"No, 280," Gabby jokes as she fetches her purse from the hook hanging beside the door. She'd heard the Chirp allotment increased. The sapient teacher considers how easily we pass judgment based on abbreviated texts these days: *we scroll, we swipe, we block, we react. Whereas letters enable longhand.*

"Hey, where are we going anyway? Am I dressed appropriately?" She glides glittery gloss across her lips. Brandon watches longingly as her matching pink nails cradle the applicator and the makeup softens her mouth. The chemistry between them builds. Brandon rises from his seated position next to her. He extends an arm behind her small waist and feels the thin fabric of her rayon dress.

"You look perfect," he says and pulls her toward him. "We're going dancing. Vamos a bailar!"

"Really? Again? Where?"

"Salsa dancing. After we eat."

Swept off her feet already, Gabby closes the door behind them.

Inside a trendy Mexican restaurant, Brandon returns from the bar with two margaritas. "Bebemos al nuevo año escolar!" He clinks the glasses together and hands Gabby one.

"We drink to the new school year?" Gabby guesses.

"Yes. And new beginnings." Brandon looks at Gabby over the rim of his green glass as he sips the cocktail.

She meets his stare. "New beginnings," she repeats, thinking back to sports bars in Chicago…hot wings, rowdy crowds, and basic nachos at best. The current scene captures her interest more than football ever did, although she played the part of local sports fan for many years, her navy sweatshirt with orange lettering still hanging up at home.

Beyond the restaurant dining area, Gabby spots a shiny dance floor and neon strobe lights illuminating its center. She takes a drink and looks over the menu. Enchiladas, tamales, tostadas, chili verde, carne asada…so many intriguing choices.

"So, tell me," Brandon interrupts her perusal. "Did you have a boyfriend back East?"

"At times," Gabby answers coyly.

"Well, does he—do they—still call you? Or visit?"

"No, the only person to visit so far was my dad."

"I see. So, you haven't had any other sleepovers since you moved here."

"Ha!" Gabby laughs at Brandon's implication. "Eddie sleeps with me every night," she smirks.

A waitress approaches their table. She smiles flirtatiously at Brandon. "Hi," the unnatural blonde greets him as if they know each other. But her face quickly loses the appearance of friendliness as she looks Gabby over. "Cómo estás?"

"Bien, gracias," Brandon answers without meeting her eyes, his face behind the menu. Sol Y Luna, the name of the restaurant, is spelled across the brown leather cover. Eventually, he collapses it and orders. "Prawns diablo con tortillas y guacamole y pescado ranchera para mi amiga."

"Tu amiga o tu no-vi-a?" The woman pronounces the last word slowly. Nosily.

"La comida, por favor."

"Si, señor," the waitress wipes the table and glares at Gabby as she turns to leave with the folded menus.

"What was that?" Gabby asks, confused by the heated exchange, the conversation and order she took no part of. "Do you know her? Did you just order for me? What is 'novia'?"

Brandon shakes his head and sighs. "Yes, I know her, sort of. Not really. I come here sometimes. And yes, I ordered for you. You like fish? It's excellent. And novia means girlfriend."

Gabby sits back in her chair. *Whoa. He comes here? He knows her? His girlfriend?* It was a lot to take in. She brings the icy drink to her mouth.

"She asked me if you were my girlfriend."

Gabby swallows.

"Yes, I like fish, thanks," she briefly responds, her head still spinning. She'd eaten a lot of it growing up. Because of her father's occupation.

"Listen, it's no big deal. I didn't say whether or not you're my girlfriend. It's none of her business. I like to dance, and so I come here on salsa nights sometimes; I've danced with her before, but that's it. We just danced. She has a boyfriend anyway, see." He pulls out his phone, taps a few areas, and shows Gabby a picture of the waitress with an older man wearing a cowboy hat. "Nuestro aniversario," the caption reads "with Coralina and Manuel."

"Okay. Um, I'm going to use the ladies' room now." Buzzed by the overload of information mixed with tequila, Gabby retreats to the restroom. A Mexican-inspired mosaic floor pattern adds to the chaos she feels. A fiesta of colors framed by white tile walls. Uncertain emotions and impressions mingle in her mind. *So, if Brandon can access a picture of this waitress so quickly, he must be "friends" with her on social media. Or he has looked her up to see that she's involved with someone, at least. And that's supposed to be reassuring to me? That doesn't disprove their relationship. This is awkward! How often are salsa nights?*

Gabby returns to the table as the food arrives—served by someone else, a male waiter. Brandon puts his phone back in his jeans pocket. "You okay, dude?"

"Yeah. This looks yummy, thanks."

"De nada."

"So, you have a reputation here, it seems?"

"Like I said, I like to dance," he reminds her.

"With different partners?" Gabby boldly inquires.

"Yes. That's appropriate for salsa dancing. Rotating partners is encouraged. But I'm here with you tonight. I only want to dance with you." Intending to comfort her, Brandon reaches beneath the table. His warm hand meets her bare leg, and suddenly, nothing else matters. Not the fish. Not the waitress. Only his fingers brushing against her thigh.

"Okay," Gabby manages to say as she begins to melt faster than the ice in her glass.

After they eat and finish their salted drinks, Brandon escorts

Gabby toward the music. There are only a few couples dancing, but Gabby can tell they're enjoying themselves: moving quickly and strutting effortlessly. There is a narrow bar top counter with stools just outside the area. Gabby sits down and faces the dance floor. Brandon mouths, "I'll be right back." It is hard to hear him above the Latin beat, so she takes in the salsa scene.

Both male and female partners contribute to the combination of moves; they each take turns showing off, separately adding their own flair. Two spotlights illuminate the floor. The Midwesterner is awestruck by the mutual respect between individuals. Each person seems to lead and follow, initiate and reciprocate. *A flirtatious banter. Sexy and classy. Like silhouettes sashaying.* The women look flashy and appealing, upscale and frilly. Flowery blouses accentuate their curves conservatively. The well-groomed men appear sleek and aerodynamic: shirts tucked into belts, hair gelled into place. Gabby leans on the bar, chin in hand. *I could watch this all night.*

Brandon returns with fresh drinks. He sits down and sets two margaritas on the bar between them. Gabby picks up the cocktail, raising the rim to her glossy lips. "Thanks," she sips, looking left at her handsome companion.

"Ready to dance?" Brandon nudges. The music fades. Gabby chews a small ice cube and quietly mulls over the question.

"I don't know the steps or what to do."

"Hang loose, I'll lead," Brandon lifts a hand from her lap, tugs at it, stands, and guides Gabby upward. "Vamos a bailar."

Reluctantly, the timid trainee rises. She follows him onto the hardwood floor as the music resumes. Under colorful lights, Brandon grasps Gabby's right hand. He places his other hand behind her shoulder, coaxing her outstretched left hand to rest on his bicep, their arms parallel to the floor. With his legs, Brandon positions one of her knees between his own. As his thighs move against hers, Gabby begins to follow the beat with her feet. Her hips hinge to and fro, matching his vivacious movement.

Gracefully, Brandon extends their interlocked hands, moving her outward. Gabby's loose hand flutters down to her side. He pulls her in again, their chests touching. And then, with his arm guiding hers overhead, she spins. Subsequently, Brandon ducks and does the same. Gabby flashes back to memories of ballet, solo on the stage, twirling tentatively. She compares the fluidity of their current co-curricular to a rehearsed routine: *This conjoint experience is uplifting!* She rises onto her toes. *Relevé!*

"Where did you learn to dance like that? And speak Spanish?" Gabby asks from the sidelines after the song ends. They return to their seats inside the restaurant.

"From my dad. In Mexico." Brandon takes a drink.

"Oh, I didn't realize you were Mexican." Intrigued, Gabby sips and listens, the citrus cooling her throat.

"Many Californians are Mexican, Miss Oliver." He chomps on ice. "Either by blood or by regional association. I think my dad is one-fifth Latino? He likes to visit Mexico, and I went down there a lot while growing up. We have family in Guadalajara, distant cousins. Or maybe we just called them 'primos?' I haven't seen them in years. But when I was younger, we'd go to these big fiestas. Mustached men would wear sombreros y botas. Women would put pretty flowers in their hair. We kids would goof around, eating sweets. And there was always dancing. Back then, my father was a master on the dance floor! He was something to see," Brandon chuckles. "Maybe you can meet him sometime."

"That's great," Gabby smiles. "I mean that he enjoyed dancing with your mom."

"No, my mom didn't dance much."

Gabby feels silly for making the assumption, this being the only story she's heard about his parents. "I'm sorry, are they not together?"

"Yes, they live up the road, actually."

"Oh, nice." Without memories of her parents dancing together or apart, Gabby finds herself at a loss for words.

On the drive home, that last margarita and the notion of carpe diem implore Gabby to ask a burning question. After all, the dance floor experience set her afire. "So, did your ex like to dance? I mean, did you two go to Sol Y Luna together much?"

Brandon turns to Gabby, raises his eyebrows, and then focuses on the road ahead. A few seconds pass before he answers. "Natasha likes to hula. It's not really a partner dance. Why do you ask?"

"Well, I don't know. Just wondering. You haven't told me anything about her. I mean it's none of my business, I suppose. But, didn't you say you were supposed to get married—like a month ago?"

"Six weeks."

"Can I ask what happened?"

"She's still in Hawaii."

"Oh," Gabby replies, unable to muffle her surprise.

"As I said, Natasha prefers to dance alone."

After a few minutes of riding in silence, the teachers arrive at Gabby's apartment complex. Unlike the last time she'd driven with him in the VW, when Brandon dropped her off at a slight distance from the door, he parks his Thing in her assigned guest space. *Right up close.* He gets out of the vehicle. Hoping she didn't spoil the evening by asking about his previous partner, Gabby thanks Brandon for taking her.

"That was fun, different, cultural; thank you for getting me out of the apartment!" She heads toward the front door of her first-story dwelling. A sensor light beams overhead. Tiny pink roses decorating the entrance become apparent as they approach. Gabby finds her keys, unlocks the door, and turns to say goodbye. She pleasantly waves with her free hand, but Brandon doesn't respond—verbally or physically.

Immobilized, he just looks at her, penetrating her with his stare. Gabby can sense sexual energy building. Brandon's reservation with words excites the talkative teacher now straddling the doorway's threshold. She recalls his precision on the dance floor and likens it to his careful choice of words and the seductive silence in between. Finally, Brandon awakens from his fixated trance. He reaches for Gabby, pulls her toward him, and kisses her—passionately, conclusively, climactically.

"Goodnight Gabriella." Then, without hesitation or elaboration, he departs, leaving his date spinning on the sidewalk.

WEEKEND TWO, SUNDAY

Sleepy and somewhat slow due to the aftermath of alcohol, Gabby walks Eddie down to the beach by morning light. Still swaying from the previous night's turns, she feels rather romantically awakened. Gabby processes the outing as she maneuvers around people along the boardwalk. Some gaze outward at waves, others downward at their phone screens. One woman films her toddler playing at the water's edge while a slightly older boy braves deeper water. He's not in the footage, and he loses his footing. "Mom!" The older brother calls out, adrift in the tide.

"Hold on," his mom says, distracted by her videography. "Timmy is jumping the waves. I want to send a picture to your dad." Meanwhile, the other kid's pants get soaked, and he struggles to swim ashore. Gabby waits to make sure he's safe before continuing her walk. The mother doesn't look up from her phone until big brother tugs at her tank top. "Billy, you're all wet!" She reprimands.

Eddie and his observant owner pass a demonstration happening on the other side of the street. Something about pesticides running into a local river. An organic agricultural brigade. Farmers—or people dressed up as farmers—line the sidewalk. Passersby honk in support or protest, drawing attention to the cause regardless. Gabby recognizes one of her students standing in environmental solidarity. Lillian holds a sign that says, "Thumbs Down to Roundup!"

Eddie pulls Gabby toward interesting smells. He lingers longer than she cares to near unbagged dog-poop piles. Meanwhile, she admires shoots of sage and lavender, taking in their natural fragrance. Letting Eddie lead the way, the contemplative teacher trails behind her furry companion. Near drowning and eco-friendly rally aside, Gabby feels girlish and giddy. She smiles at the memory of Brandon on the dance floor, his fancy footwork, his artful movements, the confidence in which he commanded her body. In hindsight, Gabby realizes she mostly just followed along. *I have to maintain some control here*, she self-talks. *I can't just let him sweep me off my feet. I must stay grounded. Come to think of it, am I just a rebound?* Eventually, she steers Eddie back home, toward the golden landscape to the east. "Come on, boy," she directs.

Back at the apartment and curious about her coworker, Gabby decides to research him online. She questions, *isn't that what interest in a 3-D person tends to lead to these days…snooping through social media as if someone's online profile and supposed friendships could tell his or her whole story? Let's see…* she navigates to Brandon's Insta-Face account. *What did he say that girl's name was last night? Oh yeah, Coraleena? Coralina?* She clicks on Brandon's list of friends. 1069. *Wow.* Compared to her 252, she wonders how he keeps up. *Does he actually know and trust all of these people—enough to look inside his life?* In contrast, Gabby keeps her social circle small, granting limited access to her home, heart, and head. Plus, she barely finds time to check in on her closest friends, their perpetual posts only intermittently catching her passing attention. She scrolls to "C." *Voilà!* **Coralina: from San Diego, went to college at Horizon University, works at Sol Y Luna, engaged to Manuel Rodriquez.** *Eh,* she concludes, *not exactly a threat or romantic contender.* Gabby looks over a few pictures and moves on.

What did he say the hula girl's name was…Natasha? She scrolls down and down, past many alphabetized women and finally to the elusive ex. *Wait, there is a Natacia, Natacha, and Natasha.* "What the hell?" she whispers aloud to Eddie who sits next to her on the couch. Gabby is amazed by the number of pretty females Brandon apparently corresponds with.

The first, Natacia, looks to be about fourteen. *Weird,* Gabby judges. *Let's hope she's a relative!* The second Natacha is beautifully blonde, a blue-eyed cover model, or possibly a porn star based on her provocative pictures. *Geez, is that her? How could I compete?* And the third Natasha is pictured wearing a grass skirt, flowery lei around her neck, and ebony hair framing her face. *Well, that must be her,* Gabby decides. She notices a picture of the two of them on a white-sand beach. Brandon looks happy, his closed-lipped complacent smile complementing the beauty of the woman next to him, his Hawaiian shirt blowing in the sea breeze of last summer.

Dear Mom,

Hi. How's it going up there with Grandma? Playing cards? Who's winning?

So, I'm writing to tell you about my date. Yes, with that surfer dude. The one who drives the convertible. Don't worry, we kept the top on, meaning both my shirt and the car, haha! But he kissed me. And he twirled me. He fed me yummy Mexican food, and of course, we drank margaritas. He even paid the bill!

Then, we went salsa dancing. I know what you're thinking…that I didn't last long in ballet. But this is different, Mom. Salsa requires a partner. I wasn't out there on my own. It was a cultural experience, or at least a regional one. Anyway, I had fun…mostly. The date got me out "on the town."

But Brandon has a lot of female friends online, including our waitress last night. That was awkward! I'm not sure how deep those virtual connections run.

I've been out of the socialization scene for a while with my head down in the books and with moving and all. And I haven't ever really gotten into the digitally-driven dating world. It just seems so superficial. If I'm going to invest time in someone, presumably long term, I want it to be worth it. But I guess we can't anticipate when people will leave our lives.

Miss you,
Gabbers

P.S. Brandon's recently single. I don't know the whole story. We'll see what happens…tomorrow at work.

WEEK THREE

TEEN DRAMA
ONLINE AND ON SET

Week Three, Monday

As Miss Oliver carries her book bags down the school's outdoor hallway, she notices someone in front of her room. Upon closer look, she sees that it is the principal imposing upon her doorway. He is standing with his arms folded. The teacher attempts to hide her anxiety and compose herself. As timing would have it, Brandon passes her on the sidewalk, and when he walks beyond Mr. Keystone, he turns back to Gabby, his eyes wide, questioning. Mr. Ritter easily unlocks his door as Gabby greets their boss.

"Good morning, sir. How are you?"

The corners of a mustache turn upward as the older man smiles. With a mix of authority and friendliness, he replies cheerfully. "Good day, Miss Oliver. Can we go inside, please?"

"Of course." Gabby sets down her bags and opens the door. "Please come in," she gestures after turning on the overhead lights.

"Listen, I won't bother you for long," the principal assures her. "I know you have to get set up, and I have to prepare this morning's announcement. But I've been meaning to come say hello, and I want to ask you something in person. I heard your third-period students are writing letters to the president of the United States? A girl I sat by at Friday's assembly told me about the assignment when I asked her how she likes the new class. I think her name was Lucy."

Gabby looks her superior in the eye. She feels a bit intimidated. "Yes, sir. I hope it's okay. These students…they're really passionate. They did research on chosen political and societal topics. They want to express themselves. I'd like to give them that chance. For instance, Lucy wrote about education and class sizes in particular."

"Hmm," the principal looks mildly impressed. "Are they writing on behalf of Heart High?"

Gabby hadn't thought of that: how the language and biases

might reflect back on the school at large, how the teens are representing the institution, good or bad. "Um, no, actually; I don't believe any of them specify which school they're attending. I didn't instruct them to. Initially, I wasn't actually going to mail the letters at all. We're comparing correspondence with President Lincoln to the current president's use of language."

Tall Mr. Keystone mulls the information over. He nods his balding head in approval. "Okay, Miss Oliver. Send them. With or without an official school seal, depending on the quality of writing, of course. You can decide that. Maybe the president will benefit from reading something in print. Good work, Oliver. Way to empower our youth!"

Whew, Gabby thinks. *I weathered two tornadoes since school let out Friday.* She puts her things away and sits down to relax for a minute. Her cell phone dings, reminding her to silence it. After all, she doesn't want to set a bad example for the students.

Of course, it's Brandon. **You okay?**

Yep, thanks. she writes back. **The boss man just wanted to tell me what a great job I'm doing. Well, kinda. TTYL. Have a nice day.** 😌

Gabby tucks her phone away and giggles to herself. *Did I just abbreviate "talk to you later," even though I've sworn against it? Did I just use slang accompanied by an emoji? Am I succumbing to teenage trends?* She considers her previous commitments to spell out words and resist the temptation to use cutesy smiley faces. For years, Gabby has attested that too much gets lost in the translation of abbreviated text messages. But she also knows that a burgeoning romance can inspire modern measures.

Refocusing her attention on work, Miss Oliver checks the seating chart to refresh. She has written brief notes on it in order to have a quick reference handy for third period. She looks over the spectrum of ethnicity, disposition, and talent represented in Room 18.

(Teacher's desk)

Seating Chart

(2)

Subject: 11th grade Reflective Writing **Teacher:** Miss Oliver **School:** Heart High

3rd period →

* outbursts in class Kenn (football	* phone use in class Adam players)			Leeland (dad in Army)
				Ember (no phone) (fireman dad)
Rhonda (blog writer)		Binah (Bee-nah) (actress)	Nadia (baby) * ELL	Nico (works) * ELL
Lillian (environmentalist)	(student council) Lucy	Stephanie (cheerleader)	Matt (techy)	
Scott (singer) * IEP				Rob (musician) * S/he

(Door)

"Good morning. Welcome back." Miss Oliver looks over the roster, noting absences. "Anyone know where Stephanie is?" The group is unusually silent. The teacher looks up over her glasses. Kenn and Adam exchange glances and then dramatically hide their faces. *Whatever,* Gabby thinks. *If they have an inkling of her whereabouts, it's probably better they keep immature remarks to themselves.*

"Did you send our letters?" Rhonda cheerfully asks while braiding her long hair beneath her black hat.

"Yeah, how about mine?" Kenn jeers from the back. "About why dress codes should be lifted, so girls can wear shorter skirts and lower-cut tops."

"Yeah, who cares if bra straps show?" Adam gives his friend a high five.

Miss Oliver bites her tongue long enough to collect her thoughts. "You are here to learn. Not to ogle or objectify girls. Dress codes are in place to maintain a respectable learning environment."

"My bedroom's a respectable learning environment," Kenn laughs.

Gabby loses her composure. "Kenn, outside, now!"

"Oh shit," Adam remarks. Since he apparently registers the seriousness of her tone, Miss Oliver feels emboldened. *Maybe his buddy Kenn should regard it, too,* she frets in frustration. *Ugh!*

"Class," the teacher instructs, "read for ten minutes. That does not mean get out your phones. Find something in print from the shelf if you don't have a book with you."

Miss Oliver walks outside where Kenn is texting while waiting. She retrieves the inhaler from her pocket and relieves her shortness of breath.

"Excuse me," she begins. "Who do you think you're dealing with? I am your teacher and your elder. This is school, not some comedy act! It's not a place for inappropriate jokes. It's not okay to make misogynistic comments in my classroom. Not in writing. And

— 133 —

not aloud. Not in reference to me, students, or in general. You have been disrespectful to me as a woman and as an educator. I expect an apology. And…a research report on the history of school dress codes! Maybe it'll help make up for the D you got on your letter-writing assignment. And no, I'm not sending it, by the way. But I might send a note about your behavior home to your mom."

Kenn bows his head silently. Surprisingly, he looks sincere, apologetic, possibly remorseful. "Sorry," he utters, paying his bail.

Miss Oliver resumes class after ten minutes pass. "Let's start over. Yes, Rhonda, I'll be sending some of your letters, depending on content and whether or not you okayed it."

Scott takes the cue, **"I hope that someone gets my message in a bottle."**

"Exactly, Scott and…The Police," the teacher smiles in recognition of her witty student, always on key despite his brain injury.

"Other than a few exceptions," she clears her throat and looks toward Kenn, "I was pretty impressed by your letters. I admire your passion and courage to research and reach out. Sometimes, what we find through inquiry doesn't fit what we previously believed, but I trust you benefited from the process and discovery. Just be sure to use scholarly articles and websites when possible. We'll talk more about quality sources throughout the year. Overall, I learned some things from your reports. Your viewpoints are interesting. I also respect your humility. Do you know what I mean by humility?"

Leeland raises his hand and waits until the teacher acknowledges him. "Humility means to admit you don't understand something. To defer to the chain of command or someone who knows better."

"Okay, yes," she agrees. "It's okay to be humble. To not have it all figured out. And yet express yourselves anyway. In some ways, you did that, Matt. By suggesting the president consult experts on matters such as energy and the environment. Others…well, you were more, let's say, confident in your approach. And that's okay. As long as you're respectful. Even if you don't care for a person in a position of power, you still have to respect that position, which brings me to language."

Matt interrupts, "Did I cross the line?"

Miss Oliver gives him a nod. "Yes, slightly. You can rewrite it after we conference, Matt." She faces the class. "Remember Frederick Douglass? Which words did he use to address President Lincoln?"

Binah responds as her hand goes up. "He refers to the president as 'sir, your excellency.'"

"Right," the teacher affirms. "Now, let me ask, did you all write that way, meaning politely, modestly?"

Without waiting to be called upon, Binah answers the question. "No, I didn't use *those* words, but times have changed. This president seems more approachable, like he's hip. Whether you like him or not, he's almost like someone I could talk straight with."

"Straight?" the teacher questions. "Are abbreviations straight? Or are they assumed? Are emoji's straight or open to interpretation? Is there enough room to address major political issues in 140 characters...or even 280?"

"True," the boy with long hair chimes in. "Things can be taken two ways sometimes." Miss Oliver considers the Robert/Roberta conundrum. She decides to call *them* Rob from now on.[24]

Lucy asks, "Are we talking about respect or shorthand?"

The instructor realizes the conversation has taken a tangent. "Well," she decides, "both. My point is your writing style tends to differ from Douglass'. I've thought about whether I want you to revise these letters, to clean them up in parts, to make them more executive." The students quietly wait in anticipation. Nico looks at the clock. Lillian winds a section of her dreadlocked hair around a pencil. "But I've decided to send them anyway, after a couple of necessary rewrites.

24 LGBT Resource Center through the University of Southern California (USC), Gender Neutral Pronouns Guide

Ultimately, it's *your* voice."

"Yesss!" Rhonda celebrates.

"I will be handing out feedback on your prewriting pages. I've invited some students to conference with me in person about this assignment. Language matters. Word choice matters. Mechanics matter. For readability. And so does content. I'll discuss the specifics with individuals as opportunity allows. I'm usually available before class, during break.

"For now, I want you to communicate your ideas to each other. And if you need the letters, I have them here. Try to have civil discourse; listen to other viewpoints before arguing your own. We can appreciate each other's work, even if we don't agree. Lillian, I want you and Adam to pair up, since you wrote about similar topics, albeit from different angles. Matt, you can join them, actually. Rhonda with Ember. Hmm, how about Nadia and Lucy? The rest of you...pick a partner, please." The teacher writes on the board.

1) Name the topical interest or issue
2) Describe something you learned through research
3) Say what you requested from—or suggested to—the president
4) Convey your approach

"In a minute, not yet, we'll share, but let's talk about number 4. Some of you try to persuade the president through ethics. You try to convince him of your credibility or of the worthiness of the matter itself. Lucy, yours comes to mind on the subject of education. We call this ethos. Others use an emotional appeal like Nadia did, concerning the DACA debate." Miss Oliver looks toward the mom in the third row. "And Ember, you highlight devastating statistics on teen depression. This is known as pathos. If you try to reason with the president—or talk 'straight' as you say it—that's probably logos. Logic, facts, or commonly held beliefs. Matt, you tried to reason about renewable energy versus fossil fuels, correct?" Matt nods yes. "And you reason with regard to rights and rigid thinking, Rob. Rhonda, you do this by drawing censorship comparisons to other countries, some of them alarming." The educator casually points toward students in order to offer examples.

"This is a very brief and basic explanation of persuasion styles, also called modes or proofs.[25] I'll refer back to it in time. But for today, decide which method you naturally took. Maybe you used all three."

Ethos: Credibility, Character
Pathos: Emotion, Anecdotes
Logos: Logic, Reason

Miss Oliver collects the letters as they leave. In exchange, she hands out KWL charts for homework: a reflective activity for students to discern what they already **K**new, what they **W**anted to research, and what they each **L**earned. She quietly mouths, "great job" to Rhonda, Binah, Ember, Lillian, Leeland, and Lucy.

Lucy takes headphones out of her ears and asks, "What?"

"Nice work—on the letter."

"Oh, thanks," the girl snaps her gum.

"And hey, Lucy, I heard about your grandma passing, I mean, your abuela. I've been meaning to say this for a while: I'm sorry. Lo siento? Sympathies. Losing a loved one is hard."

"Thank you. Gracias."

"You're welcome." Lucy resumes listening to music as she walks to her next class.

The teacher sorts the papers at her desk. She loads computer paper into the printer and quickly copies a few of her favorites. She also separates out letters from those she intends to conference with, namely

---

25 Based on the ancient Greek philosopher Aristotle's Theory of Rhetoric

Nadia and Matt. Miss Oliver muses on the merits of the assignment. *Students got to express themselves in longhand; some stood up for social justice; they researched timely and controversial topics; many wrote from humancentric perspectives; most organized their thoughts via prewriting; they detailed their wishes into requests or recommendations; ultimately, these high schoolers were given a real-world opportunity to address and petition a specific person.* But most did not revise their work after she read it.

Voices vary, the first-year teacher reminds herself. *As does everybody's personal best.* However, if she did this again, she would lead lessons on persuasion techniques beforehand, thus giving opinions a richer framework. And she would help students refine their language. She would emphasize formality and coherent focus. Miss Oliver jots notes to herself for next time and mentally titles them *on-the-job training.* She also records applicable Common Core State Standards (CCSS) for English Language Arts (ELA) in compliance with the California Department of Education (CDE).

Finally, Miss Oliver takes a red pen to Matt's inappropriate language and Nadia's spelling errors. She shall someday project excerpts from the more outstanding examples. *But for now, most of these will do,* she concludes, tucking the correspondence inside a large manila envelope. In hindsight, the novice teacher still isn't sure if trying to make students conform to polished academic writing conventions means diminishing their authenticity.

Heart High School
11th Grade Reflective Writing
101 Pergola Street SW
Palm Oak, California 90000

The White House
Mr. President
1600 Pennsylvania Ave NW
Washington, DC 20500

Week Three, Tuesday

During the morning break, Miss Oliver runs to the cafeteria for coffee. She doesn't usually leave her room much or drink a second cup. But it being her time of the month, she's especially tired and, well, agitated—hence her confrontation with Kenn the previous day. When she returns, students are gathered outside her door. Many are looking at their phones, pointing, and laughing. As she approaches the scene in her gray pantsuit, the teens tuck their cells away and sober themselves. "Time for class," she chimes in while ushering them inside with a disposable coffee cup in one hand and inhaler in the other.

Everyone sits down, but some are still chatty. Whispering secrets. Chuckling. Lively. Miss Oliver allows them to talk while she takes roll. Since it's the third week of school, and a precedence for formality has mostly been set, she figures a deviation from the normal quiet read-to-get-started routine probably won't hurt. Just as she's about to mark Stephanie absent again, the girl walks in. Her cheeks and eyes are red and puffy. Stephanie has obviously been crying. Her hair is a bit of a mess, too—the blonde ponytail off to one side.

"Nice bed-HEAD," Adam remarks from the back row. Several students laugh loudly.

"Good one," someone comments.

"Uhhh," Stephanie sighs dramatically as she slams her books down on the desk, glares back at Kenn, and then surrenders to her seat. She lays her head onto folded arms, apparently unwilling to engage in schoolwork.

"Well," Miss Oliver draws the attention away from Stephanie. "Today, we'll be looking at *Narrative of the Life of Frederick Douglass*, both a description of it and selections from Chapter Two of his memoir. This is an extension of our previous lesson about Douglass as a writer, but we're switching genres from persuasive letters to expressive stories, including song."

"Really?" Rob perks up. "We can write music? For school?"

The teacher is charmed by their enthusiasm. "Sure," she declares. "May Douglass inspire us." Miss Oliver elaborates as she passes out papers. "This project should also enhance your journal responses. I hope you're all taking time to write in both the private and shared parts of your notebooks. I will be collecting them again soon. Since I'm not viewing the personal section, I will ask you to tally the entries and communicate the total to me via a writing log. You'll also complete a self-evaluation sheet."

Narrative of the Life of Frederick Douglass
Published in 1845

"I am going away to the Great House Farm!
O, yea! O, yea! O!"

"This they would sing, as a chorus, to words which to many would seem unmeaning jargon, but which, nevertheless, were full of meaning to themselves. I have sometimes thought that the mere hearing of those songs would do more to impress some minds with the horrible character of slavery, than the reading of whole volumes of philosophy on the subject could do...."

When Miss Oliver gets to Stephanie's desk, she touches her shoulder gently, trying to capture the sad girl's attention and prompt her involvement in class. She doesn't budge. The teacher bends down and asks, "Do you want to go talk with a counselor?" Stephanie shakes her head. Miss Oliver slides the handout beneath the girl's fixed elbow and moves up the row.

As the papers are disseminated, she reminds students to put their phones away. *As usual, holding their attention is a challenge.* Gabby thinks back to her own high school daze. *Was note passing as compulsive and distracting?*

"Okay, who would like to start reading the narrative aloud?" Binah raises her hand.

About halfway through the second full paragraph, Miss Oliver recognizes the appropriateness of Binah's volunteerism. Tight curls frame her dark face as she naturally articulates the document. "Those songs still follow me, to deepen my hatred of slavery, and quicken my sympathies for my brethren in bonds." Binah's beautiful voice cracks. Rob raises a hand, indicating they would like to be next. The teacher signals for them to finish.

While Rob reads, Miss Oliver creeps back to confiscate Adam's phone. "You had one warning," she sternly whispers before plucking it from his hand and setting the device on her desk.

"Thanks, Rob and Binah." Multitasking, she resumes her stance at the front of the room. "Let's talk about this. What stuck out to you?"

"Kenn stuck out to Stephanie!" Adam jeers, either to be funny or to spite the teacher for taking his cell. Either way, he's off topic, and Stephanie does not deserve any more jabs, regardless of her disengagement and apparent culpability in whatever drama Adam is referring to.

"Adam, leave Stephanie alone. One more outburst, and you'll be sent to the office!" She holds a finger in the air. "Now, back to the narrative. What resonated with you all?"

Stephanie lifts her head, "I like the part that says, 'Slaves sing most when they are most unhappy. The songs of the slave represent the sorrows of his heart; and he is relieved by them, only as an aching heart is relieved by its tears.' It's like…ironic, right? The slaves are singing because they're unhappy, but singing makes them feel happy?"

Ember agrees: "Crying and singing can come from a similar emotion." The teacher recollects the story about Ember's mother dying in a car accident, her mom's song fatally interrupted while texting.

Miss Oliver compliments students on their insightful analysis.

Stephanie slowly raises her upper body from the desktop, sits back, and looks forward.

To verbalize his understanding, Scott begins to sing. "**Look what they've done to my song, Ma…Well, it's the only thing that I could do half-right, and it's turning out all wrong.**"

"Hey, my mom loves that album!" Lillian beams. "It's called 'Beautiful People,' right? By Melanie." The teacher is delighted by the student exchange and musical modality in which Scott learns. Surprisingly, Lillian stands and follows his lead, "**Well, if I could find a real good book, I'd never have to come out and look at what they've done to my song.**"

Alas, Stephanie says, "Amen, sister."

The bell rings; students collect their things. "Journals," the instructor reminds them. "Use Douglass as your inspiration. Write music if you want. About sorrow and/or happiness. See you tomorrow."

Stephanie slumps back into her seat. The room clears out, meanwhile Miss Oliver tidies up by straightening desks and picking up scraps of paper off the floor.

"Can I stay?" the troubled teen asks from her immobilized position. With head in arms and words muffled, she pleads, "This is your prep, right? Can I just sit in here for fourth period, maybe through lunch? I'll go to fifth period. Promise."

The teacher walks over and sits down next to Stephanie. "What subject do you have this period?"

She flings an arm outward and points next door.

"Math?"

"Pre-calc," the distressed girl specifies.

Miss Oliver ponders the proposal. *Should I allow a student to skip class? To take refuge here with me?* She looks outside and notices that kids are still passing between rooms. The warning bell sounds.

"Okay, but go tell Mr. Ritter where you are and ask for the

work." At the mention of her colleague's name, Gabby feels a little lightheaded. Stephanie agrees to the terms and wills herself upward.

A few moments later, Brandon peeks inside. "This okay with you? I mean Stephanie hanging out. She looks pretty upset."

"Yes, it's fine. I'm not going anywhere. Thanks." The final bell rings, concluding their conversation.

Stephanie returns. Meanwhile, her teacher begins organizing the art cabinet as intended. She pulls boxes of markers, crayons, construction paper, and colored pencils out onto the floor. An array of colors lend potential to upcoming projects. Alongside a pile of Sharpies, she discovers a poster she meant to hang up at the beginning of the year. Famous quotes by Michelle Obama. Gabby admires her for being the first-ever Black First Lady in the White House.[26]

"I never cut class. I loved getting A's,
I liked being smart. I liked being on time."

"There are still many causes worth sacrificing for, so much history
yet to be made."

"The problem is when that fun stuff
becomes the habit.
And I think that's what's happened in our culture."

\- Michelle Obama
First Lady,
lawyer, writer, mother

---

26 First lady during Barack Obama's presidency from 2009-2017; Quotes are from brainy-quote.com

Miss Oliver decides to hang the poster near her desk in the back-left corner. Stephanie perks up from her dismay. "What does she mean by 'fun stuff?'" the cheerleader asks curiously.

"I think Mrs. Obama may have been referring to fast food; she promoted healthier eating habits."

"Oh, right," the downtrodden girl apparently recollects. Miss Oliver tapes the corners of the black poster to the white drywall.

"She is from the Chicago area like me." The teacher attempts small talk.

"Cool," Stephanie simply says.

"Hey, do you want to chat about what's bothering you? If not, it's okay. You can just work on math. Or write in your journal. But I'll be in here, sorting these pencils and such."

Stephanie seems to consider the kind woman's outreach. She looks around at the room's inspirational sayings, encouraging students to write, read, and care. Upon the wall by the window, a large yellow scroll is tacked up, unfurling a long list of feelings. In brown lettering, the title reads "Emotional Language." Stephanie stares at the words.

"It's Kenn," she finally reveals. "He shared something secret, and now everyone knows! It's embarrassing." She glances at the pretend parchment. "Humiliating! I can't believe he'd do that to me. I mean, he's cocky in person, but that's just for show. He's actually pretty nice… outside of school and by way of text. At least with me. Well, until now."

"I'm sorry he betrayed you," she consoles. "High school is hard. Especially with the potential for private matters to be scattered electronically these days. But you'll get through this tough time."

"I guess," Stephanie hopes. "Maybe. We'll see."

"Hey, there's a song I like to listen to when I feel discouraged. Care if I play it while I organize this cabinet? Maybe you've heard it before. Perhaps you can relate to the lyrics. Music usually helps me feel better."

"Sure," Stephanie smiles. The teacher finds the track via her laptop and turns up the volume. In this case, she's thankful for easy access to online content. Female voices from Wilson Phillips fill the room:

"No one can change your life, except for you. Don't ever let anyone step all over you...Things will go your way if you hold on for one more day."

After school, Marie stops by to chat. "Hey, where were you at lunch? I had to sit by stinky Sam instead."

"Ha!" She laughs at Marie's reference to the science teacher. The stunning redhead sits down at a small desk. "I stayed in," Gabby tells, her green eyes animated. "A student ate in here with me. She was having a hard day. We listened to music and hung some posters. She made this." Gabby holds up a piece of pink construction paper.

The artwork is entitled "Pieces of my Heart." Stephanie has drawn a heart shape in red marker and then shaded and labeled sections accordingly: Family, friends, school, cheer, drama, beach, K.W. and marginally, D.D.

"Therapy in Oliver's room?" Marie cautiously questions. "With Janis Joplin? That's nice. But you do realize you can send her to the counselor's office?"

"Wilson Phillips, actually. And yes, I could, but she didn't want to go. Was I wrong to let her stay?"

"No, as long as the door was propped open. Just mind the school rules," Gabby's mentor advises. "Who's K.W. and D.D. anyway? And drama has its own section? That's funny! Who is this girl?"

"It's Stephanie Mason. She means the drama club, theater. I think K.W. is Kenn Whitehead. Not sure who D.D. is, but it's not really my business why he—or she—weighs on her heart."

"Hmm, well Stephanie should've been using her 'free' time to read. She's behind on Gatsby," Marie scoffs. "She should be more concerned with Tom and Jay, not K.W. and D.D., considering we have a test on the book this Friday."

Gabby registers the point and extends the bookish analogy: "Tom and Jay. Ashley and Rhett. Isn't that the classic conundrum, regardless of setting or time period? Safe choice or exotic intrigue?"

"Exactly, a girl must choose. But I say ask Daisy and Scarlett. Stephanie should keep up with her reading. Classic characters still star in today's teen drama."

"Do they? Or are they indeed *Gone with the Wind*?"[27] Gabby casually challenges the department chair. "Those dated characters didn't inhabit modern times, this world of electronics and Insta-Face confusion, likes and critics, private matters becoming instant public spectacles."

"Are you saying that Myrtle's death wasn't a spectacle? It was a bloody affair—all puns intended! There have always been admirers and critics throughout literary history, Gabriella. Still, I find that teaching is less about the material these days and more about raising ethical humans from the digital zombies sitting in these seats!"

---

27 A novel by Margaret Mitchell, published in 1936

Week Three, Wednesday

Miss Oliver wears school colors for game day, red and black. Though she's a Chicago Bears football fan at heart, she supports the local team. *Go Cupids!* Black dress pants and a sleeveless satin shirt hug Gabby's trim figure, her red blouse tucked in with a black belt. Slight heels and red earrings complement her ensemble. She is of average height, comparable to most of the girls in her classes, but not to be mistaken for a teenager. The sophistication of professional garb sets her apart from skirted cheerleaders.

As she sets up, placing a worksheet about modals on each desk, Miss Oliver notices that several students left notebooks in the wire baskets beneath their desks. While sipping a breakfast smoothie, she gathers the forgotten items and sits down to read the latest entries.

The teacher opens Ember's notebook. She skims over the previous entries. *Oh yeah, the angry girl. Granted, she has a right to be angry at the world for taking her mom from it,* Gabby broods. *I can relate. Although I find poetic language more calming than rants.* She flips through more lined pages. *Let's see…fireman dad. How fitting for a girl with short orange hair! New boyfriend. And, that's right, Ember doesn't carry a cell phone.*

> #5   I told Donny about my mom. I told him what happened, and he started crying. I've never seen a guy cry, except my dad. We were walking by the ball field, and he was complaining about his mom. That she's always nagging him about homework and shit. He asked me about my mom. I said she's dead. And he started crying.

> #6   So, Donny asked me to the homecoming dance. The fucking dance. I don't dance. Plus, I'd have to buy a dress. And, who am I going to go shopping with? My dad? I told Donny I wasn't going. I

mean they'll all be taking pictures and posting that sparkly shit all over Snap-Speak. Yuck. I'd rather stay home and eat tacos.

#7   Donny bought me a polaroid type camera last weekend. He said it's an early Christmas gift. He found it in an antique store downtown Palm Oak. He said this way we could take selfies at the dance.

Taped inside, beneath the last entry, there is a smiley-faced picture of Ember and a handsome young man. *Presumably Donny.* A private message sent directly.

Dear Ember,

I love this picture! It's good to see you happy. And what a beautiful backdrop. Thank you for sharing this with me. I hope you have a wonderful time at the dance. Take lots of pictures.

Enjoy,
Miss Oliver

She crosses out Ember's fiery swear words and offers alternative suggestions: homework and such, dang dance, sparkly stuff.

The next journal Gabby opens is Lucy's.

I'd rather be a "B". I see these girls with their D-cup cleavage and think, that's too much pressure to look like that. Too many expectations from guys. Most big booby girls can't help the way they look, of course. They were born that way. And I hear some have back problems because of it. So why would someone surgically "enhance" her bust? Does she not feel pretty or confident? Enough? That's kinda sad, actually. I'm not willing to undergo the operation. Like for what, men's benefit? To sell myself as sexy? Nah, I'd rather just be me, a "B." I might be stylish, but I don't dye my hair. And I don't dress in fancy underwear. I'm just 17. Do we have to do that thing?

I can tell you've given this some thought, Lucy. Good for you for being happy with your body and hair the way it is. You're beautiful! And no, you don't <u>have</u> to do any thing.

P.S. Watch the movie "Embrace" when you get a chance. It came out in 2016. Warning: The documentary is happy <u>and</u> sad, uplifting <u>and</u> disturbing. It's offers a variety of perspectives on body image, from the fashion industry to female body builders to moms after childbirth. Beauty takes many forms.

The teacher wonders if she's being too friendly with students. *Should my responses be more academic? Nah, this is not a formal essay,* she decides. *Besides, maybe these girls need someone in their corner.*

Next is Rob's journal. *Or Roberta's? The musician formerly known as Robert?* The kid from the front row.

> *Graduation is coming, and I'm scared. Scared of leaving my friends, my family, my band. But I might get accepted to colleges elsewhere, and I wanna go. I also wanna smoke pot and try blow. I think. I dunno.*
>
> *I wanna have sex, but with a steady friend or on the fly? Who wants to be with this guy? I went to a party, and they said, "let's drink!" I snuck out the back and tried to think. She likes me, but I like him, and he's with her, yeah hand me the gin.*
>
> *So, instead of responding to the prompt, I'll write a song. Will anyone else sing along?*
>
> *Everyone believes they're in this teenage world alone. Just call me, bro. I'll wait by the phone. High school is a time to figure it out. I'm confused as hell. Without a doubt. My mom says I'm quiet. But I'm screamin inside. All these impulses are hard to hide. So, I meet with the band twice a week. They need me to play guitar, but I just wanna Speak. Growl. Vocalize. And howl.*

Wow, Rob, I like the rhyme and tempo here! I'd like to see your band perform sometime. Making choices about college can be daunting. But also exciting. A chance to reinvent yourself elsewhere. As your teacher, I have to tell you to be careful regarding sex and drugs. But it sounds like you've got the rock-and-roll part down! :) I hope you can channel your frustration through music, instead of resorting to illegal substances.

Miss Oliver wonders if she's mandated to report confessions of—or allusions to—drug and alcohol usage. *Underage sex?* She makes a note on a yellow sticky: "Ask Marie about sex, drugs, and rock-and-roll." She circles it and laughs, hoping a bystander doesn't read her reminder.

She wants to give her students an outlet to express themselves without restraint, but she also aims to adhere to school rules. With a slurp, she finishes her smoothie.

One more journal...Kenn's. The kid who last wrote, "I'm an f'ing God on social media. Girls love me." Gabby recalls Stephanie's comment from the previous day, that Kenn is "nice" via text. *Hmm,* she thinks. *If the rest is "just for show," he's masquerading inside his journal, too.*

> To answer your questions, my sister's alright. My dad moved to Palm Springs. I'll go stay with him over spring break, maybe. Can't wait to see hotties by the pool! I can't blame my dad for leaving my mom. His new wife is fine as hell. Go dad!

"Go dad?" But what about mom? This kid definitely has some unresolved issues! Does he really idolize his dad for finding a "prettier" alternative? Or might he just be trying to prop himself up from the dysfunction of divorce? Context, she remembers a college professor advising her. *Consider these kids in context.*

> *I hope you get to see your dad over spring break, Kenn. Too bad he lives at a distance. I'm looking forward to meeting your mom at parent–teacher conferences.*

> *P.S. You can communicate your real feelings in here. It's confidential. Writing could help sort things out. Divorce is difficult.*

After taking roll for third period, Miss Oliver looks over her talking points. "Okay, who is definitely going to the football game tonight?" A third of the hands go up. The teacher tallies this count on the board under the heading "will go."

"Who *might* go to the game tonight?" she surveys. A few hands go up. "And finally, who *will not* go to the game tonight?" One hand slowly raises. It is Stephanie's. Miss Oliver notices that the cheerleader is not wearing her usual uniform. *Hmm*, she wonders. *Interesting*.

"Today, we're playing with modals," the upbeat instructor informs her class.

"Ooh, models! Which ones? Sommer Ray, I hope!" Kenn jabbers about an athletic American influencer. "I'd play with her!"

"No Kenn. *Modals* indicate probability. Whether or not something is likely to happen." She shows a slide with examples: should, would, may, can…. "We use these all the time, but we *ought* to do so carefully. Especially when it comes to absolutes. It's hard to own always and never."

Scott chimes in with a song as usual. **"And I-I-I-I-I will always love you-ou-ou, I will always, I will always, lo-oo-ove youuuuuuu."**

"True, Scott. Love *might* be an exception. But Whitney Houston and marriage aside, everyday commitments tend to vary. As do our opinions. So, I discourage the use of absolutes, in writing and in general communication." At the mention of love, it reoccurs to Gabby that she'd promised herself she'd *never* use abbreviations or emojis to sum up meaning in text messages. But lately, with Brandon, she has. She shakes her head of the heart-shaped daydream.

"Can anyone think of an example of a time when you a tried a food you said you'd *never* eat?"

Ember raises her hand.

"Yes, go ahead," the teacher beckons.

"My boy, um, friend, he's been wanting me to eat menudo, you know tripe, stomach lining. I said I'd *never*. But we were at his abuela's last weekend, and she made some for dinner. It smelled so good. I didn't want to be rude, so I tried it. And dang, that soup is good!" Several students verbally agree.

"Okay, interesting! Today, we're going to create modal continuums in groups. I want you to come up with a topic or question— ahem, an appropriate one—and rank your answers along a range of probability. Please initial your chosen modals. And feel free to be creative! Here's an example." Miss Oliver writes on the board.

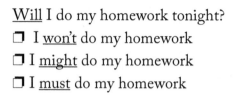

<u>Will</u> I do my homework tonight?

❒ I <u>won't</u> do my homework

❒ I <u>might</u> do my homework

❒ I <u>must</u> do my homework

Students start to chatter and discuss matters. Curious, the teacher discreetly listens to passing conversations. She overhears Leeland broach the heavy subject of a school shooting: "*Could* it happen at HHS?" He emphasizes the hypothetical. Miss Oliver recalls Leeland's letter to the president. He expressed feeling unsafe and made a case for stricter gun control.

"*Probably* not," someone answers, curbing the anxious small-talk.

Miss Oliver walks around the room. Thankful for comic relief, she smothers her laugh when Rob says, "I *never* wear underwear!"

The teacher circulates the aisles and then sits down at her desk in the back-left corner. Surprisingly, there is an essay left there from Kenn: his extra-credit assignment on the history of dress codes. And the "Ask Marie about sex, drugs, and rock-and-roll" reminder is stuck to the top of it.

When her last classmate has left the room, Stephanie asks if she can "hide out" again.

The teacher sits down next to the sullen girl. "I can't keep excusing you from class, sorry."

"Okay," she sighs and rises from her seat. "But can I come in for lunch?"

"Sure. Mrs. Burrows will miss sitting with me in the cafeteria, but it's alright."

"Thank you."

"Hey, why aren't you wearing your uniform?" she inquires as Stephanie slings a backpack over her shoulder.

"I'm off the team."

When the lunch bell sounds, Gabby warms up a Lean Cuisine meal. She scrolls through her music library and decides on Alison Krauss. *Maybe a soulful song would lift Stephanie's mood.* Gabbby sings, "**Good Lord, show me the way.**"

"Hey," Stephanie enters with a smile.

"Hello."

The girl sits down and unwraps a homemade sandwich. Then, she removes a juice box from a paper sack tucked inside her bag. Apparently, Stephanie planned ahead.

"So, want to know why I'm off the team?"

Miss Oliver is surprised by Stephanie's eagerness to talk. She again considers referring her to a counselor but decides that the trust they developed must've encouraged her refuge there again. She is glad Room 18 feels safe to Stephanie.

"Sure. If you want to tell me."

Stephanie holds up her cell phone. The woman's eyes widen. She looks at the picture and then back at her student. Gabby is speechless; she's totally shocked that the teenager would show such a sexual image to her instructor.

"Well, you'll probably hear about it, so here it is. Everyone else has seen it. Now, you have, too."

The teacher is in disbelief. *How could such a private moment be shared?* In the photo, Stephanie is presumably performing oral sex. On Kenn! And superimposed above her head are the words, "suck my PLANK!"

After work, Miss Oliver seeks out Marie's wisdom. First, she tries calling her on the school's landline phone. No answer. So, she texts: **Got time to talk?**

Her mentor sends an instant response. **Sure, be right over.**

When Marie arrives, Gabby simply hands her the sticky note.

"Sex, drugs, and rock-and-roll! Well, whatever do you want to know?" Marie questions.

"Um, let's start with the basics," she replies. "What if a student mentions drug and alcohol usage?"

"Admits to it or alludes to it?"

"In one case, just alludes, I guess. Says he'd—she'd—like to experiment."

"Well, haven't you ever tested an idea on paper? Just tried it out, rather than experience it in real life? Maybe in a fictional story, perhaps?"

Gabby answers: "Yes, I suppose I have." She thinks about her lesson plans in addition to creative writing. *Sometimes, they go well; other times, they don't.* Often, she has to revise her best-laid intentions on the spot, in order to live up to unexpected occasions.

"Every teen wants to experiment, too. And the other case?" Marie triages.

"What if a student showed me a picture of her performing a sexual act?"

"Whoa. What? Why? Wait…was this Stephanie?"

"Yes."

"Okay, I heard." Marie sits down. "And here's what I think. In case number one, the school created this class in order to give students an outlet to express themselves without the scrutiny of social media, a way to explore, clarify, and reflect on ideas. So, if a kid says he—or she—wants to try something, let him—or her—debut that thought with introspective writing instead of online or through action. Let's hope. And in the other case, fuck. That sucks. For Stephanie. Oops, disregard that pun. Ha! Here she is engaging in a lewd—but not uncommon—intimacy, and bam, it's shared! With devastating consequences to her reputation, her self-image, her confidence in confidentiality, and her comfort level. You know Queenie took her off the cheerleading squad?"

"Yes, I heard. Is that necessary? It's not like Stephanie had sex on school property or broke any rules, really, right?" Gabby wonders.

"She broke Queenie's code of conduct. Plus, there is alcohol pictured with the…dick."

"Oh, I hadn't noticed. The alcohol, I mean. I saw part of the… penis." Both women burst out laughing.

"OMG," Marie dramatizes in a pretend teenage voice. "That was some dick pic!"

"Um, yeah, *Kenn's* a dick." Gabby talks openly. "Why is *he* not off the team? I saw *him* wearing the jersey today."

"Good question. I guess football players are held to *different* standards," Marie concludes.

"As were Puritan ministers," Gabby adds. "I mean if we're talking about uniforms and public shame, it makes me think of Dimmesdale: He didn't have to outwardly wear *The Scarlet Letter.*"[28]

"Ha! Good point, but unfortunately, this isn't fiction."

When Miss Oliver picks up her purse to leave, she notices a text from Brandon. **"Hey happy hump day! Thinking of you. Send a pic-me-up! I already left school."**

"Ugh, horny men!" she hisses to herself, tossing the phone back into her pinstriped purse. *Sharing revealing photos as a prelude to exclusive dating seems like an oxymoron. Revelation can wait for in-person exchanges!*

---

28 Romantic historical fiction by Nathaniel Hawthorne, published in 1850

Week Three, Thursday

During snack break, Gabby peeks her head into Brandon's open classroom. He is hanging up a poster with information about the homecoming dance.

"Promoting the dance, I see," she cordially greets, forgiving his shallow request from the previous day.

"Yes, of course," he smiles. "Hey, I'm glad to see you. You never responded to my text."

"Nice to see you, too. But FYI, I'm not a selfie taker. I've tried it. It's hard to get the right angle. And, even when a person likes a picture of herself, it doesn't mean the recipient will. It's too awkward. That's how I feel about it anyway, sorry."

"Okay, whatever, well, how about you be my date to the homecoming dance then? In RL." Brandon sticks tape on the corner of the poster and presses it to the wall. "Wouldn't that be rad? We can take a professional picture there. You know, the wallet-sized keepsakes with little stars in the backdrop."

Gabriella shakes her head and laughs. "I am not going to the dress-up dance as your date, silly. Imagine the gossip."

"Let them talk," Brandon persists as he finishes the décor and steps toward Gabby. He casually touches her waist with one hand. "I bet you'd look fantastic in a formal."

She reddens and turns toward the passageway between their rooms.

Stephanie is there, sitting outside, back against the wall, head down in arms, apparently waiting for Miss Oliver to arrive.

"Good morning," Gabby ekes out, feeling flustered from her conversation with Brandon.

"It's not so good," Stephanie mutters.

"Okay, come inside," she welcomes, propping the door open.

Stephanie sinks down into her assigned seat and wallows. The teacher preps for a lesson on rhyme and meter, since some were enthused about writing song lyrics. She hadn't planned to present poetic elements just yet, but with the dance coming up and her own budding romance, Miss Oliver decides to give students an elevated opportunity.

She organizes her desk and finds Kenn's essay still there from the previous day. It is situated next to her rose quartz not-to-worry stone. She reluctantly opens the title page. *Wow, it is neatly formatted*, she acknowledges, noting the bibliography in back. She tries to put her opinion of Kenn aside as she grades the paper in front of her. *Let's see...* Kenn's intro and thesis are predictable, that he disagrees with dress codes, but not for reasons she'd expect. He purports that dress codes limit individuality. Miss Oliver contemplates the football uniform he wears every Wednesday; she chuckles at the irony.

Kenn refers to scholarly studies and compares grades at schools with and without uniforms. Besides his promotion of girls being allowed to "dress sassy," the essay is actually intelligently written, and without its slightly immature remarks, the teacher might've accused him of plagiarism. Instead of her usual disdain toward Kenn, she feels a bit of pride regarding his writing abilities and willingness to complete the assignment. Miss Oliver pencils, "good work" at the top. "I appreciate the time, research, and effort you put into this." *Could writing redeem Kenn?* she wonders, looking up at the former cheerleader.

The teacher walks over to comfort Stephanie. "I'm sorry about what happened to you. It was mean what Kenn did. That's cyber harassment. I've also heard it called non-consensual pornography. And it's in violation of the Communications Decency Act.[29] He shouldn't have shared your private moment. Has it been taken down from the Internet?"

---

29 Passed by Congress and signed by President Clinton, the Communications Decency Act, or Title V of the Telecommunications Act, of 1996 was designed to control pornography and obscenity in cyberspace, especially with regard to displaying offensive and/or sexual images to minors.

Stephanie lifts her head. "Yes, it has, except for the circulating screenshots, but Kenn didn't originally post it."

Gabby furrows her brows beneath her bangs. "What do you mean?"

"Well, Kenn took and sent the picture to Adam. It was rude of him to do that, sure. And by the way, he was referring to when I out-planked him in the gym. But Kenn was just trying to be funny."

"It's not funny, Stephanie. It's inappropriate. Spiteful. Defamatory. And derogatory."

"True, but it was Adam who shared the image at large. Kenn didn't know he'd do that."

The teacher is appalled. "Are you defending Kenn?"

"No, not exactly. But I still care about him, and I don't want him hurt."

Now Miss Oliver is confused. "Aren't you the one who got hurt?"

"Yes," Stephanie clarifies. "But now, my online boyfriend wants to kill both Kenn and Adam."

Hmm. Kill is a strong word. But kids can be dramatic. Miss Oliver downplays Stephanie's concern. Once students begin writing, she retreats to her desk. Teenage drama set aside, she grabs a notepad and applies the creative time to herself.

After a few startup haikus, the teacher gets an idea. On a blank page, she sketches herself. With an amateur's artistic talent for illustrations, she does her best to convey her appearance accordingly. The two-dimensional drawing depicts a smiley, thin, tallish woman with loose hair and glasses. Dressed simply and professionally, she looks symmetrical. Gabriella suddenly remembers people used to tell her she resembled one of the smart female leads on the 1990s TV show

90210.[30] Gabby always thought it coincidental that she and the actress share a comparable first name.

Feeling like a celebrity, she ponders portraits of people these days—lighting adjusted, features highlighted. *Similar to cinematography.* Her positive self-image doesn't require much tuning. She's okay with the imperfections, including a shock of gray strands coming from behind her hairline. *A picture is just an approximation. Only our 3-D selves carry depth.* Pretty pleased with her "selfie" alternative, she tears out the page, intending to "message" it later.

---

30 *Beverly Hills 90210* (starring Gabrielle Carteris, et al) was a popular series about teen relationships and topical issues.

After class, Miss Oliver notices Lucy passing out pamphlets at the doorway. She approaches the student.

"Hey, are you handing out info about the upcoming dance?"

"Hi, um, no," Lucy replies as she attempts to tuck a binder of materials into her backpack. Just then, something falls onto the floor. A wrapped condom. Before she realizes what it is, the teacher reaches for the lost item, meaning to help Lucy collect her things.

"Oh," Miss Oliver awkwardly registers what she's holding and hands it to Lucy.

"Keep it, I have plenty," the student kindly smiles as she pulls a shiny rectangular pamphlet from her bulging binder. Inside, a condom wrapper is taped to the top. The teacher quickly looks over the information being presented. There are bullet points on safe sex, both oral and penetrative. A section on STIs (STDs). A half-page spread about birth control and prevention. And lastly, a quick explanation of procreation.

"Hmm," she acknowledges, not sure what to make of the sex ed being disseminated in her room.

"I hope it's okay that I pass these out in here. I figured you'd be cool with it. I'm a Peer Mentor. And with oral sex being the hot topic on campus this week, I thought I'd come prepared to inform."

Miss Oliver is speechless. She looks down at the cover of the colorful leaflet. It reads, "Safe is Sexy."

Week Three, Friday

When Gabby gets to school, she finds Stephanie's notebook slid beneath her doorway. A secret message? A girl's desperation to communicate? The teacher likens the act to faceless text messaging. Why wouldn't Stephanie just come talk to her? She opens the notebook to the most recent entry.

> *I didn't mean to cheat on my online boyfriend. But, it's hard not to because he's not physically here. And being "textually active" isn't the same as being sexually active. I thought I could trust Kenn. I assumed he cared enough about me not to turn my life into a drama-fest. But now, here I am!*
>
> *Dillon was mad at me at first. He saw me tagged in a post about blow jobs and asked me WTF it was about. I wanted to call and talk to him, but he rarely has time. We've never talked, actually. We only message. But like, all day long. Pictures included. We started cyber dating "exclusively" last month.*
>
> *Dillon's not mad at me so much as he is at Kenn and Adam. Now that he's aware of how they upset me. How I got kicked off the team and all. He says he'd like to see those jerks dead. That's crossing the line. Right? I mean, is a virtual threat a real threat? Is oral sex with someone else against cyber dating rules? I don't know anymore.*
>
> *Dill lives up north, so I don't think he would physically do anything violent. We've only fantasized about meeting up in person. TMI, sorry. Anyway, I'm still worried. Dillon is in a gang. And he said he might come down on the bus today. So, I'm staying home just in case.*

Miss Oliver ponders if she should phone Stephanie's parents. She'd been meaning to do so, and this letter is alarming. She decides to try calling them at lunchtime. The bell rings, diverting her attention.

"Happy Friday, class. In addition to our vocab routine, we'll also be sharing some of the songs and/or poetry you wrote this week. Like I told you before, you don't have to show everything; that's why we wrote multiple pieces. When I'm done giving directions, please pick one and pair-share it with someone sitting near you. For those of you who feel like speaking up front, we'll have an opportunity before the bell. Oh, and journals are due again today."

Students open up their notebooks, some of them enthusiastically, others reluctantly. They take turns reading their work aloud. The educator walks the aisles, making sure teens are on task and not on their phones instead. *Can't they just leave the gadgets in their lockers?* She almost wishes the school would authorize her to collect cells at the beginning of the hour, but because phone use—for music, research, and recall—is allowed in other classes, the policy is not definitive. So far this year, most teachers report they haven't taken phones away because of a lack of backing from the administration.

There are so many "what-ifs" to consider writing into the policy, like what if a diabetic uses her device as a timer and alert system regarding when to take medication, or what if there's an emergency on campus, or…more commonly, what if one teacher is okay with it and another is not. Then, students play the daddy/mommy game: "But Mrs. So-and-So lets me."

Finally, Miss Oliver interrupts the chatter when she feels it has moved beyond sharing poetry and into spreading gossip. From the back of the room, she asks, "Okay, is there anyone who would like to recite his or her work?"

Nadia raises her hand. "Yes, Nadia. Thanks for volunteering."

"I wrote a song to my baby. I used the imitation method you suggested. Where we take a song and change words."

"Okay, great!" she applauds. "Let's hear it."

Just then, an older kid with a closely shaved head and baggy black jacket interrupts the class. He slams the door shut behind him. "Who's Kenn?" he demands.

Kenn apprehensively looks at the teacher and then at the intruder. She silently wills Kenn not to speak, but he does anyway.

"I'm Kenn. What's it to you?" The tall, blonde, ordinarily confident boy conjures bravado, although Miss Oliver can sense fear in his voice. She is standing at her desk, behind Kenn's, across the room from the entrance where the unknown visitor challenges her student.

"What's it to me? What's it to me, asshole? You fucked with my girlfriend, and now I'm here to fuck with you. And your boy...what's his name, Adam? Stephanie said you'd both be here. She stayed home to see me today. Guess what, prick. My cock's bigger!"

The teacher is astounded by the profane exchange. "Excuse me, this is a school setting."

The visitor glares at Gabby. "School is where Stephanie gets mocked now. School is where she's outcasted from cheerleading. School is where I knew I could find these jerks. Who's Adam?"

Miss Oliver intervenes. "I'm going to call security!" she announces, picking up the landline.

The assailant stomps over and yanks the phone from her hand, its coiled cord now dangling a receiver between the teacher and her desk. He questions the students from the back of the room, gesturing toward Kenn. "Who the hell is Adam, the son-of-a-bitch?"

Kenn cautiously looks at his friend. Adam stands and postures impressively. Shaking with worry, Miss Oliver wonders if he's enough of a threat to the newcomer. *Football gave Adam biceps, but would it provide him with adequate defense against this imposing offensive lineman?*

The older kid—*what did Stephanie say his name was*—prowls over to Adam. "You think you're funny? You think sharing a private picture is laughable? You think you can get away with it? Fuck you." Dillon—*that's his name*—pulls a shiny silver handgun out of his coat's right pocket and points it at Adam. "I'll show you who calls the shots."

Several students gasp. Ember covers her head; Lucy starts to cry, her eye makeup running. Dillon flicks Adam's arm with the gun. "You're sooo strong. You can lift a phone without consequence. Well, maybe you don't need that arm anymore!" Dillon turns to Kenn who sits next to Adam. "And how about the dick you're so willing to show off? Maybe it needs to be shortened! Maybe I should teach you both a lesson—here and now."

Miss Oliver nearly faints. She can barely breathe. She unlocks her knees and stabilizes herself against the solid desk, professionally running through emergency protocol in her head. *Fire drill? Line up students and grab the roster. No. Earthquake? Shelter in place under desks. No. Bomb threat? Don't use cell phones. No. Intruder on campus. Lockdown. Yes, that's it! Get everyone to the middle of the room. Place a green or red sign in the window, indicating whether we're okay or in trouble.* That no longer applies. They're in dire distress with no escape.

What else? Stack up furniture against the doorway? Irrelevant. Grab something heavy and fight like hell. Gabby looks around. *The fire extinguisher! It's heavy. It has ammo. It could work. And it's within reach!* But, she's a few feet away from the gunman.

Active shooter. That's the phrase. But what's the protocol? Her adrenaline pumps. They hadn't had a drill yet. It was supposed to take place soon. The teacher remembers marking her calendar for it. *This wasn't on the calendar. What am I supposed to do?* She wonders if her meager weapon would even hold up against a real live gun.

Miss Oliver feels called to protect her students…somehow. She looks around. Several kids hide beneath their folded arms or crouch under desks. Except Leeland. *Wait, what is Lee doing?* From his desk across the back of the room, he's trying to get her attention. He's tilting his head toward something. Something in the left pocket of his camouflage cargo pants. He's trying to show her without drawing attention to himself. His bulging eyes are questioning her, almost as if he's asking permission.

Miss Oliver nods in acknowledgment, indicating that Lee continue to communicate his idea to her. She's telling him go ahead, go ahead with his question. *What is it?*

Bang! Dillon slumps to the floor. Screams. Loud noises. The classroom goes dark.

Weekend Three, Saturday

Miss Oliver slowly comes to consciousness in a hospital bed. Her dad is there beside her. She tries to shake the blurriness from her eyes, the mental confusion from her memory. She turns to her father. He is holding her hand.

"What happened?"

"Gabby, you suffered a mild head injury when you fell. You fainted at school and hit your head on the way down. They said you must've fallen against the desk and art cabinet. Evidently, you knocked a metal pencil sharpener off the wall and landed on it. You had a minor concussion. But you're okay. Doctors checked."

Gabby reaches up to feel her head. There is a lump in the back. *A welt. A contusion.* Words are coming back to her now. *My head is swollen. I got hurt.* "What happened to my students?"

"Your students are fine. Luckily, the intruder is dead."

Gabby lays her head onto a pillow. An icepack cradles her skull.

A few hours later, the teacher reawakens. She looks around the vacant hospital room. She sees monitors and IV lines, but the only thing connected to her is a small nasal cannula providing oxygen. There is a bouquet of fresh flowers by the windowsill. A bluish hospital gown covers her body. The television was left on, presumably by her dad. Gabby blinks as she tunes in.

SCHOOL SHOOTING. TEACHER WOUNDED. ONE DEAD. ANOTHER JAILED. HERO OR CRIMINAL? BREAKING NEWS AT 6:00.

Gabriella looks at the overhead clock hanging beside a whiteboard noting her condition. Concussion. Stable vitals. CT scan complete. The arrows point to 5:58. She assumes that's p.m. *When did Dad fly in?* She tries to figure out how 6:00 fits within the timeline of events but gets distracted by a picture of her classroom on the TV screen.

Desks are askew. There is blood on the floor in front of her desk, where the attacker was standing when she last saw him. Notebooks and backpacks are still there, left behind in what is now a gruesome crime scene. *My safe space.* The one she dreamed about and manifested through careful planning and creative organizing. *Wait, I didn't collect journals?* She foggily questions the trivial routine before shrugging it off. The phone rings. Gabby looks to her left and sees a red light blinking on a corded hospital phone.

"Hello?" she manages, not sure of her voice. All Gabby hears is sobbing. "Hello?" she repeats.

"Are you okay? I'm so sorry. I shouldn't have told him."

The tired teacher makes out Stephanie's tearful voice. "Yes, I'm, um, okay."

"He wasn't going to hurt them," the girl explains. "I think he just wanted to threaten Kenn. And well, Adam. To stick up for me. I didn't know he had a gun. Honest. We'd only talked online. And now he's dead. I never even got to meet him. To see him. In person. He got off the public bus at school."

Gabby is overwhelmed. "I'm sorry for your loss?" she expresses tentatively.

Stephanie continues to cry. "I should've gone back to school. After I dropped off my notebook. I could've stopped him, maybe. Stopped Leeland."

"Stopped Leeland from what?" she clarifies.

"Stopped him from killing Dillon! They're saying Dillon's gun wasn't even loaded." Stephanie snivels.

Gabby tries to string together limited pieces of information. *A trespasser intended to threaten my students. With an unloaded weapon. And Leeland happened to have a gun? He defended his classmates. I fainted. No one I personally know and care about got physically hurt. Stephanie is the reason for the upset, but she wasn't even there. Her online boyfriend intervened. At school.*

"What happened?" Gabby looks around and repeats the question to her dad who is walking back into the hospital room with a soda pop. She asks it of Stephanie, who is still sobbing over the phone. She asks the television which is blaring in the background. Slowly and unbelievingly, the teacher articulates the words again, "What happened?"

Nurses come in. Gabby tries to relax into the soft pillow behind her, but the sharp edges of an icepack cut into her wound. She is helpless to her students now, unable to save Stephanie, Kenn, Adam, or Leeland.

Gabby awakens to find Marie beside her hospital bed. She's holding a coffee, two coffees. Two sweet-smelling pumpkin spiced lattes. 'Tis the season.

"Rise and shine, Miss Oliver. I brought drinks."

Gabby smiles at her friend and mentor. Marie props the bed up at the head. The recovering teacher sits upright. She reaches for the cup and puts the warm drink to her lips. "Thank you."

"Sorry I couldn't get here sooner. The kids had soccer yesterday. But I see Mr. Ritter sent you flowers. And I saw your dad in the hallway. That was nice of him to come so soon. How are you feeling?"

"Better now." She takes a second sip. "Marie, what the hell happened?"

Marie slowly swallows. "How much do you remember?"

"Just about everything, I think." Gabby locates an inhaler beside her and administers the medicine into her mouth. "Up to the gunshot, I guess. That's what I told the police officer who came by to take my statement. But there were other loud noises, too. Stephanie said her boyfriend's gun wasn't loaded?"

"Stephanie was here?" Marie verifies.

"No, she called."

"Oh, well, some nerve. That girl. Yep, apparently, it wasn't loaded. But who knew? If you threaten people with a gun, you're asking for a gunfight, in my opinion."

"But Leeland should not have had a gun at school," Gabby puzzles.

"Right. But good thing he did?" Marie shrugs her shoulders. "This is a sticky situation, worse than your awful hair." She tousles Gabby's bedhead. "We work in a gun-free zone, Gabriella. That's according to the federal Gun-Free Schools Act, dating back to President Clinton in

'94." Marie takes a deep breath and continues. "The zero-tolerance law applies to any student who brings a firearm to school. Legally, Leeland should be expelled. Supposedly, each state has the power to alter the one-year expulsion, though. So say the news reporters.

"And as a Junior, Leeland has over a year left, obviously. But the school secretary told me Leeland is old for his grade. Someone said he repeated a year because his family has moved around, since his dad's in the service. So, he's eighteen, and get this, rumor has it he actually has a permit for a firearm! But not a handgun. He's not old enough. Regardless, concealed weapons aren't allowed at schools. Evidently, Lee's parents kept a pistol in the home, but he had no right to bring it on campus."

Gabby takes in the onslaught of information. Suddenly, she has an epiphany, something she must've heard on the news at one point in her life. "What about the 'shoot first' thing, the—what's it called—stand-your-ground law? He was defending the class."

Marie shakes her head. "I think shooting 'first' only applies to defense of your home, your 'castle.' And, laws regarding standing your ground outside the home weren't adopted in California, as I understand it."

"I thought some Californians could carry concealed weapons for 'good cause?'"

"Maybe, if permitted." Marie clarifies. "But my husband says that involves paperwork—fingerprints, an interview, proof of character, special safety courses, a range qualification, and fees."

"Oh, geez. So, where's Leeland?"

"In jail."

"Wow," Gabby reacts.

"Listen, Teach," Marie reassures her with a pat on the leg. "Don't blame yourself. You are not trained as a law-enforcement agent or first responder. Your focus is on education. Writing to be exact. And well, because of the nature of your third period, you provide some basic counseling at times. Although, I suggest we sort that out with admin. You've got a lot on your shoulders. Teaching is enough of a responsibility, especially in public schools with class sizes as big as they are."

"And the other loud noises I heard?" Gabby circles back to their initial discussion.

"Probably security officers banging on the locked door. Several students texted 911 from their cell phones. Good thing they had those resources handy, albeit a little late."

Marie reaches for Gabby's hand, the one without coffee. "I'm sorry this happened in your classroom. It's horrible. A school shooting is every teacher's worst nightmare. Ugh. What a way to start the year! And isn't it ironic that your Reflective Writing course was supposed to deter dramatic behavior?" She groans in defeated disbelief.

"Yes," Gabby answers. "And, speaking of irony, Leeland just submitted a research paper on gun laws! A plea for more governmental control. He said he didn't think schools were safe enough. Because of all the attacks. Maybe that's why he took matters into his own hands."

"Really? I guess he had guns on his mind...and in his possession! Even with stricter rules though, there will be individuals who break them. But hopefully that becomes more of an exception. I feel kinda bad for the kid, despite the huge risk he took. Still, students should leave security measures to adult authorities."

"Yeah. I'm not sure how I feel," Gabby concludes, handing Marie her coffee and pulling the hospital blanket up over her shoulders.

Week Four

Picking Up the Pedagogical Pieces

Week Four, Monday

"Alright, Gabbers, I'm going now. My plane leaves this afternoon. I'll take the shuttle to the airport. Do you think you'll be okay alone here at the apartment?"

Gabby looks up from the couch at her dad. His hairline is receding, but there's still a youthful twinkle in his eye, a spark that says, "I have work to do. I love you, but I have to go." The same warm but realistic speech he used to give her as a kid.

"Fair winds and following seas," she bids her fisherman dad farewell by using a mariner's phrase she learned as a child, one she would comically mispronounce as a toddler. "I'll be fine, Dad. Thanks for making the quick trip. I'm glad you got to see my apartment again, now that it's decorated."

"Of course. And hey, Deb's painting sure looks nice! Fitting," he smiles in regard to the two roses hanging prominently above the fireplace.

"Yeah, it's perfect. Reminds me of Mom. But too bad I couldn't show you my classroom. They said the crime scene investigation should wrap up soon. I'm not sure when school will resume."

"Gabriella, be careful, please. 'It is only when caught in the swift, sudden turn of death that mortals realize the silent, subtle, everpresent perils of life.'"

"Who said that one, Dad?" Gabby always loved her father's famous quotes.

"Melville, of course.[31] I love you. See you at Christmas."

Gabby grieves her dad's departure quietly. *I'm alone again*, she sulks. *Without family. Without longtime friends. And with a helluva situ-*

---

31 From *Moby Dick* (1851) by American novelist Herman Melville (1819-1891)

ation at school! She uncovers herself and pulls a notebook from beneath the couch. She has several stashed around the house…in case of emergency.

Dear Mom,

> *Dad just left. He came out to visit me in California. This you probably already know from above. Thanks for protecting me again, by the way. Last week's shooting draws a line in my short teaching career so far: a before and after—before I ever had to deal with guns at school, and the current reality of picking up the pieces the assailant (and shooter) left behind. In my classroom! Life is painfully hard sometimes, Mom. It's hard to see Dad go back to Chicago. I wish I were in Aurora for comfort's sake: familiarity, old friends, and fall colors. I miss walking along the river in that City of Lights. But my life is here now. Temperate <u>and</u> dangerous. Think I'll be okay??*
>
> *Without the lull of the sea and prestige of overhead palm trees, without a steady job and new boyfriend—so to speak—I might otherwise retreat. But I have to muster courage now. Right? I have to go back to work. I think about you when times are tough, Momma. You said yes to chemo and second chances, although they were undoubtedly difficult and uncomfortable. Thanks for inspiring me to fight for what's good. I just hope I don't get caught in a line of fire.*
>
> *I love you. I miss you.*

Your daughter,
Gabbers

She slides the notebook back under the couch, intending to tear the lined page out later. She'd submit it to her closet collection then. Pulling a fuzzy blanket back up around her chest, Gabby drifts off to sleep.

A little while later, she is awakened by a knock at the door. She stirs and shouts, "no thank you," to the mystery visitor.

"It's me. I brought dinner. Open up, please." Brandon's familiar voice calls.

The sluggish woman rises from her leather refuge, smooths wrinkles from her sweatshirt, and makes her way toward the door. Noticing her appearance in the hallway mirror, Gabby cringes. Her hair is a mess, her wire-rimmed glasses are cockeyed, and her face is creased by the couch. *Oh wow,* she winces. *I'm a wreck!* Hesitantly, she opens the door and hides against the wall behind it. Brandon looks in to see no one at the entrance. "You can come in," Gabby greets from the crack. "But I need to shower."

"Okay," Brandon says. "I texted ahead, you know."

"No, I don't know. My phone is shut off, I think. Either way, I'm ignoring it."

"Whatever Gabriella, go ahead and shower. I'll just hang out and dish up this dinner." He walks down the short hallway and turns right into the small kitchen space as Gabby quickly makes her escape into the bathroom.

The warm water revives the weary teacher. She enjoys the rose scent of her soap. Gabby carefully shampoos the tender area of her head and slowly shaves her legs. *Brandon can wait,* she figures. *Neither of us has school tomorrow. What's the rush?* Once dried off, moisturized, and clothed in suitable—but subtly sexy—pajamas, Gabby exits the confines of her chamber. Hair wrapped in a flowery bath towel, brownish bangs dangle around her forehead.

"Nice jammies," Brandon comments about her lacy v-neck tank top and silky scalloped shorts.

"Thanks," she smiles, only half-caring about her appearance. "What's for dinner? Thanks for coming over, by the way."

"Chinese is the entree. And no problem. I've been worried about you. Did you get my flowers at the hospital?"

Gabby points to the glass doorway in back, through which Brandon can see the bouquet placed on an outdoor bistro table. "Thank you," she repeats.

"Listen Gab, it's not your fault. What happened at school, I mean. I got the gist of the story from the news. And from coworkers, of course. You can't blame yourself." He presents her with a bowl of stir fry. "Want wine?" Brandon holds up a bottle of pinot he must've brought over. He is standing on the kitchen side of the counter, presenting the optional beverage.

"Sure," she shrugs, taking a bite and chasing the food with a drink of water. "Brandon, there's something you don't know. Something probably no one knows, except Leeland."

"Oh yeah, what's that?" Brandon uncorks the wine with a pop. He pours two glasses and slides one across the counter toward Gabby who is sitting on a stool near the hallway entrance.

"I gave him permission."

"What? Who?" Brandon asks mid-bite, pausing with his fork raised halfway to his mouth.

"Leeland. He asked me if it was okay to shoot the attacker. And I nodded. I didn't realize what he was asking, exactly. But it's all I've thought about for days."

Brandon sighs, chews, sips. "Would you admit that in court? In Leeland's defense?"

"Absolutely."

After dinner, they sit on the couch and finish drinking their wine. Brandon scrolls through his phone. Annoyed, Gabby picks up a coffee-table book: *The Rewards of Teaching*. She flips through it, perusing the index. "Nope, nothing in here about school shootings," she says with a sigh of defeat.

A few seconds pass before Brandon acknowledges her. "What? Oh, right. Yeah, I think it's a rather taboo phenomenon, something no one wants to talk about. Except via the media—where everyone is talking about it. Can you believe the spin Fox is putting on this? On *our* school?"

"No," Gabby comments. "I haven't really watched the news much."

Brandon puts down his phone and looks at her incredulously. "What do you mean, you haven't seen the news? Every channel is covering it—on TV and online. It's all the buzz on social media. You should hear what they're saying about you! About how you forgot to unlock the door and how that might've spared bloodshed if security could've opened it in time."

"The door was propped open beforehand! The turn of events happened quickly. Besides, a lock wouldn't change the fact that Lee brought a gun to class!" Gabby is furious. "What exactly is he being charged with, besides breaking school rules?"

Brandon looks askance at his colleague. "Dude, I suspect he could be charged with murder."

"It was classroom defense! He stood up for us! Quelled the threat."

"Right. Well, Heart High is getting heat for not having metal detectors. For having an open campus without guarded entry points. And some people are emphasizing teachers should carry guns. In California! Because it's so 'dangerous.'" Brandon uses air quotes. "Yet, we have some of the strictest gun laws. And thankfully, the presence of guns has gone down since the Gun-Free School Zones Act started back in…1990 under Bush Sr. I think that's what I read. Keep in mind 'gun-free' doesn't apply to sworn officers, though, luckily. We definitely need protection from potential mass shooters and individualized attacks, like this insane asshole who barged into your room. But I can't see *you* with a holster around your waist. Ha!" Brandon pokes at Gabby's midsection, attempting to lighten the mood.

"It's not funny," Miss Oliver begrudges. "I looked around for a weapon. I was going to use the fire extinguisher! I wish we would've had that active-shooter drill before all this."

"I know it's not funny, especially for the class 'hero.' There are as many people rooting for Leeland as are turned against him, from what I can tell. His poor mom was hounded into contacting his dad on deployment. She had to go through the official chain of command, I guess, since Lee's father can't use personal electronics on this assignment. So many people are impacted, and you're not even paying attention, Gabriella."

"Excuse me, Mr. Ritter." The recovering teacher feels personally insulted. "I can't be the only one who struggles with this new normal, this onslaught of incoming information. Plus, I suffered a head injury; I lost consciousness. And I'm trying to process what happened on my *own* terms. I don't need the media to tell me what took place. I was there—a primary source who experienced it firsthand. And for your information, I plan to 'check my phone' tomorrow morning. I'll read news and email, too. And, what's it called, Insta-Face! I'll make sure I'm caught up on what secondary sources are saying before I go into school and see what's become of the crime scene in *my* classroom."

"Okay. Okay. I'm sorry," Brandon apologizes. "I know this is a lot to process. It's crazy. Stephanie's online boyfriend took aim at her real-life boyfriend. It's unbelievable. Even in today's times."

"Stephanie called me at the hospital. Said she never even met the deceased in person."

"Lovely," Brandon concludes. "A present-day teen romance." He gets up and fills their glasses.

"Hey, speaking of romance," Brandon raises his brows repeatedly. He plays music from his mobile and reaches a hand out toward her. The Latin beat uplifts her spirits. She unwraps the towel from her head, revealing her grayish thread. A touch of wisdom before her time, the highlight is caused by a single spot of vitiligo. Gabby quickly braids her soft hair to one side. She swallows another drink and surrenders to the moment by placing her hand gently in his. After three long days, Gabriella is finally ready to engage.

"Resist," Brandon instructs as they stand face-to-face. "I can't lead unless you push against me a little. Show strength." Gabby tightens her grasp. "This is the technical salsa step," he says. "I didn't teach you before. I wanted you to simply experience it. But I think you need to count in order to better comprehend it."

She recognizes the calming metaphors. *I will focus on dance and tune everything else out. I will concentrate accordingly.* Gabby looks up with teary eyes. "Okay. Teach me."

"The woman steps back at first," Brandon explains. "Atrás. Back, left, together. 1, 2, 3. I'll come forward with the same count. See?" He moves the coffee table out of the way and shows her. "Pause on 4. Now you come forward while I go back. Left, right, together. Adelante. 5, 6, 7."

Gabby begins to cry as they transfer weight and energy. Her back, Brandon forward. And then the reverse. Each moving to and fro. Leading and following. Resisting and cooperating. Brandon kisses her forehead. The beauty of their shared understanding both calms and revives the injured teacher. *I can do this,* she encourages herself. *I can learn new strides. With everything that's happened at school, romantically, medically, and in a world of politics and confusion, I can move onward— slowly, rhythmically, numerically.*

Week Four, Tuesday

Eddie licks Gabby's face until she opens her eyes. "Good morning, my sweet dog," she greets. After a quick change of clothes, they're out the door and walking around the apartment complex. He does his morning business; she takes in the sunrise, the sea breeze, the quiet suburban streets.

Back at the apartment, Gabby brews coffee and sits down with her phone, laptop, and TV remote. "Okay, let's do this," she tells Eddie, who is indifferent to the news his owner has been dreading. Eddie happily lays his small curly head near her leg in support. Miss Oliver sets her ceramic mug down on the table in front of the couch, right beside *The Rewards of Teaching*. She pauses.

There are plenty of worthwhile rewards, the woman reminds herself. *To expose kids to ideas, improve reading comprehension, develop analytical skills, foster critical thinking, push people toward their potential, enhance public speaking, provide a safe space for students, facilitate dialogue, promote artful expression, increase empathy, design collaborative projects, enable teamwork off the competitive field, broaden vocabulary, and to allow experimentation with writing.*

A long time ago, Miss Oliver decided that grammar, spelling, and punctuation were important, too. Important enough to teach. *Because those details help render meaning.* And keeping her job meant turning on the news: taking in the latest, juggling facts with uncomfortable fiction, and balancing others' interpretations with her own sense of reality.

The TV shows Leeland Farbinski's mugshot. He looks stoic. The headline asks: **WAS IT WORTH THE RISK? WILL STUDENT BE FOUND GUILTY OF VOLUNTARY MANSLAUGHTER? EXPELLED FROM SCHOOL?**

The speculation over Lee's "crime" undermines his courage, the teacher thinks. She flips through a few news stations, watches ABC,

NBC, and CNN, and then turns the television off.

Next, Miss Oliver clicks on her computer. She ignores ads and navigates to trusted websites, reputable news sources, including *The New York Times* and *The Washington Post*. She reads, **Armed intruder locked students and teacher in Californian classroom. He threatened two boys who had dealings with his online girlfriend. 18-year-old student who had handgun shot trespasser dead.**

Gravity of the national news sinks in. Gabby looks at a more local press. *Any further details? Los Angeles Times* reports, **Teacher suffered minor injuries. No one else hurt. School temporarily closed.** *Ugh, why me? Why us? Why Heart High?* She makes a mental note to pick up a newspaper in print, too.

Miss Oliver listens to National Public Radio, which reveals, "A court date for criminal charges is set for Friday. Due to widespread media interest, judge urges expediency, and defendant waives right to trial by jury."

Court Friday? No jury? That was *novel* news! Once again, Gabby pulls out the notebook from beneath the couch. This time, she uses it for research and documentation. But first, she carefully tears out the letter she wrote to her mom. Gabby folds and kisses it before "mailing" the correspondence via her closet. "Wish me luck, Mom," she says as it drops into the timeless trunk.

Once media outlets have been reviewed and recorded, Gabby skims over her work emails and finds a request for comment from the local paper. She ignores it for now and turns on her phone. Ten missed calls, nine text messages. *I can handle this,* she tells herself. The most recent call is from the principal, Mr. Keystone. He left a voicemail.

"Hello Miss Oliver. I hope you're feeling better. I heard you got discharged from the hospital. That's good news. I want to let you know classes will resume on Wednesday. You may want to come in beforehand and make sure your room is in order. Maintenance has sanitized it. A counselor will visit your third period. She'll use most of the hour to debrief with students and offer confidential counseling services thereafter. I've called a special all-staff meeting after school on Thursday. As you may have heard, Leeland's court date will take place on Friday. We've arranged for your substitute since you are a key witness in the proceedings. No need to call me back. Good luck, Miss Oliver."

The other voicemails and text messages are from concerned friends and family. Of course, Brandon reached out repeatedly. Gabby considers logging into her Insta-Face account but decides it can wait. She spends the afternoon baking instead. She listens to music and processes the details she's gathered. She wills herself onward with a cup of sugar, a teaspoon of vanilla, and three shakes of cinnamon.

The teacher goes to school that evening. Because it's late, she's able to scoot around the hubbub of security and scrutiny, reporters and onlookers. When Miss Oliver opens the door, the familiar smells of books and whiteboard markers engulf her senses. Janitors have obviously moved desks in order to sanitize the floor. She collapses into the nearest misplaced desk and cries. *This isn't what I planned. It isn't in the unit, and it wasn't in the syllabus.* Meanwhile, the overhead lights hum along indifferently.

Eventually, Gabby begins to do what she came in for. She cleans up the classroom. She tries to reassemble the safe learning environment her students once enjoyed. She rearranges desks into right angles, clears walkways, picks up a fallen notebook. It is Lucy's.

I became a peer mentor when my cousin got me into it. She took me with her to a meeting at the clinic, and I learned so much! I thought why doesn't everyone know this stuff? Like you can get sexually transmitted infections from oral sex. And…you can get pregnant even if a guy pulls out. Of course, you probably know this. But, I didn't! And, I don't think many of my friends do. No one wants to talk about it. It's awkward. But, the clinic is great. They give out free condoms and information plus HPV vaccines which help prevent cancer. Some of my friends get BC there now. Including Plan B. If disease and pregnancy are avoidable, I'd like to spread the word. My mom works in the field of education, so maybe I will too. I guess I am already.

Gabby recalls her conversation with Lucy about sex ed. It seems so long ago now. Still, she's charmed by the girl's willingness to mentor her peers in a non-traditional way.

She continues to straighten up—her spirits and the space. *Without being able to go back in time, we can try to pick up where we left off,* Gabby avows. *But where did we leave off? Oh yes, poetry!* She picks up the last notebook from the floor. It's Kenn's. She flips it open apprehensively.

This is me
It's hard to see
What's right and wrong
About my schlong
In the pic
For which Stephanie took a hit
I shouldn't have betrayed
Should've obeyed
Common courtesy
Before Adam took the mic from me
Instead I acted like a pig
Kinda like my dad
You dig?

Gabby can't believe Kenn admits he was wrong, albeit abstractly and pervertedly. And he even likens his actions to his divorced dad's apparent disrespect for women. *Hmm,* she thinks. *Maybe there's hope for this kid yet. Regardless, I'm glad he's alive.*

Week Four, Wednesday

As Mr. Keystone had arranged, on the first day back to class, a counselor visits third period. Mrs. Ann Bach gently debriefs on the basics of what happened; she takes questions and offers advice: resources online, books in the library, journaling as an outlet. The woman writes her office hours on the board. She also lists contact information for the social workers and therapist at school. Meanwhile, Miss Oliver takes roll, noting that Stephanie is absent.

Students want to know what will become of Leeland, but Mrs. Bach simply states, "That is for the court to decide." She says he obviously broke a school rule according to the Gun-Free Schools Act, but he also broke state law by carrying a concealed weapon without a permit. She reiterates, "Without prior authorization, Californians are not allowed to carry weapons in public." She further informs them that in California, the minimum age for licensed sales or transfers of handguns is twenty-one. "Though there are exceptions for certain uses, a person must operate within legal limitations." The counselor clarifies that even though Leeland fired the gun in defense of his classmates, it was unlawful for him to use the handgun without permission and bring it to campus. Stating and sticking with the facts stabilizes them.

Finally, Miss Oliver resumes her place at the podium. "Okay, students, let's do our best to pick up where we left off...tomorrow." She checks the clock and hands out a take-home reading assignment, verse by one of her favorite poets. At a loss for words, she relies upon literature for instruction. "Upon first read, take in the overall message and emotion of this poem," she instructs. "But then, read it again. Consider the African American author's bio. And remember what we read about Douglass saying slaves sang during his day. Pay attention to the cadence and occasional rhyme within this twentieth century piece."

Caged Bird

BY <u>MAYA ANGELOU</u>

A free bird leaps
on the back of the wind
and floats downstream
till the current ends
and dips his wing
in the orange sun rays
and dares to claim the sky

But a bird that stalks
down his narrow cage
can seldom see through
his bars of rage
his wings are clipped and
his feet are tied
so he opens his throat to sing…[32]

After class, Kenn approaches Miss Oliver at her desk. "I'd like to visit him."

"Who, Kenn?"

"Leeland." The teacher looks up from her gradebook. "Do you want me to take him any homework or anything?"

She thinks about Kenn's request and whether to assign homework to a student who may not be returning to school, to

---

32 Published on page 16 of Maya Angelou's 1983 poetry collection, *Shaker, Why Don't You Sing?* Used by permission of Random House, an imprint and division of Penguin Random House LLC.

everyday life, to normalcy. Miss Oliver momentarily meditates on the tremendous debt Leeland is paying for trying to protect Kenn. "Sure," she says, charmed by Kenn's thoughtfulness. "If you're able to, take him today's poem."

After school, Gabby has to meet with Leeland's lawyer in order to be prepped as a witness. Leeland had pled guilty to voluntary manslaughter. His trial would serve as a sentencing hearing. She would need to prepare a statement for court. On the drive, Gabby debates whether she should confess to silently giving Leeland permission to shoot. *Does it matter if I unknowingly consented to him drawing a gun?*

Week Four, Thursday

On her way into work, Gabby stops for coffee at her favorite café, JC's Java. As usual, she looks over the local happenings posted alongside the doorway while she awaits her latte. Her eyes are drawn toward a flashy flier advertising a local dance studio: "All ages and abilities welcome." The women pictured wear flowers in their hair, fitted frilly tops, and long flowing skirts. As evidenced by their smiles and group hug, they appear to be best friends, and their ages seem to span across generations. Confidently, each dancer poses with a large fan and expressive hand gesture, inviting and intriguing. Gabby thinks one of the girls in the brochure looks like Stephanie. It's not her, but the resemblance inspires the teacher to grab a second "free pass" for her student. *Maybe they'd both try it.*

"Do you like flamenco?" a blonde barista asks from behind the counter. Gabby recognizes her Insta-Face friend and remembers she is a dancer.

"I don't know it. Is that the style you practice?"

"Yes, you should attend a class! It's fun. No experience necessary. The coordination will come."

"Hmm, maybe I will. After…well, things settle down."

The supportive woman signals "okay" with a wave. Gabby thanks her for the caffeinated latte lifeline.

Stephanie comes to Room 18 early. Without words, she embraces Miss Oliver. And the teacher hugs her back. *If the former cheerleader faced scrutiny before, she definitely does now.* Gabby hands Stephanie the "free pass" to the dance studio. "It's not cheerleading, but maybe it'll fulfill the same need for song, dance, identity, femininity, and belonging."

"Thank you." Stephanie gratefully takes the pass from her. She looks it over curiously. "And, again, I'm sorry for what happened here last week."

"I know," the teacher reassures with a slight smile.

"Good morning, all. Yesterday's grammar lesson got postponed until today. And vocab Friday still stands. You'll have a sub tomorrow. As you probably expect, I'll be in court."

"Wait a minute!" Lucy exclaims. "After everything that's happened, you want us to study *grammar*?" Miss Oliver stops writing notes on the board. She turns and looks at Lucy.

"Life goes on, class! And quite frankly, thanks to…well, just because." Stunned students listen. "The syllabus says we'll focus on the mechanics of grammar, spelling, and punctuation. So, that's what we're doing! Unless you have another idea!"

"Yeah," Matt follows. "How do you spell WTF?"

Rhonda adds, "And how do you punctuate a school shooting? There was blood on the floor. Period?"

The teacher scans the space. Students are looking to her for an answer, for closure, for a group hug, maybe. "You know what, forget today's lesson on commas. In a sense. Forget this worksheet!" She slams the stack of handouts down on the lectern. "Just journal. About whatever. Play with semicolons, shift tenses, vary sentence structure, and try to spell words correctly. Or…read. Draw, maybe. Be bored, daydream! Spend this time however you want to, but don't turn to tech for filler."

Lucy raises her hand. "Why are you so against us using our phones? Other teachers let us."

Matt adds, "Yeah, especially right now, since Heart High is making headlines."

"You're so old-school," Adam calls out diminutively.

Miss Oliver sits down in an available desk. She feels weak, overwhelmed. *Haven't they been listening to the tenets of this class? Don't they understand the importance of writing and reading, not skimming over clickbait but really engaging with someone's story? Don't they appreciate the opportunity to escape sensationalism for one brief hour?*

"Listen. I know you've been glued to the news. But please use this hour for something else. And beyond that, I think you should try to avoid social media and biased broadcasts in general right now. We were the ones who experienced the shooting. Not the secondary sources reporting on it. We were here. In this room!" She taps the desk with her pointer finger. The teacher's voice begins to crack. She closes her eyes to hold back tears. "It's personal. And, it's our business. Not theirs. Not the national news anchors. Not the social-media critics. Not strangers to this campus. Not those passing judgment on Leeland without ever having interacted with him!"

"That's true," Adam unexpectedly agrees. "Me and Lee, we played paintball together. I like the guy. Even though people are talkin' shit."

Scott gets up and approaches the podium. He grabs the papers intended for the day's lesson and begins to hand them out. The heading reads, "Commenting Online with Commas: A Street Guide to Intelligent Response."

The students are relieved by the pass to relax this period. Each person is yearning for peace. Everyone copes differently. Some read; others journal, draw, or fill in the worksheet. Kenn and Adam chitchat within Miss Oliver's earshot. She doesn't mind. *On or off task, it doesn't matter. Not today. Individuals need time to process trauma.*

"Yo, Miss Oliver," Binah calls out. "Can we use the art supply?"

"Of course," she replies, carefully opening the cabinet next to her desk, the one she banged her head against.

The teacher sits down to research grief counseling and crisis intervention. She starts with websites Ann recommended. She's unsure how to handle this aftermath. College didn't exactly prepare her. Miss Oliver reads about Critical Incident Stress Management. Reactions supposedly include feeling shocked, numb, indifferent, overwhelmed, agitated, apprehensive, indecisive, and sad. *Check, check, check.* She can relate to the range of emotions listed.

Eventually, Binah stands up. Her face looks radiant and sincere. She addresses her classmates. "What up? Hey, I made this card." She holds up two yellow pieces of construction paper. The pages have been taped together, their edges artfully scalloped with craft scissors. On the front, in pink paint, Binah has written the words "Thank You." She proposes, "I thought we could, um, sign this for Lee. Maybe 'Teach' here can take it to him in court tomorrow?"

"Sure," she slowly smiles, impressed by Binah's initiative. No one objects. Instead, they simply pass the large card around the room. Gabby watches as some sign Binah's creative gesture while others pass it along. Silently, student jurors seemingly agree to disagree on the verdict over whether Leeland's actions were right or wrong.

Stephanie is there at lunch, as expected. They both eat quietly, separately, together. Miss Oliver doesn't bother her student, and the teen doesn't trouble her teacher. While Stephanie munches on lunch, she silently reads the novel she's been assigned in Dr. Burrow's class. Sandwich consumed, she looks up from *The Great Gatsby.* "You know something?"

"What is it, Stephanie?" The teacher stops working on the next day's sub plans.

"This book was written a long time ago. Let's see." She flips to the copyright page. "1925. And yet, it applies today. Sort of to me, in particular. There's this line here. It reads, 'The colossal significance of that green light had vanished forever.'"

"Yes," she acknowledges. "How does that apply to you?"

"Well, like these characters, I was part of a love triangle. And Dillon, he liked me from afar. And well, the green light. Never mind, it's silly."

"Go on," the teacher prompts, recalling the book, remembering that the green light symbolized opportunity.

"I would look to see when Dillon was online. I would look for his green dot on Insta-Face."

Without quoting the next bit aloud, Gabby knows the count of Stephanie's "enchanted objects had diminished by one." And the classic literature was connecting her to a fictional—but relatable—time and place. It was also giving her an escape from present loss.

"Do you think it's wrong for me to miss Dillon? I mean, not the violent version but a fantasy one, the person I thought he was… online. Sure, I knew he was a bit of a tough guy from his pictures, but I guess that attracted me to him, in part. And now it backfired! Literally." Stephanie shakes her head and sighs. "I feel bad for his cousins up North."

The teacher calculates the initial question. *Did Stephanie really want an answer, or does she just want to be heard?* "What is it you miss about him, exactly?"

"I miss the way he'd chat with me. He would always hit me back like right away."

"Hit you back?"

"Yeah, text me, message me, send a picture, whatever. It seemed like he loooved hearing from me. He was so interested in my life. He made me feel, I dunno, special."

"And there's a void now, an absence of correspondence," the listener reflects and rephrases.

"Yes." Stephanie begins to cry. "This is stupid! I didn't even know him, really. But I felt like I did. On a personal level. We shared so much. Details about each day. I feel lonely now."

The teacher carefully cogitates how to respond. *Dillon and Stephanie never even occupied the same room. They were always alone… together.* "I'm sorry you feel lonesome. Are there other people you could chat with, those who offer companionship and support?"

"Yes." Stephanie snivels.

"Do they make you feel special?" She nods her head affirmatively.

"My little sister likes to watch cartoons together. My mom takes me to the ballet every Christmas, and my dad, well, he's been to just about every game I've cheered at."

After school, Gabby hums an old Elvis song her conversation with Stephanie prompted: **"We had a quarrel. A lover's spat. I write, 'I'm sorry.' But my letter keeps coming back."**

Soon, Marie arrives to check on her adult student who is writing a quote on the board. Tomorrow's sub would refer to the journal prompt.

"Today's young people have a special vulnerability: although always connected, they feel deprived of attention."
-Sherry Turkle, *Alone Together*, P. 294

"Well, how'd it go?"

"Since school resumed, you mean? Well, a counselor came in yesterday. Ann Bach. She was great. And Mr. Keystone gave a speech about tests coming up and 'getting back to business ASAP.' So, I attempted to teach a lesson on commas today. I was going to talk about proofreading text messages and social-media responses, even. I designed the lesson and worksheet weeks ago. But you know...."

"It didn't fit the tone?" Marie clarifies. "The mood has shifted, Gabriella. As a parent and longtime teacher, I'll tell you that both parenting and teaching involve an imaginary set of ideals. Seldom do we live up to them. Rarely do we even realize a consistent set of norms. Things change from day to day and within each classroom dynamic. Look back at your syllabus. Rethink your lessons a bit. Maybe frame them differently." The tall red-haired sage commiserates, "I'm sorry your best-laid plans got detoured by gunfire."

After a few seconds of silence, Gabby says, "You're right. But I sort of gave third period a day off today. Is that okay?"

"For one day, sure. You all need to regroup. Because you have a bigger responsibility to third period now. A duty to discourage violence and encourage alternative conflict resolution. And regarding your comma lesson, let me tell you something, Gabby: There are two types of folks in this world. I've worked in diverse environments. I've met all kinds. Basically, it boils down to this. And you can quote me." She winks. "There are people who religiously use Oxford commas. And there are those who never will." Smugly, Marie stands. "Come on, I'll walk with you to the staff meeting."

Gabby gets up and grabs her purse.

"Don't forget your briefcase. I assume you prepared a speech, right?"

Gabby looks worried. "No."

Marie scrutinizes, sticking her neck out. "Come on. Really? You knew we had this meeting today. You know they're going to ask your opinion, what you want to see change, and so on."

Miss Oliver takes a deep breath. She feels irritated by all of the demands upon her during her recovery—to teach, to comfort, to consider school-wide security issues, to appear in court, and now to testify in front of her colleagues. She forces a smile and assures her mentor, "Don't worry, I can wing public speeches; after all, my name *is* Gabby!"

"Welcome everyone," the principal begins. He's standing at the head of a large wooden table where faculty members are gathered inside a multi-purpose room. "Let's get started. What a week it's been. I'd like to thank everyone for coming back to work, despite the strain of law enforcement officials and reporters outside. We are a team, and we will work through this, offensively and defensively. Heart High has a good academic standing, and we will continue to use the methods that help students succeed. We will also do more to keep kids safe on campus.

"As you've noticed, we have two guarded entry points now; the other access areas have been closed off. We'll be using the TSA model. Bob Wellborn, head of maintenance, finished installing the metal detectors today. Thanks Bob." Both men nod in acknowledgment. "We've hired an additional armed guard. Everyone, meet Bret Willshire. Bret, meet the staff." Mr. Keystone points toward the older newcomer. "Bret is a recently retired LAPD officer. His grandson Jabbar is a freshman here."

The principal walks around the conference room. "I've handed out a revised Active Shooter Protocol. Please update your Emergency Preparedness binders. Our drill is still on the calendar. Because it takes place so soon after real gunfire, counselors will be available to meet with students beforehand. Mary is working on specific talking points." The principal moves toward Dr. Mary Hatfield, school psychiatrist. "She's also interviewing candidates for new mental wellness positions. Thankfully, we've just been allotted the funding. We'll have an additional counselor and psychiatric social worker on hand to support both teachers and students. With that, I invite you to fill out the suggestion forms located in the middle of the table. Administrators are open to your input. This event was unique and alarming, especially for Miss Oliver who witnessed it firsthand." Mr. Keystone stops circling the room and places a hand on her shoulder. "Miss Oliver, the floor is yours."

Gabby stands and clears her throat. "Hello, everyone. Thanks for your kind words in person and via email. I'm feeling better and glad to be back to work. This experience has shaken me, disrupted students, and disturbed the nation. I will attend Leeland Farbinski's hearing tomorrow, of course." The nervous novice looks around. Everyone stares back at her.

"As most of you know, I'm new to this school, community, and state. But, we're all fairly new to these circumstances of modern times—when online exchanges may provoke bullying or violence, even on campus. I appreciate the updated security measures Mr. Keystone spoke about. I'm grateful for the counseling team's support and intervention. And, personally, I hope politicians, police, and parents do more to protect our youth by trying to limit easy access to guns. But I think this crisis is about more than weapons. It's also about relationships, online and in person. That's partly what my third-period class is designed to address…ironically. I will do my best to nurture reflective writing, digital citizenship, considerate connections, meaningful discussion, and respect for privacy."

Miss Oliver sits down. She takes a suggestion form from the middle of the table and scribbles "SCHOOL-WIDE CELL PHONE POLICY??" in red.

Gabby goes home to relax. She'd survived another day of post-traumatic strain. That night, on a whim, she searches up Stephanie's IF profile. The girl's latest post is an excerpt from the song "Love Stinks" by The J. Geils Band.

Both Rob and Scott have "liked" it. Gabby ruminates: *Well, this relational theme hasn't only come up in literature! It's certainly been expressed through music and other media!* Looking away from the screen, her green eyes seek analogous understanding. She supposes singing for relief—because of sorrow—is nothing new. *As Douglass and Angelou aptly noted.* Gabby realizes, *even though "it's all been said before" (so sing The Supremes), context tells a different story every time, therefore making Stephanie's situation both unique and relatable.*

Week Four, Friday

Miss Oliver didn't sleep. She read, journaled, and meditated on the matter of Dillon's actions, Leeland's reaction, and the strange conglomeration that would result in court proceedings. At 5:30 a.m., she gets a text from Marie.

I'll pick you up. I got a sub. See you in an hour.

Great, thanks, Gabby responds. She is glad for Marie's friendship, mentorship, and recent lifeboat response to her own internal mayday.

The tired teacher showers, dresses, and buttons her white blouse and charcoal-colored suit coat. She hides the dark circles under her eyes with her best bifocal concealer. She presses her long skirt on a short ironing board before shining her black heels. "Look ship-shape for school," her dad used to insist during her adolescence when she wore a red plaid skirt with white tights. As a single dad, Mr. Oliver was glad to clothe young Gabby in uniforms versus having to shop for and coordinate girlie outfits. Gabby first loved and then later hated the monotony of uninteresting attire among her female classmates.

"You okay?" Marie asks upon arrival.

"Didn't sleep," Gabby shrugs.

"I bought an extra latte." Marie pulls a disposable cup from between her legs. Another teeters on the dashboard. Both cupholders are full of miscellaneous items: sunscreen, lip balm, hair ties, receipts, fingernail clippers, pens, candy.

"Thanks for the lift."

"No problem. Sorry about the messy car. I blame the kids," Marie winks.

"Oh, it's fine," Gabby fibs, wondering if the peanut butter and jelly sandwich stuck to her shoe would easily unglue.

The women chitchat for a while and then ride quietly along the coast. Marie smokes an e-cigarette. Gabby watches for whales. She scans the horizon optimistically. "I've never seen a whale," the Midwesterner breaks the silence.

"Really?" Marie questions.

"No, but I've seen big fish. Sturgeon especially," she follows. Marie laughs at the comparison.

The longtime Californian shifts the conversation. "Gabby, why did you leave the familiar freshwater back East for these shark infested seas?"

"Adventure," Gabriella answers confidently. "My dad wanted me to work at the nearby private boarding school where I attended. 'It's safer,' he said. 'Plus, you'll have less students and therefore less to grade.' Maybe he was right. I could've stayed home, taught girls who paid tuition and chose a cloistered educational experience. It would've been less risky...perhaps. But I told my dad I wanted to help kids who struggle: students with special needs, language barriers, and financial hardships; teens who are trying to overcome stigmas due to tracking."

"That's noble," Marie compliments. "And a bit of a stretch for you, maybe? I mean from the small, familiar, parochial setting." She raises her eyebrows.

"I suppose. My religious upbringing was a bit sheltered. It lacked co-ed vibrancy, the politics of public schooling, and well, the technology of today."

"What do you mean by 'lacked technology?'"

"Well, we didn't have laptops in the classroom; that's for sure. And teachers taught from blackboards."

"You mean whiteboards, pre-smartboards, right?" Marie elucidates.

"No, I mean chalkboards." Gabby corrects.

"Wow. How old are you?"

"Thirty-two."

"That seems old-fashioned. And it wasn't too long ago."

"True. But my dad wanted me to interact with females after my mom passed away. All of the adults there were women. And all of the students were girls. It was the only private school we could afford. It was sort of low budget. And we got a discount on account of the head-master's husband being a fisherman, too. He was friends with my dad."

"Yikes. That must've been kinda lame—no boys? No access to the World Wide Web?"

"There were boys. I didn't live at the school full time," Gabby hints. "And we had a few computers in the lab. But I didn't get a cell phone until graduation. Actually, I bought it with grad money."

"Oh, okay. What about college?"

"College was eye opening!" Gabby exclaims.

"Right. I bet." Marie affirms. "Where'd you go?"

"Loyola in Chicago. On a scholarship."

"Hmm, Catholic."

"Yes, but I loved learning about literature and teaching," the younger woman wistfully reflects.

"Of course. Who's your favorite author?"

"Classic or contemporary?" Gabby smiles esoterically.

"Both." Marie challenges.

"Maybe Nathaniel Hawthorne and Parker J. Palmer?"

"How moral," Marie judges. "Well, here we are," she announces as they drive into the courthouse parking lot.

Gabby and Marie bypass reporters and politely decline to com-ment on the incident. They walk through the metal detectors and enter the County Superior Court by security escort. They are instructed to turn off their cell phones. Photos are especially prohibited.

There is no jury and apparently no one to represent Dillon's side, except for the prosecutor. Leeland waits up front. His back is to

Gabby. A security guard sits beside the accused. A woman is weeping to the right. "That's Leeland's mom," Marie indicates. "I saw her on the news, poor lady."

The court's wooden double doors open, and in walks Stephanie. Her sharply dressed parents follow her. Gabby notices that her female student—the cause behind the case—is sporting a semi-sophisticated looking silk blouse exposing her bare shoulders. Stephanie is directed to the left by way of passing Leeland who waves at her, his handcuffs clinking. Lastly, Kenn and Adam enter. Though mismatched in height, each witness is wearing a similar suit and tie. Despite the pretense of respectable apparel, the boys boldly sit by Stephanie's family.

Gabby can't help but notice the courtroom's resemblance to a church setting, complete with pews and pulpit, although instead of a cross hanging in the backdrop, she sees the state seal. "All rise for the honorable Judge Eckis," the bailiff broadcasts as a middle-aged female enters the room; a black robe wraps her upright figure. The chief official sits tall and taps her gavel perfunctorily.

"Greetings. This is the case of The People versus Leeland Farbinski. Through adversary process, we will review what happened at Heart High School in the city of Palm Oak, California. To summarize, an armed man named Dillon Dentaw entered a writing class and threatened two students. His gun was not loaded, but that was unknown at the time. Leeland Farbinski shot the intruder, allegedly in defense of his classmates.

"Farbinski was then arrested, and the institution temporarily closed for investigation. The defendant has pled "no contest" to voluntary manslaughter, the underage use of a handgun without supervision or consent, carrying a weapon in public, and violation of the Gun-Free Schools Act. This is a sentencing hearing."

Judge Eckis continues the introduction: "As prosecutor, Mr. Murray will present the case on behalf of The People. The defendant is represented by a Mr. Fog who has been appointed by the County Defender's Office. Mr. Fog has been to the location of the shooting. Are there any preliminary matters that need to be addressed? Any initial disclosures before this inquiry begins?"

"There is a letter, your Honor. It is from the defendant's father. It will be read by his mother when she gives testimony."

"Thank you, Mr. Murray. That will be entered as indirect evidence."

"For the record, your Honor, the student is of advanced age for his grade. Though he is only a Junior, this defendant is eighteen and therefore an adult."

Mr. Fog follows: "With that, your Honor, and for the sake of the minors here today, I would like to explain that voluntary manslaughter is less criminal than murder and is circumstantial, done purposely and with passion but not premeditated or malicious, so killing without prior intent. I want to articulate the lower level of unlawful homicide with regard to self-defense."

"Okay, that offense has now been made clear to listeners, despite impending disputes. So, unless there are further remarks, the prosecution may present," the judge directs. "And, before we start, I ask that side conversations be kept quiet in court." She looks toward the teenagers.

"Mr. Murray, are you ready to proceed based on what was stipulated and previously agreed upon—that you would ask the defendant about certain matters, in the interest of brevity?"

"Indeed, your Honor." An elderly, overweight lawyer scuffles up to the stand. His thinning gray hair glows in the bright overhead light. The hearing formally opens.

"May I have Leeland Farbinski to the stand, please?" The young man follows orders and pays respect to the judge as he nears.

"Hello, your Honor," Leeland politely addresses his arbiter.

The court clerk on cue asks, "Please raise your right hand. Do you swear to tell the truth, the whole truth, and nothing but the truth?"

"Yes, ma'am," Leeland answers allegiantly.

"Mr. Farbinski," the prosecuting attorney asks: "Do you understand the offenses to which you have pled? That you are here because you posed a danger to your school?"

"Yes." Leeland turns his attention away from the prosecutor and toward the judge. "I plead guilty."

Mr. Fog swiftly interjects: "Correction, your Honor, he pleads no contest."

"I've been briefed about your confession," she replies. "We're here to determine sentencing based on mitigating and aggravating factors. Mr. Murray, you may continue."

"In your statement, Mr. Farbinski, you told police you have a hunting license, hold a gun permit for a rifle, and you've attended a firearm safety course. Therefore, you should know how old a person has to be to own a handgun."

"Yes, sir, I do."

"Then you should also be aware you cannot carry a gun in this state without special permission, and you cannot bring a gun to a school unless employed to do so. Is this your father's gun?" The gruff lawyer points to the metallic object under scrutiny. It is locked in a clear case and situated with other evidence on a table at the front.

"Yes, sir, that's my dad's pistol."

"Did you use it to kill Dillon Dentaw?"

"Yes. I thought his gun was loaded. I didn't expect to shoot anyone. I didn't think it through; I just acted instinctively. I wanted to stop him from killing Kenn, Adam, and possibly others."

"Did anyone influence your decision, or did you act alone?"

Leeland looks out into the courtroom. He surveys the attendees. For the first time since the shooting, he makes eye contact with his teacher.

Gabby thinks back to the last time they exchanged glances. It was right before Leeland pulled out the gun, the one on display. It was when she'd given him the go-ahead without knowing what she was assenting to. Just before she fainted and hit her head.

"No. I mean, yes," Leeland answers. "I acted alone. No one influenced me." Gabby shudders.

"I see," the attorney analyzes. He reads from printed documents and then looks at Leeland to clarify. "It says here you brought your father's handgun to school as an experiment?"

"Yes. Just in case I needed it. For law enforcement. In the event of an attack. And to see if I could live up to the role of an armed officer, like my dad."

"Hmm," the prosecutor heckles. "No further questions, your Honor."

The judge asks, "Mr. Fog, would you like to examine the accused?"

"Not at this time, your Honor." Leeland is excused. Gabby notices that his lawyer is approximately forty years old, handsome, and dressed professionally but unshaven. Although they had spoken on Wednesday, it was a brief meeting blurred by her nerves.

"I'd like to call Mrs. Farbinski to the stand," Mr. Murray announces.

Leeland's mom stumbles when she gets up from the seating area. She rights herself and saunters slowly. Her dark hair hangs loose from a frazzled bun, and a beige-colored blouse covers her busty build. She tearfully swears to tell the truth.

"Mrs. Wendy Farbinski," the prosecutor begins, "I understand your husband can't be here today, but you wish to represent the both of you in court."

"Yes," she snivels.

"And I understand you have a letter to read on your husband's behalf."

The woman unfolds a piece of paper from her purse. Meanwhile, Gabby realizes she forgot the card students made for Leeland. It's still sitting on her kitchen counter. *Damn.* Outlying classmates wouldn't get to share their sentiments or support. Not in court.

```
Dear Leeland,

     I love you, but you have disappointed
me, your mother, and your country. You broke
school rules, state rules, federal rules, and
family rules, junior. You know gun safety
and firearm responsibilities are important!
I've taken you to the range and the snowy
field where I shot that bear up in the AK
wilderness. I appreciate your admiration, and
you've seen me carry a gun in uniform. It is
with pride and sadness that at eighteen you're
still imitating me like you did at eight
when you dressed up like an Army Ranger for
Halloween! I didn't expect you to unlock our
safe and put us in this predicament ten years
later. I thought you knew better. As I've said
about the armory on base, weapons should be
kept secure and used legally. I'm pleased you
ended up protecting your classmates, but it
wasn't your place to do so. We will have a
private conversation about this someday. For
now, take your punishment as it is awarded,
son. May your mistake be a lesson to others.

Your dad,
Major Leonard Farbinski
```

Leeland's mom slowly folds the letter. Each crease is audible. A weighty tear drops from Leeland's chin onto the solid oak structure.

"Mrs. Farbinski," the attorney addresses her. "Where was the key to the gun safe kept?"

"In my nightstand, tucked away," she solemnly answers. "Close at hand—just in case. I, I, sleep alone when Leonard's deployed. I have to take precautions."

"Against bad guys?" Mr. Murray queries.

The woman nods and whispers "yes."

"Well, then, if your son were a year younger, you'd be in violation of Penal Codes 25100 and 25200 for improper storage of a firearm. Because your child gained access, carried it off premises, and caused death!"

Judge Eckis proclaims, "Mr. Murray, Mrs. Farbinski is not on trial here. And her 'child' is technically an adult. Besides, Mrs. Farbinski believed the gun to be secure within a locked container."

The court reporter types feverishly. Everyone takes in the exchange of information. After a moment of silence, the judge issues a ten-minute recess, offering people a chance to use the restroom. The witnesses talk among themselves. Stephanie sits still, her head hung downward, hands clasped in her lap; both she and her parents remain closed-lipped. Kenn and Adam appear to discuss potential plays for next week's football game. Their hands flail about, choreographing the upcoming competition. Marie files her nails.

Meanwhile, Gabby shuts her eyes and broods. *I'm sorry my classroom became unsafe.* She feels mixed emotions—remotely responsible, concerned for Leeland, nervous for his mother, and resigned to wait for the legal outcome, whatever the consequences might entail. Unlike her high hopes at the start of school, the depressing situation is now beyond her control.

Proceedings reconvene. "I would like to call Kennith Whitehead to the stand," the prosecuting attorney resumes.

"Wish me luck, brotha," Kenn bids Adam farewell before theatrically making his way to the witness stand. The boys bump fists.

"Mr. Whitehead, I understand you had relations with Ms.

Mason here, and that upset Mr. Dentaw."

"Yeah, apparently. I didn't realize he had property rights to her."

"Property rights?" the attorney scoffs.

"Yeah, dawg, like they were a real thing. I thought they just messed around online. I thought she was fair game." Gabby squeezes Marie's knee. She wants to scream. And she can't even imagine how Stephanie's parents feel.

Marie mutters, "This kid. What the hell is he saying?"

"I think mouthing off is his coping mechanism," Gabby quietly postulates.

"Okay, dawg," the annoyed lawyer mocks. "My question is about the day Dillon threatened you with a gun. Did you anticipate Dillon would come to campus that day?"

"Hells no. My girl wasn't even at school. I had no clue that thug was coming in hot."

"So, you didn't ask Leeland to bring a gun, to defend you in any way?"

"Um, no way!"

The defense interposes: "But aren't you glad he did?"

The judge knocks her gavel against the bench. "Overruled. You're leading subjectively, Mr. Fog. And frankly, gratitude doesn't matter."

The prosecutor dismisses Kenn and calls Stephanie to the witness stand. "Ms. Mason, to be clear, were you aware of the intentions behind Mr. Dentaw's visit?"

"No, I predicted he would come to see me!"

"Right, well, did you know he plotted to hurt—or scare—your friend Kenn here?" The older man air quotes the word 'friend.' He is privy to the preliminary events leading up to the shooting because Leeland divulged the information in his police statement.

"I mean, Dill talked about it, but I thought that was just talk."

"So, you didn't ask Leeland here to bring a gun to school—in case there was a shoot-out?"

"No, not at all. I barely know Leeland. He's new."

With Murray's questioning complete, the defense attorney cross-examines Stephanie: "So you're saying you don't know Leeland, even though you two sit in the same classroom daily? Yet you entrusted your secrets to some guy online?"

"Yeah, I suppose, if you put it that way."

"Interesting," Mr. Fog utters.

"How did Dillon sound? Like he would do harm?"

"Well, I didn't actually hear him. I mean he messaged me some stuff."

"Oh, well, now. Did you warn Kenn?"

"No, not really."

"Did you warn your teacher?"

"I mean, I told her about Dill—that I thought he might ride down to see me. I didn't expect him to go looking for Kenn. I stayed home from school. That's why I was absent."

Gabby wonders what Stephanie's parents think. She never got a chance to phone them that day. She recalls the notebook Stephanie slid beneath her door. *Uh-oh, the alarming journal entry! Should it be on the evidence table?*

"Hmm. Did this Dillon ask about your classes, regarding where they were located and so on?" the defense demands.

"Well, yeah, I guess. I thought he was just interested."

The judge looks inquisitively at both attorneys. Finally, the prosecutor deduces, "Well, it appears Leeland indeed acted alone. It's his fault a shot was fired! I have nothing further."

"Points taken," Judge Eckis comments conclusively. "The defense may now present."

Mr. Fog approaches. "Your Honor, I would like to call my first witness, Betty Dentaw, to the stand."

Gabby hadn't noticed the girl sitting behind her. The bystander maneuvers her way forward. The young woman with sleek hair pulled into a tight ponytail now sits opposite Leeland on the other side of the judge.

"As Dillon Dentaw's only relative willing to drive here today, I have some questions for you," the defense begins. "Did your cousin plan to kill the two men sitting over there?" The lawyer points at Kenn and Adam.

"Our family is in shock. And no, he told me he only wanted to scare them," the slim teenager answers sheepishly.

"Did you know Dillon was bringing a gun down to do the scaring?"

"No, I didn't. I mean, we live together with some other kids from Oakland. But with work and um, other stuff, we barely see—barely saw—each other."

"Were you worried about your cousin getting in trouble, considering he'd already been arrested for violence?"

"I didn't think much about it. Dillon is—was—twenty-two; he owned a gun, and it wasn't taken away after he was released from jail the last time. So, I'm pretty sure he had a right to it."

The defense attorney interrupts: "I move to strike the last statement, your Honor. As a matter of law, the deceased did not have a right to carry a gun in public or bring it into a school, whether or not it was loaded."

"Motion granted. Ms. Dentaw's last statement will be stricken from the record."

Mr. Fog redirects his attention. "And Ms. Dentaw, may I ask why Dillon didn't just drive himself. Why did he take the bus?"

"He doesn't have a license. He lost it."

"You mean he misplaced it?" the attorney investigates.

"No, it was revoked."

"Well, that says something else about his character, now doesn't it?"

The defense attorney looks directly at the prosecutor and declares, "I'm done here."

"You may now cross-examine the witness," the judge prompts.

"No questions, your Honor. I'm just here to uphold the law," Mr. Murray states.

"Defense, you may progress with your points then. Ms. Dentaw, you are excused."

"Apparently the law allowed a violent criminal to keep a handgun after he was released from jail, and I take issue with that," the defense attorney asserts. "Moreover, Mr. Dentaw broke the same laws as the younger Mr. Farbinski regarding concealed carry and gun-free schools. Aren't the boys even on those accounts?"

The judge shakes her head. "Sir, we are not trying the deceased here. Dillon's record is a moot point."

"Oh, so Mr. Dentaw gets off the hook? Free and clear? A poor victim who rode for hours on a public bus with a handgun in his coat pocket, no big deal? The punk gangster threatened these students!" the lawyer exclaims, gesturing toward Adam and Kenn. "My client protected his classmates, ma'am. Granted, he committed some crimes in doing so, but Dillon is the villain in this story. And I refuse to accept otherwise!"

"Mr. Fog. You are out of line. Your acceptance or denial of the details is not in question. Mr. Farbinski's innocence is," the judge simplifies.

"You're right, your Honor. But let me add that Leeland recently moved here from Alaska where the 'shoot first' self-defense law is golden," the younger attorney bothers to mention.

"That doesn't apply, Fog. Come on," the prosecutor challenges. "We're not in Alaska *or Kansas* for that matter. The kid should not have had a handgun on him. He can't claim to 'stand his ground' when unlawfully carrying. You know it. She knows it," he points at the judge. "And he knows it!" the seasoned lawyer extends his plump index finger toward Leeland.

The defense attorney collects himself. He straightens his tie and looks around. He summons his second witness, Miss Gabriella Oliver. After she swears in, Mr. Fog asks, "What can you tell us about Leeland here, teacher? What can you tell us about his character as a member of your class?" Mr. Murray sighs loud enough to demonstrate annoyance.

"Well, I'll say he is courteous and attentive. His grade point average is 3.9. He thoughtfully responds to discussions, and his writing is thorough and well researched."

"So, he's a good student. A good student who made a bad—although that's arguable, considering the timing—choice."

The prosecutor stands up. "Your Honor, this is silly. I object. Fog is appealing to pathos. We should focus on facts here, not conjecture. The fact is Farbinski was out of line. Way out. Timing is irrelevant. Enough with the bleeding-heart bullshit!"

"Your Honor, can I please speak freely?" Gabby petitions.

"Overruled, Mr. Murray, and sure, go ahead, Miss Oliver."

"I am both thankful for—and troubled by—Leeland's actions. There are so many lessons to learn from this event. Not just for him. But for the other three students here as well. Parameters involving privacy, for one. Plus, the costs of sharing personal information. I realize we're here to ascertain the particulars of that fateful and fatal Friday. But everyone could be more accountable to his and her own decisions, dating back to before Leeland brought a gun to school, and we can plainly see how poor choices can have a detrimental domino effect. It's unfortunate Kenn and Adam conspired against Stephanie to begin with."

"Right, well, we're here now," the prosecutor curtly rebuts, "for Mr. Farbinski's sentencing, not to muse over every shoulda, woulda, coulda leading up to the lethal incident!"

"Indeed," the judge acknowledges. "This is his hearing. And so, I appreciate the sentiment and testimonies. Mitigating factors—not having a prior criminal record and accepting responsibility at the outset—

weigh on rulings here today."

"Your Honor, there's something else." Gabby wonders how her supplemental defense of Leeland might be perceived. Her heart quickens. She reaches for her inhaler, which is not nearby. She thinks about historical figures she admires—the people who stood up for those who needed their support, even when it was contentious. *Like Honest Abe.*

"Leeland didn't exactly act on his own."

Marie gasps.

"He yielded to me. He looked to me for permission."

Leeland's mom Wendy whimpers.

"I didn't know what he was asking to do. But I nodded yes."

"Thank you for being forthright, Miss Oliver. We will adjourn at this time. I am retiring to my chambers for lunch. Afterward, I will sensibly sort out the situation and deliberate in order to determine an appropriate sentence. After the recess, court will commence at 2:45."

Ready for a reprieve, Gabby uses her inhaler. And then the nearest bathroom. Over lunch in the courthouse cafeteria, consisting of plastic-wrapped turkey and cheese sandwiches, Marie asks her coworker what she thinks of the case so far. "Well," Gabby chews, "I think it was unwise of Leeland to bring a gun to Heart High, sad he felt unsafe at school, disastrous he acted in a manner which would incriminate him, too bad Stephanie didn't effectively warn HHS, and crazy Dillon endangered us at all! I fault myself for not actively intervening, not seeing the warning signs from Stephanie as serious."

"Good summary of a bad situation," Marie concurs, licking leftover mayo from her fingertips. "I'm surprised you spoke up about giving a blind endorsement to Leeland. Are you sure that was the right thing to do?"

"Sometimes, the right thing is relative."

"True. Well, we'll talk more later. Excuse me, I've got to go find a place to smoke."

"Okay, I'll probably take a walk around the courthouse. Since we have time to kill."

After the break, the women sit among witnesses and supportive spectators. They all stand to welcome the judge back. She asks both lawyers to make closing arguments. On behalf of the government, the older attorney expresses he is in alignment with the defendant's dad, meaning he agrees Leeland's actions were dreadfully disappointing, and his justifiable consequences should function as an example and legal lesson to others.

The defense implores a reduced sentence. He observes, "Here sits a kid who is barely eighteen. He is smart and respectful and feels called to enlist in the armed forces one day. A felony offense could complicate that. Time in jail would derail his plans to graduate high school with honors as well."

"He made his choices," the prosecutor surmises in refutation.

"Undeniably, he did," the Judge recaps. "Mrs. Farbinski, I invite you to come up front in order to support your son during sentencing. You may hold his hands if you'd like." The gracious judge makes handwritten notes while Leeland's mother walks forward again. She steadies herself next to her son, first stroking his hair and then cupping his hands with hers. His handcuffs rest awkwardly between them.

"Leeland Farbinski," Judge Eckis turns her attention toward the accused. "This is a unique set of circumstances. You seem like a decent kid who broke the law. Several laws. Still, dare I say, I am impressed by your courage in the classroom. And I appreciate that you looked to your teacher for approval first. Even if she didn't understand why. I think you could potentially apply yourself as an upright citizen of society someday—after you serve your time and pay your dues.

"As for the ruling today, there is evidence and testimony in favor of the government's case against you. You have admitted to primarily acting alone as you so willingly confessed earlier. This leads me to believe you did not anticipate the killing; it took place under the conditions of a "sudden quarrel," was motivated by fear, and done in order to apprehend the deceased. You appear genuinely remorseful and have demonstrated accountability for your choices and actions. I have carefully considered everything presented, and I hereby sentence you to the minimum three years of jail time in a state prison under California Penal Codes 192(a) and 193 for voluntary manslaughter.

"The felony offense results in the lifetime loss of the constitutional right to bear arms—unless pardoned. Let me be clear: In compliance with California Penal Code Section 29800 and the Gun Control Act of 1968, you are prohibited from buying or owning a firearm.

"For the crime of carrying a concealed loaded weapon, you are charged the maximum $1,000 in accordance with Section 25850. Because of the context of this unusual situation—you hold a permit but not for this gun, it was your father's and not otherwise unlawfully stolen, your lack of criminal history, and your happenstance defense— I've reduced the CCW felony to a misdemeanor under the Wobbler clause. With regard to Sections 29610 and 29700, possessing a pistol without consent, you will be fined an additional $1000.

"I take discharging a firearm on school grounds very seriously, as it is a grave offense, a crime that falls under Title 18 of the U.S. Code and more specifically Title 20, Section 7961, detailing gun-free requirements in education. California's adoption of the Gun-Free School Zone Act is PC 626.9. For this violation, I sentence you to an additional three years."

"Six years!" Gabby murmurs to Marie.

"However." Everyone waits in anxious anticipation. "The court has discretion as to how those terms will be structured, and I've decided they can run concurrently. Furthermore, the final two years will be suspended and thus served under mandatory supervision, a strict form of probation. Due to overcrowding in state prisons and pursuant to

Penal Code 1170(h), you may serve your one year in the county jail closer to home, which I find to be a reasonable and fair consequence."

Leeland's mom audibly sighs in relief.

"In summary, your total jail time results in one year, followed by two years under mandatory supervision, and fines totaling $2,000. Plus the loss of gun rights." With that, the judge taps the gavel and announces, "Court adjourned."

Weekend Four, Saturday

Gabby snoozes into Saturday. She is mentally and physically drained after the emotional week, which was finalized by Friday's courthouse culmination. The exhausted teacher pets her pooch in the comfort of their full-sized bed. She reaches for a new paperback on the nightstand and begs, *Fiction, take me away!* She is reading *The Split* (2019) by a Floridian female novelist from the Midwest.[33] Gabby likes the story because the author highlights nuances within relationships and the risks of taking sides on national issues.

Gabby and Eddie lounge around awhile. Her bedroom fantasy has always included a good book and coffee. But…she eventually checks her phone just to see if anyone has beckoned her out of post-traumatic school-shooting malaise. And indeed, Brandon has.

Pick you up at 6:30?

Hi. What? Why? She curtly answers.

I thought you were going as my date to the dance, he reminds her with a round, yellow, winky face.

Oh yeah, Gabby simply responds without punctuation or emoji conclusion, thus leaving connotation open to interpretation. *The homecoming dance.* She rolls her eyes at Eddie who unmovingly reciprocates apathy.

I signed you up to chaperone, Brandon beseeches.

Gabby pauses. Both irritated and optimistic, she replies, **Thanks.**

The bookworm reads the day away. She avoids thinking about school. Eventually, she stretches her legs and sits upright in bed. *What to wear?* she deliberates, somewhat indifferently. Moseying over to her

---

33 https://www.randiharvey.com/books

closet, Gabby tries to muster enthusiasm, finally deciding on a pink sequined top and black dress pants with pink pumps and pink gemstone earrings. It seems to fit the date-night/chaperone-duty combo.

That evening, Brandon arrives in a brown suede jacket, cactus-print collared shirt, big brass belt buckle, and tan slacks with cowboy boots. *Western fancy.*

"So, how was court?" Brandon broaches as they get into his car, the top up this time.

"Heart-wrenching."

"How so?"

"Oh, one example," Gabby feigns nonchalance, "was witnessing Leeland's mom holding her kid's cuffed hands while he was sentenced to a year in jail."

"Dude, one year, that's less than I expected."

"Plus fines, probation, and the loss of gun rights. I think he could've spent six years in jail, but the sentencing got reconfigured."

"Wow. I wonder how his armed dad overseas feels, considering it was his gun, right?"

"Yeah. Probably disheartened. He sent a letter. Leeland's mom read it in court. His dad knows guns have their place. In the right hands. But Leeland broke the rules."

"Do you think he feels proud of his son at all?"

Gabby looks out the window. "I'm not a parent, and I can't say for sure. Overall, his letter sounded disapproving."

"Makes sense. Is that how you feel, too? About guns in general?"

"Well, I'm no stranger to hunting. I grew up eating venison my dad shot. I followed him around in the woods and hid out in the cold deer blind. While reading, of course. But shooting for sustenance and taking a human life are two very different stories."

"No doubt. Hey, did you tell the judge what you told me? About Leeland asking you for permission, so to speak?"

"Yes. It might've lowered his punishment a little. But coming forward with that wasn't easy." Gabby suddenly remembers lines from the play Binah performed in: *The Tomorrow People.*

Marie's son, as Tim, had asked, "Are you going to keep your job? Qualify to be a teacher?" And then Binah answered, "Yes, and then carry on teaching…But I wouldn't mind it being a bit easier."

They drive along quietly past the beach. Poisonous but pretty oleander flowers divide the lanes. Brandon fidgets with his phone, trying to find a song to fit the mood.

"I wish you wouldn't do that," Gabby finally says after watching him look down at his device several times.

"What?" he inquires. "Wish I wouldn't do what?"

"Use your phone while we're on the road."

"Sorry, I was just searching for a song I thought you'd like. Never mind!"

Brandon reaches across her and places the cell into the Thing's open glove box next to a wad of surfboard Sex Wax. He comes up with another way to break the silence: "So, I'm assigned to the snack bar. And, I think you're at the lemonade stand?" He notes their separate duties as they travel together toward the evening's function. Still reflecting on the court charges, Gabby feels numb, unready to fully participate. As they near the school, she tries to reassemble the parts of herself she'll need for the event—her roles as supervisor, secret girlfriend, and…potential first responder.

"Wait, I forgot my pepper spray!" she panics.

"What?" Brandon inquires, thrown off by the change of subject.

"We need to go back. I forgot it on the counter, sorry. Please turn around."

"Gabby, you don't need Mace; we're just going to a school dance, not some shady alleyway night club!" He takes the next freeway exit.

"Yeah, but what if…what if I need to defend myself, the students? I bought a container of pepper spray this week. I thought it would be good to carry, in case of emergency."

Brandon turns into the paved lot, parks the car, and looks at Gabby. "Listen," he puts a hand on her thigh, "I realize you're probably still shaken by what happened, but it's safe in there." He signals toward the stucco building where students are lined up outside. "There are cops on duty. You don't have to provide any defense."

When they walk in through the cafeteria's double doors, security officers prompt them to pass through a metal detector. Brandon's belt activates the alarm, and students turn to see why. He's quickly ushered through.

Miss Oliver spots Ember on the steps leading down to the makeshift tile dance floor. The lunch tables have all been cleared and stacked on the side. It's dim in the large room, aside from the colorful strobe lights being projected from a DJ booth on stage. Gabby can tell Ember is having a good time with her boyfriend. They are laughing together, and the young woman is nicely dressed in a gold gown, despite the dress-shopping worries noted in her journal.

Lucy greets her teacher and gestures toward Mr. Ritter. She must've noticed them walk in together. She raises her eyebrows in astonishment and then nods knowingly. "Cute," she smirks. "Right this way, Miss Oliver," the teen directs her toward the lemonade counter. As a representative of student council, Lucy helps coordinate event logistics.

Nadia and Nico hang around the drink stand. "I see you two got a night out together. That's nice," Miss Oliver makes small talk with the young parents. Nadia is wearing a cream-colored dress with a lace overlay flattering her full figure. Nico's suit looks a little big, like he borrowed it from someone taller. They regard each other admiringly.

Every once in a while, Brandon gazes up from the snack bar, which is about forty feet away from Gabby's post. Between concessions, he glances at her, and she reciprocates his toothy acknowledgment, girlishly forgetting her previous safety concerns.

"Your teeth won't always be so white," Marie wryly jeers upon walking up for a glass of juice. She obviously saw Brandon and Gabby exchanging smiles. "Just you wait; coffee will stain those pearls of his, too! He's attractive now, sure. But give it ten years and a gut full of beers! I've seen what can happen to a handsome man. Ha! I've been married a while." She winks and sips her lemonade. "Hey, I'm surprised to see you here. After yesterday. But I'm glad you're grinning again."

A popular rap song summons dancers to the floor. Binah is quick to rally her friends, and they all appear to know the words. With hands in the air affirming the shared sentiments, they jump and shout the lyrics, each student an instrument in motion.

"You heard of Square Footage?" Matt asks Miss Oliver, who admires the dancers' energy. He hands her six quarters in exchange for the yellow beverage.

"What?" she replies, trying to communicate over the loud music.

"Square Footage, the rap artist. He's big-time right now. Speaking up for social justice and stuff. I follow him on Insta-Face. I like his Daily Squares."

"No, I haven't heard of him," the teacher admits. What do you mean 'daily squares,' like food, meals?"

"No," Matt gently giggles. "They're motivational prompts. Four sided. Square says with every concern, big and small, there's 1) the issue, 2) an ideal resolution, 3) a small step toward change, and 4) personal responsibility."

"That's cool." She sways to the beat, trying to rise to the hip occasion.

Matt raises his glass to her. "You stick with me, Miss O. I'll keep you in the know."

With that, and because of a lull in customers, Gabby wanders over to the snack table. "Have you heard of Square Footage before?" she asks Brandon.

"Haven't you noticed the poster in my classroom? 'F' squared, baby!"

Accepting she is apparently in the dark with both music and math, Gabby resumes her position as the citrus server.

"Hey, can I buy you a drink?" Brandon follows her and flirts.

"Got a dollar fifty?" she smiles in response.

About an hour into the function, and after the homecoming queen and king are paraded through the cafeteria, Scott hoists himself onto the stage up front. He takes the microphone from Lucy, who was just announcing the court winners, and he begins to sing the lyrics of a well-liked song. Without music playing to back him up, Scott renders a karaoke version of Lorde.

"We'll never be royals...That kind of luxe just ain't for us. We crave a different kind of buzz."

Scott quickly draws a crowd, and students sing along to his lead. Soon, he is the main attraction as the crowned winners depart the stage. Matt films the change of scene on his smartphone, and Gabby notices a "live" banner scrolling across the bottom of Matt's device.

"Hey, he doesn't sound bad! He's actually in tune," Rob compliments. They stand in front of Brandon and Gabby at the lemonade counter. Rob is wearing tight black skinny jeans and a red Guns N' Roses crop top.

On the drive home, Brandon asks Gabby what she thought of her first dance at Heart High.

"I thought it was awesome when Scott sang acapella over the mic, even though parts of the song were inappropriate."

"You mean it was awkward, comical maybe?"

"No, courageous. Scott has a gift for melodic memorization. And he doesn't care if people laugh. I just love him," Gabby pats her chest with both hands.

"You're such a hopeless romantic," Brandon teases amicably.

"Well, yeah! I'm giving you a chance, aren't I?"

Brandon grins at her witty comeback.

"But hey, what does it mean when someone is 'live' on a cell phone?" Gabby asks her slightly younger date. "Like when Matt was filming Scott tonight."

"That the recording is being streamed on a social-media site."

"Then and there, unedited and without permission from the people being captured?" Gabby is naïvely surprised. While waiting at a stoplight, Brandon looks at her dubiously.

"But it's not like he's a celebrity in a band," Gabby continues. "Those who don't know Scott might not appreciate his musical contribution. I mean out of context. He was performing for the school, not the screen. Who's viewing it?"

"Well, it depends on Matt's settings, I suppose. It might just be his friends and family, and if he tags Scott, then his too, or it could be public."

"But…" Gabby can't find the words. She sits with the friction she feels—her want to shield Scott from possible embarrassment and the realization that it's out of her hands. *Once again, social-media sharing has the power to turn a high-school moment into a public spectacle.*

The unsettled teacher and her homecoming king venture inside the apartment for a night cap. After a couple small glasses of alcohol, Gabby forgets her concern for Scott's vulnerability. Brandon picks up an empty wine bottle from the coffee table and places it to his mouth like a microphone.

"Hey, hey baby. I wanna know," he stands, trying to rouse her, **"if you'll be my girl."** He moves his hips seductively. Brandon repeats the lyrics of a familiar tune from one of Gabby's favorite classic movies.

She can't help but laugh at his raunchy rendition of *Dirty Dancing*.[34] He motions for her to join him.

"Fine," she agrees, her eyes playfully rolling, despite their twinkle. Gabby feigns reluctance to romance. "But no lifts," she teases, rising from the couch.

Gabby puts both arms around Brandon's neck as he hums the tune by Bruce Channel. They move their feet slowly, without choreography and reminiscent of the high-school dance, complete with amateur adolescents groping. She surrenders to the song and opportunity to dance with Brandon. *After hours.* He holds a hand above her head and caresses it downward with his warm touch. But unlike Baby, Gabby doesn't laugh at the ticklish sensation. Instead, she kisses Johnny's—Brandon's—neck, inviting his closeness, his candidness, his continuation of dirty dancing.

---

34 A romantic movie from 1987, starring Jennifer Grey and Patrick Swayze as Baby and Johnny

Weekend Four, Sunday

Brandon leaves the apartment by early light. *The surf must be calling*, she supposes. With a frothy cup of dark-roast coffee, Gabby gets to work. She picks up Rhonda's journal.

Domains

There are three dimensions, three worlds in which most of us high schoolers are currently living: the real face-to-face present, the virtual Insta-Face membership, and the in-between posts existence. While living in the space between shares: We take pictures, we imagine reactions, we connect and disconnect from the present and virtual versions of life, multi-tasking within multiple magnitudes.

Static

Life is unlike social networking because when we say something aloud, we don't always know if the listener or listeners "like" it. And we definitely don't know how followers would feel about the conversation. That listener might later tell others, and those people might further comment on and/or misinterpret the grapevine game of telephone. But the original speaker cannot easily track her influence, good or bad. There is no timeline of commentary or suggested reading to research. She cannot edit or delete her input either. RL exchanges aren't filtered through SM.

To be (seen) or not to be

Pretty much every teen I'm friends with has undergone some sort of small crisis concerning social media. Panic about not being seen, not feeling liked, not appearing popular, or not looking perfect. We can delete or inactivate profiles, but everyone I've talked to about these anxieties says they eventually reactivate their accounts in order to resume communication and correspondence online. Tis the times.

Hindsight

So, I've been thinking...this class is called Reflective Writing. And, I already write reflectively, well sometimes critically or analytically, online. I love having a blog! Even if no one reads it. But people do. They really read it! And, I try not to worry about whether they like my words or not. Writing is my coping and processing mechanism. It works for me. But, it's not for everyone.

Others cope through socialization, church, nature, music, sports, travel, etc. And, that's okay. What you're trying to do in here is encourage writing, regardless. And, I think that's good, too. Because maybe some of my classmates are untapped writers. With all the turmoil in the world today, people need outlets.

I typically use an online forum, but I have an appreciation for opposing viewpoints. Journaling privately obviously worked for your mom, but in the end, she decided to share her words with you. Through that transaction, they were no longer private. I think deep down everyone wants to be heard, seen, appreciated.

Dear Rhonda,

Thanks for these existential entries, but I don't believe my mom made her journals accessible because she longed for posthumous fame. She hoped I'd learn from her perspective and mistakes, since she couldn't live longer to raise me into my teenage and adult years. Her words have raised me. They have connected me to a mother I wouldn't have known much about otherwise. So, in a way, you're right. By transcribing her thoughts, she made herself known. To me.

But she did not put herself on display. If I compile some of her pieces into a shareable literary collection, she could leave more of a legacy. And I would do that for the sincere sake of poetic inspiration.

I'm glad writing helps you along, too. Blogging or jogging, I agree humans need active outlets. But social media is another story. And while we live in a world where likes and followers suggest value and credibility, good writing still speaks for itself.

After that silent intellectual exchange between teacher and student, Gabby feels inspired to write an entry of her own, a letter to her first teacher.

Dear Mom,

I've been reading student journals. They are handwritten and heartfelt. But some teens express that they grapple with modern-day habits.

Truthfully, technology gives me anxiety, too. Maybe it's because I don't fully understand it. The ins and outs of electronics, the Internet, Blue Tooth, and the mysterious Cloud. There's so much to keep up with. And even if I could comprehend yesterday's tools, it'll be a new set of norms tomorrow.

There's such a learning curve, and my preference for printed material makes the hill higher. People are hardly reading hardbound and paperback books anymore, Mom. They tend to skim from screens. Can you believe it?

As soon as I've learned how to minimally use a device, I have to upgrade it. A person has to buy new gear to keep up with trends. And everything is wireless now! I feel like a curmudgeon writing this at my age, but I miss tangibility.

Before there were MP3s (music files) and online radio stations, there were tapes and CDs (and in your era, 8-tracks,

*records). Real music you could hold, artifacts bought from the store
and carried home. Album covers and inserts for fans to read, lists of
song titles to mull over, timeless pictures of musicians, there on the
shelf or in the car, available for collection.*

*People these days are minimalists—meaning they don't
have much to show for depth—but they are also hoarders of
information: twenty digital photos for every one we'd take with 35
mm film and five online news subscriptions for every local paper
bought at the corner market. Oh and the endless emails! It seems
like nothing is special when everything is accessible.*

*At times, electronic connectivity feels like an invasion of
privacy and plea for attention. Just because I don't yell something
on social media (a platform where you can share ideas and pictures
with everyone you've ever known or wanted to know) doesn't
mean I'm trying to hide it. I just think certain opinions require
development before distribution. Hence, good old-fashioned
journaling and friendly person-to-person letter writing!*

*I've always loved texture. Found items. Keepsakes.
Clippings. Actual photographs. The written word. Even as a young
girl, I was old fashioned. Because I take after you.*

Thanks for the memoirs, Mom.

*Nostalgically yours,
Gab*

With memorabilia in mind, Gabby pulls out an Indigo Girls CD
from underneath her TV stand. *Surely, this will lift my spirit,* she antici-
pates, looking at the worn case. After wiping the backside on her shirt,
she inserts the disk into an open CD player on her entertainment center.

**"I offer thanks to those before me.
That's all I've got to say...."**

At 10:05, Gabby gets a text from Marie. She stops dancing around the living room and looks at her phone, hoping it's Brandon coming back.

Happy birthday! *Oh yay*, she beams. *Someone remembered!*

Thanks. Hey, how'd you know it was my birthday?

I got a notification on Insta-Face. How else? Haha!

How personal, Gabby snarks, recalling her hanging wall calendar with loved ones' birthdays noted on it. She then realizes her dated record is admittedly limited when compared to social networking reminders. *Eh*, she shrugs, appreciating the electronic efficiency. Just then, a text comes through from Brandon who must've also been alerted online.

Hey sexy. Sorry I had to run. I had a surf date planned with the bros. Happy birthday btw. XO! See you mañana. Last night was rad! TTYT.

That's it? She thinks. *No card? No gift? No bueno!* Gabby opens up her Insta-Face app to see a bunch of basic birthday wishes. She also notices a picture of Brandon and his "bros" on the beach. Posted five minutes ago.

Sighing, Gabby walks outside to the collection of apartment mailboxes as Eddie piddles along the way. Wearing slippers, she inserts her key and turns it to find a single greeting card inside. *Well, at least someone thought ahead.* Excitedly, she opens the beige envelope with its little Buddha stamp and wax seal. On the card's front cover, it reads, "No matter how hard the past, you can always begin again." A quote by Jack Kornfield.[35] That was her dad, dependably nurturing with wise words. And inside, he had written a genuinely sincere sentiment. Gabby displays the postmarked present on her small kitchen counter next to a bouquet of flowers she carefully cuts from a rose bush just outside.

Gabriella snuggles up to her dog. "I guess it's just you and me today, bro," she says aloud. "Maybe we'll take ourselves out for ice cream." She looks up at the rose painting.

The thirty-three-year-old woman thinks back to her fourth birthday, the last year her mom was strong and healthy enough to celebrate her daughter's special day. Gabby remembers their old Buick Regal stuffed with helium-filled balloons. Her mom drove up to the midwestern preschool honking. Gabby was outside for recess, her pink jacket buttoned up tight. Across the passenger side window, her mom had written, "Happy Birthday!" in silver marker with a little balloon drawn at the top. *Inside the balloon was the number four.* They were going shopping for a fancy dress. And at the mall, they would share a pretzel dipped in nacho cheese, Gabby's gooey-good kid favorite.

---

35 American author Jack Kornfield is known for his books about Buddha's teachings. Buddha (Siddhartha Gautama) was a philosopher, spiritual teacher, and religious leader from ancient India.

Week Five

Rethinking Protocol

Week Five, Monday

"Good morning. As you know, I was absent Friday because of Leeland's court date. You probably saw it reported on the news. Since it is public information, I can say Leeland has a felony on his record. To be clear, he was sentenced to one year of jail time, $2,000 in fines, two years of strict probation, and as I understand it, he can never own a firearm."

No one reacts. They wait.

"That said, he plans to take correspondence courses and earn his GED—general educational development, also called a graduation equivalency diploma. Oh, and I think Kenn brought Leeland the poem we read last week?"

Kenn manages an unenthusiastic half-smile.

Miss Oliver takes a deep breath. "I'm, um, sorry for the interruption within our class." She tries to refocus on the curriculum. "Before the shooting, Nadia was about to sing a song she wrote for her baby. She said she'd replaced some words within familiar lyrics. Can we go back to that, please? Back to the moment before…plans changed?" The redirection feels forced, but Nadia reciprocates.

Nadia smiles. "Cantar? You want me sing about Cielo?"

"Yes, please, that would be lovely."

"Silencioso mi bebé. In the loud world. When bad news blows, into me you curl. If ICE calls, mi bebé won't fall. Mama has Cielo through it all." She sings in tune to the nursery rhyme "Rock-a-Bye Baby." *About immigration and customs enforcement!* Miss Oliver can only imagine Nadia's world outside of school and her worries regarding the new baby. Nico looks downward in embarrassment.

"Hey, I wrote a song, too," Rob unexpectedly interrupts Nadia's deportation lullaby. "It's not as sweet, but it's real."

"Do you want to share—I mean sing—it, Rob?" the teacher asks.

"Sure." They open their notebook. "What happened in here has got us down. This is no time to clown around. So, Stephanie, we have to ask, what was it that you said last? 'I'm not a tramp or a tease!' Yet some are calling you a sleaze. We get it's not all your fault. Kenn and his friend shoulda got caught. Put in their place. But not in this space. We're here to learn, I suppose. Just trying to discern. Who knows? Leeland, boy, he dropped the mic. Now, what will become of his life?"

Silencio. The class is shocked by Rob's rendition. They have broken the ice.

Finally, Rhonda remarks, "I'm sorry, but the whole lead-up to the shooting is ridiculous! An out-of-town thug who's never met Stephanie comes to town to defend her? He rides in with shining armor that's unloaded? And Leeland just happens to bring a gun to school that day. What are the odds?"

Matt answers, "Yeah, Rhonda, what are the odds? What are the odds those students in Texas or Florida or Connecticut or Colorado saw it coming? They didn't. Acts of violence are random and sad. I read on ABC News there have been more than four-hundred school-shooting incidents in the last decade, according the Center for Homeland Defense and Security. Sure, our situation is different because this Dillon character only planned to threaten a couple of guys, not cause mass murder. But he used the wrong tool."

Kenn exclaims, "He was an f'ing tool!"

Lucy politely raises her hand. "What about Leeland? He brought a gun to school. I mean it worked out in our favor. But it's still wrong. People are calling him a hero, a vigilante, but I don't agree."

Miss Oliver responds, "You're right: Leeland was in the wrong. That's why he's paying the price in jail and through probation, in addition to fines and the loss of rights. And that's why we have metal detectors now. So it doesn't happen again—hopefully. And you're spot on, Matt and Kenn. Violence in school is tragic. Dillon definitely used the wrong tool and approach in order to defend Stephanie."

"You suckers are so stupid!" Adam blurts out. The teacher is taken aback by his blatant insult. "Rhonda, Leeland probably didn't just bring a gun that *one* day. It's the day he got caught with it! Dude was probably packin' for a while. He took the Fifth on that detail."

Miss Oliver hadn't really thought of the extended possibility. *How long had Leeland been carrying?* She knows Adam is referring to the Fifth Amendment, and he's correct; Leeland didn't further incriminate himself in court.

"That's unfortunately possible, I suppose, Adam. But please don't call people 'stupid.'" The teacher checks in: "Stephanie, are you okay if we continue this conversation?" Muted, she nods agreeably.

"Let's think about this. What could Dillon have done differently? Furthermore, what might Leeland have done differently?"

Binah raises her hand. "Dillon coulda waited for Kenn and Adam outside school."

Kenn laughs. "That hothead didn't want to have a friendly talk!"

"He coulda punched you outside then. Still woulda been better."

"F. you, Binah," Adam defends.

"Well," she insists, "you two deserve some payback for messin' with Steph."

Adam glares at her. Miss Oliver resists the urge to step in, to dominate the discussion. Instead, she tries to increase uptake by letting students build upon ideas.

"What if," Lucy propositions, "Dillon would've just like reached out to Adam online? Or Kenn. Or both. Just said, 'Hey, what you did to embarrass my girlfriend was wrong.' Like that. Like 'stay away from Stephanie' type thing?"

"She did it to herself," Adam jeers. "This two-timey tramp made HEADlines first!"

"Dude, stop," Kenn rebuts. "Leave her alone, man."

Binah redirects the argument away from Stephanie by saying,

"Yeah, that woulda been nicer, Lucy. Dillon mighta been a bad guy, but that hoodrat ditn't deserve to die."

Kenn contests: "He threatened me with a gun! What else could we have done?"

"Dillon should have stayed out of it. Since he did not live here," Nadia abstractly adds.

Matt stands. "Yes, and let's not forget Dillon had no permit to carry a gun. Plus, according to the news, he had a criminal record. Violent priors? The firearm should've been taken away! Based on his background. He's was a walking red flag. His gun rights should've expired when he was previously arrested."

Rhonda changes the focus: "So, Leeland wanted to try out carrying a gun? 'Just in case' he needed it for self-defense. Like it was some kind of a personal challenge? To see if he could provide protection? First of all, how ignorant! He didn't have a permit for that pistol, let alone a concealed-carry license. And everyone knows you can't bring weapons to school! He must've known he might get expelled and derail his future. What the hell? If he wanted to play 'tough-guy,' he could've—I dunno—gone to the range, shot there, under supervision, in a safe place...or maybe carried a Nerf around as an experiment?"

Miss Oliver silently mulls over Leeland's mental stability alongside his adolescent need for identity formation. She understands Leeland idolizes his father, a soldier who actually earned his right and rank. She remembers reading about the concepts of identity crisis, rebellion, experimentation, and role confusion in an educational theory class. The teacher wonders what the late developmental psychologist Erik Erikson would say about her students.[36] She checks the time. "Any other thoughts?"

---

36 Erik Erikson (1902-1994) is credited for the notion of psychosocial development stages, ranging by approximate age: trust versus mistrust (0-1), autonomy versus shame and doubt (18 months – 2/3 years), initiative versus guilt (3-5), industry versus inferiority (5-12), identity versus role confusion (12-18), intimacy versus isolation (19-40), generativity versus stagnation (40-65), and ego integrity versus despair (65+).

Nadia raises her hand. "Stephanie should not have trusted Dillon. He was too far away, too bad, too unknown. Like a mystery."

Miss Oliver nods in approval. Stephanie musters the courage to speak on her own behalf. "I know, okay! You're right: Nadia, Binah, and Matt. Jesus! I'm sorry. So many things went wrong. With Kenn. With Dillon. With Leeland. What now?"

Unexpectedly, Scott belts out, "**Love bites. Love bleeds. It's bringing me to my knees. Love lives. Love dies. It's no surprise.**"

Rob sways and whispers, "Def Leppard, nice!"

The teacher takes over. "What now? That's a great question, Stephanie. And the rest of you made some good points as well. Unfortunately, guns were brought on campus and someone died. The school has thankfully addressed this issue by controlling where people enter and exit. Everyone is subject to scrutiny. We have more security. And students have been reminded of the rules. We will have a drill soon, and counselors are here to help if you'd like to meet with them privately. But, let's talk about non-violent tools. What resources *do* you have to work through this? To move forward? To work on yourselves? As classmates, friends, romantic partners, social-media users, and digital citizens?" She walks over to the whiteboard and picks up a green marker.

"We can write," Rhonda opens. "We can also pray. Even if I don't regularly do it, I know it makes my mom feel better."

"Yes, prayer tends to set good intentions and provide calming relief." Miss Oliver supports the spiritual proposal.

"We can make art," Binah suggests.

"We can talk it out?" Lucy vocalizes.

"We can read for exposure and example," Lillian intellectually interjects. "There's a lot published on related subjects these days, fiction and non."

"Podemos trabajar," Nico expresses.

"I'll be lifting weights and practicing football," Adam contributes.

"Exercise is a great stress reliever! I personally enjoy walking," the teacher relates.

"We can sing," Rob adds.

With that, Scott dedicates a song to Stephanie. **"I only wish my words could just convince myself that it just wasn't real, but that's not the way it feels. Operator...."**

Miss Oliver wonders if any of the adolescents would recognize the words of Jim Croce. Appreciating student input regarding how to cope, she hums the next line. Tears well in Stephanie's eyes as the bell rings. She mouths "thank you" to Scott from across the room.

The class felt disconnected after the distressing incident, but Gabby welcomes recent contributions. She'd been so focused on her own recovery, on the school's response, and on Leeland's litigation; she hadn't offered her brood a chance to really express themselves. Though intense, the alarming turn of events resulted in increased safety precautions, personal responsibility, careful considerations, and difficult but necessary debriefs. *Tomorrow would give students a fresh start, a second chance.*

With newness in mind, Miss Oliver moves the desks into group seating configurations. She assigns those she wants to keep a closer eye on up front, of course. She also designates a creative corner where kids can draw or color during downtime. She sets out colored pencils, blank paper, and pages with meditative designs. And for artistic inspiration, she includes books by Shel Silverstein[37] and Brian Andreas.[38] *Instead of turning to tech for distraction, these teens can make art from imaginative stimulation.*

---

37 Shel Silverstein was an American writer, poet, and cartoonist known for his playful children's books. He lived from 1930-1999.
38 https://www.storypeople.com

Revived by the change and potential connectedness that may ensue, the teacher pulls out the old syllabus. She begins crossing items off, scratching them out, taking a red pen to her own work. She writes three new goals: collaboration, digital citizenship, and accountability. She researches ideas online, excitedly taking notes along the Internet's journey. *Let's see: Digital Citizenship = relationships and responsibility. Media Literacy = comprehension and application.* Further exploration would verify her basic understanding of these concepts. *Why didn't college quite cover it?* They'd read plenty of Piaget and other dated material about adolescent and cognitive development[39] but not so much about teens navigating the electronic era. *Or how to guide them.*

Miss Oliver prints related articles, highlights suggestions, writes in the margins. Artful lesson planning is her multicolored palette again. The possibilities feel empowering. With a teacher's notion of Universal Design, meaning multiple modalities painted into the pedagogy, she prints a new portrait of Reflective Writing and adds a subtitle: within a Digital Age. Gabby prides herself on cultivating a Growth Mindset instead of her usual hesitant and cautious stance toward electronics, especially in academia.[40]

By way of her roundabout research, Miss Oliver happens upon a documentary called *Screenagers*.[41] Intrigued, she tabs the site, plans to pay to watch it, and would try to host a screening at school.

Teachers leave. The campus quiets. Gabby comes to a stopping point. And then her phone dings, reminding her of the time and her hungry dog back home.

---

39 Jean Piaget (1896-1980) was a Swiss psychologist known for his research on child development and the idea of constructivism in education. Constructivism means building upon a person's prior learning and experiences.
40 With a Growth Mindset, a person believes he/she can development new skills and approaches, regardless of setbacks. According to Carol Dweck, American psychologist and Professor at Stanford, Fixed and Growth Mindsets show people's reactions to challenges. A Fixed Mindset is a rigid stance, an emphasis on basic traits, or an assumption of limited abilities.
41 *Screenagers* (2016) was created and directed by physician Delaney Ruston. It is about raising a teenager in a techy world. The film suggests solutions, and the website offers resources. Its sequel, *Next Chapter* (2019), focuses on understanding challenges, lowering stress, and empowering adolescents within the context of a digital age.

What are you wearing? Brandon asks.

The same professional garb I've been sporting all day, she responds colorlessly.

You're no fun, dude. Make something up!

Feeling tired, Gabby deflects, **I'm still at work. What are you wearing?**

He quickly texts, **a leopard speedo and snakeskin cowboy boots.**

Really? Her pulse quickens. She's aroused at the thought of him unclothed.

Maybe, he answers ambiguously.

Nice details. A for adjectives!

Ha! Says you, the English teacher. Want a picture?

No, I'd rather leave you to my imagination. But thanks for asking before sending something provocative.

Wow. You really are different than most chicks!

Gabby wonders if that's an insult or compliment. Either way, she replies, **yes, I'd like to think so.** ☺

Giddy Gabby goes home. That night, she pulls out her favorite shoe box. In the absence of footwear, there are precious photographs inside. Pictures of her as a child, her parents together as a young couple, her mom pregnant…Gabby giggles at the fashion trends and big hair of the late 1980s and early '90s. She studies her family members' faces, their smiles, their old house in Illinois—the last place they all lived before her mom got sick. She slowly shuffles through the printed memories and reads her mom's handwritten descriptions on the back of each. "Gabriella as Raggedy Ann." She imagines her mom holding a pen, its blue ink transferring onto the now distant memory, which was captured about a year before her ovarian cancer diagnosis. With love and with Halloween on the horizon, adult Gabby posts the kid picture on her refrigerator door.

Week Five, Tuesday

Feeling oriented toward the future, having taken time to process the incident, read the news, witness the verdict, and restore her willpower, the reenergized teacher is finally ready to publicly comment on Leeland's case. She'd finally email that local reporter back. *Was it too late?*

As Miss Oliver mulls over what to write while she drives to work, a familiar song plays on the radio. *Where have I heard this before? Oh yeah, the school dance! It's Square Footage!* When the funky track finishes, the DJ says, "and there we have it, folks, everyone's favorite rap activist! Remember to chew on your daily squares today, listeners. As things come up, be sure to ask yourself: What's the issue, what's an ideal resolution, what's a small step toward change, and what is my personal responsibility in the matter?" *That's it! Gabby* determines. *I'll use these prompts as a guide!* Before class, she composes an email to the Palm Oak Press.

```
Hello,

     Thank you for reaching out to me. I
apologize for my delayed response. As the
teacher who experienced the local shooting
firsthand, it is important that I say
something.
     Please know that Heart High takes safety
on campus seriously. Since the troubling
incident, we've increased security and support
for staff and students, thanks to additional
funding. Ideally, everyone will feel safer
as a result, which is what Leeland Farbinski
wanted—the freedom to relax at school without
worry, the comfort of protection. I am
thankful for my job and my life.
     Gun violence is a complicated issue;
```

however, this scary situation was loaded with more than ammo. For those privy to the graphic details, let this be a lesson in making better choices by deciding when it's wise to stand up for someone, to which extent, and what the consequences could be. Actions leading up to the armed intrusion were associated with relationships: privacy concerns online and personal matters between students.

As an educator, I am committed to teaching the tenets of digital citizenship, facilitating important discussions, being more communicative with school counselors, providing resources to parents, enabling artistic opportunities, and encouraging both problem solving and stress relief through reflective writing.

May we all become more mindful.

Sincerely,
Miss Gabriella Oliver

Before pushing send, the teacher decides to defer to her boss. She forwards the draft to Mr. Keystone for approval first.

Miss Oliver looks over her lesson plans: *TSWBAT institute new classroom norms and begin a collage project.* After most of the students walk in and mill around, she greets them.

"Hi, as you can see, we have a new seating arrangement. You're grouped into three or four for a purpose. I hope to foster a better sense of community in here, and I want you to listen to each other's viewpoints. You each have skills to offer the group. We'll be working on some collaborative assignments soon. Please find your name and sit down according to the chart I've projected up front."

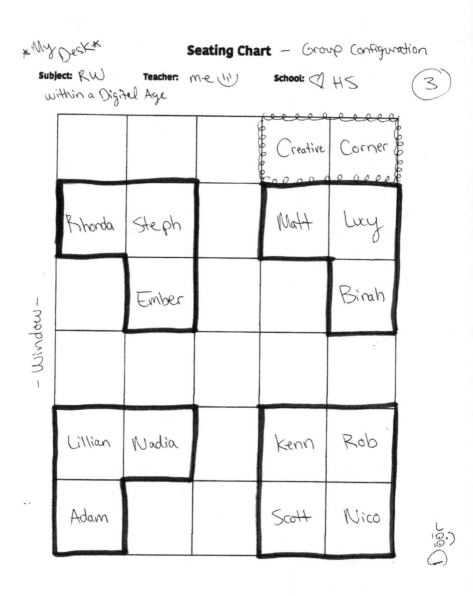

— Window —

Creative Corner

Rhonda | Steph

Matt | Lucy

Ember

Binah

Lillian | Nadia

Kenn | Rob

Adam

Scott | Nico

They find their seats: Some grumble about their designated desks; others chat with new neighbors. The teacher takes roll and then changes the slide to show the updated class website. The boldfaced text at the top says, "Reflective Writing within a Digital Age." There is fine print beneath the title. Miss Oliver asks Rhonda to read it aloud.

"We have to find a way to live with seductive technology and make it work to our purposes. This is hard and will take work. Simple love of technology is not going to help. Nor is a Luddite impulse." - Sherry Turkle, *Alone Together*, P. 294

"Wait, what's a 'Luddite?'" Lillian inquires.

"Luddites lived during the early 1800s. They were afraid new machines would threaten their existing jobs. It's basically a term that refers to people who are wary of change, of progress," the teacher clarifies.

"The quote is about balance, right?" Rob asks. "Being open to technology but not overdoing it?"

"Yes," Miss Oliver affirms.

"Nice job with the site update, Miss O. I see you've finally learned how to log on to the World Wide Web," Matt teases affably.

"Well, thanks. In addition to assignment specifics, you can now correspond with me and each other—after school."

"This is cool, but I have to tell you, most teachers already utilize expanded sites," Rhonda contextualizes.

"I realize that, but I originally envisioned this low-tech class differently. And now, I'm deciding we can use technology to enhance, rather than just distract from, our layered lives. I'm trying to embrace a new normal after what happened; I want to give you thinking points going forward. We will be learning about digital citizenship, and as you can see, I've posted links for you all to read tonight. For those who have limited access to the Internet at home, I've printed some info in both English and Spanish." The teacher glances at Nico. It occurs to her then, in a flash of brainy brilliance, that links *do* connect us. By providing access—to each other and resources. *Of course they do!* But in light of Nico's second language, the concept is made clearer.

"With this new seating arrangement and online forum, I want to establish a fresh set of class norms—rules for us to live up to in here. You'll still be developing verbal-linguistic and intrapersonal-thinking skills, but what are some *interpersonal* ideals we can agree on?"

Stephanie raises her hand. "Respect and, um, privacy!" She manages a closed-lipped smile, widening her eyes as if to say she won't consent to anything less.

"Definitely," Miss Oliver affirms. "A slight change in habits does not equal a reduction in expectation or change of heart. Privacy and respect apply to journals, in-person dialogue, and online conversation, right?"

"Yes," Rhonda qualifies: "We should not make comments on-line that we wouldn't say civilly in person."

"True that," Matt happily confirms. "And the site is just for our class; not to be screenshot and shared elsewhere." He looks toward Kenn.

"Speaking of phones," the teacher follows, "I've told you before, and I'll say it again: I don't want to see your cells out. There's no reason to use them in here. Not for research or music or otherwise. I'll be sure of it. They are too distracting when we're trying to focus. I want to boost social relations, not social-media use. We have laptops for looking things up, if needed. And dictionaries! There's value in meeting a word's alphabetical neighbors, you know? So, one warning! If I see your phone out afterward, I'll hang on to it—in my desk drawer—for the rest of the period." She reminds Adam with a stare. He meets her eyes and rolls his own.

"That seems fair," Ember acknowledges.

"No, it's not!" Adam disputes. "My phone, my property."

"My class, my rules," Miss Oliver spars.

"Whatever, lady. But your boy Ritter over here," Adam motions toward the room next-door, "he lets us use earbuds and listen to music while we solve math problems. It ain't a thing. Actually, music helps me focus."

"Me too," Rob adds.

"Fine," the teacher concedes. "I'll play classical compositions on occasion when we write. But I've seen what happens when students go to change a tune. You get caught up in whatever is calling out from the face of your phone."

"Oh man, that's so true," Matt supports.

"Yeah," Lucy agrees.

"Okay," Miss Oliver redirects the topic. "How about language norms? In group discussions, within the class at large, and with me?"

"I think there could be less sarcasm coming from some of the guys?" Stephanie suggests.

"Yeah, and less demeaning comments about girls, too," Lucy calls out. "Honesty" and "sincerity" are added to the list of ideals being compiled on the board.

"We should write this shiznit down on a poster!" Binah declares. "Hang it up to remind us!"

"Great idea," Miss Oliver applauds. "Binah, will you please hand out one sheet of construction paper to each table? Every group can distill key points down to select standards of accountability. Then, we'll tape your interpretations together." Binah agreeably gathers and distributes art supplies.

After about twenty minutes, the teacher steers her students' attention back up front. She alerts them to a function on the class site. "See here, you can later click on the assignment due Friday: <u>Found Art(icles) Collage</u>." Miss Oliver hovers over the link until further details appear.

Lillian relays the directions as her instructor passes out rectangular pieces of cardboard: "Print, transcribe, or cut news headlines, quotes, and graphics from various forms of media, preferably those published rather recently. You can also include applicable website headings. Artfully assemble them onto a small poster board. Then, staple a short essay to the artwork describing how and why you think these articles and/or topics relate. What is the overall theme or message? You may use social media (print it at home) but not constrain yourself to such. Please include a bibliography with at least three sources."

"Is this similar to composing a found poem?" Rhonda clarifies.

"Yes, exactly," the teacher confirms. "You can work in your small groups or choose to do it alone. If approaching the project from a cooperative perspective, you'll have to creatively share the work and tell me who did what."

Stephanie raises her hand while formulating a non sequitur: "So, are we doing our personal writing online now? Like on this site? I'm not sure I want people to read that."

"Good question. No, we are not. You will still write *to me* and *for yourself* by hand. That is not changing. Reflective writing is the premise of this class, privacy is paramount, and we will continue that routine. There will be a balance of electronic and printed assignments. I've come to accept writing can put us back together, regardless of its form."

"Oh, speaking of writing," Stephanie raises her hand again. "I have my letter. You know, to the president or whatever. It's way over-due, sorry." With a minute left before the bell, the former cheerleader holds up a stapled document.

Scott happily sings, **"Yeah, there's better days shinin' through. These are better days, baby. Better days with a girl like you."** Miss Oliver thanks him for the Springsteen song as students depart.

What are you concerned about in the world, in the United States? What would you like to happen or to change, if you could help the cause?

I would like to see the First Lady address girls about positive self-image, boundaries, equality, and empowerment. I suppose she must have wisdom to offer on these subjects, and she's in a position to share it.

For one, the First Lady could promote a thing called "No One Eats Alone." The positive program encourages kindness, respect, belongingness, and acceptance in schools. But, I've only just heard of it through this research. I've eaten alone (well, with you, Miss Oliver) for a while now.

How would you respectfully advise the president on the matter?

I'm not writing to the president. <u>I'm writing to his wife.</u> Thanks for the chance to do so.

Write your letter.

Dear Mrs. President,

Hello. I'm the girl from Heart High School. You've probably heard of me. I made headlines twice, once among my peers and once on national news. Both stories were shocking and unpleasant. This awful experience has devastated me more than anyone knows. No one wants to eat alone:<u>https://www.nooneeatsalone.org</u>

I'm reaching out to you because I hope you can help girls like me deal with cyber harassment. I feel I was bullied when a boy texted something private to his friend, and then that friend posted it on social media. To make me look bad. They never really got in trouble. But from that point, I was judged because of a sexual choice, one I thought would be better than going all the way. It was never meant to be public. It was disrespectful for them to distribute, and it resulted in a horrible domino effect. And it wasn't even my private parts that were showing! Now my reputation is forever haunted by one "indecent" act.

What about my good grades, my (former) position on the cheerleading squad, my roles in school plays, my love for family? Those things should count. Yet no friends from cheerleading or drama stuck up for me. The only individual who did was the guy who got killed. Although he wasn't innocent. That's like another topic.

I shouldn't have trusted a guy I'd never met in person. I shouldn't have given him so many personal details about where I go to school. I wish someone would've warned me: "Online is a place for human contact but not intimacy" ("How Evil is Tech," New York Times article by Brooks 11/20/2017).

Anyway, perhaps you could better address the issue of social media popularity because it's causing severe depression and anxiety in teens, especially girls ("Uptick in Teen Depression," NPR, All Things Considered, 11/14/17). Also, I read about the Intimate Privacy Protection Act (IPPA) which was introduced by a Representative from CA in 2016 as an amendment to Title 18, the United States Criminal Code. Has that bill passed yet? It has to do with online abuse, particularly sharing porn without permission. What about the ENOUGH Act from 2017, a federal statute with the same intent? It's obviously wrong to share sexually graphic images without some body's consent, but is it like officially unlawful?

When it comes to gender equality, I think females should try to create a positive sense of self and not let males ruin it. Right?

We need courage, and we need a spokesperson. We need to stand up to meanness, offensively and defensively. Let's go, girls!

Sincerely,
Stephanie

P.S. Have you heard of One Billion Rising? It's a global campaign to stop bad treatment of women. My cheerleading coach is planning to participate. Maybe you could help promote that movement, too?

After sitting with Stephanie's letter, holding its tangibility, taking in the timely relevance, and relating it to today's world, Miss Oliver recalls something a sage professor once said: "Empathy is the center of an English Language Arts curriculum." She connects the principle with the present: *Indeed, empathy is often at the heart of writing, outreach, reading, and the circulatory response.*

Week Five, Wednesday

Before school, Gabby checks her inbox. Mr. Keystone had replied.

```
Dear Miss Oliver,

Way to represent the school! And support your
students. Well written. Go ahead and send your
email to the press.

Btw, counselors are working on implementing a
schoolwide mindfulness program within their
suicide-prevention and life-skills lessons.
We are also in the process of setting up gun-
violence prevention training which is designed
to help people recognize and report warning
signs. You'll be kept in the loop.

Thank you,
Mr. K.
```

The students will continue collages, discuss digital citizenship, and pledge to uphold a code of conduct. First, Miss Oliver gives time to work on projects. She offers stacks of magazines and local newspapers. They busy themselves cutting and gluing, printing and assembling. Halfway through the period, she segues into a discussion about the previous night's homework.

"Okay, let's put away the art supplies and switch activities here. Regarding your reading, what did you learn about the concept of digital citizenship?" The students noisily clean up scraps from their desks. The teacher realizes she should've given them a timed warning and a longer period of transition, but Rhonda is already raising her hand.

"I think it's basically about courtesy to each other online," the class blogger announces over the din.

"Well, that's a good way to put it. Can anyone give us some examples?"

"Yeah, like not hatin' on people: not embarrassin', mis-represent'n, plagiariz'n, or ghostin'," Binah expresses informally.

"Definitely," Matt, the tech whiz, concurs. "Pausing before you push send."

Stephanie raises her scissors. "So, it's simply about kindness and honesty?"

"Yes, those are all tenets of digital citizenship." Miss Oliver writes vocab on the board.

"Like good manners online?" Lucy clarifies.

"Yep," the teacher approves, "but wait, what exactly is 'ghosting' again?" She turns to Binah.

"It's when someone don't answer, like leave you guessin'. It drives a girl insane not knowin' where she stands. Some cats don't like to respond. They rather avoid questions and issues. Just ignore you. I mean me, anybody."

"Word," Kenn surprisingly agrees while looking toward Stephanie. He is dressed in the team's red and black jersey, advertising the evening's football game.

"So, you're saying these ghost-like acts happen when friends would rather disappear than address uncomfortable topics by…text?"

"Yes, you know, Miss O," Matt confirms with a nod, trying to bridge the generational gap.

"Well, avoidance seems wimpy and disrespectful," the teacher judges. "The friend could at least say, 'I don't feel comfortable answering that question right now' or make a point to speak in person, right? I believe people owe each other more honesty and reciprocity—as friends, family, and/or romantic partners."

"Yeah, props," Binah agrees.

Lucy stretches bubble gum between her tongue and index finger. "Something I've noticed lately is a chica will post something on s.m. when she means to say it to just one person."

"That's so frickin' dramatic," Ember snarks.

"I get what Lucy means," Rhonda clarifies. "Chicks and even dudes will make comments about coded personal matters only meant for a select few or even one person. Like they're hoping someone in particular will see it. But the rest of us wonder what the heck it's about."

"Do you find that entertaining or annoying?" the teacher marvels.

"I don't know, maybe entertaining because it's an unsolved mystery, like watching a soap opera or telenovela," Lucy compares before putting the gum back in her mouth.

"It's annoying, now that I think about it," Rhonda remarks. "It clogs up my feed."

Hmm. Miss Oliver likens the anticipative action to fishing, hoping for a bite from a particular breed, depending on the bait. She pictures her younger self casting a line at the lake, flipping the bail, waiting for a tug, her wrist ready to reel. Then, she senses a snag. Something else beneath the water. *A stick, maybe?* The metaphorical memory fades.

"I underlined some words from reading, Miss." Nadia politely redirects the discussion as she articulates "appropriate, responsible, etiquette, and ethical." The group identifies unfamiliar definitions and voices brief examples of concepts as they may relate to Internet use.

Then, the teacher draws their attention to a poster that has been hanging up in back all year. She moves it to the front of the classroom next to their Ideals Collaboration *(the "shiznit")* from the previous day: The purple calligraphy reads, "Is it true? Is it necessary? Is it kind?"

"Part of your homework is to ponder this poster and these prompts whenever you send an electronic message today." She notices

Rob inking the words onto their arm like a tattoo.

Seeing this, Scott sings a familiar Steve Miller Band tune. "The question to everyone's answer is usually asked from within. But the patterns of the rain, and the truth they contain, have written my life on your skin!"

"Thanks Scott, great song. So, the other aspect of your assignment is committing to—or at least attempting to follow—a code of conduct online and via text." Miss Oliver passes out the printed pledge. "I cannot hold you to this promise, but I can offer it as a way of orienting yourself on social networks. Based on what happened with Steph, Kenn, Adam, and in general. Please tape this slip of paper inside your notebook, within your bedroom, to your home device, or directly onto your phone. Oh, and FYI, the last line of criteria is rightfully there because you're minors."

Social Media Code of Conduct
I will not share any photo, content, or comment that is:
Mean
Untrue
Illegal
Violent
Racist
Sexist
Homophobic
Pornographic

Signature: _____

A small line of students awaits the teacher after class. Adam hands back his unsigned contract and simply says, "Nice try, but no thanks." He doesn't stick around to debate it.

Rhonda approaches next. "He's such a negatron! But at least he didn't crinkle the paper. You can reuse it." She gives Adam grace. "Hey, so, this is good and all, but what about comedy and sarcasm for satire's sake? Are we not supposed to watch, like, or share it?"

Miss Oliver holds onto Adam's blatant refusal while processing Rhonda's sophisticated question. "Hmm, I hadn't thought about that. I guess you'll just have to use discretion."

"Fair enough," Rhonda remarks.

Next up is Ember. "You know this doesn't really relate to me," she quibbles. "The whole digital thing. I don't go online—much. Why should I care?"

"Well, if we're talking about social networking, neither do I, really. Only rarely do I log in to Insta-Face. But we do use computers sometimes, right?" the teacher smiles. "And your friends are online. And you've said your boyfriend is. And society is. So, we're going to talk about the terms. Because someday, you'll have a job, and you'll need to use the Internet—and probably a cell phone—for work or otherwise. So, you'll want to be smart about it. Think of it as an educational investment in your future."

Ember shrugs. "Yeah, I guess," she concedes.

"Whether we like it or not, technology is a requirement in today's world."

At noon, Miss Oliver goes to the lunchroom. It has been a while since she accompanied her coworkers for a meal. Sam, the science teacher, has pulled up a rusty metal chair next to Marie. He is speaking nonstop as the veteran English teacher attempts to read while eating. Gabby suppresses a snicker upon seeing Marie's snubbing of Sam. The newcomer sets her compartmentalized tray down with a thud. Marie beams at the sight of her friend.

"Hey, look who it is! I thought you'd sworn off school lunches."

"Nah, I can no longer resist tater tots," Gabby jokes.

"Stephanie's eating elsewhere today?" Marie verifies.

"Yeah, it appears that way." Gabby signals outside where Stephanie and Rob sit atop a boulder, both wearing pony tails.

"Nice," Marie observes.

"So, I changed the seating arrangement, the Reflective Writing syllabus, oh, and I updated the class website this week."

"Wow, you've been busy! You must be feeling motivated again then?"

"Yeah, I want to foster a better sense of community—both online and in person."

"I like group projects," Sam interrupts. "You ladies should stop by the lab after school sometime. Maybe we can all brainstorm on a Science-English project?" He wipes a bit of sour cream from his mouth.

Marie secretly squeezes Gabby's arm, muffling a laugh and clearly siding with her department ally.

Instead of "stopping by the lab" as suggested by Sam, Miss Oliver decides to go to the evening's football game. She rushes to and from home first, in order to let Eddie out and change clothes. The teacher returns wearing school colors—a red sweatshirt with black jeans. The bleachers are already pretty full by the time she gets back and makes her way out to the field. Surprisingly, she sees Stephanie in the stands. The girl's not in uniform, but she appears to be having fun with friends.

Gabby chooses an open spot next to some enthusiastic parents. She munches on popcorn and looks for recognizable players. When cheerleaders sing the pep song and coax home-team fans from their seats, Gabby hears Stephanie's voice behind her. "Cupids have begun, Cupids, number one...." Unwilling to retire her school spirit or support, the former cheerleader pronounces every word loud and clear.

Toward the end of Reflective Writing class, Miss Oliver checks in with students who are happily working on their art collages. "Is anyone—or any group—done with either the art or essay portion, or maybe even both?"

Kenn raises his hand. "I'm pretty much done with the collage part. I need to do the writing yet. And the—whatcha call it—biography."

"You mean bibliography," Rhonda corrects.

"Right, well, here's my poster." He has apparently chosen to work alone on the project. When he holds it up, none of the students show particular interest in the star player's work. They are busy arranging their own creative pieces. The teacher walks over to see it up close. A colorful banner catches her eye.

"I won't lie," he hands it to her. "My mom helped me find the sites. She said this theme—or whatever—would be good for me to learn about. Because of what happened and all. Plus, it's related to what you had us read."

Curious, she looks it over. Considering Kenn had done a decent job on his extra-credit dress-code paper, she doesn't discount his effort, even without the written requirement attached. By now, Miss Oliver knows Kenn's intellect outweighs his affect.

He has printed articles and definitions in regard to cyberbullying and sexual harassment. The collection includes pictures from various websites and poem entitled "Betrayal" by Lang Leav.[42] Scholarly information comes from the Cyber Civil Rights Initiative,[43] the National Women's Law Center,[44] and something called Fifty Shades of Silence.[45] The teacher looks forward to learning more about the subject via his citations.

A BETRAYAL

I cannot undo
what I have done;
I can't un-sing
a song that's sung.

And the saddest thing
about my regret-

I can't forgive me
and you can't forget.

- Lang Leav

---

42 Lang Leav is a novelist and published poet from Australia.
43 The Cyber Civil Rights Initiative provides support and resources to victims of non-consensual pornography. There is a helpline number, removal guide, and legal information listed.
44 The National Women's Law Center is a non-profit organization located in Washington, DC. It promotes gender justice and equity through a network of advocates committed to improving the lives of women and families.
45 50 Shades of Silence is a website dedicated to information about how to address, discourage, and remove revenge porn. There is a documentary by the same name. Both are based on the personal experience of Darieth Chisolm. Numerous resources are listed.

"Look okay?" He asks sincerely. She is busy reading the fine print.

"Yes, Kenn. This is impressive, and the poetry is a thoughtful touch. I didn't realize these sites existed." She hands the collage back to him.

"Thanks and yeah, me neither. Hey, there's something inside, too. It's for Steph," he says, appearing nervous. "Since she's been ignoring my texts."

Stephanie looks up. Kenn opens the display board. It had been folded over to thicken the collage. Inside, revealed in iridescent silver Sharpie, he has written the words, "I'm sorry."

And, just like that, by way of a research assignment, Kenn apologizes to Stephanie. It isn't private; it's on display for the class to see, but unlike social media, the message is tangible. Stephanie could, in fact, take the collage home and tape it on her bedroom wall.

But first, Miss Oliver would hang the poster up as a resource for students. *Hopefully the information would dissuade Kenn and others from photographing or sharing nonconsensual pornography in the future.*

That afternoon, as anticipated, the school holds an active shooter drill. It is not during third period, but the simulation takes place in Gabby's class as it does everywhere on campus. Her fifth-period students realize the resonance the training has in Room 18.

Parents were informed via email earlier in the week, and they could object to their children participating by signing and sending a form back to school. Otherwise, HHS had parents' passive consent. Mr. Keystone announces the drill and proceedings over the PA system. Miss Oliver takes a puff from her inhaler.

"Hello, Heart High. This period, your teachers will be going over lockdown safety procedures with you. The purpose is to empower both educators and students alike, should someone threaten our school. We want to inspire a sense of calm, care, and confidence on campus. We will not be using any props here today, folks. This is not a real-time simulation and should not feel like a scary situation. It's a slow-motion walk-through, an opportunity to discuss concerns. We have a safety team in place, which includes myself, the vice principal, two counselors, a nurse, our security team, and liaisons from the local police department who are here today with EMS responders. We will be walking around campus and checking on you during this drill."

In a stone-faced, surreal state, Miss Oliver reads protocols and relays what to do when. The approach is intended to minimize stress, not to recreate trauma. The run/hide/fight model and concept are explained in detail. The teacher talks about what students could and should do if an intruder is somewhere on campus—run and hide while maintaining accountability—versus what might happen if an armed assailant were within close proximity. She does not refer back to what really took place when two individuals took aim among a different set of students. *That day did not follow protocol.*

The school day closes, and Marie stops by to chat. She sets her black briefcase down next to her coworker's desk. While waiting for Gabby's attention, Marie uses her finger to trace a broken-heart-shaped pencil carving upon a student's wooden desktop. Before addressing her friend and mentor, Gabby comes to a stopping point with typing up assignments on her newly interactive class website. "Hi," she finally greets, swiveling her chair and switching her brain from business to social mode.

"Hi," Marie replies with an empathetic smile. "You doing okay?"

"Yep, thanks," Gabby responds, trying to both hide and convey her annoyance at the invasion upon her workday wrap-up.

"Well, I can see you're busy." Marie stands to leave, picking up on the teacher's desire to get back to business.

"What's up?" Gabby wonders.

"Nothing, really. Just checking in...after the training and all. Hey, want to go out for a drink, relieve some stress?" Marie asks.

Gabby considers the friendly offer and opportunity to unwind outside of school. "Sure." She closes her laptop.

The two women decide to meet for a margarita at Sol Y Luna. On the short drive over, Gabby fondly remembers her time spent with Brandon there. She giddily recalls his hand on her bare leg beneath the table—a simple touch which shifted the previously professional association between them. And then, they danced and braved their first kiss. Lost in the memory's daydream, Gabby walks up to the bar where Marie is fiddling with her phone. They order, and an older woman serves their cocktails: Marie's on the rocks and Gabby's blended. The return customer is thankful not to see the weird waitress from before.

"What did you think of the drill today?" Marie begins. She darkens the screen on her device but leaves it within reach.

"It was...procedural," Gabby concludes. "But no amount of prep can prepare us for a real attack," she adds defeatedly.

"True, but I suppose it is good to discuss possibilities."

"Unless the act of even broaching the topic traumatizes students," Gabby argues. "Especially after the recent incident."

"So, you're saying, wait and see? Handle situations if they arise?" Marie seems skeptical of Gabby's implication.

"Maybe it's better than living in fear?" the younger woman postulates. "I don't know. Can we talk about something else—besides shootings at school, real or imagined?"

Marie's phone lights up. It's her husband, Todd. **Do I need to pick up the kids now?** he asks.

Marie shakes her head. "Clueless," she says aloud and points at her cell. "Todd has no idea the younger boys have dress rehearsal for the elementary play!" She sets the device down and vents to Gabby. "He probably doesn't remember the elementary play is tomorrow night, even though Steven—the oldest kid—and I have posted about the event. It's like Todd doesn't see us, doesn't realize what's going on in our lives. I mean, come on, I made the costume for Peter Pan![46] I sewed the damn thing twice because it didn't fit the first time! And Todd couldn't click 'like' when I posted a finished picture of it on Insta-Face?"

"He hasn't seen the costume in person?" Gabby inquires, confused by Marie's irritation.

"Well, yeah, I've had the green fabric and brown felt around the house for a month, but I mean online. Todd hasn't publicly acknowledged it. The play is a huge deal for the kids. The least he could do would be to share the flier! It's little Stan's first big role. Plus, I 'like' all Todd's posts. To show him *I* care."

"I see," Gabby nods, trying to understand their modern family dynamic—on and off screen—as Marie texts Todd back. **No, they have play practice! I'll get them later.**

It occurs to Gabby that social media is a love language of sorts.[47] *It serves as a way to process daily life, express commitments, and, in turn, receive affirmation for personal effort. That is, when the right people show interest. Posts and shares co-depend on approval from particular readers. Todd's lack of like offends his wife.*

"Anyway," Marie tunes back into her previous conversation with Gabby, before Todd's text interrupted them. "What do you suggest we do to prevent gun violence then?" She forgets or ignores her friend's request to change the subject.

"Um, at school, what Mr. Keystone talked about today and at the

---

46 A story about a boy who would not grow up, originally based on a 1904 play and novels by J.M. Barrie

47 *The Five Love Languages* (Words of Affirmation, Quality Time, Receiving Gifts, Acts of Service, and Physical Touch), written by Gary Chapman, published in 1992

staff meeting is wise. Even though armed guards and metal detectors might seem extreme to some. At large, I think buyers of guns—and maybe even ammo—should have background checks, regardless of where they purchase their weaponry, meaning in stores, online, or at shows. Granted, I'm no expert, and I know that's not entirely applicable to what happened with Leeland, but here's what I've been thinking about…since you asked. It applies to that Dillon gangster who should not have had access to guns after he got in trouble with the law." Gabby pulls out an inhaler and takes a puff before continuing her ideological viewpoint.

"No one complains about teachers being fingerprinted before they take a teaching job. Everyone agrees kids ought to be in good hands at school, right?" Multitasking, Marie peeks at her phone and then looks back at Gabby, dividing her attention but showing curiosity in the analogy her coworker is trying to make. "So, why do some take exception to background checks for gun owners? Isn't it also important for people holding that kind of power to be accountable to their past, their records, their potential? The Commission on Teacher Credentialing would not give clearance to a person with a criminal record, so why would a gun dealer authorize a criminal to hold so much power? Doesn't the general population deserve a right to safety?"

"Great point!" Marie approves, raising her drink. "A similar case could be made for driving licensure. Meaning meeting requirements and regarding responsibilities. It's a privilege to drive—and teach. But first, you have to pass those tests."

Week Five, Friday

Miss Oliver is entering an extra-credit opportunity on the Reflective Writing website for anyone willing to read and write a book report on *Amusing Ourselves to Death* by Neil Postman—either the original or the twentieth anniversary edition which was published in 2005.

Stephanie comes to third period a few minutes early and happily approaches the teacher. "I went to the class!" she beams.

"Which one?" Miss Oliver verifies.

"The dance lesson you told me about. That Spanish Gypsy class. Flamenco. I went last night."

"Oh, right. I forgot about the free pass. I believe it's still on my coffee table. How'd you like it?"

"I *loved* it. The experienced instructor was really good at snapping her hand fan open! It's called a pericón. And everyone was so friendly! There were women of different ages. I was one of the youngest. But there was a little person, too. You know, a dwarf." She whispers. "And an enthusiastic lady with, like, a real British accent! The dancers were—what's the word—diverse. Like Puerto Rican and Nepalese, Irish and Caribbean, Guyanese and Mexican, Filipino and Native American, Vietnamese and Indian. Like from India! All were welcome—big, small, short, and tall!" The bubbly student smiles at her spontaneous rhyme. "I mean, it's kind of like cheerleading because there's a sisterhood of sorts and choreography and such, but the group seems less judgmental, like more accepting of different body types, not so cookie-cutter. One pretty lady was wearing a red shirt that read, 'Empowered Women Empower Women.'"

"Awesome. That sounds amazing! I'm really glad you went," the teacher kindly responds. She's pleased to see Stephanie so perky again.

"Yeah, and there's something else there too, an energy. I can't really explain it. But it's exciting! Maybe I'll journal about it."

"Hello. Happy Friday. Here is today's quote. Please think on it and respond in your journals. Do you agree or disagree? Why? How?"

To move forward together—as generations together—we are called upon to embrace the complexity of our situation. We have invented inspiring and enhancing technologies, and yet we have allowed them to diminish us."

- Sherry Turkle, Alone Together, P. 295

As the teacher monitors students, Stephanie shows her an entry in the "for me" section.

> *Flamenco is a kind of historic dance. It is sassy and sexy, but not in a bad way. It's feminine, accepted, and respected. Physical and mental activity. Repetition. Footwork. Rhythm. Intention and attention. Confidence and courage. Emotional expression. Attitude. It's about mood. Beat, gaze, and grace. A story set to song.*

There is a sketch of a circle next to the writing. Numbers surround it like a clock; some are starred. Stephanie has labeled it "Bulerías."

"You just now wrote that?" Miss Oliver asks.

"Yes, that's what I was trying to tell you. About the energy in the dance studio. I think the coach called it 'duende.'"

"Really? Wow. Then, what's 'bulerías' mean?"

"It has to do with rhythm, the twelve counts."

"Interesting. This is poetic, Stephanie. Lovely. Consider sharing it with your dance class." The girl smiles, and as she closes her journal, Miss Oliver notices a flower pinned behind her ear.

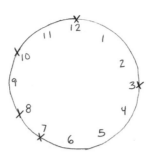

"Okay students, please put your notebooks away and give me your attention." Rhonda scurries to finish scribing. "So, we've talked about the detriments of phone use upon privacy, time, and mood. There is also a lot of research showing other factors: eye strain, bad posture, attention span, reading habits, poor sleep, loneliness, and the worst are depression, anxiety, and even suicide. I'm passing out an excerpt from a study entitled, 'Have Smartphones Destroyed a Generation?' It was printed in *The Atlantic* in 2017. It is based on the nonfiction book *iGen* by Professor of Psychology Dr. Jean M. Twenge. The book was also published in 2017. We will take turns reading the article aloud. You've already responded to a quote from it in your journal. Remember the line was about emojis versus facial expressions? Oh, and Ember used the article for research when writing her letter to the president."

Lucy volunteers first: "The arrival of the smartphone has radically changed every aspect of teenagers' lives, from the nature of their social interactions to their mental health. These changes have affected young people in every corner of the nation and in every type of household."

Matt verbalizes: "The allure of independence, so powerful to previous generations, holds less sway over today's teens, who are less likely to leave the house."

Miss Oliver relays more from the article: "The results could not be clearer: Teens who spend more time than average on screen activities are more likely to be unhappy."

The students are stunned. Just when they thought their "Teach" was embracing tech, she hits them with these striking statistics.

"Whoa, Miss O. This is pretty heavy," Matt summarizes.

"Yes, it is."

"Well, at least I'm on the right side of history!" Ember muses.

"We'll see!" Lucy reacts. "Don't be so snobby about not using a phone. I still think it's a good resource."

"She isn't saying it's a bad thing, guys," Rhonda surmises. "Just that we have to interact more, isolate less, and balance RL with virtual space?"

"That's right," Miss Oliver confirms. "Technology is ubiquitous, but it has its place. We're so ingrained in it, we may be overlooking the costs."

In response, Scott continues his Steve Miller Band song from earlier that week, **"You live in a world of illusion where everything's peaches and cream. We all face a scarlet conclusion, but we spend our time in a dream."**

"Precisely, Scott. Now writers, for the weekend, I give you these homework assignments. One, if it applies to you, try to resist your phone and/or the Internet in some capacity, be it with time, use, or apps. I encouraged you to do this before, but just while waiting in lines. This time, take a media fast. See how it makes you feel. And two, journal about that. Record your honest feelings about abstaining from electronics. Who knows, maybe you'll discover that the experience is more enlightening than excruciating! Maybe you'll find more time to read."

Wearing new leather boots laced up to her knees, Dr. Burrows walks in after school. She sits down and pulls out a form from a folder. "So, it's time for your performance review. I'm here to grade your classroom management." Miss Oliver looks around at the empty space and smirks. The department head takes a red pen from her tall sock and starts marking boxes on the document.

"Engaging subject matter? Check."

"Fair to students? Eh, mostly," she kids.

"Resists making personal texts and calls during class? Wait, do you even have a phone?"

Gabby takes her device from a desk drawer, holds it up, and points to texts that had gone unnoticed until now. "Sorry, I didn't see these," she apologizes in response to Marie's request to do the review earlier when students were actually present. Gabby also sees a text from Brandon asking if she'd like to hang out on Sunday.

Marie shakes her head. "Well, you won't be marked down in that category! Ha! However…you missed a notification from your supervisor!" She pretends to be perturbed. Gabby considers the fact that Marie could've called on the school phone, but she doesn't bring it up.

"Hey, supervisor, let me ask you something…do you still allow students to use their cells in class? I mean after the shooting and the information counselors sent home about irresponsible uses of tech?"

Marie inhales deeply. "Haven't you seen my red Cell-Free Zone poster?"

"No, I guess I haven't noticed it." Gabby thinks back on the times she observed her mentor teach.

"Oh, it might've fallen behind the bookshelf. Too bad." Marie shrugs, playacting. "Listen Gabriella, there's theory, and there's actuality. I like that my students can easily look up a word electronically. You, on the other hand, have dictionaries handy." She gestures toward a small bookcase dedicated to Merriam-Webster. Marie whispers: "Dare I confess that I sometimes let kids read and listen to stories on their… PHONES?" Marie gasps theatrically. "If they forget their books, they can usually find the day's passage online. That's a good thing, in my opinion, because reading time doesn't go to waste. And some people are better listeners, more auditory than visual learners. So, audio books and e-readers are allowed in my room, especially if a kid has an IEP stating so.

"I teach literature; these are current times. Phones are a resource, Gab. They can widen access to content, so that's how I rationalize it. I'm sorry if this goes against your personal philosophy. Maybe I'm doing a bad job as your boss. But, using tech is just…easier. It's convenient, albeit distracting at times, I give you that. It's always available in our pockets, though. Well, except for yours."

Gabby looks down at her blue blazer and long matching skirt. "I don't have pockets." Both women laugh. And with a sense of mutual understanding, they agree to disagree. Marie signs off on the form and heads out to watch her son play Peter Pan.

So far, the indoctrination experience had tested Miss Oliver—her values, habits, intentions, and teaching practice. It had stretched her further than she could have ever expected in these first five weeks. Her worldview had widened, the new job having already aged her. Exposure to students expanded Gabriella's reality and resumé. She would be required to write up an introspective piece to go along with Marie's assessment. Gabby feels like nothing short of a book will give her the space to tell the story.

That evening, the teacher mails the construction-paper card to Leeland. First, she looks over the student signatures. *Nothing offensive or overly negative. Mostly words of gratitude and commiseration.* Then, she signs it herself.

Dear Leeland,
Thank you. And good luck.
Sincerely,
Miss Oliver

WEEKEND FIVE, SATURDAY

Gabby works on lessons for the upcoming week. She readies journal prompts and homework assignments, typing them up to be inserted as time and space allow. With the last five weeks behind her, she realizes plans aren't fixed. Still, some ideas include asking students to reflect on:

- What is your "brand" on social media? Think about what you're posting. Is it positive and inspirational? Are you raising money and awareness for worthy causes? Are you prompting people to venture outside, get creative, or go somewhere specific? Are you making people laugh or wonder? Or are you potentially causing upset—defensiveness, anger, sadness, exclusion? How are you contributing and consuming?

- Is there something you've posted that could cost you a job or college admission if an employer or academic official saw it? Something offensive, derogatory, or inappropriate? Even if it's a repost? Scroll down your timeline to identify a list of what could be misconstrued about you. Consider deleting negative content. After all, social media offers your digital resumé. It conveys your values and preferences.

- Who has access to your profile page? Who does not? Who should not? Why not?

- When was the last time you stood up for someone, even if it was hard or unpopular? This could've been online or in person. At school, home, or elsewhere. How did you feel before, during, and after the event?

- What are ten things you're thankful for?

Gabby grabs her list of errands, purse, and inhaler. With reusable shopping bags in hand, she opens the apartment door and says adiós to Eddie, reassuring him she'll be back with treats. Long ago, after her mom passed, Gabby decided farewells were important. She never leaves a place without saying goodbye. Just in case.

Upon driving through the intersection near a local grocery store, she spots a familiar face. *Wait, is that…Ember?* As Gabby drives up, she confirms it. Ember is standing on a street corner collecting money. On the sidewalk, firefighters hold big signs requesting that motorists "Fill the Boot." She rolls down her window. "Hi Ember!" Gabby grins at seeing a student outside of class.

Ember forces a smile. Her braces show silver rubber bands tightening her teeth. "Hey. Want to donate to muscular dystrophy?"

"Sure," Gabby checks the light. *Still red.* She reaches into her purse. "Good to see you!"

"Yeah, thanks," Ember replies unenthusiastically. "My dad makes me do this every year. It's hot. It takes all day," she begrudges.

"Well, I'm sure he appreciates your help. Here's ten bucks. Good luck."

"Thanks." Ember stuffs the bill into a rubber black boot.

Gabby parks and goes in for groceries. She's planning to make pizza, *Chicago style.* She grabs deep-dish dough, sauce, cheese, pepperoni, canned olives…

"**Hello, is it me you're looking for?**" Gabby gazes upward from her crouched olive price comparison and notices Scott towering above her. "**I can see it in your eyes. I can see it in your smile.**" He's right in tune with Lionel Richie. And he's wearing a dirty maroon-colored apron with the store's white logo printed across his chest.

"Hi Scott! I wasn't looking for you. But I'm glad you found me! I didn't know you worked here! With Nico?" She stands, lifting her plastic shopping basket from the floor.

"I'm takin' what they're givin' 'cause I'm workin' for a livin'."

Miss Oliver is again impressed by Scott's lyrical repertoire at the ready. "Huey Lewis, right?" She quizzes him.

He smiles back, seemingly delighted by her musical knowledge and general friendliness. Just then, an older employee rounds the aisle. "Scott, we need you on three. There's a spill. Some kid stomped on ketchup. Come on." Scott follows his supervisor, limping along the pickle section.

"Alright," Gabby reviews her list aloud in the car. "Groceries, dog food, oh yeah...I wanted to get a second charger for my cell, to leave at work." She remembers seeing an electronics store on the main drag to and from school. She drives in that direction and soon pulls into a strip mall.

PHONES, COMPUTERS, ACCESSORIES the business advertises. She opens the glass door and hears a ding-dong chime alert the cashier of an incoming customer. The young man has his back to her as he organizes different-sized batteries behind the counter. The shop seems empty otherwise.

"Hello," Gabby greets. "I'm, um, looking for a phone cord."

"What kind of phone?" the gel-haired clerk asks, turning toward her. "Hey, Miss Oliver!"

"Matt! Hi! You're not going to believe this, but you're the third student I've seen today!"

"We're everywhere," he jokes. "How can I help you?" She sets her device down on the counter. "I just need a cord for this."

"A wall charger or a computer connection or...one for the car?"

"For school. I mean to plug into a socket there."

"Right over here," he leads her down the first aisle, picks up a small plastic package and hands it to her.

"Thanks. You found it so quickly," she makes small talk.

"Yep, that's my job. How's your day going?"

"Good, just running errands and, um, running into students at the same time, I guess."

"Ha! Hey, if you want to see more of us, you could come to open mic night tonight at the coffee house next door. Rob's going to perform."

"Oh, really. Singing?"

"Yeah, and Rob's buddy plays guitar. But the guy…girl? Is not in our class."

"What kind of music?"

"Um…alternative rock? Although it won't be the whole band."

"Hmm, I'd like to see Rob on stage. But do you think it's weird if I watch?"

"Why, because you're a teacher?"

"Yes, and I'm older."

"It's open to the public. I go sometimes. They'll be glad to see ya. I can text Rob right now, if you want. I've gotta ask if they want me to record them tonight."

"No, let's not, thanks. If I go, it'll be a surprise."

"Okay, Miss Oliver. The show usually starts at seven. Maybe I'll see ya then."

Gabby goes home, unloads the groceries, and rewards Eddie with a treat. To earn the meaty prize, he shakes with both hands. She contemplates asking Brandon or Marie to join her for coffee later but decides it might be awkward to walk in with another teacher as her date, *and Marie probably has family plans.* Her kids' weekend soccer schedule seems to consume her. Gabby would have to go it alone.

What to wear? She fingers through her colorful T-shirt drawer, looking for cool concert memorabilia. *Hmm, Sting, Stevie Nicks, or Slayer?* The fact that she even has a Slayer shirt could be a surprise to students. Gabby reflects back on the heavy-metal show and the long-haired guy who bought her a ticket. He went to the mosh pit and came back with a ripped shirt. *That's when we decided to buy souvenirs.* She hopes the coffee scene would be less aggressive.

The evening light looks pretty upon palm trees as she drives into town. With the wind picking up, the fronds sway above the sidewalk. Gabby is grateful for the invite out, even if it is a little odd for her to show up unexpectedly. She likes Rob and appreciates Matt's support of his classmate. The parking lot is fuller than it was during the daytime. She parks her Nissan, uses an inhaler, and walks into the café.

Gabby orders an iced tea and notices a microphone set up on a mosaic patio floor. *How nice,* she observes, comparing the al fresco area to snow drifts beside buildings in Chicago. She makes her way outdoors and takes a seat. She doesn't recognize any of the five people seated there, although she wonders if Rob's parents are among them. Matt arrives and sits down in the chair next to her. He's sipping a blended chocolatey drink. "What up, Miss O? I'm glad you came. Not a lot of people here. See Rob yet?"

"Hi. No, I haven't," she answers. Matt starts setting up a tripod. He pulls it from a cloth case and then removes a high-tech camcorder from another bag. "Nice equipment."

"Thanks. It's what I do: electronics," he qualifies, signaling toward his workplace. "Go, go, gadgets!"

"Wowsers!" Gabby winks.

Matt chuckles at the TV show reference, an inside joke with shared understanding. "Hey, that's the guitarist over there," he motions to a person with a purple mohawk.

"Okay, cool. Hey, Matt?" Gabby broaches an uncomfortable question.

"Yeah."

She clears her throat. "Does Rob like to be thought of as male or female?"

"Ya know, Miss O, I can't say for sure. Depends on how long you've known Rob, I guess. We grew up calling him 'him,' so I still do. He's my neighbor. I got him this gig, actually. Because I work next door. And I've been helping him create a web presence."

"Web presence?"

"Yeah, to attract followers and all."

"Oh, right."

"He's big on IF."

It takes a moment to translate, but Gabby soon realizes Matt means Insta-Face, social media. She finds his input about Rob's gender fluidity interesting and decides she should probably ask Rob directly.

Just then, Rob walks outside the café. They're wearing leather pants and a cut-up orange tank top with homemade fringe at the bottom. Their rock star hair hangs loose. They notice her, and their eyes widen. Rob smiles, looking pleased to see fans in the small audience.

"Slayer, really?" Rob asks upon sitting down nearby.

"Yeah, I went to a concert once. I mean, one of their concerts. It was...something."

"I bet. Hey, good to see you, Miss Oliver. Matt told me you might be here."

"Ma-att," the teacher sounds irritated. "I thought we were going to surprise..." she doesn't know whether to say him or her. "Rob."

The vocalist registers her considerate non-gendered hesitance. "It's okay," they assure. "Glad you can rock out with us."

When the music starts, Gabby compares the tune to a slower Metallica song she likes, but she can't remember the title. The electric guitar and amplifier seem slightly out of place within the coffee crowd, but the teacher tries not to judge genre. Back when she worked at a bookstore café in college, open mic nights were mostly poetic: intellectual more than musical, but lyrical, no less. This was different.

Loud, bold, lively. She thinks about how brave Rob is—to sing, to fancy fringe, to come out on stage and in life.

Weekend Five, Sunday

Gabby remembers Brandon's desire to "hang out," but she doesn't want to initiate a plan or text exchange. *After all, the weekend's homework assignment was about resisting one's phone.* Nonetheless, she gets a message from Marie.

Nice paragraph in the paper! Brava!

Thanks. ☺

Do you have an online subscription? In order to see it?

No I don't, but I'll be sure to pick up a copy. And an extra one for my dad.

The teacher thinks back over the previous weeks and how far the Reflective Writers have come in the short time since the shooting. She recalls Rhonda's astute suggestion that people use writing as a tool for problem solving. Gabby definitely agrees. While waiting on Brandon, she distracts herself by reading what Rhonda has to say on her blog entitled *Opal Mood*.

WARNING: Do not ingest this unconsciously.

I'm sitting here typing this on my laptop with multiple tabs open to different sites. Meanwhile, my phone is on my bed next to me often alerting with its soft hum of breaking news. And I'm paused right in the middle of that one Monty Python movie where the obese man goes into the restaurant and can't stop eating. It's called *The Meaning of Life* (1983). So funny and gross and true.

My parents are downstairs in the living room. They're watching the news on tv, while scrolling through their favorite sites on separate tablets. My dad likes sports; my mom prefers spirituality. Dare I say society has become that man in the movie? Except instead of food, we're gorging ourselves on information and sometimes regurgitating it without necessarily understanding the gist.

These devices are like evolutionary extensions of us. It's just the way it is, I guess. But sometimes I'm struck by it all. Being born into Generation Z, this is the norm. But I'm told it used to be different.

Nowadays, we're reliant, dependent, addicted to this need for a free flow of communication. Not only do we crave and consume it, we also require it to convey our own opinions, no matter how crazy they might be. Perhaps we need some filters?

I'm not talking about full-on censorship, blocking or unnecessarily removing info. I'm not encouraging "fake" labels at whim either. I'm referring to seriously fact-checking and flagging bogus falsehoods. Especially those that may do harm to our health. Like, calling out hate speech from violent extremists. Monitoring forums for conspiratorial disinformation (like the First Draft organization does). To warn us before we overindulge in an idea. In order to foster further research and deeper thinking.

At school, our teachers do a good job of allowing everyone the chance to speak while keeping it respectful. They won't tolerate overly negative or mean words. If somebody makes a statement, teachers usually challenge the person to explain

and support it. I believe more people could be
called out for their counterfeit claims.

That's why I thought it was wise when a social site
recently added a warning sign to a politician's
misleading Chirp. It reminds me of the fat guy in
this movie I'm watching. He's eating everything.
He needs somebody to say, "Hey, maybe you should
stop, because this might make you — and others
watching — sick!"

In this country, we're allowed to express ourselves
rather conveniently. A variety of platforms make
this easy. People are able to find outlets for
their ideas and feelings. That's a good thing. But
all of these possibilities create a problem for
our intake capacity and digestion ability. I've
decided we need help managing the massive amount
of material coming at us. Because some of it is
puke!

Wow, Gabby appraises. *What a fascinating peek into Rhonda's household! And great movie analogy!* She realizes this recent blog entry comes with some contradiction, considering Rhonda's plea for freer expression detailed in her letter to the president. *Rhonda does try to qualify what she means, though*—Gabby challenges her inner critic—*by maintaining openness with some safeguards.*

The teacher recollects the quote she had students respond to on Friday. It was about generations moving thoughtfully forward together with an awareness of complexities. It was also about the pros and cons of tech. *Rhonda shows maturity in her writing. She looks at issues from multiple angles. And she credits teachers.*

There are no comments in reaction to Rhonda's postulation. Gabby would try to remember to check back. Meanwhile, she searches for First Draft. It is a non-profit coalition and global network of investigative journalists. Then, she clicks on to read about cybersecurity teams within social-media companies. Apparently, "Big Tech" is not always liable for what individuals post. "Operators are not publishers" of content. *Or something to that effect.*

As Gabby understands it, private providers and interactive users are protected under Section 9 of the Communications Decency Act of 1996.[48] And Title V is what regulates indecency in cyberspace. She'd read this on Wikipedia and gleaned info from elsewhere.

It was a lot to process, and Gabby wasn't sure if she had all the details straight. She refills her coffee. *Could accountability immunity change? Administrators of Insta-Face must have some responsibility to moderate, right? Via independent fact-checkers? Trustworthy AI programs? Or a panel of people who maintain diversity yet discourage needless discord? In order to prevent violence, track repeat offenders, thwart attacks, lookout for illegal activity, police for predators, watch for obscenities, and curb false advertising? There should be some checks and balances, right? No place is completely lawless! And what about data being collected and secretly shared from sites? That sure seems shady!*

Gabby gazes upon a framed quote on her counter, courtesy of her dad, of course. It was a grad gift he thought applicable to her teaching venture.

When the power of love overcomes the love of power, the world will know peace.

Jimi Hendrix, American Musician

Socratically, Gabby asks herself: *Can elected representatives set basic rules—in the name of safety, security, and civility? If not, then who controls online content? App stores? What is their code of conduct? Is there*

---

48 ...as noted in Section 509 of the Telecommunications Act that year, which was updated and interpreted from Section 230 of the Communications Act of 1934.

a set standard across platforms? Across nations? Do the same policies apply to all users, regardless of status? Wait, did the Intimate Privacy Protection Act—or something similar—pass? Will Stephanie's letter be taken seriously enough?

Rhonda begs the complicated question: With the power to influence at our fingertips, who's in charge these days? *No one? Everyone?*

Feeling puzzled, Gabby silently recites the Pledge of Allegiance and asks herself, *is our "one nation under God" still "indivisible?" Or is it under command of social-media sway and support? Liberty reigns? For all? Where's the justice? Who does is serve? And on what does it stand?*

Specifically, Gabby queries who is looking out for kids. She recalls her dad saying some of his fishermen friends now support illogical theories because of their increasing interaction with unbridled misinformation, their reliance upon message boards and fringe forums versus sound sources. *I thought the ol' guys were more grounded,* she sighs. *And these fellas are fathers, too! What are they telling their grandchildren? Is truth even identifiable anymore?*

To find answers, Gabby learns a little about the FCC, ISPs, and the EFF: The Federal Communications Commission, Internet Service Providers, and the Electronic Frontier Foundation. The latter is another non-profit: activists who defend both expression and privacy. This prompts her to research the notion of free speech under the First Amendment, business rights, digital civil liberties, net neutrality, and so on. As a grown-up girl who was once orphaned by her mom, she knows unforeseen situations will arise and require adaptability. *Regarding the blossoming world of tech, "every rose has its thorn."*

The inquisitive teacher comes across an organization called the HONR Network, a non-profit helping to protect people from online abuse that stems from hate, hoax, or harassment, especially accusatory claims which are defamatory and unwarranted. "Wow," she exclaims to Eddie: "These are concerned citizens doing noble work!" Next,

Gabby clicks on a news organization called Truthout. Its "about" page proclaims editorial independence and critical analysis. The in-depth revelatory reporting efforts are said to be reader-supported, action-oriented, and donation-based, free of advertiser backing. She tabs the site. *But wait, there's something else: Article 19!* Her brain is full. Eventually, she closes the computer, uses her inhaler, and meditates on the multifaceted matter.

Rhonda raises interesting points of consideration and contention: Is it good to provide some governance over media—preferably from officials with politically unbiased intentions—or better to let people try to figure out what's true for themselves?

As a student of literature, Gabriella tends to humbly heed the warnings and insights of literary luminaries like George Orwell (1903-1950)[49] and his teacher Aldous Huxley (1894-1963).[50] *When it comes to authority and technology, their futuristic fiction is timely and telling.*

Around lunchtime, Gabby surrenders hope for seeing Brandon. *Oh well. Maybe he forgot.* But, being the daring dancer he is, Brandon eventually takes the first step.

Hey whatcha doing? Wanna come over here?
Sure? When?
Soon. Now?
Okay, maybe in a bit, where do you live?
587 Vista St. On the west side of town - third condo on the right once you pull into the complex.
Should I bring anything – to eat or drink?
No I have some stuff. But bring your bikini. For the jacuzzi.

---

49 Eric Blair (writing under the pen name of George Orwell) was an English novelist and critic known for his dystopian social science fiction novel *1984* (1949).
50 An English writer and philosopher remembered for his dystopian social science fiction novel *Brave New World* (1932).

I don't have a bikini.
Ha! Well I'd like you to swim naked, but it's a community pool.
I have a bathing suit, just not a two-piece!
Darn!

Darn? Whatever, Gabby decides. *My navy one-piece is cute!* She readies herself, packs a beach towel, and heads out. Feeling adventurous, she cracks open the sunroof on her purple Pathfinder. *The day has come to see where Brandon lives.* She knows what a condo is—*basically an apartment a person owns.* Beyond that, she isn't sure what to expect.

After pulling into the driveway and over several speed bumps, Gabby sees that the front of Brandon's condo looks newly painted, well landscaped, and inviting. She knocks, but the red door isn't latched, so it opens slightly when her knuckles meet it. "Hello," she calls, not wanting to barge in ungreeted.

"What's up? I'm stoked you're here. Come in," Brandon answers from inside. He stands shirtless at the kitchen counter, slicing lemons.

"Hi," Gabby steps inside, wondering whether to remove her sandals. Because it's a warm day, she's wearing a striped summery romper, the kind where the shorts and top are connected.

"Hey, you can put your bag and purse on that chair," Brandon nods toward a recliner. "Try this," he insists, handing her a mojito spritzer.

"Okay, thanks," she takes a minty carbonated sip.

"Let's sit in here," he walks toward the couch. The layout is open, so his kitchen, dining area, and living quarters are connected. Gabby notices a surfboard theme throughout. Even her cocktail glass has a blue wave pictured on it.

"Cool place," she compliments, sitting on a brown loveseat next to Brandon.

"Thanks. It's pretty bitchin'. Lived here about two years now." He sets his glass down on a sleek wooden coffee table in front of them.

"Selena, play Jack Johnson."

"Selena?" Gabby inquires. "Yeah, she's my roommate," he kids, "a.k.a., my smart speaker. I renamed her." The music starts to play.

"Oh," Gabby takes it in. "Is she always listening, then?"

"Unless I turn her off."

"Well, then, I won't say anything too provocative," she flirts, trying to relax, admittedly feeling somewhat uncomfortable at the idea of being audibly spied upon.

"Please do. Selena can handle it," Brandon jokes and then leans in for a mouthy kiss. They make out for a few minutes.

Gabby eventually sits back against a striped Mexican-style blanket, wipes the wetness from her lips, and takes a drink. "With Selena here, it feels like there's another woman in the room." Brandon laughs. "You know, it's funny," she says, "I can recall a time when we'd have to dial the radio station to request a song or band. Do you remember that?"

He looks off to the side and then shakes his head. "No, not really."

"Well, maybe it was more of a midwestern thing. But I'd phone a local channel, one I knew my friends were listening to, wait on hold or call back if the line was busy, and then ask the DJ to play a certain something. Usually for someone. I could do a shout-out over the air, too. And then, wait for it to play."

"That's thoughtful. Who would you shout-out to?"

"Oh, friends, boys, classmates."

"Which song would you request for me?"

"Good question. Maybe something by the Beach Boys?"

"Ha!" he laughs. "Tubular! Selena, play the Beach Boys."

"And this shout-out goes to a cute guy at school, from Gabriella Oliver," she pretends to announce over her drink-microphone.

"Come over here and kiss this cute guy," he teases, placing a hand behind her pony tail and pulling her toward him. As their tongues share space, Brandon gets a call, which is broadcasted over the speaker.

"Call coming from Natasha, connected to Brandon Ritter's iPhone," a female robot voice relays.

"Ugh," Brandon rolls his hazel eyes at the interruption. "Sorry, I should've put my phone on do-not-disturb mode."

"It's okay," she lies.

"Let me just take this really quick."

Gabby is aghast. *Isn't Natasha his ex?* She gets up to locate the inhaler in her purse.

"Hi, yeah, Tuesday is fine," she hears him saying. "No, I'll be at work. Just open the garage. It's in there. You know the code. Okay, have a safe flight. Yeah, you too." Brandon puts his device down, adjusts the settings, and then wipes his hands on his board shorts. The music has stopped playing, and a silent awkwardness hangs about the room.

He goes into the tiled kitchen. Gabby hears water dispensing from the fridge. Brandon drinks. She waits. He brings her a glass of cool tap water. "Sorry, what were you saying about the, eh, shout-outs, the radio, the requests?" He seems rattled.

"I believe we covered that. Are you okay?"

"Yes, I'm fine." He smooths his brown mustache with two fingers. "Just embarrassed. As you may remember, Natasha is—was—my fiancée. She's coming by the house to pick something up next week. A box of her things. I don't plan to see her."

"Oh, it's alright, no biggy," Gabby acts nonchalant.

"She lives in Hawaii now; she decided to stay there after the wedding, the one we cancelled. It's all good; I mean, it's good for her there. Fitting. She likes it. The lifestyle, culture, and all. She's Hawaiian."

"I see," Gabby acknowledges. "Why did you two split up again?"

"It's…a long story, really."

"I'm an English teacher. I like stories. I mean, if you want to tell it."

Brandon inhales, closes his eyes, lets out a sigh. "Okay," he yields. "But, let's have another drink. How about by the pool? I'll tell you over there."

"Sounds good," Gabby agrees to the change of scene. And change of clothes. She undresses in the bathroom, slipping into her blue suit with anchors on it—purchased at Navy Pier back in Chicago. She pushes her breasts up high into wire cups and admires herself in the mirror. *Not a bikini but not bad*, she thinks about her conservative display of cleavage.

Brandon keys in a code on the gate pad, and they enter the fenced pool area. There is a family sitting on the other side of the concrete, and there are a couple of kids playing in the shallow end of the pool.

"Hey, looks like the jacuzzi is open," Brandon happily observes. They toss their towels onto lounge chairs and step into the steamy water. "Nice suit," he admires.

"Thanks," she smiles. Becoming aware of her looks, Gabby wishes the transition lenses of her eyeglasses weren't foggy. She changes the subject: "It's convenient you have access to a pool and all."

"Yeah, it's rad," he agrees. "Comes with the HOA's—Home Owners' Association's—fees and perks."

"Cool. Must feel nice to own your own place. So…what about Natasha?" Gabby reminds him, curiously.

"About that." He takes an icy drink from the cup he carried over. "Basically, the dynamic changed between us. And she wasn't ready to commit."

"What do you mean by dynamic?" Gabby prods.

"Well, we had an open relationship before."

"Open?"

"Yeah, we both dated around some. Non-exclusively. And it worked for a while."

"It did?"

"I suppose. We agreed to the loose conditions. But then, I

asked—we decided—to make it monogamous, to marry. She was going to move in here when we got back from Hawaii."

"Hmm."

"But she decided to stay on the Big Island, to reconnect with old friends. And…lovers."

"Really?"

"Yeah, she has a new boyfriend now. Old boyfriend. Whatever."

"Wow."

"It's over, it's fine, for the better." He raises his eyebrows insinuatingly, finds her hand under the water, and interlocks their fingers. Holding her grasp tightly, Brandon looks up at the afternoon sky and leans back against the hard confines of the hot tub.

Week Six

Armed and Resourceful

WEEK SIX, MONDAY

Dr. Burrows peeks her head into Room 18 as Miss Oliver shuffles through copies. "So, I see it's official," she happily greets.

"What's that?" the younger teacher looks up.

"You and Ritter. Insta-Face says he's 'in a relationship with Gabriella Oliver,'" she air quotes.

Gabby's jaw drops. Before she has time to properly confirm or deny social-media monogamy, Marie soberly changes the subject. "Well," she looks at her smartwatch, "we can talk romance later. But hey, you know the virus that's going around abroad?"

"Yes, I think so; I heard something about it," Gabby replies apathetically, still shocked by Brandon's online announcement. She wasn't exactly watching the news over the weekend.

"There's a rumor that if it becomes a problem," Marie pauses, "we, um, might have to switch to distance learning, online classes. Keystone just warned me. He said not to say anything, but I have to tell someone! WTF, right? Good thing you got your class website updated! Are all your prep periods included on that, or just Reflective Writing?"

"Wait, what?"

"Well, the virus can be deadly, I guess. For some. So, if contagion travels here, we'd have to decide whether to close the school—stay at home, go remote, prevent the spread. But don't worry about it today. Not yet."

Marie continues down the outdoor passageway. Her heeled footsteps reverberate in the classroom. Gabby's not sure how a foreign sickness could possibly affect Heart High from such a distance. *Could the virus go…viral?* The bell rings, so she shelves the worry for later.

At break, Gabby gets on her computer. She scans news headlines and then checks Insta-Face. She's never been on social media at work, and she's pretty sure the petty pastime is against policy for paid employees. The teacher looks around to make sure no one is watching.

Marie was right: Gabby's romance with Brandon had been declared. And his status update has 17 likes so far, mostly from people she doesn't know. Except for the school secretary, Mrs. Gonzalez. *Secret's out.* She wonders if the majority of Brandon's friends only care that he's dating again after his recent breakup. Gabriella Oliver is but a tag to them. She's an unknown, except for her profile picture and brief bio, if they bothered to click further out of curiosity. Or if they recognize her name from the news. *Geez, this is real! But am I just a presumed rebound?* She uses her inhaler.

From the list of likes, Gabby taps on the other name she knows—Marie Burrows. And there, she sees several shares: one to promote a book club Marie must attend or support, another for a writing camp a former student is leading over winter break, and author pages her supervisor follows. Some are big name writers both women find influential. All with emboldened thumbs-up approval.

On her colleague's timeline, there's a recent screenshot posted. It's a reply from Stephen King. *About writing! Avoiding adverbs. And... telepathy?* To think, *Marie had a conversation with King!* Even though she holds a doctorate as a subject-matter specialist and seasoned teacher, *he's...famous!*

Gabby realizes something she hadn't fully considered before, or at least not in a positive way. *Social networking removes pretense. It promotes causes like the ones Kenn and Stephanie conveyed. And it can encourage art.* Although she still believes respect matters and earned credentials count, Gabby now appreciates that Insta-Face can open channels of communication between like-minded members from different strata.

"Hello, Reflective Writers. As you may recall, we began this class with an informal intake about writing. And I'm glad you're all journaling more as a result of our discussions here." Miss Oliver holds up a college-ruled notebook as an example.

"Here's a survey I've adapted from Common Sense Media Education."[51] She passes out sheets of stapled paper. "It asks how much time you spend online: For comparison to our earlier inquiries; in contrast to writing privately for clarity, therapy, and creativity's sake; and in relation to our ongoing dialogue about technology's toll."

Scott picks up on the theme by singing: "**Come writers and critics who prophesize with your pen...don't speak too soon for the wheel's still in spin.**"

Rob credits his classmate's contribution: "Bob Dylan again, perfect! The times are certainly changing. Hopefully for the better."

---

1) What do you do online?

> use social media
>
> do homework
>
> research
>
> read for interest
>
> watch streaming videos
>
> email
>
> text/message/chat
>
> play games
>
> listen to music
>
> other

---

51 Common Sense Media is a non-profit, research-based organization that serves as an online resource for parents and teachers. The website offers advice, information, and tools for digital citizenship along with book, movie, and TV show ratings.

2) From the list, what do you do most often?

    a)

    b)

    c)

3) What are your family's rules or policies concerning technology? Note specifics or mark as not applicable (n/a).

    Time spent online
    Sites you're allowed to visit
    Who you can chat with
    Posting policies
    Privacy settings
    Photo sharing
    Cyberbullying
    Inappropriate/pornographic content
    Sleeping with your cell

4) Do you have Internet access on a computer, tablet, or interactive video game console in your bedroom?

5) What excites you the most about the digital world?

6) What could you cut back on, regarding phone and Internet use?

    a)

    b)

    c)

The class spends a good fifteen minutes filling out the survey. Meanwhile, Miss Oliver passes out a Family Media Agreement, courtesy of Common Sense and recommended by a school counselor. It is about taking care of devices, staying safe online, thinking before responding or sharing, being mindful of time spent on screens, and communicating openly with family members.

Upon seeing most students have completed the survey and skimmed over the agreement, she voices, "I will be emailing your guardians a link to this contract, in case you, ahem, lose it. I hope it helps you and your family work out an arrangement. I want them to feel supported, too. Especially after what happened in here, and the uncomfortable things that led up to it. So, parents will be alerted to the Common Sense site for information on privacy settings, home assistants, location services, parental controls, and installing filters on networks. I will also be sending home an additional link to HealthyChildren. org where the American Academy of Pediatrics offers a Family Media Plan in English or Spanish."

"Gee, thanks," Adam slumps.

"You're welcome," Miss Oliver bows. "Most kids tend to appreciate limits. Once they get used to them." She invites students to discuss their survey responses with classmates sitting nearby: "How do your answers compare? Do family rules vary among members of your group? Are there device-free areas in your house, such as the dinner table? Do you have an electronic curfew?"

Gabby remembers her colleague's comments from last week and this morning. *I wonder what Marie's household looks like.* She understands that as a mom, Marie is dependent upon her phone for kid-care logistics; and as a teacher of literature, an authority in her field, Marie advocates for reading in any form, paperback or paperless. *But how does she go about enforcing rules with her own children?*

Although her mentor begrudges the diversions inherent in mobile phone use, she yields to the new normal. However, Gabby knows that even looking at one can scatter a person's attention across apps. *And multitasking at home or school impedes focus.* She is not yet a parent, but Miss Oliver would rather her "kids" tune into class.

Adam announces that, so far, his family doesn't have rules; his parents use their cells during dinner, and sometimes he plays violent video games into the night. He also boasts about being able to watch pornography. He claims he uses a tablet for that. "Bigger screen, bigger babes." Adam reports that his parents don't hover over or check his devices. And when his friends come over, "It's game on!" he says shamelessly. Adam looks up to see the teacher listening in. "Hey, porn's not new," he defends with a sinister smirk. "What's fairly new is being able to stream it live." Classmates sitting nearby aren't phased by Adam's unabashed confessions, so the woman swallows her desire to react.

Walking around the room, Miss Oliver listens to other student-led conversations. Nadia and Nico like to video chat with relatives. Scott watches music videos. Lucy says she's not allowed to send bathing suit pictures. Kenn admits that after being grounded from his mobile for a week, his mom now monitors his cellular activity via a parental app on her phone. Rhonda relays a story of an "asshole" she had to block from her blog. Ember and Lillian don't have much to share on the subject.

After talking it over, Matt decides to set his social-media profiles to "friends only." Rob offers to help Scott consolidate his six Insta-Face accounts, despite his forgotten passwords. Binah says she'll think twice before posting medical updates about her dad because she now realizes the confidential info isn't meant for all of her theater friends to read. Stephanie commits to playing fewer games online. And several teens concede they could cut back on texting.

Miss Oliver takes mental notes about student behaviors and the diversity of family rules regarding electronics. Recognizing a real need for media literacy and screen-use limits, she wants to stimulate greater conscientiousness within their wired world. *Mindful moderation.*

Although the teacher has wavered on tech's role in her own life and still feels conflicted at times, she understands adolescents are growing up with an unprecedented set of evolving norms and nuances therein. She has tried to serve as a resource to her pupils. But she wonders how the idea of online classes would upset individual households. *Yikes!* She doesn't dare think it further. *Not yet,* Marie had said.

"Well, guys and girls, we've talked about some important stuff this period and since the start of school in general, especially in these last few weeks. Remember reading the passages about Douglass and Lincoln? That seems like so long ago now! I hope you become better digital citizens and more reflective people because of our discussions, your journal entries, and the recent materials being sent home. In addition to writing, we will study media lit more. It'll help you make better sense of what's on the Wild Wild Web."

"Yeehaw!" Kenn exclaims.

"What worries me about excessive screen use is that it is generally unguided, uncensored, and unprotected. We've seen what can go wrong. Plus, as an English teacher and booklover, I'm concerned kids are reading less due to their preoccupation with technology. Granted, there's some good stuff out there, including access to inspirational influence. But you have to ask yourself why you're on an app: is it educational, productive, creative, safe, and supportive? Is it worth your time? Are you responsibly using tech as a tool for thoughtful engagement? Did you do your homework first?"

"Sometimes," Lucy answers on behalf of the group.

"Okay, to be clear," Miss Oliver delineates, "I'm not discouraging listening to music or interesting podcasts while you exercise or do chores. And I'm not criticizing family movie night, where everyone sits down to watch a show on TV. If popcorn and blankets are shared, it's a group experience."

"Video games are a group experience," Matt argues.

"If you're *alone* in a room with the remote control?" Miss Oliver interrogates. "I understand that gaming offers a way to escape and explore fictional worlds. Electronic games can be scenic, strategy based, challenging, creative, and even cooperative. I'll give you that, Matt. But screen play can also become highly addictive and isolating; in fact, there's tons of research on the subject, particularly when it comes to violent rivalries. But we can agree to disagree about the 'social' aspect of modern Mario."[52]

Lucy asks the teacher how often she checks IF. Miss Oliver answers: "More than I used to; maybe two or three times a week now?"

"You mean a day?" Stephanie verifies.

"No, a week. On average."

"But social-media stories only appear for a day!" Lucy can't relate to her instructor's infrequent habit. She's incredulous: "You'd miss updates!"

"I guess so. But I tend to prefer other types of storytelling. And things that last. Anyway, the bell is about to ring, so here's your journal prompt for tonight."

If you were a parent of a teenager, what rules would you set? Referring back to the survey and contract, please come up with a guideline for your hypothetical kid. What are your policies regarding time spent online, allowable sites, who he or she can chat with, what is okay to post, which photos can be taken and/or shared, what to do about instances of cyberbullying (witnessed or received), and whether your child could sleep with a device.

---

52 (Super) Mario Brothers was a popular arcade, and then Nintendo video, game in the 1980s.

Gabby wonders what her parents' rules would be in the face of contemporary technology. *That's if I were younger and if my mom were still alive.* The subjunctive to-be verbs and distant hypotheticals leave her guessing.

Dear Gabriella,

Look at you, my sweet child. You're almost five now. Yet you've been holding a pencil correctly since you were two. I love to watch you write, practicing numbers and letters. "Look Mom, I made a 5!" you exclaimed from the kitchen today. Inside a little pink purse, you carry mini journals. Pads of paper undecipherable to anyone else. But, you'll sit on the couch and read them aloud to stuffed animals. I can't wait for you to have children someday! Or patients. Or students.

Today, you told me you don't wish to be a mom because you don't want to bleed like I do (during my menstrual cycle), but you might become a doctor or teacher when grown up. What I can't tell a budding five-year-old is women bleed, regardless. And patients bleed. And, students, well, they're human, too. Life is messy, with or without babies. Warning, child: there will be blood.

I know my decline is scary, and I'm sorry. I hope you find solace in writing now <u>and later</u> in life. I just wish I could be there to read it.

In every person's journey, there is a turning point. A before and an after. For me, there was something bigger than cancer that divided my existence. Something greater than all the great books I've enjoyed. Something more formidable than blood. It was you.

I don't have long now. Doctors tell me it's time to say goodbye. So, I leave you this letter, these journals. Your dad promises to safeguard them until you're in high school. You can also have my jewelry, the pieces you like to try on. And my pretty dresses. They're yours to keep.

I hope my words buoy you from time to time. As much as I fear you seeing the darker side of me, it's worth it for you to read the rest—the epiphanies I experienced, the joys, the heartbeats that led me here. I don't have much else to pass down, so I gift my accounts of life and limited perspective on it, my exposure to the world these last forty years.

I carried you in my womb, on my breast and hip, and if I can somehow come back to this earthly place, I'll try to carry you onward—beyond the inevitable blood and tears, throughout your coming years.

Love,
Momma Rose

Author's Commentary

Generally, 3-D teachers have permission to utilize intellectual material and refer to real-world events at will. Because this book is set in an English classroom, the references, online resources, data, quotes, and citations are meant to be educational and contemplative in nature. With that in mind, some of the profits will be donated to scholastic programs.

Miss Oliver's lessons and thinking points are socially valuable for comment on and off the page (potentially in book club discussions). Out of respect and consideration for the work of authors, artists, musicians, journalists, psychologists, public figures, organizations, et al., I consciously kept excerpts small and diligently gave credit where it is due. I aim for an integrative art appeal.

As is evident in the novel, music is a powerful vehicle for communication, inspiration, correlation, and stress relief. Regarding Scott's inclination to sing, his character is a unique invention. It took creative craftsmanship to work his witty contributions into the dialogue, and the poetic lyrics were reformatted for prose. Appropriate within the context of each exchange, they are not just decorations. Clearly, the songs help Scott build a rapport with classmates. Music also encourages Rob's expression as a non-binary individual. As you saw, Rob and Scott connect through this shared interest.

Scott is a survivor who is doing his best to participate. His renditions, along with other carefully chosen and situated lyrics (easily accessible online), give the text a multimedia feel which readers should find fitting for this literary study of technology's toll. Certain tunes are directly tied to themes. I cannot imagine this story without Scott, hence the dedication. He transforms the classroom experience.

Scott's Playlist
(in order of his musical contributions)

"Shelter from the Storm" by Bob Dylan

"Lola" by The Kinks

"Hello, Goodbye" by The Beatles

"Roxanne" by The Police

"Make You Feel My Love" by Bob Dylan

"Another Day in Paradise" by Phil Collins

"The Times They Are A-Changin'" by Bob Dylan

"Shallow" by Lady Gaga and Bradley Cooper

"Photograph" by Nickelback

"Message in a Bottle" by The Police

"Look What They've Done to My Song, Ma" by Melanie

"I Will Always Love You" by Whitney Houston (Dolly Parton)

"Royals" by Lorde

"Love Bites" by Def Leppard

"Operator" by Jim Croce

"Better Days" by Bruce Springsteen

"Jungle Love" by Steve Miller Band

"Hello" by Lionel Richie

"Workin' for a Livin'" by Huey Lewis and the News

Other Song Snippets
(in order of auditory appearance)

"Hold On" by Wilson Phillips
"Down to the River to Pray" by Alison Krauss
"Return to Sender" by Elvis Presley
"Love Stinks" by The J. Geils Band
"It's All Been Said Before" by The Supremes
"Hey Baby" by Bruce Channel
"Galileo" by Indigo Girls
"Every Rose Has Its Thorn" by Poison

Epilogue and End Notes

I strived for accuracy and believability within the court scene and as the lawful stipulations apply. The court case is unrealistically sped up for the sake of pacing, entertainment value, and the day-by-day structure of the story. Legal details are conveyed through the filter of a third-person narrator, Gabby's introspection, and the interpretation of characters. Although presented as such, not all of the fiction should be taken as plausible. By raising the stakes for Leeland and hopefully increasing engagement with readers, I admittedly took some artistic liberties and relative risks when composing and editing certain chapters, hence these thoughtful disclaimers.

Books about human conditions often broach uncomfortable subjects. Letters to the unnamed president are intended to draw attention to language, encourage longhand, give characters a political voice, develop personality, and show that teenagers care about pressing issues. Their correspondence is incomplete and opinion-based, which is typical of teens, representative of hurried curriculums, and indicative of multi-tasking inside overpopulated classrooms. Nonetheless, the pupils bring up good points and timely topics worth researching further. Here are some of the sources used to write that section. As the author, I am not necessarily endorsing these websites, the online content, or any stances students take. If you want to look up a link, and its URL (internet address) becomes outdated, please search for the wording therein. Other sites and sources for this assignment are embedded within the letters themselves (including Matt and Ember's).

Adam's Letter

https://en.wikipedia.org/wiki/Clean_Power_Plan
https://www.nytimes.com/interactive/2017/06/01/climate/us-biggest-carbon-polluter-in-history-will-it-walk-away-from-the-paris-climate-deal.html
https://www.nytimes.com/2017/06/01/climate/trump-paris-climate-agreement.html
https://www.nytimes.com/2017/06/03/us/politics/republican-leaders-climate-change.html
https://www.epa.gov/newsreleases/epa-review-clean-power-plan-under-president-trumps-executive-order
https://en.wikipedia.org/wiki/United_States_Climate_Alliance
https://www.epa.gov/clean-air-act-overview

Binah's Letter

http://thehill.com/blogs/pundits-blog/economy-budget/335618-the-trump-budget-cuts-social-security-plain-and-simple
https://www.hhs.gov/answers/medicare-and-medicaid/what-is-the-difference-between-medicare-medicaid/index.html
https://www.nytimes.com/2017/08/15/us/politics/cbo-obamacare-cost-sharing-reduction-trump.html?mcubz=0
https://www.verywell.com/what-is-bac-bronchioloalveolar-carcinoma-2249362

Leeland's Letter

https://www.dhs.gov/mission
http://thehill.com/blogs/blog-briefing-room/news/283388-homeland-security-chief-makes-push-for-gun-control-following
https://www.atf.gov
http://smartgunlaws.org
https://www.journal-news.com/news/national/assault-weapon-assault-rifle-what-the-difference/LPXLAj8ZcHkPn2rLn3bOGK

Lillian's Letter

https://www.theguardian.com/environment/2011/feb/04/man-made-greenhouse-gases
https://www.nps.gov/pore/learn/nature/climatechange_action_home.htm
https://www.climate.gov/news-features/understanding-climate/climate-change-global-sea-level
https://www.noaa.gov/news/international-report-confirms-earth-is-hot-and-getting-hotter
https://www.ucsusa.org/resources/whos-fighting-clean-power-plan

Lucy's Letter

http://www.aasa.org/SchoolAdministratorArticle.aspx?id=10850

Rob's Letter

https://en.wikipedia.org/wiki/Equality_Act_(United_States)

Rhonda's Letter

https://www.wired.com/2017/04/internet-censorship-is-advancing-under-trump
https://webfoundation.org/2015/08/italys-internet-bill-of-rights-a-step-in-the-right-direction
https://www.nytimes.com/2017/12/05/business/china-internet-conference-wuzhen.html
https://slate.com/technology/2016/11/how-the-internet-works-in-north-korea.html
https://en.wikipedia.org/wiki/Dark_Ages_(historiography)
https://en.wikipedia.org/wiki/Frederick_Douglass#cite_note-32

Stephanie's Letter

https://www.nooneeatsalone.org
https://www.nytimes.com/2017/11/20/opinion/how-evil-is-tech.html?smid=nytcore-ipad-share
https://en.wikipedia.org/wiki/Intimate_Privacy_Protection_Act
https://speier.house.gov/_cache/files/6/5/65a8c4d9-76f9-4b94-a3d9-8992c0cda799/78A5388EDDE97F5A37682073289D32AD.the-enough-act-one-pager-11-27-17-002-.pdf
https://www.onebillionrising.org

Kenn's Collage

https://www.50shadesofsilence.com/internet-safety
https://www.cybercivilrights.org
https://nwlc.org
https://www.langleav.com

A Selection of General Citations
(in order of mention in the book)

"Uptick in Teen Depression Might Be Linked to More Hours Online" from *All Things Considered* on National Public Radio by Patti Neighmond, hosted by Elise Hu, 11/14/17: https://www.npr.org/sections/health-shots/2017/11/14/563767149/increased-hours-online-correlate-with-an-uptick-in-teen-depression-suicidal-thou?sc=17

The Tomorrow People (a television series presented as a radio play) by Roger Price, 1973. Season Two, Episode Two, "A Changing Picture," featuring Elizabeth Adare and Philip Gilbert as Elizabeth M'Bondo and Tim. The first quote is from 9:58-10:08, the second from 11:48-12:27. https://www.youtube.com/watch?v=7D3-T7-QQkw
https://en.wikipedia.org/wiki/The_Tomorrow_People#Cast

"Have Smartphones Destroyed a Generation?" from *The Atlantic* by Jean M. Twenge, 9/2017: https://www.theatlantic.com/magazine/archive/2017/09/has-the-smartphone-destroyed-a-generation/534198

The Lincoln Institute, Civil War, Mr. Lincoln and Freedom, Frederick Douglass. The American History Project of the Lehrman Institute, Online Library Archive by Richard J. Behn and Kathleen Packard: http://www.mrlincolnandfreedom.org/library/mr-lincolns-contemporaries/frederick-douglass

Narrative of the Life of Frederick Douglass, Chapter Two. Page By Page Books (public domain), Copyright 2004: https://www.pagebypagebooks.com/Frederick_Douglass/The_Narrative_of_the_Life_of_Frederick_Douglass/Chapter_II_p3.html

Communications Decency Act: https://en.wikipedia.org/wiki/Communications_Decency_Act

Screenagers (2016) and *Screenagers: Next Chapter* (2019) documentaries, created and directed by physician Delaney Ruston: https://www.screenagersmovie.com

First Draft News: https://firstdraftnews.org/about

Electronic Frontier Foundation: https://www.eff.org/about

HONR Network: https://www.honrnetwork.org

Truthout: https://truthout.org

Article 19: https://article18.org

Common Sense Media: https://www.commonsense.org

Family Media Plan, American Academy of Pediatrics, HealthyChildren.org:
https://www.healthychildren.org/English/family-life/Media/Pages/How-to-Make-a-Family-Media-Use-Plan.aspx
https://www.healthychildren.org/English/media/Pages/default.aspx

SELECT WEBSITES AND RESOURCES USED IN DEVELOPMENTAL RESEARCH

LGBT Resource Center through the University of Southern California (USC), Gender Neutral Pronouns Guide: https://lgbtrc.usc.edu/trans/transgender/pronouns

Giffords Law Center to Prevent Gun Violence: https://giffords.org/lawcenter/gun-laws and specifically https://lawcenter.giffords.org/minimum-age-to-purchase-possess-in-california

Everytown for Gun Safety: https://everytown.org/about and particularly https://everytown.org/issues/guns-in-schools

California Legislative Information: https://leginfo.legislature.ca.gov

National Association of School Psychologists (NASP), Best Practice Considerations for Schools in Active Shooter and Other Armed Assailant Drills: https://www.nasponline.org/resources-and-publications/resources-and-podcasts/school-climate-safety-and-crisis/systems-level_prevention/best-practice-considerations-for-schools-in-active-shooter-and-other-armed-assailant-drills

"Cyber Civil Rights Initiative Joins Miami Law" by Miami Law Staff Report, 8/20/2015: https://www.law.miami.edu/news/2015/august/cyber-civil-rights-initiative-joins-miami-law

"The Privacy Hierarchy: A Comparative Analysis…" from University of Miami Law Review, Volume 73, by Katherine A. Mitchell, 2/15/19: https://repository.law.miami.edu/cgi/viewcontent.cgi?article=4569&context=umlr

"Five Lessons from the Justice Department's Big Debate over Section 230" from *The Verge* by Adi Robertson, 2/19/20: https://www.theverge.com/2020/2/19/21144223/justice-department-section-230-debate-liability-doj?campaign_id=158&emc=edit_ot_20210120&instance_id=26211&nl=on-tech-with-shira-ovide&regi_id=128018689&segment_id=49814&te=1&user_id=079a63f8cc88c98a8a1a4163c0982ee3

"Our Latest Steps to Keep Facebook Groups Safe" by Tom Alison, 9/17/20: https://about.fb.com/news/2020/09/keeping-facebook-groups-safe/?campaign_id=158&emc=edit_ot_20210202&instance_id=26671&nl=on-tech-with-shira-ovide&regi_id=128018689&segment_id=50832&te=1&user_id=079a63f8cc88c98a8a1a4163c0982ee3

"Employees Fear Mark Zuckerberg's Commitment to Free Speech is More About Protecting the President Than His Company's Ideals" from *Bloomberg Businessweek* (pages 50-53) by Sarah Frier and Kurt Wagner, 9/21/20

"Post-Trump, a New Focus on Big Tech" from the Business Section (page A17) of the *Los Angeles Times* by Brian Contreras, 11/8/20

Additional Resources for Teachers and Parents

Parenting in the Screen Age, a book by Delaney Ruston, MD (2020)

reSTART Rehab, a treatment facility for video game addiction and screen dependency, located in Washington state: https://www.restartlife.com

Tips from a Youth Life Coach: https://www.jenniferbutlerlc.com/post/bullying-vulnerability-and-social-media

Podcasts on Parenting Adolescents: https://www.jenniferbutlerlc.com/podcasts

Cyber Civics: https://www.cybercivics.com

Braver Angels: https://braverangels.org

Center for Humane Technology: humanetech.com

The Social Dilemma documentary: thesocialdilemma.com

Wait Until 8th: https://www.waituntil8th.org

We Start Now: https://www.westartnow.org

Sandy Hook Promise: Protecting Children from Gun Violence: https://www.sandyhookpromise.org

CONTRIBUTORS

Zaydrian Davis - Heart High School poster (84) and Earth drawing (114)

Zoey Davis - smiley hearts (depictive of a daydream), 153

Debra Wright - rose painting, 50

Siena Ureño-Clayton - photo of Ember, 148

Jesse De Alba Jr. - photo taken with Siena, posing as Ember's boyfriend Donny, 148

Norman Clayton - photographer who took and designed the Polaroid-type picture of "Ember and Donny"

Nitaña De Hato Rey - sketch of bulerías flamenco rhythm, 267

Jared Barkan - drawing of Stephanie Mason, 36

David Reeser - sketches of Miss Oliver, Frederick Douglass, and other art

Blue Jay Ink - historic image of Abraham Lincoln (from November, 1863, a fair-use reproduction), 76

Lang Leav - "Betrayal" poem from Pinterest (with permission from the author), 259

Darieth Chisolm - 50 Shades of Silence banner, 258

Dr. Jean Twenge - reviewed applicable quotes within article excerpts, pages 66, 109, 267

INFLUENTIAL READING
(some of the books I enjoyed while working on this project)

Textbook by Amy Krouse Rosenthal

Big Magic: Creative Living Beyond Fear by Elizabeth Gilbert

Daring Greatly and *The Gifts of Imperfection* by Brené Brown

The Wisdom of Sundays by Oprah Winfrey

On Writing: A Memoir of the Craft by Stephen King

Amusing Ourselves to Death by Neil Postman

Alone Together by Sherry Turkle

Unselfie: Why Empathetic Kids Succeed in Our All-About-Me World by Michele Borba

American Girls: Social Media and the Secret Lives of Teenagers by Nancy Jo Sales

Girl, Wash Your Face by Rachel Hollis

Lives of Girls and Women by Alice Munro

Are You There, God? It's Me, Margaret by Judy Blume

Educated by Tara Westover

This Will Only Hurt a Little by Busy Phillips

Inside Out by Demi Moore

A Book of American Martyrs by Joyce Carol Oats

The Split by Randi Harvey

Life by the Cup by Zhena Muzyka

Islands Apart by Ken McAlpine

The Circle by Dave Eggers

Leaving Home by Garrison Keillor

Love in the Time of Cholera by Gabriel García Márquez

To Kill a Mockingbird by Harper Lee

HONORS AND GRATITUDE

A special thank you goes to the survivors from Marjory Stoneman Douglas High School in Parkland, Florida who speak out in peaceful protest of gun violence with regard to prevention policies and life-saving legislative action. Thank you for encouraging youth voter registration and community leadership. Sincere condolences for your dear losses on the tragic day of 2/14/18. Social media has helped get your meaningful messages out, and that is a great thing.

Your March For Our Lives movement is necessary and timely. The public-health crisis deserves attention. Although this is a different story, one with a twist on the gun-violence epidemic, its fiction grew from our shared values of school safety, compassion, and mental health. As you've proven, high schoolers care about national issues. I hope I do a decent job at giving these characters—your fictional peers—political and passionate voices.

https://marchforourlives.com

Miss Oliver is named in honor of Iliana Olivares, a Californian English teacher I worked with and befriended one summer-camp. Ms. O. and I shared recess duty, had our own children at camp, and joyfully combined our ESL classes for karaoke.

Momma Rose is named after Amy Krouse Rosenthal, an acclaimed author my daughter and I admire. As an innovative artist, imaginative writer, wife, and mother, she definitely understood the passage, limitations, and transcendence of time. Like Rose (and Gabby), Rosenthal was also from Chicago. She famously encouraged people to **"make the most of your time here."**

For more info, please see: https://www.whoisamy.com and https://www.amykrouserosenthalfoundation.org

Sadly, both Olivares and Rosenthal died due to cancer (in 2016 and 2017 respectively). May they live on through their literary namesakes.

Marie's role is meant to commemorate strong women I've known—the mamas who can manage kids at home, stressors at work, house chores, life's predicaments, personal goals, and the pressures of present-day relationships. It is no coincidence that several of my close friends have the middle name Marie/Mari. Furthermore, two mentors by the name of Mary also influenced my writing. They too fit the motivated mom description noted here.

Coda

This book is loosely set in 2019, on the edge of a new decade. It was mostly finished and undergoing predetermined revisions when the coronavirus changed life as we knew it. We didn't expect serious health concerns, catastrophic chaos, a plot twist in our routines, or the turning (off) of events. Once COVID-19 took over our news alerts, email content, lesson plans, texts, posts, and prayers, technology became our lifeline—to education, protective information, for shopping, entertainment, exercise, and connection to others outside the home.

Irony is a writer's companion: I continued to tout tech's potential toll while largely dependent on it during quarantine. As an author, part-time teacher, wife, and mother, I still think finding a balance between time spent online and unplugged is key. Although I admittedly struggle with resisting tech's tug at times, my convictions haven't changed, and research supports this thesis. Privacy and safety issues can increase with reliance upon Wi-Fi.

We're all adjusting to new norms in a technologically driven society. We've felt distracted and overwhelmed by it. The Internet is keeping us "connected" and unfocused, regardless of the distance between teacher and student. The pandemic has proven remote learning should not equate to screen time all day. While online resources can come in handy, clicking on links is not ideal instruction. That was an emergency and temporary response to school closures. A decent substitute. It got teachers and parents by—barely. But this story is not about a pandemic. Although the coronavirus is hinted at toward the end of the story in order to approximately situate it historically, there is a two-month discrepancy in the timeline of fact versus fiction.

To each their own stance on the subject, their own experience in this social (media and distancing) experiment. This novel offers a window into Miss Oliver's world. Fictional characters and setting aside, it shows the demands upon public-school teachers due to class size, special needs considerations, language barriers, gender dynamics, gun threats, and the challenge of holding students' attention, despite the buzz in their pockets.

As you have read (or will read if you flipped to the back first), Gabby didn't expect what would happen in her classroom either.

DISCUSSION QUESTIONS

Engagement and Relatability

At what point did you really get into the story?

What are some of your favorite lines or passages? Why do these resonate with you?

Which songs did you connect with? How do dance and music play a meaningful part?

How did the additional resources shape or enhance your reading and understanding?

What does this novel prompt you to learn or think more about?

Characters

Which character do you most relate to and why? Who would you want to be friends with?

What are Gabby Oliver's values? How do they compare to Marie's?

Do you believe Brandon and Gabby are compatible? Why or why not?

Who has power and status in the story? Why? How is it challenged at times?

What are some examples of maternal or mentor relationships? Why are these significant?

Why is Matt's character essential?

What do you think about Kenn's behavior? Adam's?

How do you feel about Leeland's actions?

Interests and Assignments

Miss Oliver admires President Lincoln. Which historic figures do you appreciate?

To what extent do you agree or disagree with any of the student letters or journal/blog entries? Why are these issues important to you?

Miss Oliver says she prefers positive, rather than political, posts. Are those descriptions mutually exclusive? What do you enjoy seeing shared from friends online?

Gabby tells Brandon that some of the student letters (to the president) are idealistic. Why is it hard to live up to our best ideas?

Thinking Points

Miss Oliver writes (to Rhonda), "We live in a world where likes and followers suggest value and credibility." To what degree do you agree or disagree?

What are some pros and cons of using tech? How does this apply to your life?

What are some reoccurring themes in the novel? How are the topics of respect, privacy, and reflection developed? What larger lessons or moral elements are explored?

If a social-media post drastically impacts a school environment, do you think students should be held accountable at school?

Please refer to the journal prompts throughout the book, including those that are listed at the top of Weekend Five, Saturday.

Takeaways

Does this novel inspire you to journal more? Use tech less? Change your habits in other ways? Enforce stricter screen rules for your kids? Disallow phones in class?

What would Miss Oliver's situation be like during the pandemic? Would she have an easy time teaching online, or might it be difficult for her to provide distance learning? What about Mr. Ritter? How could each student's life be uniquely impacted by reliance upon tech for school?

How are you making the most of your time here on Earth (as suggested by Amy Krouse Rosenthal and mentioned in the epilogue)?

Who will you recommend this book to and why?

NOTES

Notes

About the Author

A married mother of two, dance enthusiast, and a U.S. Coast Guard veteran, Tamara loved school as a student in Michigan, and she enjoys it as a part-time educator in California, hence the setting of this novel. She earned an associate degree from Ventura College, plus a bachelor's and teaching credential from CSUCI. Tamara has worked as a substitute teacher (in private, charter, and public schools), taught English as a Second Language (ESL) to international students at summer camp, tutored college-aged learners, volunteered as Parent Club Secretary for her kids' school, and co-chaired a fire-wives auxiliary. A lifelong writer, Tamara has published local articles, participated in poetry readings, won a countywide inspirational essay contest, presented penned pieces at dance exhibits, and performed on stage via *USA Today's* Storytellers Project.

Email: tamaramillerdavis@despitethebuzz.com
Website: https://www.despitethebuzz.com
Facebook: https://www.facebook.com/despitethebuzz
Instagram: https://www.instagram.com/tamaramillerdavis
Goodreads: https://www.goodreads.com/book/show/58341719-despite-the-buzz

To find out more about Tamara, her writing process, and her path to publication, consider listening to Episode 18 of the Confident Healer podcast:

https://www.theconfidenthealer.net/tamara-miller-davis-on-writing-empowerment-and-publishing-her-first-book

If you enjoyed this novel, please take a picture of yourself with the book and post it with a kind review or your favorite quote as the caption. Hashtag the title: #DespiteTheBuzz

CPSIA information can be obtained
at www.ICGtesting.com
Printed in the USA
BVHW011334280922
648152BV00001B/2

9 781736 372203